Counter

E

Liz Martinson

Thank you to my beta readers and their feedback:

Judy, Robin, Katy, Sarah and Lesley.
Thank you to Robin for final proofreading.

Any errors left are my responsibility.

Thanks to Jo and Jack for use of their piano and Dilys for the
guitar.

For Mum and Dad for the love and support they always gave
me.
Gone but never forgotten

Contents

Chapter One:

The morning sun poured through the windows of the large room, giving promise of yet another hot day. Two men sat at a table scattered with used coffee cups and sheets of paper, the efficiency of the air-conditioning making them unaware of the growing heat outside. Propped against the edge of the table was a guitar and in one corner stood an upright piano. Nineteen-seventy-nine was a good year for rock bands and a particularly good year for Tunnel Vision. But equally, that meant writing more songs, performing at more venues. Nic Daniel, lead singer with the group, and the main songwriter, was working that morning with his long-time friend and lead guitarist, Andy Lawlor.

Nic threw down his pencil in disgust and ran an impatient hand through his already tousled, shoulder-length thick black hair. 'It's not good enough. It just doesn't sound right. What am I missing?' A frown marred his handsome features as he sat back in his chair, lifting his long legs to rest bare feet on the edge of the table where his elbows had been. He stretched hugely, wide shoulders cracking after sitting in one position for so long.

Andy fiddled with a paper cup, turning it round and round on the polished wood of the table before looking up, shaking his own long brown hair back from his strongly boned face. 'Nic.' He sighed and hesitated, regarding his friend and working companion of many years consideringly. He'd a pretty good idea of what was wrong but was uncertain whether or not this was a good moment to bring it up.

Nic looked impatient. 'We're off on the European tour in, what, three, four weeks? When we get back, we need to record and get this new album out before the British tour. Ahh!' Nic threw up his hands. 'We need more tracks anyway, but I'm stuck with this one. I really think it has the makings of a great song, but-'

'Hey, hey, hey, leave it for now, okay?' Andy dropped the cup and aimlessly pushed his papers into a heap. 'We can always work on it while we're abroad.'

'I guess.' Nic picked up the guitar and a stream of silver notes filled the room as he went over and over the bit that was bothering him. 'I'm tired anyway.'

'Late night?' Andy knew it had been.

There were shadows under Nic's eyes and this morning when Andy had arrived, he'd still been asleep. Eventually he'd appeared, rumple-haired and bare-chested, to offer apologies

1

and drink several cups of strong, black coffee. Now he was irritable and edgy. Hardly surprising.

'Yeah, late night.'

'A chick?'

Nic nodded sourly.

'Where'd you meet her?'

Nic grinned in rueful apology at his friend. Putting down his guitar, he swung his legs to the floor and stood up, moving lithely over to the drinking fountain in the corner and filling a paper cup with chilled water. 'Ginger's.'

Ginger's was a nightclub they both occasionally visited. There was no shortage of women there who were willing to be picked up by either Andy Lawlor or Nic Daniel, but with Nic it seemed to be a bit of a habit recently, and all one-night stands at that.

Moving restlessly to the window, Nic gazed down three storeys into the garden at the back of his London house, in which he not only worked, but lived as well. The garden was a tangle of greenery. It looked cool outside but he knew it was not.

'And?'

Nic turned, his grin fading. 'Where's all this going?' He gestured widely with his arms outstretched, the water threatening to spill onto the polished wood floor. 'All these women! Where's it all *going*? What's the *point*? Are you happy? Is this what we wanted, what we've worked so hard for?' He returned to the table and sat down, his face intense. 'I'll tell you, sometimes I get sick of it. And if you ask yourself the question of why they bother with us? It's only because of who we are, what they can get out of us.'

'Yeah, well, I'm quite glad to hear you say that,' Andy observed dryly. The moment *was* right, he decided, squaring his shoulders. Before he could change his mind, he began to speak. 'You ask me where it's all going, and no wonder. For you, recently, I'd say downhill! It's all smoky nightclubs, booze and so many women 'til I guess you can't tell one from another. You're stale, you're bored and yes, you're getting arrogant! You're letting too many people fawn round you these days, doing everything you say, and it seems to be going to your head.'

'Be careful what you're saying!' Nic snarled, half-rising from his chair to confront his friend.

'I'll say what I want to, especially if it affects *my* livelihood as well as your own. You and I, we've worked together for years now. What is it…sixteen, seventeen years? And how long have we known each other? Twenty years, Nic, twenty years. I know you

2

inside out. And if I say you're changing, then you're changing. You never used to be like this. You always kept a sense of...of proportion about it all, by going up to the Lakes, walking, whatever! But you haven't been to Bleathwaite for months now. I've been up there more often than you and last time I went, Sam was a bit concerned. Some papers are beginning to make a point of following you around because they know they might get a good story involving you and the latest woman in your life, and to put it in Sam vernacular, he thought nowt to that!'

Nic recoiled, more hurt than he cared to admit by Sam's terse criticism. 'Andy!'

'C'mon, just listen, will you? Let's get this finally sorted out now it's come up? Carry on like this, and you're gonna lose fans and you'll lose them fast. They'll sense you no longer care and believe me, they'll find someone else. Because remember, you're not just a good song to them, you're an escape and they want to know you care. Not only that, but the edge will go from your songs, you'll struggle more, like with this one, because you're hungover, tired out, jaded or quite simply can't be bothered!'

Nic continued to glare at Andy, taken aback by this unexpected attack, although he was uncomfortably aware there was more than a grain of truth in what he was saying. He tipped his head back to drain the cup, his throat working as he swallowed the water.

Andy impatiently pushed his chair back from the table. 'Tell me, *when* did you last go north? *When* did you last go walking, which you once claimed was what saved your sanity in this mad world of ours? *When* did you last see Sam? Listen, you're falling into the trap which is always there in our profession. Too much adulation. Too much drink. Too many women. Too many opportunities to do drugs-'

'Stop right there!' Nic's voice was filled with fury. 'You know, you *know* I don't do drugs!'

'Okay, okay!' Andy lifted a placatory hand. 'You don't do drugs. Yeah, I know. But for how long?' He looked very serious now. 'You never used to drink this much either. And you've always had a bit of a reputation for women, yes, I know that, but *now*? As I said, do you honestly know *who* you're in bed with these days? When will the boredom or whatever it is that's wrong with you lead you to give in to drugs as well?'

'*Never*. That I do know, whatever else you lay at my door.'

Andy regarded him steadily then sighed. Yeah, perhaps that was right. Nic hated the whole drug scene, after the first two guys they'd had in the band had indulged far too often, performed badly and nearly wrecked the group before it had even taken off. That wasn't what Nic wanted. He wanted musicians who would be prepared to put performing first, as he himself had always done until recently.

'Okay, okay. Maybe I accept you won't be tempted on that front. And sleeping around, yeah, why not? It's great. But *cut it back*, okay?' Andy gave him a quick grin, one eyebrow raised. 'Remember what you owe the fans. Don't end up in clubs every night, drinking too much...being so hungover the next morning you can't get up on time for working sessions!'

'Andy, if this was *anyone* but you...' Nic breathed, his voice dangerously low.

'Yeah, but it *is* me. Well, it's me saying it to you, but you may as well know others are saying it to me.'

'Who?' His fist hit the table.

Andy shrugged, his gaze remaining steady. 'Ian. Jon. Jon said the other day you couldn't give a damn when we were trying that song out for recording. He was in quite a temper, didn't you notice?'

Uncomfortably, Nic recalled his disinterest, caused by another late-night drinking session, another woman. Jon, he remembered, had eventually thrown down his drumsticks and walked out, swearing volubly, and to be quite honest, Nic hadn't even cared to find out the reason why, had just been glad to call a halt. But it seemed *he* was the reason. And yes, now he remembered, Ian, his bassist, had given him a silent look of contempt and left as well. He sat staring blindly across the room, shocked by what he'd just been told.

Andy was right! How had he sunk into this? He certainly hated drugs with a passionate intensity that was surprising to many, but after all, what was alcohol but just another drug? How had he slipped into the trap of drinking so frequently and so freely? It shamed him to think the other members of the group were beginning to think he was letting them down. He'd never, ever intended that to happen.

'Nic?'

'Yeah, yeah, yeah.' Nic shook his head impatiently. 'So you all think I'm letting you down?'

Andy hesitated. 'Pretty well, yes. And you're charismatic on stage. I mean, without us, *you* could probably still survive-'

'Nah!' He was quick to vehemently deny this. 'We're a sound, all of us. The fans all have their favourites anyway.'

4

'*You* could probably still survive,' Andy repeated impatiently, a grin crossing his features, 'but I'm not sure *we* could! It's important for us to keep you straight, okay?'

'So?'

'Keep your feet on the ground. Cut back, okay?'

Nic ran his hands over his face to avoid looking at his friend. 'Andy, you're a hard man,' he muttered through splayed fingers.

'Someone's got to say it before it's too late,' Andy replied simply, gathering up the papers they'd been working on. 'I guess there's not much point in going on with this?'

Nic sighed deeply. 'I guess you're right in what you're saying. I don't know...I do know I'm not totally happy these days and I don't know why, but it's not boredom with my music or the group. Never that. I'd like to find...' For a long moment, he was silent, eyes staring into the distance. 'Hell, Andy, is it so impossible to find someone who'd love me just...ah, I must be mad! Forget it. Nothing but sentimental drivel.'

'What are you trying to say?'

Nic got up and restlessly wandered over to the window. He swung round. 'I guess I always thought, somehow...I always thought one day I'd find someone who'd...' His voice died away and he dropped his gaze from his friend's direct stare.

Andy looked at Nic consideringly. 'Who'd love you just for yourself, kid?' he asked softly, sadly. 'How could that ever be? The only way is if you met someone who doesn't know who you are and you're too well known for that. It would take a miracle, and miracles just don't happen. You'll never meet anyone who doesn't know who you are.'

'Yeah,' Nic said equally softly in reply, 'it *would* take a miracle, wouldn't it?' His face was tired.

'But jumping into bed with every woman who offers isn't the answer. Look, get away up north, have a talk to Sam, go for a few walks. You always said it kept you straight and you haven't been up there for months. You've slipped into bad habits, that's all. We've only noticed because all this is new for you.' Andy's voice was sympathetic.

'Maybe.' Nic was noncommittal. 'Can't go north anyway, until we come back from abroad. Too much to organise in the next month and I can't spare the time. But yeah.' He sighed and stood up, punching his friend on the arm. 'Tell the others not to worry. I'll pull it together. But I feel...I feel...oh, I don't know...' He shrugged and touched the pile of papers on the table. 'Look, for now, yeah, we'll pack it in. I'll go out for a ride on the bike. If I can't get up north, that's the next best thing, and I've got time enough for one now as long as I get back for my three o' clock meeting.'

'You do that.' Andy, too, stood up. He'd thought Nic just needed a warning, a pep-talk, but it seemed there was something deeper here. Nic seemed depressed and lonely. He knew all the women who latched onto him were after prestige, their own hour in the spotlight, material goods, and only in him as a means to this end.

In the same position himself, Andy knew only too well fame had its own drawbacks and could make you feel very isolated. Nic, it seemed, was apparently hankering for the impossible.

'Yeah, you do that,' Andy repeated, watching Nic as he swung his tall body round and headed for the internal staircase which led to the basement garage. 'Take care, friend,' he said softly. 'Take care.'

Chapter Two:

Jessica Farndale turned onto her drive and stopped the car, her eyes widening in consternation and surprise.

In front of the garage, totally alien and completely out of place, was a large motorbike. Contemplating this sleekly black and powerful invasion of her property uneasily, her eyes flickered from the bike to the front of the house and back. She wasn't expecting visitors but anyway, no-one she knew would possess such a vehicle and there was no-one to be seen, so whose was it, and, more to the point, where was the owner?

In spite of the heat of the late August afternoon, Jessica shivered. She'd always felt motorcyclists to be rather threatening. Shaking her head impatiently, her thick, honey coloured hair swinging over her face, she opened the door, her feet crunching on the dusty gravel of the drive. The silence was absolute; not even the birds had the energy to sing.

Advancing slowly towards the bike, Jessica reached out a long-fingered, delicate hand and touched the gleaming tank. Where *was* the owner? Slowly Jessica turned and once more surveyed the front of the cottage, which looked peaceful enough. Hesitantly, she walked to the door.

Peering cautiously through the windows, Jessica could see everything looked as she had left it early this morning, when she'd set off for rehearsals in London. Unlocking the door, she opened it carefully, listening for any strange noise, trying to sense if there was another person in the house. Moving softly upstairs, she opened the doors to all the rooms. No disturbance at all. Dust motes danced lazily in the beams of sunlight coming through the windows, and lit up the shining wood of the dressing tables. The crisp linen on the beds gave off a faint perfume of fresh air and lavender.

Downstairs again, still moving silently, with muscles tensed, Jessica checked the sitting room. The baby grand piano stood at one end of the room and she thought of the pieces she'd been practising this morning, working through them with David Brunskill almost note by note, beginning the long process of building up her own interpretation for the next series of concerts in the new year.

Shaking her head, dismissing thoughts of music, she crossed the hall to the kitchen. The quarry stone tiles on the floor glowed warmly and the honey coloured wooden units caught the

7

sunshine and filled the room with light. There was no sign of an intruder anywhere. No sign of theft, and no sign of vandalism.

Aware of a release of tension, Jessica leaned against the sink and ran a tongue round her dry mouth. Turning on the tap, she filled a glass with water, drinking slowly as she stared out of the window which overlooked the front garden. The house might be quiet and undisturbed but that still didn't solve the problem of whose bike it was and where he...it *had* to be a he...was now.

Jessica shrugged. Now she knew there was no intruder in the house, other thoughts came to mind. Perhaps he'd broken down, tried her house for help, left the bike and gone to look for assistance elsewhere. It was hardly the weather to try pushing such a large machine any distance. Mind you, he'd have a long walk...the nearest villages were Northrush and Chipping Mickleton, both about five miles distant.

Wandering down to the other end of the long room, where a dining table and chairs stood in front of French windows leading into her large back garden, she set the glass down and moved to unbolt and unlock them, thinking ruefully that any burglar would have found her a poor target. She'd no television. The only thing that was worth stealing was her stereo system. Now that would...Jessica froze.

There *was* someone, after all. Someone in the garden. She could see him lying in the shade of one of the trees. She stretched out her hand and groped for the support of the table. Hesitating, she considered ringing the police. It was the most sensible thing to do. Certainly, a lot more sensible than the sudden surge of hot anger that swept through her at the sight of the recumbent figure, so oblivious to the fear and worry he'd provoked in her.

How dare he drive his bike onto her property and leave it there, sneaking round the back to lie sunbathing in her garden, scaring her witless? Without stopping to think, reacting blindly to the fear she'd first felt, which was now fuelled by anger, Jessica finished opening the windows and strode into the garden until she stood about six feet away from the prone figure lying in relaxed abandon and quite obviously asleep.

He was tall, dressed in a close-fitting black tee shirt and black jeans. Wide-shouldered, slim-hipped, bare-footed. The jeans were soft and worn, and contoured his body in an understated but immensely sexy way.

Jessica paused, swallowing suddenly as she realised not only was she blatantly assessing the sleeping man, but was

8

finding him undeniably attractive. Something coiled inside her, shocking her with its intensity.

He had strong, tanned arms, one flung above his head, the other by his side. An equally strong face, thin and square-jawed, with high cheekbones and a wide, finely-cut mouth. Thick black hair curled down to touch his shoulders, longer and far more unruly than the hair of the sort of men Jessica usually came into contact with.

His impact on her was as unexpected as it was disturbing and she drew in her breath sharply, uncomfortably aware of the sudden slam of her heart against her ribcage and these strange new sensations, which were most definitely not fear, moving from the pit of her stomach throughout her body, almost taking her over. A long moment passed as she continued to watch him.

Finally managing to break the strangely mesmeric effect he seemed to have on her, she stepped forward and prodded him on the leg with the toe of her shoe before retreating rapidly to a safe distance, glad she was able to rekindle her anger.

'What do you think you're doing?' she asked in a curt voice.

Intense blue eyes, framed with thick, black lashes, snapped wide open in alarm then screwed up in protest against the glare of the sun. The man's arm fell over his face to shield it and in one swift movement he rose fluidly to his feet and stepped back into the deeper shade under the tree, staring at Jessica with those incredible eyes.

'Whooaa,' he breathed out slowly, his voice deep and softly caressing. 'Have I died and gone to heaven, or what?'

In his turn, and as blatantly as Jessica had assessed him whilst he slept, he continued to stare. He took in her fall of thick blonde hair, her green eyes and her tall, slim figure with its generous curves outlined by the thin cotton dress that skimmed her body before flaring out over her hips and swirling round tanned legs which seemed to go on forever. He took no account of the blaze of anger in the green eyes, or her full mouth held in a tight line of annoyance, as his eyes flickered slowly to her feet and back again, a definite awakening of interest plainly obvious on his face.

'Hey,' he said easily, a faint smile lifting the corners of his mouth, confidently expecting the usual response from her once she realised who he was. This irritating breakdown of his bike might prove very interesting, very interesting indeed. His stance was assured and slightly arrogant, one hand hooked into the pocket of his jeans, the other reaching to push his tumbled hair

9

back from his face. But the reaction which came was not quite what he'd expected.

Jessica glared at him in disbelief. Was that all he could say? *Hey*? 'Look,' she said cuttingly, 'would you mind explaining exactly what you're doing? Here, in my garden, with your...your bike on my drive? Don't come any closer!' She panicked as he stepped forwards.

He spread his hands in a wide gesture of apology. 'Look, lady, I'm not going to hurt you or anything. I'm sorry, I honestly didn't think anybody would mind. My bike's broken down. Rather drastically, I'm sorry to say. I can't go any further. I was hoping to use your phone. No-one answered the door, so I came round to see if anyone was in the garden.'

'And when you found there wasn't you should have gone, so why are you still here?'

'Well, hey, no excuse.' He shrugged and grinned at her, blue eyes crinkling at the corners, then pushed his fingers a second time through his thick black hair. 'The garden looked so pleasant...it's hot...I didn't know where the nearest phone was...so I just...'

His easy manner, his assumption that what he'd done was quite acceptable, but especially his casual amusement, irritated Jessica thoroughly. She ignored a small voice at the back of her mind suggesting he hadn't been so very unreasonable after all. That she had, in fact, worked out for herself that this was probably the explanation for the bike's presence in front of her garage, and interrupted him forcefully. 'So you just trespassed! Well, Mr...whoever...you *can* use my phone, I won't deny you that. Then you can move yourself and your bike to the bottom of my drive and sit there and wait for your help.'

'My name's Nic,' he said slowly, 'Nic Daniel. Nic without a k. Daniel without an s.' His eyes narrowed as he watched her carefully, waiting for a reaction. Again, there was none. Jessica continued to glare at him with undisguised hostility. A momentary flicker of amazed disbelief, followed by uncertain surprise, crossed Nic Daniel's face.

'Right, Mr. Daniels. You see those open doors? The phone's inside, on the island half way down the room. Pick up your stuff, go and use it and then get out. Please.' she added with perfunctory and slightly desperate politeness, for she just wanted this man gone. He really was having a most disturbing effect on her emotions and she wasn't sure she liked it. She trembled slightly, her stomach still unsettled.

10

He stood there in his black tee shirt and jeans, bare arms folded across his chest, looking at her steadily. 'Daniel.' The dark-haired man repeated mildly. 'Nic without the k. Daniel without the s.'

'Quite frankly, I couldn't care less. In five minutes, I don't ever expect to see you again, so what your name is and how you spell it is a matter of supreme indifference to me. Move!'

He stayed where he was, gazing at the beautiful, angry woman in front of him as he tried to process the fact that, once again, she'd shown no flicker, no sign whatsoever, that she knew who he was.

Running the tip of her tongue nervously over her lips, Jessica realised he reminded her of his bike. Powerful. From her point of view, uncontrollable. Slightly menacing. But...oh, beautiful to look at. 'Go and use the phone, will you? Otherwise I will, to ring the police!' Jessica said desperately.

Nic moved forward, looking slightly dazed. 'So you want me to go sit at the bottom of your drive? Lady, it might take a couple of hours or more for my help to get here, and it's rather hot. Couldn't I...?'

'No!'

'Okay. I'll use your phone and then get out of here,' he said tightly, his initial attraction to this uncooperative beauty fading away into annoyance. It seemed this just wasn't his day! First Andy, now this! With a look of contempt at Jessica, he walked over to where his helmet, jacket and boots lay on the grass. Picking them up, he strode with arrogant and fluid ease across the lawn and disappeared into the cool gloom of the house.

Jessica followed him and stood just inside the French windows, and as Nic sat down on a chair, pulling on his socks and boots, she watched the movement of his hands in fascination, a strange feeling of intimacy filling her as he performed the simple task. It seemed she was unable to take her eyes off this man, who had intruded so abruptly into her very quiet, very sheltered, existence.

Leaving the helmet and jacket lying on the table, he turned to the phone, crisply dialling the numbers with his lean, tanned fingers.

For one brief, shocking moment, Jessica wondered what it would feel like to have those fingers touching her. Her face flaming, she dropped her eyes quickly, unable to believe the direction of her thoughts. This wasn't the sort of man she'd ever

11

met before, or the type she would ever seek out. He didn't come under the headings of conventional and non-threatening.

But reluctantly, Jessica found her eyes drawn back to him again, instinctively recognising the power of his body as he sat on the chair waiting for the phone to be answered, appreciating the long, tangled hair and his passionate mouth. She was, quite frankly, bewildered.

Running an impatient hand through his thick hair, scooping it up and back, away from his face, obviously something of a habit, he gazed unseeingly across the room. Suddenly he straightened and leaned forwards. 'Hi. Put me through to Josh, please.' There was a brief pause, then, 'Josh? Is that you? Nic here. The bike's broken down. Badly...no, no, I'm okay. I just need someone to come and collect me in the van so we can get the bike back.' He listened attentively, long fingers tapping restlessly on the worktop, flicking glances round the room.

His eyes rested briefly on Jessica standing by the table, now slowly drinking from her glass of water and still watching him. Her face coloured as he looked at her, and his mobile mouth tightened. Passing quickly over her, he focused on the blaze of colour and light visible through the open window. 'Yeah...yeah, I thought they would. It's too bad, but there's nothing to be done about it now, is there? Yes, I know, I'll deal with it. I have access to a phone here, so just give me the number, okay?' Nic's voice developed a sharp note of impatience as the conversation progressed.

Looking round, he saw a pad of paper and a pen lying to one side of the phone. Pulling it towards him he wrote down a number then repeated it back. 'Okay. It's better if I call with the excuses than you. Now, how long before you can arrange for the van to be here? Two, maybe three hours? I don't know...hang on, I'll ask.' He covered the mouthpiece of the phone. 'Where am I?' he asked brusquely.

'Five miles west of Chipping Mickleton, on the B7713 to Northrush. Northrush is about another five or six miles further on from here. This house is called Keeper's Cottage.' Jessica said flatly.

He turned silently back to the telephone with a bare nod of acknowledgement.

Jessica listened as he repeated the information she'd just given to him before she wandered miserably into the garden and sat down on the bench against the house wall, resting her head against the warm, old stone and closing her eyes.

He was a frightening man, arrogant and irritated in manner. Nic Daniel. Nic Daniel. She let the name drift slowly into her mind. And yet...frightening or not, he was also a very, very attractive man, with his lithe restlessness and his quick smile, his wide shoulders and slim hips. Even that unruly mane of untamed hair suited his strong features.

Not like her to think that. No *good* her thinking that. She recalled his contempt, justifiably directed at her for sending him out of the garden into this heat. But anyway, she imagined he wasn't the sort to bother with her. He was far too worldly and sophisticated. Why was she reacting like this anyway? She struggled to regain her usual cool, detached composure.

After a few minutes she felt a light touch on her shoulder. Startled she looked up.

'Right,' Nic spoke coldly. 'I've left some money for the calls by the phone. Josh said he'd be out with the van in about two or three hours.

Jessica nodded silently, her eyes moving over his stern face. He turned, his jacket slung over his shoulder, his helmet loosely held by his side, and strode to the side gate leading to the front of the house. 'Then I'll get out of your way. Thank you for allowing me to use your phone.' He spoke over his shoulder in the same quiet, cold voice.

'Oh, but...' Jessica rose to her feet, holding out her hand as if to detain him, wishing she could turn the clock back.

But Nic Daniel either didn't hear or didn't choose to hear. A click of the gate and he was gone.

His cold implacability struck to her very centre, but he was right, she acknowledged miserably. She hadn't given him a chance. Hadn't listened to his explanation or his apology even though maybe her anger had initially been justified. Nic Daniel wasn't dangerous...at least, not in the way she'd first thought. She had an uneasy feeling, however, he might've proved dangerous in another way, and might be very difficult to forget.

Lifting her heavy hair from the nape of her neck, Jessica sighed. It was so *hot*, even here in the shade, and it was no good sitting here with all these regrets. It was too late now. She was unlikely to speak to him again...see him again...and in two or three hours he would be gone from her house and her life. Strange, then, that even as she tried to comfort herself with such thoughts, her regret deepened.

Okay, *so what*? Exasperation filled her. She'd felt attracted to him. *So what*? He wasn't her type. Not at all. Hang on to that thought. Previous male companions had aroused no such torrent of feelings, of just about out of control emotions, which were almost unpleasant. She shook her head in annoyance and rose tiredly to her feet.

Going into the kitchen, she winced as she passed the phone with two pound notes laid neatly and insultingly beside it. Almost against her will, she moved to the kitchen window and looked out. Nic Daniel was sitting on the gravelled driveway just where it joined the road. As she watched, he lifted a hand and rubbed it wearily across his forehead before scooping back his hair again, then dropping his head to rest it on his arms.

Jessica stood there in the cool kitchen and bit her lip. The sun was beating down. He must be so hot. He was wearing black clothes. And he'd looked tired back there in the garden. There'd been a faint bruised look underneath those incredible blue eyes.

She began to feel increasingly uncomfortable about the way she'd behaved. Turning abruptly away from the window, she went upstairs to shower.

Chapter Three

Nic's mood, which had improved with the ride and the initial sight of Jessica, had by now thoroughly soured again. He shifted uncomfortably on the hot gravelled driveway. The sun beat down, burning through his clothes and sweat slicked his face. He stared at his feet encased in hot leather boots. Essential for safe motorcycling, not an enjoyable prospect when faced with anything up to three hours sitting here. He was thirsty. He was hungry. He was tired.

Today. What was wrong with the day that it had gone so sour, from the moment he'd woken up late and realised Andy was waiting for him, that song which wouldn't come right, his friend's totally unexpected, although he had to admit thoroughly justified, attack on him, and now *this*?

Nic's life was a hectic round of tours, song-writing, rehearsing, recording, decision making. He was always surrounded by people. Wherever he went, it was almost impossible not to have someone approaching him and making demands. He'd taken himself off at frequent intervals to his haven of peace and tranquillity in the Lake District, and there renewed himself.

Until recently, when he'd felt the loneliness of his life, the impossibility of being able to look at the woman by his side without wondering if she was there just because he was Nic Daniel. Well, wake up! Of course that's why she was there! Any hopes for a genuine relationship had gradually begun to die.

His thoughts wandered idly, picking over the events of the morning, moving on to the episode in the garden. At least that girl hadn't wanted anything from him. Except for his departure of course, he admitted wryly. And she hadn't recognised him, hadn't known his name.

Shock jolted through him, and Nic straightened abruptly, staring blankly up the drive at the house as it finally sunk in. S*he hadn't recognised him*!

He shook his head in amazement. There *was* someone in the world who didn't recognise him! What Andy'd said couldn't possibly happen, unbelievably just had!

He sank back against the wall. Yeah, hey, and guess what? She was an out and out pain in the neck. There was no other way to describe her. So what if her blonde loveliness had taken his breath away? What if she looked sexy enough to want to sleep with? Not much good, if she was such a sour puss.

Stupid woman! Why couldn't she understand why he'd come into her garden? A lot more pleasant than waiting at the side of the road or pushing his bike goodness knows how far in this heat! He knew these lanes. You could go for miles without sight of a house or a phone box.

Nic gave a hollow laugh. A miracle, Andy had said. But what if the miracle was no good? Maybe God liked a little joke now and then, he thought sourly, and dropped his head to rest on his folded arms. He shut his eyes and tried to blank out his mind. He'd had plenty of experience of waiting in his lifetime. A little more wouldn't hurt. Except it was so *unbearably* hot!

Twenty minutes later Jessica was back in the kitchen, leaning against the sink. She felt cool and refreshed and had changed into shorts and a loose top. Nic Daniel didn't seem to have moved and he looked extremely tired and uncomfortable.

Jessica stared at him, the same thoughts as before darting all over the place. He frightened her. A dangerous man. Not her type. Not her type at all. He *disturbed* her. He made her uncomfortable with the effect he had on her, and she wasn't sure she liked that. He was better left out there.

But…she really couldn't. She couldn't leave him sitting at the side of the dusty road in this heat for the next two hours. He wouldn't *physically* harm her, she knew that now. Sighing, she straightened up. It was a matter of basic courtesy to invite him back in to wait where it was cooler, until this friend appeared to pick him and his bike up.

It took her a lot of courage to turn and walk down the kitchen, out of the French windows and through the gate that led round to the front of the house. Her sandals scrunched on the gravel.

Nic raised his head and turned to watch her approach, his face blank, with a derisory curl to his well-cut mouth. His face gleamed with sweat and his tee-shirt clung to his back. He wasn't going to give an *inch*!

Despite his discomfort and hostility, he was still able to appreciate the shapely length of her legs and the slim, curvaceous figure, now more fully exposed by the top and shorts. She really was incredibly beautiful, his miracle woman. Nic sighed wearily. A pity they hadn't met under different circumstances. And what did she want *now*?

Speaking abruptly, before his expression could frighten her into retreating, Jessica said, 'I'm sorry. You were right. I should have listened to you properly instead of getting so steamed up. I'm...I'm going to have some lunch. Do you want to..?'

Her voice died away as Nic continued to stare impassively at her. Surprise and interest stirred inside him at this unexpected twist to events. Perhaps the afternoon would turn out better than he'd expected...there would be time to get her to bed, maybe, before Josh appeared...and he would have little compunction about leaving her afterwards.

Jessica swallowed nervously and stared down at the toes of her sandals as his eyes, blatant and intrusive, now assessed her and stripped her. Although she wasn't quite sure what it was in his look, she knew it was making her very uncomfortable and causing a flush to creep up her skin.

'Do I want to what?' prompted Nic flatly.

She glanced quickly at his handsome face and just as quickly away. His expression was still hostile.

'To come back in? And...and have something to eat? It's so hot out here and...and you've still got a long time to wait, so...so I thought...' Again, she faltered, feeling nervous and uncertain.

At last he sighed, uncoiled his long length and slowly stood up, a good few inches taller than Jessica. 'All right,' he spoke laconically and gestured to her to lead the way back into the house. Anything...*anything*...was preferable to spending the rest of his time out here and, hey, this began to show some promise.

Once back inside, Jessica indicated a chair. 'Won't you sit down?'

Silently, still watching her from under lowered lids, Nic sank down onto the chair and stretched out his legs.

'You can...you can take your boots off again if you like.' Jessica bit her lip. His deliberate, cold silence made her nervous.

He raised his eyebrows, shrugged, then leaned down to unbuckle, with some relief, the heavy boots. He put them with his helmet and jacket, next to his chair, and flexed his hot feet on the cold quarry tiles of the floor.

'Would you...would you like something to drink?' Jessica's voice verged on the desperate in the face of his continued silence. 'Orange juice? Wine? I've got some beer.' She gestured towards the fridge.

Continuing to regard her steadily, assessingly, Nic felt extremely glad to be out of the hot sun. The floor felt wonderful to his feet and already he could feel his face cooling down. But he really didn't see why he should let her off so easily. That twenty or so minutes in the full heat of the sun had been punishing and now it was her turn to suffer. And the guiltier he could make her feel, the better, surely, her capitulation would be?

Her green eyes stared back at him, completely guileless and tinged with nervousness, giving him a twinge of conscience. Trying to dismiss it, he was dismayed that it lingered, even grew stronger.

Just as she felt the silence would last forever, he nodded his head. 'Do you have any fizzy mineral water? Half and half with any fruit juice would be welcome, thanks.' He'd had enough alcohol last night.

Jessica was relieved to be able to turn away from that disturbing stare and busy herself taking a bottle of water and some fruit juice out of the fridge. She tipped them both into a large jug, adding plenty of ice-cubes, then returned to the table to fill his glass.

'Thanks.' Nic spoke briefly, taking his glass and drinking deeply.

'I was going to have some salad. Is that okay?'

Again, she was on the receiving end of his cool stare. Again, he shrugged and spoke in the same flat voice. 'Thank you. Yes, that would be fine.'

He continued to watch her, legs sprawled, arms loosely folded across his broad chest, as she moved round the kitchen, taking salad ingredients from the fridge, washing them, carving pieces from a cold, roast chicken. Quite deliberately, he still didn't speak a word and Jessica began to feel more and more uncomfortable.

She brought plates, salad, chicken and fresh, crusty, French bread to the table before sitting down opposite the ever-watchful Nic.

Pulling his chair to the table, he took a piece of bread, helped himself to the salad and began to eat appreciatively. Jessica picked up her knife and fork, then put them down. She poured herself some of the fruit juice and drank a little. Then she took a piece of bread, nervously shredding it onto her plate.

Nic stopped eating and watched her hands, then raised his eyes to meet her worried green ones. 'Why don't you relax?' His tone still remained cold as he picked up his knife and buttered his own bread, his strong, lean-fingered hands dextrous and controlled, the complete opposite of Jessica's.

'How can I?' Jessica burst out. 'You're sitting there saying nothing at all and looking at me as if...so...' She lacked the experience to explain in words what she felt about the type of

18

looks she was receiving from the cold stranger opposite, but she knew she didn't like them. 'You're making me nervous!'

'Me? Huh! I can't believe that. You're as hard as nails, lady.' He bit into the bread with his strong white teeth and resumed his blank stare, knowing what he said was totally unjustified. Anyone less hard than this wide-eyed innocent would be difficult to find. A babe in arms, he decided now, eyeing her more carefully from under his lashes, briefly wondering how long it would take to seduce her and, after all, whether he could be bothered.

Jessica swallowed hard to prevent the sob she felt rising in her throat from escaping. She stood abruptly, her chair scraping back harshly on the tiles, and fled into the silent tranquillity of the sitting room. Moving blindly across the room to the windows at the far end she rested her forehead on the cool glass, her face burning, her throat tight.

Why, oh why, she thought in anger and dismay, as despite attempts to control them, the tears escaped to trickle slowly down her cheeks, had she thought she could cope with the likes of Nic Daniel? He was way out of her league and he was obviously determined to rub in her initial poor behaviour. Her thoughts whirled round in her head. She should never have invited him back in. But Jessica admitted to herself, if she was totally honest, she'd invited him not only because of politeness and because she could see he'd been suffering in that blazing sun, but also in the hope that perhaps they could…start afresh.

Well, it seemed it wasn't to be…and it didn't make it any better that she'd brought it on herself. If only she'd listened to what he'd said without being so determined to throw him out.

He was being so *unbelievably* unfriendly, looking at her all the time in such an insolent manner, and…and there was definitely that something else in his look that she still couldn't quite work out, but it wasn't pleasant.

She swallowed. If she stayed in here, hopefully he'd finish his meal and have the sense to go back into the garden until his friend came for the bike. Jessica knew she couldn't face him again and that it'd been a mistake to invite him back. She lifted her fingers and wiped the tears away with a thumb and finger, but others followed.

In the kitchen, Nic stared at Jessica's chair crookedly standing two or three feet from the table and then at her abandoned plate. Slowly he put down his own knife and fork and folded his arms across his chest, impatiently flicking his hair back from his forehead with a quick movement of his head, everything

Andy had accused him of that morning flooding back. Hard. Arrogant. Treating women badly. Oh, yeah.

'Well, Nic, proud of yourself?' he murmured softly, a sudden flush crossing his high cheekbones. He hadn't really meant it when he'd commented she was as hard as nails. It was quite obvious, from the minute she'd been able to think straight, that she regretted what she'd done and was embarrassed about it, and *that'd* happened before he'd finished phoning. Deep inside, feelings of shame and remorse stirred and pushed through the layers of arrogant indifference which had built up almost unnoticed over the last year.

But *why* the twinges of conscience? What did he care?

Well, partly what Andy had been saying, of course, which had made him take stock of himself, but…

…it was her. Somehow, she was getting to him. Her courtesy. Her quiet movements. Her eyes, so clear and honest. Her trustfulness. She was…restful. She was gentle. He shouldn't have behaved like that, he really shouldn't.

He shook his head in annoyed disbelief. Come on! He could have any woman he wanted, without caring how he behaved! He paused, dropping his head. And look where it had got him, he thought bitterly. What was it he'd asked Andy this morning? When could he ever be sure, if a woman said she loved him, that it wasn't simply what he could offer that she loved?

What else had he asked? Wasn't it possible to find a woman who would love him for himself?

That'd take someone who didn't know who he was, Andy had replied, which would be a miracle. And yet the miracle had, unbelievably, happened.

But surely not this sleeping beauty living in her rose-clad cottage, unawakened and innocent. That wasn't his scene. She wasn't his *type*.

So, okay...what was his scene? The vapid blondes and brunettes he'd been going around with just recently? Absolutely not. That was the whole problem. He was running scared, panicking as he searched for something elusive, something he wasn't sure he could put a name to but was sure he'd recognise when he saw it.

Had he recognised it now? Certainly, he was fascinated to realise this girl, this woman, was gentle as a startled fawn, totally straightforward and open, totally *innocent*! So different, so utterly different.

And ignorant of who he was.

Could he make her love him just for himself, he wondered now? It might be...interesting. There was enough here to be going on with, to see where it went. It was simply too tempting, it really was. After a few more moments, Nic unfolded his arms and followed Jessica out of the room.

Feeling a hand on her shoulder, Jessica jumped. Gently Nic turned her round. She opened tear-washed eyes. He held a large, clean tissue in one hand and used it to wipe away the tears while with his other hand he gently steadied her chin.

'I'm sorry,' he said softly. 'That was really unforgivable of me in view of the fact you'd asked me back in and fed me, after I'd frightened you. Here,' he pushed the tissue into her unresisting hand, 'keep it.' His fingers briefly caressed her jaw before he stepped back, one dark eyebrow raised, a faint smile lifting the corners of his mouth. He knew, very well indeed, how to turn on the charm and he wanted, quite badly now, to make amends and have her thinking well of him.

Interest and wonder stirred in him again. *She didn't know who he was*! What would it be like to make love to someone who didn't know who he was? What would it be like to make love to someone who was so unassuming, so different to the women he usually met? The novelty of the idea began to be unbelievably exciting. This was his chance to find out!

'Th-thank you.' Jessica sniffed and blew her nose. 'I'm sorry to be so...so silly, but you...you...'

'Yeah, I know.' He ducked his head, looking taken aback as the shame touched him again. 'I was being unkind. Deliberately unkind,' he added, with an unaccustomed and surprising honesty.

'Well, yes, you were. But I suppose I deserved it,' Jessica acknowledged generously before rushing on. 'I didn't know whose bike it was, you see. I d-didn't even know where you were. I thought maybe someone was in the house. I was frightened and then I saw you lying there, in the garden, so...so...*oblivious* to everything! I-I didn't know what you...you might do...and these days...I live alone and this is a fairly remote house. I didn't want to take any risks.' She raised bright, tear-drenched eyes to him, a tremulous smile touching the corners of her mouth, her utter sincerity shining on her face.

Nic caught his breath, staring at her in amazement. Come on, how naïve could you get, he thought. This couldn't be for real. She'd just admitted to living alone, that the house was remote, not that he hadn't known that already, all the while with those wide green eyes fixed trustingly on his.

He shook his head in disbelief, at her, at himself, as he realised all at once, with blistering clarity, that if he *did* try to seduce her it would, plainly and simply, be wrong! Immoral, almost. If he wanted…if he wanted…

There was a long silence as he continued to stare at her, trying to work out these unfamiliar feelings. There was a sudden and unaccountable desire to protect her. A sudden fierce longing to *talk* to her, to get to know her better, to find out if she...but normally he didn't waste time *talking*! That really wasn't what he'd intended when he'd followed her in here. No, he'd still intended to…to...He shook his head a second time, unable to quite believe the direction in which his thoughts were heading. Real knight in shining armour stuff, he jeered silently at himself.

Jessica shifted uncomfortably under his stare, screwing the tissue round nervously.

Eventually, Nic sighed. 'I suppose you took a risk rushing out the way you did. But I did try to explain,' he added quietly.

Jessica's face flamed again. 'All right, yes, I admit I should have listened. But I've apologised. Can't you accept that and stop treating me as...as...'

'Someone I felt a little annoyed with?' he finished for her, with a faint smile, evading the truth of exactly how he *had* been treating her. 'Oh, yes, I'll try. Now look, I really am hungry. Will you come back and eat something?'

Jessica smiled a little shakily and their eyes met and held for a fraction of a second. She put her hand on the frame of the window to steady her suddenly trembling body and turned quickly away to walk down the room. Nic took a deep breath and swallowed hard, before following her back to the table.

Slowly, in a silence that was no longer threatening, they finished their meal. Jessica produced some coffee then Nic leaned forwards, elbows on the table. 'You know,' he spoke rather abruptly, 'I'm afraid I don't even know your name. I'm sorry...'

'Jessica. Jessica Farndale.' She held out her hand.

Startled, Nic took it in his. Jessica had only intended to offer a brief handshake, an automatic response to giving her name, but Nic continued to hold her hand in both of his. She blushed furiously and tried to pull away but Nic was quite strong enough to prevent her.

'Hello, Jessica Farndale,' he said gravely. 'Perhaps we could start again?'

Chapter Four:

They took their coffee to a bench at the bottom of the garden. It was set under some apple trees, with a view over both the garden and the rolling barley field to the wooded hills beyond. The lawn lay coolly green, stretching between the seat and the warm stone of the old cottage.

Nic glanced round. 'This is amazingly beautiful. You're lucky to live here. I'd like to live in the country if it was possible.' He startled himself by realising this was still true of him.

She stole a quick look at him, sitting in casual relaxation with long legs stretched out and crossed at the ankle. His arm rested along the back of the bench and his head was half-turned away as he looked out across the fields. To her, still somewhat intimidatingly, he exuded confidence and an aura of success and power, as if he knew exactly what he wanted and always got it. He was being pleasant enough at the moment, but she was no more sure now that it was a good idea he was here than she had been previously.

'You must live in a town, then?' Oh, brilliant, Jessica, she chided herself. Scintillating. Add that to her earlier performance as a harridan, and he would be off so fast once his friend turned up, she wouldn't have a chance to even say, nice to have met you, do call again and goodbye!

Her lack of conversational powers didn't seem to worry Nic as he turned to her with a grin. 'Yep. Unfortunately,' he shrugged lightly, 'the biggest of them all, London. I have to be central, it's essential. But I do have a house-' He suddenly cut off what he'd been about to say. 'I have to live in London...my job...'

Jessica couldn't imagine what his job might be. He seemed too unconventional for a business man, too powerful and confident to hold down a run-of-the-mill office sort of job.

'What *is* it you do?' she asked with curiosity.

'Um…' he paused, uncertainly, as it hit him again. She didn't know who he was. So, what to say, now? Having discovered her ignorance, he rather wanted to keep it that way for now. The whole set-up was intriguing, although he really wasn't quite sure where it was all going. 'I have to be based in London…' Oh great, he'd already said that. 'I, er, I work in the music industry, on the recording side,' he continued, with some desperation. True, in a vague and roundabout way.

She was looking puzzled, her great, wide eyes fixed on him. The truth rose up in response and with a great effort of will he pushed it back down. Okay, he wouldn't lie to her…somehow, he found he *couldn't* lie to her…but he would evade the truth. Once she knew, it would change everything. It always did, he thought desperately. He'd never know then if it was him or what he could offer, and therefore he'd be back at square one. *She mustn't know.*

He knew he wasn't really making much sense. He wasn't trying to be impressive, but it didn't matter. A feeling of elation swept through him as he suddenly relaxed. He took a deep breath and felt better than he had in months. Here, he didn't have to be on guard all the time. Here, he could just be himself. It was like an enormous weight suddenly evaporating. A black cloud being pierced by a dazzling sun. Another Bleathwaite. But with Jessica.

'That's a coincidence…I…I also work in music…' She was uncertain how much to say about her burgeoning career as a rising star in the classical world.

Nic looked startled. 'In music?' A feeling of panic rose up inside him 'What do you do? Where?'

'Here quite a lot of the time, but London as well.'

Although an increasingly well-known and successful concert pianist, a sheltered upbringing had, Jessica knew now with some bitterness, made her shy and uncertain of herself except when she was on the concert platform. There, with the piano as a means of communication, she was able to reach out to anyone, but she didn't enjoy the limelight, the parties, and the publicity that went with her growing fame. Living out here gave her the excuse of a long journey, in either direction, as a reason for not becoming too involved with it all.

Realising Nic had asked her a question, Jessica dragged her attention back. 'I'm sorry?'

'Do you have to spend much of your time in London?'

'A fair bit. It varies. I…at the moment I have to go up a couple of times a week. But it doesn't take too long, not long at all, from here. When you get on the motorway.'

'Why do you have to go up only twice a week?' What on earth could it be that she did?

'I play the piano.'

Nic reached out for her hands and held them in his, turning them over, looking thoughtful. He rubbed his thumbs absently over her wrist, massaging first one side, then the other. She played the piano! Would their worlds collide? Obviously they

24

hadn't, as yet, if she didn't know who he was. His mind raced over various possibilities, none of which fitted in with going to London only twice a week and being home this early anyway. Unless…maybe she was a session player? That might explain it.

Jessica swallowed, glad she was sitting down. Her breathing quickened as she stared back, incapable of pulling her hands away, incapable of speaking, as she tried to cope with this non-stop maelstrom of feelings Nic Daniel seemed to rouse in her. One minute meltingly happy, with tremors of unfamiliar excitement flickering through her, making her achingly aware of everything he did, everything he said. The next moment, nervous, uncertain, unsure of herself, but for once in her life desperately wishing it wasn't so.

He lowered her hands, but still kept hold of one as he reached for his coffee, and they sat in silence for a few moments, Jessica strangely content to allow her hand to rest in his, Nic drinking coffee and thinking hard. The piano. A memory jiggled. Nic put his cup down on the grass. 'What sort of music do you play?'

Jessica hesitated. 'Classical.'

His head whipping up, he stared at her. 'Where do you play?'

'Just recently I've been playing with the Metropolitan City Symphony quite a lot. That's what I'm doing at the moment. Rehearsing, that is. But I-I do other concerts.'

He looked at her sharply. One of the biggest orchestras in the country, she had to be good to be asked to play with them. 'I've been to some of their concerts...' his voice died away, sudden realisation crossing his features. 'I went to their series of Beethoven concertos last year,' he continued almost accusingly.

'Um, yes. They...I...'

He stared at her in startled recognition. 'You! It was you who played them! I remember now. The soloist was blonde and now I remember your name! You're a brilliant player!' How ironic that he should recognise her, but she didn't recognise him!

'Do you like classical music?' she asked.

'Mmm?' He pulled his attention back to Jessica's question. 'Oh, yes. I like most music. I know people are only supposed to like one thing or another, but I genuinely like nearly everything. What about you?'

'I only really know about classical music. I'm an only child and my parents were classical musicians themselves. They thought classical was the only kind to listen to. Luckily, I love it, but what with practising so much, and their rather intense views, it means I haven't really listened to much else. I like some of the songs I hear...pop music, I suppose. Mike says I'm hopelessly ignorant.'

'Mike?' Nic reached out an idle hand, unable to resist touching the heavy fall of blonde hair. Jessica shivered at his touch and shifted restlessly on the seat.

Sensing her nervousness, his hand immediately fell away, and he gazed absently across the fields, realising anew this girl couldn't be rushed. Nor would she want to follow him immediately to bed. If he wanted to...if he wanted her...his thoughts were confused, their direction unclear. This hesitation was new for him, he realised with wry honesty.

'Mike and Andrea. They're friends of mine from when we were at music college.' Jessica remembered the lonely nights studying, listening to the laughter and plans of the other students, too shy, too unsure of herself, to join in. It had been like that until part way through her second year when Andrea had bumped into her in the local supermarket. Andrea had soon seen through the cool facade to the lonely and uncertain person underneath and had taken Jessica in hand. Slowly she'd guided her towards more suitable clothes and make-up, turning her into a stunning beauty. Andrea had also taken her to parties, but Jessica's reserve had continued to be an obstacle and although various men had shown an interest in her, nothing special had developed, nor had any relationship developed in the four years since she'd left and been building her career. At nearly twenty-seven, Jessica would have been deeply ashamed to admit to anyone she was a virgin, but it was true.

'Andrea teaches music at a comprehensive in London. Mike writes rock music, plays the guitar, and although I don't know anything about the sort of standards he needs to be a success, I think perhaps he's rather good.'

'Rock music?' There was startled interest in Nic's eyes as his attention sharpened. 'What does he do?'

Jessica looked surprised at his response. 'Do you particularly like that kind of music? I must admit some of the stuff Mike writes seems good to me and the tunes are catchy enough. But as I said, I don't know much about it.'

'Yeah, I like rock music. As I said, I like most kinds. Yes, I enjoy rock music.' He tailed off in some confusion. A few seconds of silence passed. Nic sat forward, forearms resting on his knees. 'But look...tell me more about you...where do you play when you're not with the Metropolitan? How do people get in touch with you? And tell me...how much work do you have to put in when you have a concert coming up?' His look was intense and interested.

Jessica laughed. 'You don't want to know much, do you?'

But under his determined questioning and quite obvious interest, Jessica began to tell him about her life as a rising young soloist, at the same time giving him glimpses of the rather isolated upbringing she'd had from two parents determined to give her every advantage for her career that they hadn't had. The trouble was, they hadn't considered living as part of her education and as a result, as he'd so quickly come to realise, Jessica was reserved and shy, lacking in experience, shunning the limelight.

'But you're in the limelight when you perform,' Nic commented, curious to know how she handled that.

'Yes, but I can cope with that.' She sat up, her eyes alight, her long-fingered hands gesticulating as she put her point across. 'Strange, isn't it? When I'm performing...oh, it's hard to explain. I can communicate easily when I use the piano. I suppose I *hide* behind the piano, maybe use it as a shield, but it's more than that. I feel an obligation to please the audience and when I do, it makes me happy, so I think maybe then I do even better. Do you understand?' Jessica asked softly.

'Yes. Yes, I do,' Nic replied somewhat abruptly, turning his face away. More, he thought, than you realise!

'It's the parties afterwards I find difficult. Well,' she admitted candidly, 'I wouldn't mind them so much if you hadn't got to make sure you speak to this person, or that person, so as not to cause offence! Luckily, I'm rising above that now...people have to come and speak to *me*!' There was gentle self-mockery in her voice as she smiled at Nic.

They sat in companionable silence for a while, then Jessica looked at him. 'You know,' she said rather abruptly, 'you're not at all what I thought you'd be like...to talk to, I mean.'

'What on earth do you mean?' His eyebrows lifted in surprise.

Oh, I don't know...' she flushed. 'I thought you'd be superficial, a bit hard maybe. Cynical. Dangerous, possibly.'

'Why?' Recently, if only she knew, he could be all of those, he thought, and, according to Andy, more than that...also uncaring.

'Don't know really. I've always thought your type were like that.'

'My type? What on earth do you mean, *my* type?'

27

'You're...' she hesitated. 'You're obviously a lot more sophisticated than me. You're very good-looking. I usually...I don't...I avoid people like you,' she said in a rush, colour staining her cheeks. 'You frighten me a bit, I suppose.'

Nic stared at her for a long moment. 'Bit of a sweeping statement, Jessica,' he said at last, uncomfortably aware of how close to the truth she was.

And if she found out, if she knew who he was, what he did, and read some of those stupid stories, exaggerated beyond belief, that crept into the papers?

Exaggerated?

Mmm, just recently?

Andy's words burned in his brain again, and he knew someone as innocent, as...as *unworldly* as Jessica clearly was, would be frightened off. He didn't want that. He wanted to find out what it would be like to get her into bed, knowing it would only be because she loved *him*. He didn't know how he was going to manage that, how long it would take him, but somehow, somewhere, he would. And she wasn't to know, she *mustn't* know, who he was.

His miracle.

'Sweeping statements?' she replied slowly. 'I'm not sure. You have a...' she stopped, confused, reluctant to speak so freely when after all, she hardly knew him. Yet somehow, she'd found him easy to talk to, despite the good looks and the sophistication which, strangely, both attracted and repelled her.

'I have what?' His eyes fixed steadily on her, compelling her to continue with what she had begun to say.

'Your manner can be rather peremptory,' she finally said, blushing furiously again. 'As if you expect everyone to jump to do your bidding.' What on earth had made her say that? Except that it was true, and she was always a painfully honest person.

A look of surprise crossed his strong face, followed, briefly, by a look of almost shame. Here was another one who, it seemed, could see straight through him and wasn't afraid to tell him.

Jessica reached out and touched him lightly on the arm. 'N-Nic? I'm sorry I said that, because I really think you're not like that. Not underneath. It's a veneer...but underneath you're kind, pleasant...I think...I think probably loving, too...' she stammered, unable to extricate herself from her outspoken observation of his character.

'No,' he said grimly. 'No, don't say sorry. I think maybe you said just the right thing.'

He was intrigued by her honesty and insight, shaken that she could see these things about him, be saying these things to him. Yes, he *was* too used to people jumping the minute he snapped his fingers. Women especially. And yes, he *had* become arrogant in his attitude to them. If he was honest, arrogant with everyone around him. Andy...*and* Jessica...were right. Over and over again, this day was reinforcing the unpleasant image of what he'd become. He only hoped it wasn't too late to reverse that image.

But they'd all put up with it! *Why*?

His mouth tightened. He knew why. No-one wanted to upset him, or to trigger his recently gained reputation for bad temper.

Except Andy.

And, now, it seemed Jessica as well. She didn't care if she offended him. She didn't care what she might lose by it, because she had no idea what there was to lose. She was a pure and totally unspoilt woman, and whatever he'd initially intended had, he realised, been shelved. He was finding himself unaccountably drawn to her quiet simplicity, her honesty, her values, all of which were making him question where he was going and what he was becoming, just as Andy had done. He wanted to get to know her, to....to... He mentally shook himself. He wanted to see her again, but the timing was lousy. He was due to go abroad and...and in the meanwhile, she might find out who he was before he'd had time to show her...to show her what? That he *could* be what she thought she could see in him? Kind? Pleasant? Loving? And, yeah, she *was* right, it was all there, just somehow had got buried.

At that moment a horn blared from the road at the front of the house, breaking into his thoughts. Jessica stiffened and Nic sat back with a sigh, glancing at the gold watch encircling his strong, brown wrist. 'It must be Josh!' he exclaimed in dismay. 'I wasn't expecting him yet!'

He stood up and Jessica collected their mugs. Walking silently back to the cottage, Jessica stole a sideways look at Nic's stern, dark profile, that glorious hair tumbling wildly to his shoulders. There was no way, she thought despairingly, that someone like him would want to bother with her...she had to be too quiet for him, and they probably liked doing completely different things...and anyway, she'd blown it again, must have done, with what she'd just said to him. He'd gone very quiet since then. What was wrong with her today? In half an hour, maybe less, he'd be gone and that would be that, but for an hour or so,

29

they'd got on so well and she was drawn to him in a way she didn't fully understand.

Jessica put the mugs in the kitchen before following Nic through the side gate. He was standing by the bike talking to a slim man with long brown hair pulled back into a ponytail and bright, darting eyes.

As soon as she came through the gate those eyes fixed on her and moved consideringly from her head, over her body, to her feet. Jessica flushed and hesitated. It was the same assessing way Nic had looked at her, when he'd first woken up and later, before lunch. She didn't like it. There was a lack of respect in such a look and it made her feel very uncomfortable.

'Managed to find a piece even out here, I see.' The man didn't make any attempt to lower his voice and his look was mocking.

Jessica decided most emphatically she didn't like him.

Nic glanced over his shoulder and smiled reassuringly at her. 'Cool it, Josh. It's not what you think. She's not that sort of chick. Lay off, okay?' He spoke with easy authority.

Josh raised his chin in disbelief. 'Come on Nic, I thought you had more sense than that! You should know by now they're all that sort. Don't worry, I'll-'

'Maybe in our usual circles, Josh, but not here, not this time, not now. Just shut up, okay?' Nic's mouth tightened and his voice was sharp as he interrupted.

'Okay, okay. If you say so.' Josh shrugged and spread his hands, letting his gaze slide once more over Jessica before he turned away to wheel the bike down the drive to the van. Nic was always like this these days! Bit your head off for nothing! There was once a time he would speak to you civilly. He'd only been trying to help out, make a joke of things!

Jessica shivered in the heat, wrapping her arms round her body, overcome with a strong feeling of disquiet. Here it was again. Nic changed completely, was different somehow, when he was talking to this Josh. Worse even than she had thought. Definitely hard, with that sophistication and arrogance too much in evidence. It was as if he'd suddenly retreated behind a wall. This was what she'd been trying to say to him only minutes before, but more extreme. Now there was no trace at all of the gentleness and rather puzzling loneliness she'd glimpsed in him back there in the garden. *This* man most definitely frightened her. She shook her head sadly and turned to go back to the kitchen.

'Jessica! Hey, Jessica!' A note of panic in his voice, Nic strode up the drive. Josh was nowhere to be seen, presumably securing the bike in the van. Jessica looked at Nic warily.

'I'm sorry about Josh.' Nic stopped close to where she'd paused to wait for him. 'He's only trying to take care of me. I...er...sometimes I'm bothered by...um!' He raked his long fingers through his hair and frowned.

'It's not up to me to criticise your friends,' Jessica said stiffly. They stared at each other before Jessica shifted and half turned away. 'I certainly don't wish to be a...*bother*...to you. I'll say goodbye then.'

'Jess, Jessica.' Nic's voice deepened, deliberately caressing. There was so little time. He had to resort to what always worked best with women, what he knew he was an expert in...seduction. He caught hold of her arm. She stared at his hand, still uncomfortable and unable to find words to respond to what she instinctively knew was a falseness in both his voice and gesture. Raising large eyes to Nic's face, her face flushed, her lips slightly parted, she looked at him doubtfully.

Nic drew in a sharp breath and pulled her closer to him. 'Oh, Jessica,' he murmured again, his suave seduction forgotten as he whispered her name roughly under his breath. He bent his head and gently lowered his mouth to hers, kissing her softly and undemandingly, his arms sliding possessively round her passive body, before giving way to a protective gentleness under the clarity of her gaze.

A mocking laugh rang out through the still air, causing Jessica to stiffen and pull back in sudden recoil and Nic to raise his head and swing round, a blaze of anger twisting his features as he swore at his friend. 'Josh! I said keep out of it!'

'Not that kind of chick, you said! Yeah, right! Any chick's that sort of chick when they're around you! And come on, we all know you love it until things get out of hand and you want out! That's when you need me, isn't it?' Josh hit back, still smarting from Nic's sharpness.

'What's eating you this afternoon, man? I said *back off*! What part of that don't you understand? This girl can't cope with the likes of you! She's different!' He swung back to where Jessica had been standing, only to find her gone. 'Don't interfere! Get in the van and keep out of my hair! I don't need your help on this one!'

In fact, Josh couldn't have said or done anything worse. Nic knew she would be frightened off by him, and, he admitted sourly, his own furious reply. With another dour look over his shoulder at

Josh, he went through the gate and into the kitchen. Jessica was nowhere to be seen. He went back into the garden, quickly moving down to the bench where they had drunk their coffee.

She was sitting there, arms wrapped round her knees, staring out across the fields.

'Jessica?' Nic touched her shoulder.

'Look, just go will you' she said flatly. 'I've rather gathered that this is all pretty commonplace to you and that you usually use this Josh to...what was the word? Oh, yes, *disentangle* you. Well, not everyone falls for your looks and charm that easily, you know. I don't think...I didn't try...oh, just *go!*'

'Please, what Josh said...it sounded bad but it's not quite what you think.' His voice was pleading.

'It sounded pretty clear to me.' She turned cold eyes towards him. 'I think my first impressions of you were right,' she continued, flatly condemning him. 'Arrogant and hard. And, it seems, a womaniser as well.'

'Please...' Nic repeated helplessly. He could see the hurt etched in the proud set of her head, in the full lower lip slightly thrust out and in the tenseness of her hands. Thanks to Josh he'd lost the precious ground gained this afternoon and now didn't have time to win it back. 'All right, I'll go,' he acknowledged heavily. 'But I'd still like to see you again. I enjoyed this afternoon...you did too, you know you did...and you don't really understand what Josh meant. I haven't time, now, to explain and I can't...it'll be some time before I can get in touch again. I'm going abroad soon and I'll be busy until we go. But when I come back, please, *please*...can I come and see you again? I-I hope you don't mind, I wrote your number down earlier-'

'No.'

'Jessica...' His hand reached out towards her as a sense of panic filled him. He wondered at it even as he pleaded. Drawn by something in his voice, she turned to look at him, staring up into the brilliant blue depths of his eyes, startled by the despair she saw there.

'What's the point?' she shrugged, resisting still. Then, disturbed by the pleading she'd just seen, she dropped her head and muttered so quietly Nic hardly heard, 'If you want to come back sometime...I suppose it's up to you.'

Nic bent forward, his hand gripping her arm. 'I'll come.' His voice was a promise. 'I'll come. But now...I really have to go. I have to get back to London.' Unwilling to have her change her mind, and now short of time, Nic stopped, then turned and walked away. A few moments later, Jessica heard the sound of the van engine start up and gradually fade into the distance. She stayed where she was, staring blindly out over the fields.

Chapter Five

Nic paced the floor of the hotel room wondering how he was going to explain to Andy about Jessica. He wanted to leave this afternoon, get back to London in time to watch her playing. The date of her first concert in this new series of the new year was engraved on his brain. *She* was engraved on his brain, no matter how hard he'd tried to banish her this last four, five months, and he wasn't quite sure himself how it had happened, so what to say?

Andy, lying on the bed, laughed at him. 'C'mon, Nic, what's eating you? Things have gone brilliantly on this tour. You've pulled yourself round, pulled yourself back together, we can all see that. It's all gone brilliantly well so you can't be worrying about that, can you?'

'No. No, I know it's gone well-'

'You've been better than ever, I reckon. Had them all eating out of your hand, hanging on every word.' Andy interrupted, gazing thoughtfully at the ceiling, legs crossed, hands behind his head. 'In fact, you seem to have gone to the other extreme! Hardly drinking...and how come you suddenly stopped chasing women round so *completely*? I know I said some harsh words, but I didn't mean you to quit everything, you know!'

'Yeah...' Nic hesitated, stopped his restless pacing, resumed it again. How...*how*...to explain? Andy'd just laugh at him. Tell him he was deluded, that he'd imagined it, built it up out of nothing.

'C'mon, Nic. I'm flattered to think this sudden turnaround might be attributable to me, but somehow, I don't know, I don't think it is. Well, not all to me. I didn't want to ask before...we were all holding our breath, waiting to see if it would last...but now I want to know. Why so hard on yourself? *Was* it just what I said?'

'Some. Oh, yeah, some. You made me think...'

Andy's eyes followed Nic's restless pacing. He could detect a note of hesitation, knew by the restless energy that something more was at the back of this. Gone were the hangovers, the shadowed eyes, the dull apathy which had been spoiling his friend's performance. He knew he had influence on Nic, but he also guessed something else had happened as well.

'That day you went off on your bike and broke down,' Andy began slowly, thinking back, 'the day I spoke to you...Josh said you were at some chick's house?'

'Yeah.'

'Someone you knew?'

Nic stopped, his back to Andy, before slowly turning to stare at his friend, hands thrust into the pockets of his black jeans, hair wild. 'No,' he answered slowly.

'Who was she?'

'Her name's Jessica.'

Defensively spoken. Andy sat up higher, punching pillows before settling back with his arms once more linked behind his head. 'Jessica. Right.'

He looked thoughtful. Her name *is* Jessica. Not, *was* Jessica. Now that meant Nic was still thinking about her. And he'd certainly changed! Yeah, too much for it to be just his little homily, no matter how much Nic had taken that to heart. *Is* Jessica. Very little drinking. No women. This wasn't Nic. So what had happened? *No* women…?

'Can it be possible you've changed your little ways because of this *Jessica*?' Andy's voice was mockingly incredulous and full of disbelief as he glanced across at his friend.

Had he? Or because of Andy? Or both of them? How did he know? 'Maybe,' Nic answered shortly, turning to stare out of the hotel window.

A shout of laughter greeted his reply. 'For a woman you met once for how long? C'mon! You have to be joking?'

'Look, Andy-' Nic began hotly.

'Yeah, yeah, yeah.' Andy flapped his hand. 'Look, I've never heard you play so well before on stage...you put new meaning into everything and it's inspired all of us. There must be a reason, I grant you, but come on, be careful here. You've only met this girl *once*! This just doesn't sound like you.'

'I don't know. I don't know, I really don't. Maybe she *has* had an effect on me. She…she made quite an impression. She's different. Honest. So gentle, so innocent-'

'Aw, bring on the violins and the sunset, man! So gentle! So innocent!' Andy laughed again. 'You wouldn't know what to do with gentle, innocent girls, not anymore!'

'Come on, that's a little hard!'

'No way! Leave the girl alone. If she is so innocent, she doesn't need you hanging around. You'll destroy her.'

'Andy!' Nic growled, his voice full of menace as he clenched his fists and swung round to face his friend lying on the bed.

'Be honest. This is a hard world of ours, my friend.' Andy shrugged, an eyebrow rising sardonically, 'and face it, recently, your reputation ain't been too good!'

Nic's shoulders slumped. 'Yeah, and that's what worries me. My reputation, which you were the first to bring up and talk to me about. And you were right. I *was* going downhill. I know it's all been pretty bad until just recently, but hey, you made me think, and Jessica made me think some more, okay? No-one can fault me on this tour. The papers have had nothing to pick up on!'

'It'll take more than one good tour and a few weeks of clean living to shake off the press!'

A silence fell between them. Nic dropped down to sit on the edge of the bed, chewing on the corner of his thumbnail, a frown creasing his handsome face as his blue eyes stared into the middle distance, seeing a small Cotswold cottage, a garden filled with sun and roses, a girl sitting waiting for him. Like a flaming fairytale! What *had* happened to him? *Was* it just the novelty value, or was it something more? He'd felt…he'd felt, this last four months, that he had to live up to her standards, but he had no idea how he was to explain that to Andy, and the conversation so far wasn't helping.

He dropped his hand and turned to look at his friend. 'Andy,' he began slowly, hesitatingly, 'do you remember what you said, that it would take a miracle to meet up with someone who didn't know who I am? Well, Jessica…s*he* doesn't know who I am.'

Andy shot upright, concern on his face. Who was this woman he'd met who could fool his friend like this? What was she after? When they'd had their heart to heart back in August, Andy had sensed Nic was depressed, wanting to find someone who'd love him just for himself. Yeah, he'd said it would take a miracle, and miracles quite simply didn't happen. Nic didn't need some scheming broad to trick him into believing trash like this when he was down and vulnerable!

'Hey! That's something else. Nooo, I can't believe it! Come off it, don't try telling me she doesn't know who you are!'

'Why not?' Nic spoke sharply, standing up and moving to throw himself down into a chair instead, his long legs stretched out in front of him. 'Why shouldn't it be possible? Not everyone's heard of us, or if they have, they're not necessarily interested enough to remember or care....'

'Under the age of...say, forty? And even above that age? Come on, Nic! This humility comes across stra-a-nge from you!' Andy drawled out his words.

'Look,' Nic said hotly, 'she's totally wrapped up in her music. She was brought up very intensively by elderly parents. She plays

36

classical piano. Come on, you must have heard of her...Jessica Farndale?'

Andy shrugged and shook his head. Rock music was his whole world. He wasn't like Nic, who prowled round strange gigs, folk clubs, concert halls, to find inspiration and ideas, or, come to that Adam, who still had an interest in classical piano.

'She's quiet and shy, she doesn't like parties. She hasn't a lot of social confidence. She knows nothing about rock music. Andy, it's true! *She didn't know who I was.*' Nic's voice was harsh with intensity as he tried to erase the look of disbelief he could see on Andy's face.

Andy rolled off the bed and wandered over to the window, unsure of what to say. *Could* it be true? Could it be possible that Nic really had met someone who was ignorant of who he was?

'Well, okay,' he admitted slowly, turning to look at his friend. 'Maybe. Maybe. But Nic...' he shrugged, 'she's just a chick. Why all the sackcloth and ashes routine? Why not wait until we get back and go see her, do whatever you want?' As you usually do. It lay unspoken between them.

Nic rose agitatedly to his feet. 'It's not just that. It's not just she doesn't know who I am, although that's a big attraction. I got the impression she's been brought up a bit out of touch with the real world. I told you, her parents were elderly...they kept her a bit isolated. She's beautiful, and as a performer, she's confident enough. I know that because I've actually seen her play, but...I don't think she's had a lot of experience with men.' Nic bit on his lower lip and deliberately avoided the astonished gaze of his friend.

'And now she's met you!' Andy shrugged and rolled his eyes. 'Heaven help the girl! But surely, you must have got her into bed by the end of the afternoon and ruined all that sweet innocence anyway?'

Nic fists clenched. 'Cool it, Andy! No! I tried telling Josh...she just isn't like that! She's...transparent. Good. Gentle. And that means,' his voice dropped, 'it's me that'll have to change, perhaps. And I don't want her finding out who I am, either, until...until...if...'

Andy shook his head in disbelief. 'Now I've heard everything! The cynical Nic Daniel being defensive about a woman's virtue and suggesting *he* has to change his lecherous ways! Nic Daniel, *soul-searching*. You seem to have fallen in love,' he said slowly, one eyebrow raised. This was becoming more puzzling by the minute.

Nic stared back at him for a long moment, then 'Yeah...maybe I have, at that.' He shook his head and an expression of bewilderment crossed his face. 'But I *can't* have...I only saw her for such a short time. I was glad, at first, that we were coming away. I was so mixed up and I thought it would give me time to rationalise the afternoon, get her out of my mind. But all that's happened is that she's in my mind constantly!'

This was unbelievable! Andy shook his head. 'Be careful here. I really can't take this tale that she doesn't know who you are. Hey, after what you said to me...maybe it's wishful thinking, okay? You just *hope* she doesn't know who you are. Look-' He stopped. How to say he thought Nic was laying himself wide open to being hurt? This woman not knowing who Nic was...it seemed an impossibility as far as Andy could see, and he just couldn't accept it.

'I swear, she didn't recognise me. There wasn't a flicker, there wasn't a sign, and she's far too transparent to have covered up. Maybe at first, but later on, when we talked...no. She didn't know who I was. But it's not just that. It's the fact she...she's so unspoilt...I'd like to just try, see what happens, where this takes us, okay?

'Nope. Leave it! You're bad news.'

'I said I'd change if I had to! And she liked me. We were doing fine.'

'Yeah?'

'Until Josh turned up,' Nic said bitterly. 'I don't know what got into him, mouthing off about finding a piece, looking her up and down as if she'd come out from under a stone or something. He frightened her.'

'Look, Nic, Josh did you a favour. And he surely did this girl a favour! He stopped you messing up her life.'

'Who says I would? Tell me that, Andy! Who says I'd mess her life up? This is...different.'

'C'mon, Nic! Get real, will ya? This is *you*, remember?'

'Look, I tell you, we were doing okay. I...she made me feel...different. I didn't have to pretend. I didn't have to impress. And I surely didn't need Josh coming along all macho and making out she was bothering me.'

'Yeah, yeah, I know!' Andy rolled his eyes to the ceiling and sighed. 'But be fair to Josh, you usually do need rescuing. You're always getting mobbed by some female!'

38

Nic gave him a look of resignation. 'Occupational hazard! But...it makes us pretty conceited, you know that? I reckon at first I was a bit of an arrogant bastard with Jessica.'

'You were?' Andy asked with feigned innocence. 'Now I wonder where you got that idea from? You? Arrogant? Well, well, well!'

Nic swiped a hand at Andy. 'Oh, get your dig in,' he said sourly. He ran his hand through his hair and turned to gaze sombrely out of the window. 'It's no good, we're finished here. There's tomorrow...the press conference and the interviews in the afternoon. You can take over. I'm going back today. She's performing tonight. It's the first in her new series of concerts. I'm going home and I'm going to see her. I can't wait any longer to find out if I'm just chasing a dream, or if she's really like what I remember...' He looked pensive, then grinned wryly. 'Or maybe she's completely forgotten who I am. I'll organise a flight back to London. Say what you like...stress, loss of voice...I don't care, only do this for me?'

'Well, thanks! Do I actually have a choice in this?' Andy strode over to his friend and held out a restraining hand. 'Nic, I'm serious when I said leave the kid alone. If she is as innocent as you say, you're bad news for her, my friend. You don't know the meaning of the word faithful.' And if she's not quite so innocent, you're better away from her before you get hurt, because you're not as hard as you like to think, Andy thought, and you're wide, wide open at the moment to being badly hurt.

Nic gazed back at him steadily. 'I'm tired of it all, I told you that. Not us, not the group or performing, but the hangers-on, the women. That's what I was trying to say that day...they all want something out of us, don't they? None of them want you just for yourself. But Jessica...she might, do you see? I mean, if she does like me, it's because I'm *me* and not some...some glamour figure to be sucked dry of favours. I want to find out. I want the chance and I meant it when I said maybe I'd have to be the one to change. If that's what it takes to get my chance, then I'll change.'

The two men stared at each other for a long moment before Andy shook his head and shrugged. 'Oh, get lost, will you? You'll be no good to me as you are in any case. I'm only amazed you've lasted this long and didn't renege on us sooner.'

'Thanks. Thanks, Andy.' Nic gripped his friend's hand and received an affectionate cuff over his head.

'Yeah, yeah, yeah. You just be careful, young Nic. You just treat that kid right, okay?' And I hope she's as honest as you say she is, he finished silently.

'Okay.' Nic turned, looked back once more at Andy's serious face, and was gone.

Chapter Six:

In her dressing room, fifteen minutes before the concert was due to begin, Jessica brushed powder over her cheeks and sat back to survey the results. Green eyes stared steadily and rather sadly back. It was nearly five months since she'd first started working on these pieces for recording and now this series of concerts. Eighteen weeks and two days to be exact. The day she'd met Nic Daniel and come to life, experiencing feelings that had never happened to her before that day.

Since then, she hadn't been able to get him out of her mind, even though she'd neither seen nor heard from him again. She knew he'd said he was going abroad and hadn't expected to hear from him for a month or two. But nearly five *months*...Jessica sighed, full of regret.

Despite the fact he'd frightened her a little, that she'd felt out of her depth, Jessica was disappointed. Sometimes when in London, she'd caught sight of a tall, dark-haired man on the street and she'd turned, foolishly hopeful that it might be Nic. Every time her phone had rung, in the month or two after they'd met, she'd rushed from wherever she happened to be, in case it might be him, but as time had passed her hopes diminished.

She was puzzled, though. *He'd* been the one to seek her out in the garden, before he'd left with that hateful man who'd come to collect the bike. *He* was the one who'd begged to be allowed to come back.

Shaking her head, she stood up, impatiently smoothing down her black velvet dress. So he'd changed his mind and it was time for her to *forget* him! She simply couldn't understand how one man could have come to dominate her life like this. It was ridiculous. It was ludicrous, even. She'd spoken with him for what? A total of a couple of hours, was all, so how could someone dominate her world for nearly half a year?

Jessica had never been in love before and although she realised something here was different, she didn't understand falling in love was possible in such a short time. She shrugged, flexed her fingers and rotated her wrists. No doubt once away from her he'd decided she was a total idiot and he'd do better to keep away. Her hands trembled slightly. They always did before a concert. She moved to the door of her dressing room. It was time to join David. The orchestra was already in place, tuning up, and the concert was soon due to begin.

41

David Brunskill, the guest conductor, waited in the anteroom, eyes darting everywhere, missing nothing. A murmur of voices and the sound of instruments being given their final tuning reached them from the orchestra as Jessica came to a halt beside him.

'Hello,' he greeted her absently, his eyes still restless, looking through the doorway to the concert platform, frowning as a violinist hurried past, late. Looking back to the orchestra, now including her in their restless movements.

'David,' Jessica acknowledged. They worked well together. He always brought out the best in her.

'Ready, Jessica?' David turned to her.

She laughed and held up her trembling hands. 'As much as I ever am at this stage!'

David held up his own hands and grinned ruefully. 'Snap! I know the feeling. Hey, you played really well at the final rehearsal. The first pieces are brilliant. You've brought in an element of real sorrow. To be honest, I'd wondered if you were ready for some of them...' he hesitated and looked at her curiously. He'd been about to add that in his view, some of the pieces needed maturity and a degree of experience that he'd initially thought Jessica maybe hadn't yet had. He'd been wondering if she was over-reaching herself, playing them at this stage in her career, but it seemed somewhere, somehow, she *had* gained the necessary experience and the emotion. However, he didn't mean to pry, hence his hesitation, but he wondered where, and with whom. Jessica was too shy, too innocent, too frightened, in a way, of letting herself become deeply involved, which might, in the end, hold her back. And yet, and yet...*something* had happened to change her since rehearsals had begun.

'Mmm,' Jessica nodded, sensing his curiosity and immediately withdrawing. She didn't want to admit to David she knew her playing, always technically brilliant, was gaining that ever-important element of emotion, as he'd just mentioned. The ever-important element which he'd always told her could take her right to the top. And that was thanks to Nic, she thought ruefully, and the emotions he'd unleashed in her, the pain he'd caused her by his non-appearance.

She realised David had started to speak once more. 'But try to put a little more joy into the second half, hmm?'

She nodded. David grinned at her, turned and took a deep breath which he slowly released. With sudden energy, he moved forwards, ran lightly up the steps and onto the rostrum amidst a

42

burst of applause. Then it was Jessica's turn to come onto the stage, acknowledge the applause and take her place at the piano, close to David. Silence fell. David tapped on his stand. There were a few coughs and rustles. The orchestra settled themselves with their instruments. David raised his baton before bringing it down in crisp command. Jessica concentrated her thoughts on the subsequent burst of music and banished Nic from her thoughts.

The melancholy chords and haunting refrains of the mix of short, but somewhat sombre piano pieces in the first half lent themselves to her feelings of sadness and strange sense of something lost, especially the Chopin Raindrop Prelude. She threw her feelings into the music and was greeted at the end with rapturous applause. Shaken, amazed at the depth of emotion she'd found, Jessica took bow after bow.

She spent the interval alone in her dressing-room, avoiding the conductor's curiosity and trying to quell her apprehension. As David had said, there was no problem with the first part of the programme but she knew as well as he did that she hadn't been doing well with the second part in rehearsals, the part which shouldn't even have been of concern. Lighter, happier, more cheerful music which she was playing well, but without the necessary spark.

At length she rose determinedly and returned to the anteroom. Whatever she felt had to be put to one side now. Well to one side. This time she couldn't draw upon her emotions to make the music better. To another round of applause she took her place once more at the piano.

There. The first piece played. And Jessica knew it had been a disappointment after the first half. Oh, she'd played with her usual technical brilliance, but without any of the joy needed to lift it beyond a competent recital, it lost its lustre. Why couldn't the whole programme have been sombre? She knew she'd lost part of the audience. She could always sense it, feel the restless movements, hear the suppressed coughs. They'd heard what she was capable of and wanted better than she was now giving them. She was dreading the next item, a wild, entrancing and *joyous* piece of music.

Jessica raised her head, flexing her hands again, experiencing a surprising and debilitating loss of confidence, familiar enough to her in everyday life, never previously felt once she was up on the concert platform. David shot her an anxious glance, one eyebrow raised. She nodded slightly. She was as ready as she would ever be.

Waiting for her cue, her eyes wandered over the first few rows of the audience. She recognised the critics from the Gazette and the Opinion. If she didn't pick up, first half or not, they'd tear her to pieces. She bit on her lip. There was her agent. Her eyes moved on, suddenly paused and came back to the dark head of long and tousled hair, bent over the programme. The man raised his head and looked directly at her. Their eyes met. He smiled brilliantly at her as he realised she'd seen and recognised him.

Nic! Nic, at last! But why now? Why after all this time?

Jessica stared unbelievingly. Nic raised his programme in a salute and blew her a kiss. A sudden smile broke out on Jessica's face, illuminating her features in a glow of light. At that moment David turned almost imperceptibly towards her, warning her to be ready. His eyebrows flew up in surprise at the change in her. Jessica couldn't stop smiling. She lifted her hands and began to play.

'Jessica!' The orchestra finally left the stage after tumultuous applause, a couple of encores and several curtain calls, and once in the anteroom David advanced towards her and caught her hands in his. 'That was brilliant! To be honest, I thought the first half would be by far the strongest. You've been doing well with the other pieces, but tonight you were fantastic!' He leaned forwards and kissed her on the cheek.

Jessica smiled at him, her eyes shining. 'Thank you, David.'

'Something happened, didn't it? Between that first piece...which was competent, shall I say,' he grinned at her, 'and the next one. I noticed. You were almost apprehensive, I could sense it, then next time I looked at you, you had a grin from ear to ear and your playing...!' He shook his head. 'Whatever happened?'

'Oh, David, it's not important.'

'Not important! When you ended up playing like that? Come on, Jessica.'

But again, she wouldn't satisfy his obvious curiosity and laughingly evaded further questions before returning to her dressing-room. A quick freshen up, a drink of mineral water and she hurried eagerly to the room set aside for hospitality when the critics, agents and friends came round to offer congratulations, and the success or otherwise of the concert could be gauged by what was said...or in some cases, not said.

Nic would surely come. All he had to do was go to the stage door and ask to see her. Graham would get a message to her. He might just let him in. After all, there weren't that many people who would be here tonight.

She pushed the door open. Her agent had already made his way from the audience and stood expansively opposite the doorway. 'Jessica!' Rodney Allbright was round and bouncing, with a balding head and round, silver-rimmed glasses that added to his gnomic appearance. 'Darling! That was just wonderful!'

'Thank you, Rodney.' Jessica grinned as she picked up a glass of red wine.

Rodney shot her a keen look from under his shaggy brows. 'Your first piece in the second half lacked a bit of go, but then! Oh, my! You put a lot into it after that. I've never heard you play quite so well. There'll be a few offers coming in now, on the strength of that.'

She smiled her thanks and sipped the wine, turning as she heard the door open.

Only David.

'David!' Rodney surged forward again, dramatic, flamboyant, but as an agent, very astute. 'A wonderful piece of conducting, wonderful. When are you..?'

Jessica lost interest in their conversation and stood where she could watch the door. The room was soon busy with the usual crowd of well-wishers, all full of congratulations, questions and comments thrown at Jessica, and at each other, while all the time sharp eyes searched the room for someone important that it would be politic to speak to or be seen speaking to. It all seemed so artificial to Jessica but as always, she smiled and responded with perfect courtesy.

'My dear! Brilliant! Absolutely brilliant! James! Haven't seen you for ages...'

'Meg! Did you go to that new production of Henry's?'

'...never heard Jessica play so well, have you?'

'Oh, there's Mark Enfield of the Echo...must just have a word...'

'...and there he was! Yes, sitting just behind me. Mind you, it's not the first time he's been seen at classical concerts. He sometimes gets ideas for his own songs. He's supposed to be a very good musician, you know.'

'I reviewed his last British tour. Have to say I was impressed. And I've heard this latest foreign tour has been brilliant...'

'Jessica, darling! We have to go now. It was super. We'll see you soon...'

Every time the door opened, Jessica looked up, heart pounding, but every time, it was someone else. There was no sign of Nic. As the next half hour passed, her elation gradually seeped away, leaving her feeling cold.

Why had he come to listen, why had he blown her that kiss, if only to disappear afterwards? But then, perhaps his response tonight had been an automatic one? Josh had implied he enjoyed a lot of popularity with women. Nic had told her he came to classical concerts. So, just because he'd been in the audience tonight didn't mean anything. She'd read too much into seeing him. She'd been a fool to imagine he was there because of her. A fool!

She continued to smile automatically and make mechanical responses to the comments and congratulations, her head beginning to pound. Soon, to her relief, the crowd of people began ebbing away until eventually only David was left.

'Jessica?' He paused tentatively as he moved towards the door. Jessica flashed him a bright, artificial smile. 'Are you okay?' David's voice was concerned. He noticed the elation had gone and she was looking depressed. Her behaviour tonight had been erratic, very unusual for Jessica. Normally self-controlled, quiet and reserved, her recent sadness hadn't escaped his notice, nor the joy which had swept over her in the second half of the concert. Now this. He was worried. 'Are you okay?' he repeated anxiously.

'Oh, yes,' she said, her voice catching slightly. 'Just tired, you know. I'll get off home now. Well, I will when I've changed.'

'Are you *sure* you're okay? You seemed really happy earlier, and now...' he shook his head, looking puzzled, not wanting to probe but uneasy nevertheless.

Jessica sighed and her shoulders slumped. She didn't have to pretend with David. Working together as intensely as they did, he knew every part of her, delved into her and brought out every ounce of emotion and feeling she had. It was hardly surprising he didn't want to let go now. This was something he didn't know about, an unknown element, and he wanted to find out what was going on.

'Really, David, I am okay. I...saw someone in the audience tonight. It was someone I met, oh, about five months ago now. I thought...it was silly of me really...I mean, if he hasn't made contact with me since then, why should I ever think he'd come specially to see me tonight? I know he goes to concerts...he told

46

me...and anyway, why should he bother with someone like me?' Jessica pressed her thumb and fingers over her eyes and turned away, tears spilling down her cheeks.

'Oh, Jessica.' David put his arms round her and rocked her gently. Good grief! A man, and by the sound of it someone who'd managed to break through her reserve and touch the real Jessica buried somewhere deep inside. Well, David owed him some thanks. Whoever it was had unleashed emotions in her which had enhanced her performance beyond belief. But Jessica...dear Jessica....she was always so unsure of herself. The blame lay with those parents of hers who had cocooned her from real life for so long.

'Look in the mirror sometime, will you? You're beautiful, you're talented, you're intelligent. There's no reason at all why someone shouldn't find you very desirable!'

'Then why,' Jessica spoke flatly, staring down at her clasped hands, 'hasn't he come round to see me tonight?'

'Well, perhaps there's a reason?' David suggested gently.

'Perhaps,' she answered listlessly. 'The truth is more likely that I caught his eye by chance tonight and read too much into it.'

'Had he given you any reason to expect him to get in touch?' David was worried about this. As she was so quiet and self-contained, and, quite frankly, so inexperienced, it was indeed possible she'd read too much into not only seeing him tonight, but also into their previous meeting, he thought sadly. She was always polite and friendly with the men she came across but it had been clear to him that until recently, no-one had touched her very deeply. Now she was swinging from elation to despair about someone, it seemed, she'd only met briefly, months ago. He really needed to find out more about this.

'He begged me, David.' She caught his look of surprise, tinged with disbelief. '*He did*. We...our meeting got off on the wrong foot, rather, and I didn't like him much. But then, you see, we spent some time together and...oh, never mind that bit. We talked a lot. He was interested in my piano playing. A friend came to pick him up and he...the friend...was a bit unpleasant. From what he said, it seemed maybe my first impressions were probably right. Anyway, he was going then, so I said goodbye and left them to it, sorting out the bike...oh, I forgot, I never said, his bike had broken down which was why he was at my house in the first place.'

What? David thought incredulously, watching the play of emotions across her face as he listened to her rather garbled

47

account of what had happened. A *biker*? Jessica and a biker...with an unpleasant friend...but then, what was he doing at a classical concert? This was getting more and more intriguing. 'And?' he prompted.

'He followed me. Back into the garden. He pleaded with me, asking to see me again. He seemed...lost, somehow. Lonely. So I-I said yes,' she finished in a small voice, seeing the worry and disapproval on her friend's face. 'Despite his rude manner, I-I sort of liked him.'

David hugged her, thinking rapidly. 'Jessica...is this wise? I mean, a biker. I can't see it somehow, love. Not your type, I wouldn't have thought. Perhaps it's just as well he didn't come round tonight?'

'No, you're right, he isn't my type,' she admitted frankly. 'He scared me, to be honest-'

'Was he threatening you?' David interrupted sharply.

'Oh, no.' A smile flitted across her face. No, he hadn't threatened her. No, he scared her because of the *emotional* effect he had on her and because of his arrogance. She knew what David was thinking, imagining. 'He isn't perhaps the usual type of biker. I mean, he wasn't a Hell's Angel, if that's what they're called.'

'That's what they're called. Are you sure? How would you know?'

'Oh, come on. I know I'm a bit sheltered, but there are some things I do know about life.'

He thought for a few more moments. This was amazing, but he didn't know what comfort or advice to offer. Whatever the reason this man had in coming to the concert tonight, it didn't seem as if seeing Jessica was one of them...and apparently, he hadn't been in touch for months. Could it all be a ploy, to get her hooked? But then why, or for what? If this biker was intent on something nefarious, rape, robbery, whatever, why the elaborate absence? What could he hope to gain by that? No. He shook his head. That line of reasoning didn't seem to work. 'This man...the one in the audience...could he have a reason for not seeing you since the summer?'

'He *said* he was going abroad...but for five months? It seems a bit dubious to me!'

David hesitated. 'Possible, though,' he conceded at last. 'People do go abroad to work, you know. I believe the rates of pay are very good in Germany for plasterers, builders and suchlike.'

48

How to explain to David that somehow Nic didn't fit into this picture? Jessica smiled faintly and patted his cheek. 'Thank you, David. For listening to me and trying to help. Go on, now. Stephanie will be wondering where you are. I'm okay. After all, nothing's different tonight from any other night. I'm going to get changed and then head off home myself.'

David searched her face. 'If you're sure?'

'Sure. Go on. I'll see you next Wednesday.'

'I still think maybe it's better this man hasn't been in touch again. I can't see he's the right sort of person for you, I really can't, even if, as you say, he isn't a Hell's Angel type. Okay, yes, I understand he's had some effect on you, but...' his voice tailed off. How to say that perhaps the novelty, the very forcefulness of the encounter, had stirred her emotions for the first time in her life, that she would easily get over it?

'Whether he's the right person for me or not, I'll never know now, will I?' Jessica spoke lightly, opening the door. 'Come on, no more worrying. I'll survive.'

He kissed her lightly on the cheek. 'Take care. Are you sure...?'

'Go,' she smiled and pushed him gently out of the door.

With one last reluctant glance, David left the room, Jessica following behind. Outside the door of her room, he stopped again. 'Jessica...'

'Go home, David. We all have to suffer the pain of rejection. It's just come a bit late to me, that's all.' Her smile was rueful. David gave a faint smile in return, patted her shoulder and continued down the corridor.

Changing quickly into jeans, a sweater and jacket, Jessica followed in about fifteen minutes.

'Goodnight, miss,' Graham called from his over-heated cubby-hole of a room, as she passed the door. 'I hope your car's not far off. It's pouring down out there, and bitterly cold.'

'No,' Jessica said quietly. 'I was lucky tonight and found space in the Montpelier. Goodnight, Graham.' She pulled the collar of her jacket up round her neck and stepped out into the deserted, rain-lashed street. Head down, Jessica walked quickly down the road.

The sound of rapid footsteps gaining on her from behind made her feel suddenly nervous and she quickened her pace. The footsteps quickened as well. Panic rose up in her and she started to run. Muggings were becoming only too common on the streets of London and it was dark and, on a night like this, deserted. A hand was laid on her arm. She swung round, ready to lash out or kick, about to scream.

'Jessica! Hang on!'

She froze, then slowly lowered her fists.

Nic stood there, his hair drenched, raindrops running down over his high cheekbones, his nose, his mouth. His jacket was dark with rain and he looked chilled to the bone, his shoulders hunched under the soaked cloth, one hand thrust into his pocket. He eyed her cautiously, his other hand still on her arm.

'Jessica?' A question hovered in his voice as he spoke her name for a second time, a faint smile flitting over his mobile mouth. 'Hey, we always seem to go into combat mode when we meet!'

'You're...you're soaked!' Jessica said foolishly.

The rain fell steadily and a cold wind swept up the street, rattling a polystyrene cup along the gutter, but Jessica no longer noticed. A glow of joy, a tremor of awareness, rose up to fill her with warmth. Her lips parted and her eyes shone. Nic smiled in response, his eyes crinkling in the way she remembered, his whole dark face lighting up. He glanced at his shoulders. 'I am a bit,' he agreed ruefully. 'You were a long time. I thought you'd be out sooner.'

The glow faded from Jessica's face as all her doubts rushed back. 'Yes,' she said stiffly. 'There were a lot of people who came round. I saw you in the audience,' she added hesitantly.

'I know. You played well...brilliantly, in fact.'

They stood in the rain, staring at each other.

'I thought you'd come to...maybe to see me...but then you didn't come round afterwards. I didn't...I wasn't sure. It's been so long and...you never came backstage, so I thought maybe you were sorry you'd said you wanted to see me again.'

He looked surprised. 'But I told you I wouldn't be in touch for a while, because I was going abroad.'

'For...for five months?'

'Four. But the month before I went...I had too much on. I'm sure I told you. I wasn't actually due back until Monday but I came ahead. I only got back at six today. I knew you were performing and I wanted to hear you. I've had a ticket booked ever since they went on sale,' he added simply.

The realisation he'd made her his first priority slowly sank into her consciousness. She searched his face with eyes suddenly hopeful again. 'You could have come round after the performance, you know. I...expected you, after I'd seen you. I didn't know quite what to think when you didn't come.'

'I...er, I didn't know...I always thought you waited patiently for the stars to emerge from the stage door.' In truth, there were too many people who would have recognised him if he'd gone backstage. Recognised him, and then made sure that Jessica knew who he was. Gossip. News headlines. They would make mincemeat out of this lovely lady, he knew that without a doubt.

Still standing in the rain, aware of cold trickles running down his back, he continued in a low, rapid voice. 'I'm sorry if you expected me before this. I had to see you and I came as soon as I could. I hope you...If you'd rather, I'll go?' Nic looked at her, one dark brow raised questioningly, unused to this humble supplication, uncomfortably aware of Andy's cynical remarks.

'No!' Jessica surprised herself with the force of her response.

He looked down at her, the beginnings of a smile on his clean-cut mouth, the doubts and confusion of the last weeks disappearing. It was amazing, she was just as he remembered and, for whatever reason, he was attracted to this girl as he hadn't been to anyone for a long, long time. Maybe because she was beautiful. Yeah, right, strike that! Definitely because she was beautiful. Maybe because she was honest, maybe because she really seemed to be his miracle, liking him for his own sake. Perhaps all three.

'I'm glad you said that because I've been thinking about you quite a lot. Look, what are you doing now? Couldn't we go somewhere and talk?'

'Where?' Jessica asked helplessly. 'We're soaked. I'm...' she gestured at her jeans and trainers. 'I was going home actually.'

Nic spoke impulsively. 'Come to my flat.' As soon as he'd spoken, Nic wished the words unsaid. As he'd told both Josh and Andy, she wasn't that type. Not yet, not now. Nic knew he needed to move carefully with Jessica. In any case, there was too much around in his flat that would tell her instantly what he did, who he was. He watched her carefully as she tensed and bit on her lip, dropping her eyes.

He would have been surprised at how close she was to saying yes and hoping she could carry it off when she got there. Attracted to Nic she might be, but she could very easily recognise that his experience was way beyond hers. Pretty well everyone's experience was beyond hers, she thought ruefully

Relieved that her hesitation gave him the chance to back out, he spoke rapidly. 'No, it's all right. I'm sorry, I shouldn't have suggested that. In any case, you're tired. Come on, I'll take you to your car. Tomorrow. I'll come down tomorrow, if that's okay?'

They turned and moved down the road together, Nic walking close to Jessica's side.

'Why, yes. Yes, of course you can. I'll...I'll...yes.' Jessica was aware she was babbling. She raised her head and pushed her wet hair out of her face smiling warmly, joyously, her whole face lighting up.

Nic drew in a sharp breath. Tomorrow. She'd promised him tomorrow.

Chapter Seven

The day dawned cold and clear. Sometime during the night the rain had blown away and stars had emerged. Now, frost skimmed the grass and the ploughed fields, and the trees made long shadows in the thin, early morning January sun.

Jessica had just come out of the shower and was pulling a sweater over her head when she paused, listening. An engine, deep, growling, held on the very edge of power, its note dropping, then dropping again almost protestingly, to a throbbing murmur. Moving quickly to the window, she saw Nic swing the large, black bike onto her driveway and bring it to a silent halt.

Cheeks flaming, she pulled on her jeans and ran downstairs in answer to the ringing of the doorbell, flicking her wet hair back over her shoulders. It wasn't yet nine! The only reason she was up at all was because the thought of seeing him today had caused her to wake up far earlier than she would normally have done after a concert. What did he mean, turning up so early?

She opened the door to find Nic standing with his back to her, running his hand through his long, thick, unruly hair, surely even longer now than when she'd first met him. But oh, how it suited his strong face and sexy smile! He turned and that smile blazed across his face, causing her to catch hold of the door frame as her whole body registered his presence.

'Hi.' A flash of uncertainty took him by surprise and his smile faded as he hesitated, then gestured at the frost-slicked drive and whitened grass. 'It's cold out here today,' he commented lamely. 'It was a cold ride down.'

'Hi. Come…come in, do. Come in. Yes, you're right. It's cold. There's frost on the fields.' She stood to one side as he entered before shutting the door, suddenly intensely shy as she watched him removing his boots, before unzipping and stripping off his leathers. Underneath, he wore black again, as he'd done every time they'd met. A fine black merino sweater that moulded itself to his broad shoulders and slim waist, and well-fitting black jeans.

Nic straightened up, his confidence returning, and smiling again, he stepped forwards until he was close to her. 'Well, hi, Jessica Farndale,' he said softly, looking down into her face, his hand reaching up to very gently touch her cheek.

She bit her lip and dropped her eyes, stepping back hastily. 'You…you must be cold.'

Nic's mouth twisted in wry amusement and he shook his head slightly. He really had to remember to approach her gently and cautiously, this one.

'I was going to light the fire in the sitting room,' Jessica continued, slightly wildly, 'but you've come too early. I've only just got up...I'll do it now. You're cold. We'll need the fire, but the heating's on, too.' She turned and led the way into the room he vaguely remembered from his first visit.

Like the kitchen and dining area, the room ran from the front to the back of the house and again, like the kitchen, there were French windows overlooking the garden, bare now of flowers, with skeletal trees lacy black against the blue sky, and russet soil powdered with frost.

A large fireplace was central to one wall and it was to this Jessica made her way, to kneel on the rug and apply a light to the logs and kindling already waiting. After a few tense moments, the flames caught, and with a crackle the logs started to burn, sending yellow flames and blue smoke up the wide chimney.

Nic looked round appreciatively. In front of the window which faced the road stood a baby grand piano. The ceiling was beamed and the furnishings had obviously been chosen carefully to fit in with the house as well as to provide comfort. He prowled the length of the room, stopping now and then to look more closely at a painting or to pick up a photograph.

Sitting back on her heels, Jessica watched his restless exploration. She shook her head. This man. So different to anyone else she'd known. Here. Now. With her. Now what to do? What would he expect? She licked suddenly dry lips, feeling panicked and so unsure of herself it was almost pitiful.

'Who's this?' He picked up a picture of a long-haired man and his female companion, people he wouldn't have associated with Jessica.

'Mike and Andrea. I told you-'

'Yeah!' He snapped his fingers. 'He's the rock musician. She teaches. You met up in college. I remember.' He moved on and came to a photograph of an elderly couple, standing arm in arm in front of the bench at the bottom of Jessica's garden.

'My parents,' Jessica supplied, before he could ask.

'Where do they live?' He examined the photo closely. 'You have a look of your Dad. Do you get on with them?'

'They're both dead. They had me late in life anyway, but my mother got cancer shortly after I went to college and there was nothing they could do. She died within six months. My father was quite a bit older than she was, and he died a couple of years ago. This used to be their...our...house. I inherited it.' She sighed. 'I got on with them okay but they were strict, and determined to give me the best musically that they could, once they realised I had some talent. It was lucky, I suppose, that on the whole I wanted what they wanted. But...I became very isolated and also very intense and...' she hesitated.

For a while she'd been very bitter, when Andrea had shown her what life was all about and she realised everything she'd missed out on, but she'd got over that, to some extent. However, moments like this tended to cause the resentment to well up in her again, especially as she hadn't exactly moved on, still living as she did in her childhood home.

Nic put down the photo and looked at her. He could identify with her sense of isolation, even if the cause was somewhat different. Continuing his restless prowling, he said, 'I'm sorry to hear they're dead. Any other family?'

'No. Both my parents were only children themselves. It seems to run in families, doesn't it? It's something I'd one day like to break...' she paused again, uncertain about talking of children. Oh, no! She hoped he wouldn't think she was dropping hints. She blushed painfully.

Without appearing to notice what she'd said, he finally stopped in front of her stereo system and whistled softly in appreciation, running his finger along the rack of LPs. He flicked one out and slipped it onto the player. The room filled with the soft sound of Debussy. Jessica rose to her feet and hovered by the door.

'Would you like some coffee? Some breakfast even?'

'Come and sit down,' he suggested softly. 'Never mind coffee, something to eat. It'll keep. Hey, come here.' He held out his hand to her as he moved back to the fire, now blazing strongly, and fixed her with his compelling blue eyes, exerting all his charm.

Her stomach lurched in response and she moved slowly forwards and perched on the edge of a chair, part of a group set round the fire. Nic sank down onto the floor at her feet, crossing his long legs. She was as taut as one of her own piano strings, he thought.

'Do you practise a lot?' He indicated the piano now with a dip of his head, sensing that talking about music would be a good way to make her relax.

Jessica nodded. 'Mmm, yes, every day, I have to otherwise my fingers lose their suppleness. And I use it for trying out new pieces before starting rehearsals. David comes down to help, to decide with me which ones suit us both, or the requirements wanted, such as a particular composer. We work out a rough programme and I run through it a few times to see how it all goes together. David will listen and when we're happy, we start rehearsals proper.'

'David? The conductor from last night?' Nic felt a mild stab of unaccustomed jealousy. He was surprised. So soon? But then, although he'd only met her once before, he'd been thinking often enough about her. He sensed, he *knew*, he was on the brink of something different here.

'Yes. Well, guest conductor, really. He won't be tied down and he's very much in demand, but he does do a lot with the Metropolitan. He's brilliant,' she continued, her eyes shining with enthusiasm. 'He has a gift of really bringing out the best in me.'

A further twist within Nic. This David must know her well. 'If you work so well together, you must really like him?' It was like probing a sensitive tooth. He knew his questions might bring him pain, but he couldn't stop. And in some way the pain was exhilarating because it was such a novel sensation.

Jessica laughed. 'Oh, yes, we get on well together. But David has the gift of bringing out the best in everyone, you know. That, quite simply, is why he's such a great conductor,' she added gently.

'I probably asked before, but how long do you rehearse, once you've worked out a programme and before the concert itself?'

'Me? Oh, a lot. I work and work on a piece, building it up how I want to play it, how David wants me to play it. We have to compromise, sometimes.' She grinned, already relaxing. 'I go up to London to work on the concert piano at Metropolitan Hall. When David's happy, when I'm happy, we schedule full rehearsals with the orchestra. We try to allow some extra time, so if things don't go well we don't end up edgy and not happy about the performance. I tend,' she added ruefully, 'to get somewhat engrossed when I'm rehearsing and the rest of the world goes by unnoticed!'

Nic laughed. 'Yeah, I know-' He stopped abruptly. The feeling, he'd been about to say. 'It must be hard work,' he finished quietly, hoping she hadn't noticed his hesitation.

They continued talking about music and about Jessica's plans for the future before moving idly onto other topics, discovering and exploring what each of them liked in music,

56

discussing books and films. Conversation flowed easily between them.

Eventually, a silence fell. The logs crackled and one settled with a small crash, sending a shower of sparks flying up the chimney. Jessica stared into the flames, her cheeks flushed with the heat.

Nic watched her. He'd been waiting for a long time to see her again, to see if the attraction he'd felt for her before was still there. It was. And what's more, he *liked* her. With a sudden intake of breath he rolled onto his knees and slid his hands up her arms to rest on her shoulders.

'Jessica...' he breathed her name softly, his face suddenly intent.

Jessica shot him a startled look. Evading his arms, she jumped up in agitation and moved rapidly to the other end of the room to stare out at the frosted garden, her back to Nic, her heart pounding.

He wanted to kiss her. She knew it. She wanted to respond to him, she knew that too. Her whole body trembled with longing, but...she was so inexperienced he would simply find her laughable.

He'd find her laughable anyway, now she'd made such a fool of herself. She hugged her arms tightly round herself. Sensing Nic was a sensual man, she realised he was probably looking for a physical commitment from her beyond any she'd been asked for before. Jessica thought maybe she'd be happy to give it...eventually. When...*if*...their friendship deepened. But he wasn't like her other male friends and she wasn't sure what to do...Oh, *why* couldn't she relax? Why, at her age, didn't she know what to *do*?

Nic stared at her back as he silently swore at himself. He knew he'd made a mistake already. A bad one. He was rushing his fences, just what he knew he shouldn't be doing. They should have just kept on talking...but he wanted to kiss her so badly. To feel those soft lips under his own again. To find out if she could respond.

'Jess? Jessica?' His voice was soft and cajoling. 'I'm sorry.'

'No...' Her voice was muffled. She muttered something he couldn't catch. Nic hesitated, wondering if she was frightened or just unawakened. He was honest enough to admit if she couldn't respond to him physically it would be a considerable obstacle. He was a passionate man who enjoyed making love.

57

Go on, or retreat? He ought to retreat. He knew he shouldn't rush her, but perhaps now the subject had been brought up...he grinned wryly and, rising silently to his feet, he padded over the carpet and gently laid his hands on her shoulders to turn her round. His hands slid onto her neck and his thumbs caressed her jaw before his strong fingers gently lifted her chin until, reluctantly, her eyes met his.

'Jessica...' he hesitated. Perhaps he ought to leave it. No. It was time to find out. He went on firmly, his voice strong. 'Jessica, I'd rather we were honest about this. If you don't like me trying to kiss you...if you'd rather I didn't because you physically dislike it, then tell me.'

Jessica made a little sound of protest.

Nic's eyes searched hers. 'So,' he breathed, 'you don't mind?'

Relief flooded through him. It was only inexperience, innocence. That, he could cope with. Jessica was important to him. He wouldn't destroy her. Experience he could give her, and her sweet innocence he wanted to preserve.

Slowly, not touching her in any other way other than his hands softly caressing her jaw, he kept his gaze locked with hers and lowered his head.

A shiver ran over her and her breathing became rapid. She felt helpless, wanting to feel his lips on hers, and watched, mesmerised, as his face came down. At last he closed his eyes, thick lashes fanned on his cheeks and, still gently, still slowly, let his hands drift from her neck and graze down her body to settle lightly, unthreateningly, on her hips as his beautiful mouth closed softly over hers. Another shiver ran over her skin and her hands half lifted in an instinctive desire to hold his lean body close to hers.

'That's right,' Nic murmured against her lips. 'Come on, Jessica. Hold me. Put your arms round me.' He reached down and caught her arms, lifting them to his waist. Hesitantly she placed her hands on his hips, feeling the waistband of his jeans through the fine wool of his sweater as Nic, in his turn, gathered her close to him. He smiled at her. 'That's not so bad, is it?' Then his smile faded and he stared deep into her eyes before lowering his mouth once more and moving his lips gently over hers.

Jessica's mouth parted. Waves of pleasure spread to every part of her body, her nerves were on fire. His tongue moved across her lips, entered her mouth then tantalisingly withdrew. Enough, enough. So far, no further. Let her enjoy this.

58

She pulled him even closer, her hands sliding up to the back of his head and burying themselves in his thick hair.

Nic's shoulders lifted as he drew in a deep breath. His legs suddenly trembled and joy shot through him. So, the response *was* there. He felt, he *knew*, deep within her, there was a sensuality waiting to be released. He knew he wanted it to be his. He wanted it to be him who awakened her, who protected her, who cherished her. Even stronger, now, was the determination to wait until Jessica was ready. He wouldn't rush her to give herself too soon, whatever he'd hoped for today.

'Oh, wow,' he breathed softly, 'why were you afraid? You *were* afraid, weren't you? The havoc you cause, it's me who should be afraid of you!'

Jessica flashed him a glance from under her lashes, unconsciously seductive, and ran her tongue over her top lip. 'I'm...I'm not afraid, not really. Not of you. I'm...you...' Her voice trailed away and she shook her head.

'Come on,' Nic dropped his forehead to rest on hers. 'Tell me?' His voice was softly caressing. Jessica shivered in his arms, her face flushing with embarrassment. She shook her head again.

'Jessica...?' Her name, murmured low under his breath, was a plea for her confidence.

'I've been out with a few men,' Jessica began uncomfortably. 'They were usually musicians...I went to discos at college and sometimes out for a meal, but...'

'But?' he prompted softly.

'But I told you my parents neglected the other side of things...growing up like everyone else. If you have a talent you tend to become isolated, you see?' Jessica looked at him anxiously, drawing her head back. 'I'm not trying to be...to be...'

'It's okay. I know what you're trying to say.' He pulled her back to rest against him. More than you realise, he added silently to himself.

'So when I was a teenager, I missed out on parties, pop music, going out with friends...boys, boyfriends. Growing up. Making mistakes when making mistakes don't matter, because you're all at the same stage of learning, aren't you? College wasn't much better. I was already performing by then and still had to practise, practise, practise! And by then I was different from everyone else anyway. My clothes were all wrong. I didn't know how to join in. Andrea and Mike helped. It was only after I met Andrea that I went out at all, but...I always feel out of my depth with men. I don't know what...I feel I can't...' A silence fell.

59

Nic waited before asking patiently, 'Can't what...?'

'You're extracting my confession drop by drop, aren't you? If a man...if a man makes a pass at me, I don't really know what he expects...and what I should *do*! I usually...all the other men I went out with have been different to you anyway.' Safe, Jessica suddenly acknowledged in a stunned realisation of the truth. The few men she had been out with had been dull, conventional and *safe*. Jessica had never really enjoyed herself with them but was too shy and insecure to try attracting men like Nic. Nic, who only had to look at her to cause her insides to melt into trembling longing. 'I don't usually get involved with men like you,' she confessed in a rush, 'and I feel stupid.'

'You're doing okay,' Nic said softly under his breath, holding her close again, moved by her admission. 'You're not stupid, Jessica. Just do what you feel you want to do. If things are right, you'll *feel* right. If things are wrong, just stop. It's that easy.'

'It feels right when you kiss me. I've never enjoyed being kissed before until last summer when you...but I always thought it was because I didn't know...It's not been much fun...Ohhh, I'm not used to talking about these things!' She turned her head away, colour staining her cheeks again.

Nic drew in another unsteady breath and pulled her face round to his, dropping his mouth once more over hers, this time more demandingly. The kiss was longer, deeper, and Jessica followed her initial instincts, allowing her lips to part, accepting the gentle thrust of his tongue in her mouth, all those lovely and unaccustomed feelings exploding yet again through her whole body.

Hardly surprising, because ever since she'd seen Nic Daniel asleep on her lawn, a whole river of unaccustomed feelings had been sweeping through her, despite her wariness of him. And now her worry that she wouldn't know what to do melted away in the warmth and gentleness of his embrace, and she gave herself up to the sheer enjoyment of it.

At last Nic pulled away. He dropped his forehead down to rest on hers again and held her silently, his breathing ragged. As his breathing became more even, he stepped back, looking into her face. 'Jessica, we have to stop, we really do. But don't get the idea it's because you've done something wrong. It's quite the opposite. I need to cool down a bit!' He laughed shakily, unused to putting a brake on his physical desires, but knowing he had to, that to push her now would be easy, but he'd lose her forever. 'Just promise me from now on you'll do all your practising with me, okay? That's going to be one of the rules, as far as I'm concerned.'

Another first, asking her for and being prepared himself to give a commitment. Nic couldn't bear to think of bringing hurt to her innocent eyes by betraying her with someone else, nor could he bear the thought he might be liberating her emotions enough for her to contemplate enjoying this with another man.

They moved back to the fire. The LP had long since finished playing and the only sounds were the crackle of the logs and the soft ticking of the clock.

'You say you've never been out with anyone like me before?'

'No. Safe men. Unthreatening. Boring, probably. Certainly nothing like you. I never felt like this ever before.'

'Felt like what?'

'Oh, Nic. Confused. Excited. Melting. Worried. Unsure. As if I'm on a cloud!'

'So, I'm not safe and maybe you feel a bit threatened?' He flashed his sexy grin.

'A bit. But it's more because you so obviously have a greater experience of life, you're a lot more sophisticated than me. That has to be obvious, surely?'

'Yes. But it doesn't *matter*. I like you as you are and I can show you...over time, not now, not straight away. When you're ready. I'd always prefer it if you were honest and tell me what feels right, or what you aren't happy with. But...if I seem like this to you, why did you want to see me again?'

She looked at him consideringly and dropped her voice to a low murmur that he had to strain to hear. 'You seem lonely. But maybe most of all,' she added, somewhat helplessly, 'I can't really help wanting to see you. Something's happened to me that I don't really understand.'

Nic looked at her, surprised again by her perception, glad of her confession of need.

'Now I've upset you,' Jessica said in a small voice.

'Far from it.' Nic kissed her hair, slowly stroking the thick strands of gold and winding them round his fingers. Jessica was acutely aware of his touch. Her head sank onto his shoulder. 'Far from it,' Nic repeated.

His mind wandered back to the talk he'd had with Andy back in the summer. He'd changed since then, got back to his normal self. Jessica had given him hope, even though they'd spent such a short time together. It was as easy to be himself with Jessica as it was with Andy, the rest of the group, Sam up at Bleathwaite, the

61

hills. The only things he valued in his whole glittering world, and he'd found his way back to them and now had her as well. Now, it would be good to head up to the house in the Lake District and blow some of the cobwebs out of his mind, but there still wasn't really the time. They had to record the new album before the British tour. Strange, though, the way things had worked. If he hadn't gone into that downward spiral, Andy wouldn't have had a go at him, and he wouldn't have gone out on his bike and met Jessica

She broke his reverie. 'You're actually very gentle with me. And understanding. More than I thought you would be, to be honest. Which is...nice. Thank you.' She touched his arm. 'Tell me more about yourself. I don't know anything about you. Well,' Jessica laughed, 'except which composers you like and which books you read! Tell me about yourself. When you were young. Your family?'

'Ah,' he smiled gently at her. 'My Dad left my Mum before I was born. Hate to say it, but I don't know who he is and I don't really care. Mum brought me up with a good few slaps round the head. Did me no harm. I was a bit of a tearaway, I suppose. Growing up in the rough end of Preston wasn't...easy. Never had any sisters or brothers. Mum had an aunty, but she died when I was about twelve. Then Mum died when I was in my mid-twenties. I was very sad about that. She was a good lady.'

Jessica murmured sympathy, rubbing his arm. 'What else?' She asked. What else do you like doing?'

'Riding my motorbike,' Nic began slowly, 'out in the countryside. I need the country, the space. Always have done. I like walking, too.' Not that he'd done much recently but with Jessica's help he would find his way back. Was *already* finding his way back. 'Music. I better warn you, music can dominate my life.' Now he ought to explain.

'That's nothing to me,' Jessica's laugh rang out. 'It tends to dominate mine, as you know! How? Tell me about it?'

'Well, I like it...I'm always listening to music...going to concerts...' His voice trailed off lamely. He realised he couldn't tell her. He couldn't, he couldn't. Not now. Not so soon. Not until she knew him better, trusted him more. She was rapidly becoming too precious to lose.

Jessica looked at him, puzzled, as he failed to substantiate his claim that music dominated him.

'I work in recording, I think I already said,' he continued, speaking rapidly. 'It involves a lot of time, a lot of going over stuff.

Track mixing and layering and stuff.' True enough. He and Andy spent as much time on the technical side as they did on the performing side.

'Yes. I know.' she sighed. 'When I make a recording, it's hard enough doing re-plays, or re-takes or whatever they're called, never mind about being the ones who have to make it sound right. Do you-'

'And I enjoy kayaking.'

'*What*?' Quite honestly, she hadn't really identified Nic with any of the things he was telling her about. Parties, yes. Nightclubbing. Definitely women. But biking? The countryside? Walking? '*Kayaking*?'

'Why not?' Nic was defensive. 'It's challenging. I need it to relax. I need to keep pretty fit for what I...I like to keep fit. I don't go in for wild parties, you know. It seems very hard to convince you of that. I really don't know why you're so fixed on thinking I do.'

All half-truths. He hadn't been kayaking since a year or so ago...eighteen months ago? Which was also the last time he'd been properly walking, the last time he'd visited his second home, the last time he'd seen Sam. And be honest, there'd been plenty of parties, although not particularly wild. He'd slipped into apathy and bad habits. Andy had been right with his criticism. And Nic himself knew his recent drinking habits, and everything else, hadn't been making him happy.

'Girlfriends?' Jessica asked quietly, in a subdued voice, amazed at her own temerity.

There was a long silence. Finally, Nic stirred and spoke in a depressed voice. 'Well, yes, Jessica. And, I'm sorry, but plenty of them. They like me and...' He shrugged. He didn't need to say he was attractive to the opposite sex. With his looks and animal magnetism Jessica knew he would never lack a willing partner. 'But I wasn't seeing anyone when I met you. And while I was abroad, I didn't get involved with anyone.' He grinned ruefully. He knew that'd puzzled Andy, until Nic told him about Jessica.

Now it was Jessica's turn to be silent. He'd been honest and it hurt. But then, what had she expected? That someone as charismatic as Nic had lived a celibate life? Of course he'd had girlfriends.

'But I won't play around,' he assured her now. 'If I'm going to see you, I won't be going round with anyone else. If I decide it won't work, then I'll tell you. I'll cut loose before I look for anyone else.' His voice was rough with pleading and he raised her head so he could look directly into her eyes. He'd never bothered to say this to another woman and wasn't even sure why he was so intent on making this point again, even more definitely.

Jessica stared back into the intense blueness of his eyes, seeing his desperate need to convince her, sensing, as she had before, the raw loneliness within him. 'Okay,' she said slowly. 'So now what? Bearing in mind I *haven't* had plenty of boyfriends, as I already told you, and my experience is...pretty limited?' She managed a wry smile even as she ducked her head, her cheeks staining with colour.

'Ah!' He waved his hand in dismissal. 'That's not important. I told you, I'll teach you, but only what you're happy with. We get to know each other. I'll take you walking. Do you like walking?'

'Yes. Yes, I do. Walking, yes. And books, reading. We...we like a lot of the same kind of films and music, too. It's good. I'm surprised. But I've never been kayaking!'

'Why shouldn't we like some of the same things? It's you judging me, just by my appearance. Just because you think I look sophisticated, dangerous, whatever, doesn't actually mean I *have* to be. And I'll take you kayaking, as well,' he added as an afterthought.

'Mmm.' Jessica laughed. 'I suspect there are bits of you I shall continue to be suspicious about! But yes, you're right. Perhaps I am being unfair.'

'I'll have that coffee now. Maybe some toast?' Nic ran a hand through his hair and sat back. This soul-searching was cathartic but it surely made him hungry!

Jessica stirred and sat up, face glowing. 'Okay. It won't take long.' Greatly daring, she leaned forwards and swiftly kissed his cheek before disappearing into the kitchen.

After a few moments, Nic again started to prowl restlessly round the room. Still keyed up from the four months he'd spent abroad touring, and his hurried return yesterday in time to watch Jessica play last night, he wasn't as yet able to fully relax. And now this! He'd certainly got a physical response from her but normally he wouldn't have called a halt at that point, to resort instead to self-restraint and confession!

There was some music on the piano. Nic sat down on the stool and looked casually at it. His eyes were about to flick away when he stiffened and leaned closer. This wasn't Jessica's. It couldn't be. He scanned the sheet before picking it up and looking at the one underneath. He began to hum softly under his breath, his hand picking up the rhythm and tapping it out on his knee.

Other sounds filled his head, layering over the main tune. He saw a pencil on a nearby table and strode across to pick it up.

Sitting down again, he altered a note, then crossed out a couple of words, writing substitutes underneath. A frown crossed his brow and he hummed again, his fingers itching to play the tune on the piano. But he didn't want Jessica to hear. This was good! It was obviously original because it was hand-written. Whose was it and what was it doing here? He bent once more and wrote a suggestion down.

'Coffee's ready, Nic.'

Startled, Nic looked up. Absorbed in the song, he hadn't heard her come in and now she stood next to him, looking at him curiously.

'Mmm, yes. This...it can't be yours? I, um, I can read a bit of music. It's not classical. It's a song. There are words.'

Jessica leaned over and glanced at the music. 'Oh, that's Mike's.'

'Mike's? Oh, yeah, of course.' He got up from the piano stool, reluctantly placing the music back on the piano and following Jessica back to the fire, where she had put the mugs of coffee and a plate of toast on the stone hearth.

'Mmm. That's probably something he's given up on or lost his temper with. He'll have abandoned it and in six months' time he'll come back raving and wanting to know where it is. I keep everything he leaves here in a file so if he changes his mind and wants to work on something again, we can find it.' She grinned.

'Does he often get impatient with his work?' Nic leaned forwards and picked up one of the mugs, still excited by the song he'd just seen.

'Yes, if something isn't going right.'

'You said he was a rock musician, didn't you? Is he in a band at the moment?' Nic sipped his coffee appreciatively.

'He had a band but they weren't any good. The other players, I mean, not Mike. They didn't have Mike's dedication and talent. I do think Mike's probably got a lot of talent. He plays the guitar himself, but when he's writing something, he quite often hammers out a tune on the piano first. It's his passion, all he ever wants to do.'

'Is he working at the moment?'

'I don't know,' Jessica shrugged, looking sad. 'He does session work for quite a few well-known people but nothing lasts. He's too good, too individualistic. He's either got to find some others as good as he is or get a toe-hold in a good band. His ambition is to play with a group called Tunnel Vision. Apparently they're his idea of perfection.'

Nic choked on a mouthful of coffee and shot her a sharp look. 'Do you know their music?'

'No. Although I keep meaning to educate myself. Mike and Andrea helped me such a lot in college and I owe it to them to try to understand what they like. They often come to my concerts.'

'What about Andrea?' Nic relaxed, lying back in his chair and taking a bite of the crisp toast.

'She teaches music in a comprehensive in London.'

'Oh yes, I remember now. Does she like it? You hear so much about discipline problems in schools these days.'

'She has them eating out of her hand. Mike goes along and helps some of the boys with a group. She's even had me in a couple of times to give demonstrations. She's amazing. There's never any trouble in her lessons.'

Nic looked thoughtful. That piece of music on the piano had definitely been good. Jessica was probably right in her estimation of Mike's talents.

Later in the day, when Jessica was upstairs, Nic quietly took the two pieces of paper from the piano and on the back he wrote the name and address he'd found in Jessica's telephone book, under the entry for Mike and Andrea, then he folded them carefully and slid them into a zipped pocket on his leathers.

Chapter Eight

Andy strode into the workroom and put his guitar case on the table. 'Hi,' he said, snapping the clips open and lifting the lid. He pulled out a gleaming steel-string guitar and ran his fingers across the strings. A river of sound shivered through the room.

Looking up from the notes he was making, Nic grinned. 'Andy.'

'Hey, man, you look busy.'

'Yeah. I'm just looking at this song again, by that guy Jessica knows. Mike D'Arsace? Shall we get in touch with him? We said we would.'

Andy had been as excited by the song as Nic was, when he'd brought it back that first time he'd been over to Jessica's house and found it on the piano. They'd begun recording their new album and a couple of the songs would benefit from extra guitar input, which Mike could provide. They were even wondering about recording Mike's song as an extra.

'Yeah, yeah, but no rush. We can leave those songs over 'til last.' Andy bent his head and picked out a string of notes that echoed round the room, soft, evocative. It was a new song, unfinished yet, the last one for the new recording, a love song, a haunting ballad. 'I like the start to this,' Andy commented, playing the main theme again and again. 'If the rest is as good, you've written a winner here!'

Nic's head was on one side as he listened to the notes. 'Hold it! There! No, no...back a bit. Yeah...play that bit again.'

Andy repeated the phrase again and again.

'Try it with a sharp instead,' Nic commanded, intent.

Andy knew exactly where Nic wanted the replacement. He repeated the run, substituting the new note, playing it as before, several times.

'Better?' Nic asked.

'Yeah, maybe.' Andy wasn't so sure. 'Write it down, okay? When the rest is done, we'll see. Maybe, maybe not. How's Jessica?' He finished playing abruptly, laying the guitar down in its plush-lined case. He suspected this song had been written with her in mind, suspected Nic was taking this girl seriously. It seemed he'd been wrong about her and he was glad.

'Pretty good.'

'You treating her carefully?'

'I'm treating her carefully.'

'Going over tomorrow?'

'Yeah.'

A silence fell. Nic made notes, Andy fiddled with pieces of paper, a pen, his case.

Nic looked up, irritation on his face. 'You want to talk?' he asked.

'I want to know this…does Jessica know who you are now, what you do?'

Nic stared at his friend before dropping his head once more to look at his notes. He didn't continue writing.

'Nic?'

'No.'

'I thought you told me you'd tell her?'

'My, my, my! What would I do without you to keep me on the straight and narrow? Look, Andy, you have no idea how carefully I'm having to tread, you really don't.'

'Aw, c'mon!' Andy spoke over his shoulder as he made his way over to the drinking fountain in the corner of the room and ran himself a cup of cold water. 'You've been seeing her for what, three months now? Four? Surely things are well established enough to tell the girl? You know, it could be a pretty good conversation point after you've made love to her.' He stood with his back to Nic as he drank deeply, then wiped his mouth with the back of his hand.

A silence stretched between them.

'Nic?'

The silence continued. Andy slowly turned and stared at his friend, his eyes narrowing. Nic kept his head bent over the score he was working on, a tell-tale flush of colour slowly rising up his face from the open collar of his black shirt.

'Nic? You *are* sleeping with Jessica, aren't you?'

Nic caught his bottom lip under top teeth and ran a hand through his hair, sighing deeply. Andy's mouth fell open and he walked slowly back to the table, sinking into the chair next to Nic, his gaze fixed on his friend's face, studiously averted from him. '*Nic?*'

'Andy!' Nic exploded, leaping up from his chair and moving away to the window, his hands clenched into fists. 'I *told* you, remember? I *told* you she was different. I mean, go back a few years, okay? Say, back to when you were thirteen, fourteen. You remember those dates, then? When we were trying to find out what it was all about? Yeah, well, I'm back to that, give or take.

68

You know…how far did you let him go, this date? Ah, shut your face!'

By this time, Andy was splitting his sides laughing and Nic's face flamed. He scooped up an empty paper cup and threw it at his friend's head as Andy doubled up, hardly able to speak. 'Nic, Nic, tell me I'm not hearing this! Tell me it isn't true! Oh my goodness! What's this worth to the Daily Echo? Or Music Machine? Oh, man, would they *love* to hear this!'

'Yeah, well. Just as well I trust you, isn't it?' Nic said sourly, leaning back against the sill. 'Now you understand just how carefully I'm treading. Imagine if I told her well, hey, look, Jessica, I happen to be a rock singer of several years standing and if you read the right papers you might discover I have a bit of a bad reputation with women and I'm surely not known for fidelity? Okay, I tell her that, I won't see her for dust! Yeah, I *know* she ought to know. I'm so scared I'll lose her once she knows.'

'C'mon, Nic! Once she knows who you are, she'll stick like a limpet! They always do!'

'Not this one,' Nic said grimly, as he shot his friend a sideways look and returned to the table, head bent once more to his music. He knew it would be almost impossible to convince Andy of Jessica's integrity and other-worldliness that was like a balm to him after all the years with the brittle and sophisticated women who'd recently filled his life. And it was her very integrity and other-worldliness that would make her back off…from fear, from ignorance, from distaste. Nic shrugged. It wouldn't matter what the reason was, he knew she'd go. And by now she was far too precious to him to risk losing her. Ah, come on, time to admit it…bottom line, he'd fallen in love with her.

It was hard, very, very hard, to hold back physically, but in the end he thought it would be worth the wait, worth building up her confidence and trust in him. Worth living up to her standards. Then, *then* she might not be so quick to leave.

'Tell her,' Andy said, finally getting his mirth under control.

'May find I have to,' Nic muttered. 'But look, you'll have to meet her. Then you can judge for yourself, okay? I think you'll be surprised. This isn't my usual type and I'm not sure…' he was hesitant to speak aloud about her growing importance in his life.

'Oh, hey,' Andy said, shaking his head and lifting his guitar out of its case again, his long fingers pulling magic from the steel strings which gleamed in the sunlight, notes and chords spilling out, shivering through the room. 'I just can't believe this. Last July, you were bumming around so much the whole band was worried

69

that you were on the verge of freaking out and losing it. Now here you are telling me you haven't slept with Jessica, yet I know you've been going down there, what, nearly every night, since we came back from Europe. How can you stand it?'

'Not every night,' Nic was impatient. 'Three, maybe four times a week, is all. And yeah, okay, I find it hard, I'll be honest. But she…she *is* inexperienced. She was brought up pretty much apart from kids her own age and pushed to become a performer. And, yeah, she's good, you know, but when we all had the chance to mess about and grow up, she didn't, and I really don't want to frighten her off. There's a lot of sensuality in her, but I want her to be the one who sets the pace and her to be the one to have the confidence to go ahead.' Nic's voice was quiet. 'She lacks confidence in herself when it comes to personal issues.'

'What's she look like, Nic?' Andy was curious. He couldn't imagine Nic going for someone with no looks, but equally couldn't imagine someone with no looks lacking confidence.

Nic eyed him and grinned. 'Don't worry, my friend, I ain't lost my touch,' he said. Digging in his back pocket he pulled out a page torn from a magazine and unfolded it, laying it on the table in front of Andy.

He put his guitar down and leaned forward. 'Oh, wow!' he breathed.

It was a publicity shot. Jessica stood, wearing a sweeping black dress, diamonds around her neck, one hand on a magnificent Bechstein grand piano, thick blond hair loose upon bare shoulders, her wide green eyes looking directly into the camera and a soft smile on her face.

'Classy lady,' Andy murmured. 'Yeah, you haven't lost your touch, that much I do see. What I don't understand is how she can doubt herself?'

Nic sighed. 'From what she's said, it's simple. She was kept apart from her peers. No dances, no parties, no pop or rock, no shopping trips, no back seat at the cinema, no giggles with the girls…'

'C'mon, Nic! This isn't the Victorian era, you know!'

'Her parents were mediocre talent. She wasn't. In fairness to them, they saw that and tried to make sure she had every advantage. She started performing and entering competitions at an early age. This meant a private tutor as she was travelling all over. So not even school. She hasn't said a lot about it but I can read between the lines. When she went to college to study theory, she found it hard to join in. It was this Mike's partner,' Nic touched the song he'd taken from Jessica's house with his long fingers, 'Andrea, who took her under her wing and tried to draw her out. Succeeded up to a point in that Andrea brought Jess into the twentieth century regarding clothes and make-up, but wasn't able to provide the sexual experience.'

'So why not educate the girl yourself and put her out of her misery?'

'I am doing. Slowly. She needs to trust me and be prepared to give herself totally- '

'Why? Get her into bed a few times, you'll be gone. Who cares if she trusts you or not?'

Another long silence filled the room.

'I care.' Nic's voice was low.

Andy stared at him, unable to think of anything else to say. This seemed serious. He'd never known Nic so involved with anyone before.

Chapter Nine:

As Nic had confessed to Andy, he was finding it hard to restrain himself physically, but if he'd known it, Jessica was beginning to find it almost as hard. Nic had awakened her. She discovered she was a deeply sensuous woman and, although she realised she still had a long way to go, she was learning fast. But still, something held her back, and she thought it was the way he kept her apart from his life in London. He never invited her to his place, even though he knew she was often in town. They never met up anywhere in London. He never offered to introduce her to his friends. He was evasive, and always dodged questions which were too direct about his London life. Odd, and it could make her feel uncomfortable, as if somehow, he didn't trust her or like her enough. Or thought she wasn't good enough for his friends? She even wondered if he was involved with drugs, somehow, as well as his job in recording, and wanted to keep her apart from it.

So she held back.

Today was one of the wonderful days Nic had come down to hers for the whole day. They'd planned a walk, which they both loved, being capable of eight or more miles, and usually throwing in lunch at a pub or cafe

'Are you ready?' He stood now by the door, waiting for Jessica to fasten her boots.

She glanced up and grinned. 'Yes, just. Where are we going today?' She loved it when he could spare her a full day, which wasn't often. Usually he came down in the evening and was gone by midnight. But he'd lost the tired and lonely look that had been in his face when she'd first met him, which was good, and he seemed more peaceful and relaxed.

'I thought we'd drive as far as Clivegate, park outside the village, then walk up the scarp to Elmwood. We could have lunch there, if you like. We'll come back along the edge and drop down by Otterham. That suit?'

'Sounds great.' Jessica pulled on her fleece and shut the door behind her. Nic caught her by the arm and kissed her briefly before leading the way to Jessica's car. His bike stood in its usual place on the drive.

The late April sky was clear and blue and the sun surprisingly warm. It was only a short distance to the honey-coloured village of Clivegate, with its thatched cottages and tourist shops, tucked under the edge of the hill.

Nic locked the car and glanced up the hill. 'We'll be ready for our lunch when we've climbed that!' He laughed with sheer pleasure. 'Look! The beech trees are out.'

For a moment they both stood to look at the fresh, sharp green of the new beech leaves gleaming in the bright sun, beckoning them on into the woods.

Since he'd found her again, in January, they'd spent as many days that Nic could spare like this, happily walking in the area, talking, getting to know each other. Jessica loved that, despite her reserve about him keeping her separate from his London life. Not only that, having originally doubted his claim to love walking and be a walker, she'd had to admit if he wanted, he could walk faster and further than she could, although he always matched his pace to hers and kept the distance to something she could be comfortable with.

This morning was no different. Panting, laughing, they reached the top of the hill. Turning to survey the valley laid out below, Nic stretched his arms high above his head, his face flushed and his hair blown back by the wind. He pulled Jessica to him so her back rested against his chest and nuzzled at her hair.

'Fresh air!' he exclaimed. 'I feel better now!'

Jessica laughed. 'You really do need this, don't you? Initially, I wondered. I thought you were just being nice to me, but no, you need it.'

'Yep. It's my escape.' And I can't understand how I let it slip away from me, he admitted to himself, still feeling it was unbelievable he'd found this girl and through her, his way back to the principles he'd always tried to follow. He seriously wondered if Andy's concern would have been enough.

Maybe. But Jessica had certainly tipped the balance. He knew everything in his life had improved as a result of knowing her. His work, especially. He hadn't realised quite how dismayed the rest of them had been with him. His moods had been affecting his song-writing, his playing, his performance.

'From what, Nic?'

'Hard work,' he said briefly, after a long pause, remembering the long session yesterday with Andy. They had nearly finished the ballad and it would, as Andy had suggested, be good. Perhaps their best yet. And yes, it had been written with Jessica in mind. In fact, he wanted to call the song simply 'Loved One'.

Moving away from him, Jessica sighed and went through the gate leading into the beech wood which stretched from the lip of the hill all the way to the village of Elmwood.

'Nic! Primroses!' Her momentary annoyance forgotten, Jessica stared entranced at the scattered pale-yellow flowers on the banks each side of the path.

The sun slanted down through branches, lighting the flowers, making them seem even more beautiful.

'Ohhh,' breathed Jessica. 'They're lovely.'

He swallowed and reached out his hand to find hers. He was finding so much pleasure in sharing little things like this with her. 'Look closely, you'll see a few violets, too. See, there...near that tree root?'

They stood in silence for a few minutes, then Jessica sighed in pure pleasure. 'I always feel so privileged when I see something like this. It's not like flowers in the garden. They're designed to flourish. But these little things, I always feel they have such a struggle and then every year they push through yet again.'

'Mmm, yes. I know what you mean. I feel a bit the same.'

'You know, you're constantly surprising me!' Jessica teased. 'Why?'

'Because you've turned out to be so different to what I expected.' She laughed up at him. 'Here you are, enjoying the fresh air and sunshine and little flowers struggling through in the woods.'

'And I keep telling you, your initial impression was wrong and unfair. Let it go.' This was too close to the bone. Andy had given him a conscience about not telling Jess and it was beginning to intrude all the time, spoiling his simple enjoyment of the day.

She glanced at him, sensing his withdrawal. He sounded annoyed. His face was expressionless and his mouth was held in that straight line she'd begun to realise meant he was angry.

'I'm sorry,' she said in surprise. 'I didn't mean to upset you.'

'You haven't,' he said with difficulty.

'Oh, but I have,' she responded swiftly. She turned to face him and caught hold of his hands. He avoided her eyes, looking down at the brown beech mast which thickly carpeted the ground.

Slowly he raised his head and smiled faintly, her honesty forcing him, as always, to be equally honest in return. 'Sorry, Jessica. Yes, you did annoy me a bit.'

'Nic...' Jessica began slowly. 'You're very touchy about me teasing you, saying you're sophisticated and worldly. But...you are, you know. I've told you before, you have this air of power, of command, but you somehow want to deny it to me. I don't really understand...' she hesitated, wondering whether to say it, deciding anyway to go ahead. 'I'm not really your type, let's be honest. So I wonder…why you stay with me, why you chose me? And having chosen me, why you won't share your life in London with me?'

Nic shifted restlessly and sighed. 'I don't want the type of woman you seem to think I do. And as to why I stay with you, that's your insecurity based on your upbringing, I suspect. I've told you, I love you simply because you're fresh and unspoilt, I really do. You bring me joy and…and peace, and I don't ever want you to change and I won't ever abandon you. Not now. I couldn't. I…' He stopped and shrugged. No. He couldn't. He couldn't bear to lose her and he was so frightened she would shy away immediately she knew.

'Thank you, Nic,' Jessica murmured, touched by what he'd said and recognising it probably *was* her own insecurity that made her worry about why he was with her.

'So…nothing more to say, really. London's not important now. It will be, one day. But for now,' he shrugged. 'I need you. Just you, with no interruptions. You think you're dependent on me because you see me as someone out of your league, but have you ever considered I see you as out of *my* league because you're so pure and good? As well as beautiful, darlin'.' He pulled her into him and swayed gently, his face buried in her gold hair which smelled of lavender, his hands slowly moving up and down her back. 'You worry about me going, leaving you, but so do I! I worry you'll be the one leaving me. Don't you realise that?'

Yes. No. Why? Look at him, she thought. Tall, wild black hair, a face to die for, even *she* could see that, despite her innocence and lack of experience. Broad shoulders, slim hips…he was saved from being too perfect by the intelligence in his blazing blue eyes, his strong features and lilting half-smile, the creases at the corners of his eyes and in his cheek on one side, but the whole was simply dazzling.

Jessica tried to accept what he said, but she failed to see what Nic saw, due again to the lack of confidence she had in herself. Failed to see her own beauty. Failed to value her own gentleness and honesty. All she knew was that compared to other women, she was…she was too quiet. Too shy. Too gentle. Too impatient of the glitter and surface social exchanges which meant nothing.

Which were all the things Nic loved about her.

They stood entwined, each lost in their own thoughts, his anguished and fearful, hers self-doubting and fearful. Yet both had begun to realise they had deep feelings for each other, if they could overcome the obstacles.

If Jessica did but know it, Nic's obstacles were probably the greater. He hated her questions about his life in London, but acknowledged, as he'd said to Andy, her right to ask. For now, though, he was still determined she shouldn't know who he was. It would only convince her she'd been right about him all along and probably frighten her away. Sophisticated, powerful, dangerous to know! He kept telling himself there was time enough for the whole truth later. Enough that she knew he and Andy worked in recording. That was as close as he wanted to get. Pushing it all to the back of his mind, Nic blanked out the sudden image of Andy staring at him accusingly, and ignored the doubts about the longer he left it, the harder would be the telling.

Eventually, with soft kisses, they drew apart.

'Trust me, darlin'?' His voice was soft and pleading.

Staring at him, Jessica nodded reluctantly. 'But...' she paused uncertainly before sighing. 'I don't like it. I worry what it is you seem to want to hide from me.'

Another soft kiss, another murmured plea to trust him, and they finally drew apart to continue the walk, conversation continuing more generally, more subdued, as could often happen when Jessica questioned Nic about his own life away from her.

It took another hour to reach the pub, an old building with a dark, smoky interior. A blazing log fire provided welcome warmth and light. They sank down onto chairs near the fire. Nic bought some drinks before they consulted the menu.

'I can't decide what to have!' Jessica exclaimed, her usual gentle good humour and kindness now restored by the cold, sunny air and the exercise. She ran her finger down the selection thoughtfully.

'I have no such problem,' Nic announced with cheerful relief at her smile. 'I'm going to have the Ploughman's.' He closed his menu and leaned backwards to place it on an empty table behind them. 'Jessica...' he hesitated. This was one thing he could give her.

She looked at him enquiringly.

'I don't know how much time off you have when you're rehearsing, but I was wondering...there *is* somewhere I want to take you. It's important to me and I'd like to go there fairly soon if you want to come too.'

'Sounds intriguing.' She smiled across at him, a feeling of relief flooding through her as she realised the importance of what he was saying. 'Anywhere I know?'

'That I don't know. I don't know if you've ever been there. It's Cumbria. The Lake District. *Have* you ever been?'

'No,' she said slowly. 'No. We never went away much when I was young. It always interfered, you see, with lessons and practice.' She gave him rather a sad smile and he suddenly felt sorry for her. Love her music she might, but she'd missed out on so much else, thanks to her loving, dedicated, careful, *stifling* parents.

'I've a house there,' he said abruptly. 'I've been meaning to tell you for some time but-' He fell silent as the waitress came to take their orders. Jessica stared at him, her mouth parted in surprise, completely forgetting the menu in her hand.

Head down, Nic said briefly, 'Ploughman's, please. Jessica?'

'Wha-? Oh, yes. Umm, I'll have the ham sandwich.'

The waitress scribbled down their order and smiled at them. 'It'll be about ten minutes, all right?' she said cheerfully, as she turned away.

Jessica looked at Nic. 'Come on. What were you saying? You have a house? In Cumbria?'

'Mmm.' He nodded, taking a long drink and smiling at her. 'Will you come with me? I'd like to show it to you.'

'I thought you said you lived in London?' She avoided his eyes and fiddled with the cutlery left by the waitress.

'I do, nearly all the time. But when I can, when work allows and I'm not abroad, then I go up to the house. It's a special kind of place for me, somewhere I can be totally alone.'

He'd been back there twice since he'd met Jessica. Sam had asked no questions about his long absence. His wife had cleaned and taken care of the property and made sure, when Nic finally returned, that there was food in the cupboards and a fire in the hearth. He'd felt refreshed and renewed, had walked all day and slept all night, deeply grateful to Jessica that unknowingly she had pulled him back from the brink of self-destruction.

'And you're asking me to...?' Her voice trailed off.

'Yes, Jessica. I'm asking you to go there with me.' His hand covered hers and he smiled gently into her eyes.

Jessica was silent. A motorbike. A place in London. A house in the Lake District. As Lewis Carroll might write, curiouser and curiouser!

'I don't invite anyone there unless they're special.'

77

Flushing, she looked down at their clasped hands. 'Thank you, Nic,' she said in a low voice, acknowledging his compliment.

'Here you are then.' The cheerful voice of the waitress broke the silence that had fallen between them, placing the Ploughman's lunch and the sandwiches down on the table. Turning away, she suddenly stopped and looked back, dipping at the knees to try to see Nic's face. 'Have you been in here before, then?' she asked, a note of puzzlement entering her voice.

Nic seemed not to have heard and turned away to gaze into the flames of the fire, his shoulders stiff. Jessica looked at him and then back at the waitress and shook her head. 'No, not me. What about you, N-?'

'No,' he interrupted quickly, his back still half turned away from the waitress. 'No, I've never been here. Only driven through and seen the place from the outside.'

'Funny,' the waitress commented. 'You sort of look familiar.' She was still trying to get a good look at Nic before turning and walking off, looking puzzled.

The waitress retired to the bar and carried on a low-voiced conversation with the landlord, both of them obviously trying to decide why the waitress felt she knew them.

'It's really worrying her,' Jessica giggled, taking a mouthful of the crusty sandwich.

Nic looked annoyed. 'It's a nuisance!' he said, with irritation edging his voice.

'Oh, come on, Nic! It's hardly anything to get upset about.'

Not for Jessica, Nic admitted as he ate, wondering if he was about to be accosted with a cry of 'Now I've remembered where it is I've seen you before!' And if he was, then how he would explain things? He wondered if it was possible to leave but realised that would take just as much explaining. What should have been a pleasurable meal became a tense ordeal. He began to eat quickly, hoping they could leave the pub as soon as possible.

Usually it was all right, going out where no-one expected to see him. He glanced down at his black jeans, the fine black wool sweater, the black fleece flung on the stool beside him. The colour itself was a give-away, he supposed, but it was the colour he always wore and he wasn't going to change that, not now. And his hair, of course.

Jessica broke the rather tense silence. 'Nic, about the Lakes. I'd like to come. When were you thinking we could go?'

He shrugged. 'Whenever. Soon. Next Thursday, or at the weekend, or even the weekend after that. I'm fairly free at the moment but I wasn't sure what you had in the way of commitments?' He and Andy had just spent an intense three months working on new material and they were both tired. A break would do them good before tackling the final stretch.

'I've just finished a recording. We've already started work on another concert for the summer, but I could probably persuade David to put it on hold for a few days. It's only him and me at the moment.' She hesitated. 'Although we've not much time for this...it was a late request and David agreed because they were let down by someone else...still, a few days shouldn't matter. I've never asked for time off before,' she said, in sudden amazement.

'If you could arrange it then? Maybe make it the weekend after next, to give you time to sort it with David?' Nic placed his knife neatly on his plate and watched impatiently as Jessica took another careful bite of her sandwich. 'Just one thing...when we go...could you perhaps keep it to yourself? Not tell anyone where the house is?'

'What on earth for?'

'I prefer to keep it the way it's always been, with just Andy, Josh and me knowing where it is,' he said evenly. 'And you now, of course. All I'm asking is that you just keep the whereabouts to yourself. No big deal, is it?'

She looked at him steadily. 'Why does it have to be kept quiet, Nic?'

Because if it wasn't a secret, Nic thought, there would always be the risk of someone hanging round waiting to see him, like there was in London. But Cumbria was a different matter and he didn't intend, ever, to publicise his place there. He had to have somewhere to go where he knew he would never be accosted and could relax, be alone, be himself.

'I just like to know if I go there I can relax and not worry about anyone else turning up,' he finally answered, rather shortly.

Who would? Jessica wondered as she silently finished her sandwich, recognising he was feeling evasive again and would answer no more questions on that subject. But...it still seemed odd to her, to keep a house that no-one knew about, just to guard against "anyone else turning up". Did it matter if they did? Most people welcomed visitors. Did he fear someone finding him? Was this place somewhere to run if things in London got too...difficult? This seemed a bit weird.

'But you're prepared to take me there and risk me knowing where it is?' she asked eventually.

'Yes, I trust you. But...I'd just prefer it if you didn't discuss the place with anyone else, if I do.' He shrugged helplessly, a look of pleading on his face. 'Does it *matter*, asking that?'

'Well, no...but...would anyone really want to rush up there to see you anyway? They'd know you'd be back in London soon, so...?' she tried again.

A lot of people would, Nic thought wryly. And it's impossible to make Jessica understand without filling her in about things. 'Probably no-one would bother, sure. Put it down to paranoia, okay? Finished?' Nic rose to his feet.

Gulping down the last of her drink, Jessica stood up, flustered by Nic's obvious determination to leave quickly.

The waitress hurried forward. 'Was everything all right?' she asked pleasantly. 'You know, I still think I've met you before, but I can't think where.'

Nic smiled perfunctorily and dug into his pocket for some money. Hurrying to the bar, she put the money in the till and started to count out the change. The landlord was reading a paper but suddenly jerked upright, an exclamation bursting from him. He turned to the waitress and pointed something out to her on the page he was reading. She bent forward to look at the photograph he was pointing to and read the few lines underneath it. She raised her head and stared at Nic before looking at the landlord.

Nic swore softly and turned to the door, pulling Jessica with him. 'Keep the change,' he called over his shoulder.

'But I know now...' the waitress began, her mouth hanging open.

'Hey!' the landlord called excitedly. 'Don't go just yet...'

But Nic was gone from the dimness of the pub into the thin spring sunshine. 'Come on Jessica,' he urged, moving forward down the lane.

'Is everything all right?' she cried, looking back over her shoulder. 'He seemed to want you to go back.'

'No, no, everything's okay. Come *on*,' he said again, impatience tingeing his voice.

Jessica, puzzled, followed him. As she glanced once more over her shoulder, she saw behind her the landlord and the waitress standing in the doorway of the pub staring after them, excitement on their faces.

By the time they'd finished the walk it was late. They drove home as the sun sank behind the far horizon, turning the sky to a deep blue. A few stars shone brightly.

'There'll be a frost tonight.' Jessica said flatly. She sounded tired. It had been a silent end to the walk. Her mind had been occupied for most of the afternoon with the strange incident in the pub, plus the request that should she go with Nic to the Lake District, she was to keep quiet about where. No-one to tell, really, apart from David and maybe Andrea. She'd not seen Andrea for a long time, partly due to the work schedules of both and partly due to spending time with Nic. Andrea knew about Nic, although, uncertain as to where the relationship might go, Jessica had been cautious, telling her friend simply that she'd found someone who enjoyed walking and music, and they were seeing each other for the time being.

Nic was grateful Jessica hadn't noticed the landlord reading the newspaper in the bar and seeing something in it obviously linked to him. Despite his luck there, he knew Jessica would soon start asking questions again. Too much had happened and he began to feel there was no way out but to risk confessing.

If he could have read her mind, he would have had his suspicions confirmed. She'd decided enough was enough. She wanted to know why he kept her away from his London life. She wanted to know why he had a house, apparently to be kept secret from all but a very few people...who had to keep a house *secret* anyway? She wanted to know why he had to run from London on occasions and hide away. She wanted to know why the landlord and waitress had run after them after their hushed conference at the bar.

All this needed clearing up as far as she was concerned, but her heart sank as she realised how intractable Nic was about it. Should she let it drop as she'd always done until now? But Jessica had never lived with lies. It might be part of his world, but it wasn't part of hers and this was one thing she wouldn't give way on. If he wanted her, he would have to be truthful.

Glancing sideways at her, Nic was aware of her preoccupation and he was desperately hoping she wouldn't force the issue, while at the same time deeply sympathetic to her worries and concerns. He had to admit, it was all a bit askew and if the roles were reversed, he'd certainly be wanting answers to a few questions!

When they arrived back, Jessica took herself off to have a bath, still silent, still deep in thought, leaving Nic to start a meal in

81

the kitchen. She came downstairs to find him lying on the settee in front of the newly-lit fire.

'Okay.' He sprang to his feet. 'Everything's under control in the kitchen. I'll have a shower, if you don't mind.' He kissed her briefly and disappeared, postponing the inevitable.

When Nic returned, his black hair wet and slicked back from his strongly-boned face, she silently served the meal. They ate slowly, Jessica holding back on the flood of questions forming in her mind, Nic reluctant to start any conversation which he knew would somehow lead inevitably to a showdown. They drifted back into the sitting room, taking with them the remains of a bottle of wine. The fire was now blazing briskly, shadows flickering in the corners of the room and a faint smell of wood smoke lingering in the air.

'Try listening to this,' Nic said, slipping a cassette into the stereo. He had brought a few of his own cassettes for her to listen to and so far, she'd enjoyed most of them, a range of music far removed from her usual experience, a mix of rock, pop, folk, jazz.

Jessica sat down next to Nic and leaned her head on his shoulder, trying to banish her feelings of foreboding and now, like Nic, willing to accept any diversion to postpone what she felt was becoming inevitable. He slipped his arm round her and stared into the fire.

'I'll invite Andy down sometime, if that's okay?' he suddenly asked, remembering his suggestion to his friend that he and Jessica should meet.

Jessica looked up startled. 'Why, yes,' she answered slowly, careful not to show her surprise as she wondered at this new development, suspicious whether it was simply a distraction from the real issues or an opening to discussion. 'Yes, I'd like that. How about if we invite Mike and Andrea at the same time? I haven't seen them for a while. And if Andy's got a girlfriend...?'

'He has, but he won't be bringing her. And no, we won't invite Mike and Andrea.' He hastily tried to amend his peremptory manner. 'Sorry. Sorry. Do you mind? I'd like to meet them...but later on. I don't want to share you at the moment.'

'But you're prepared to share me with Andy?'

'He's different,' Nic pleaded. 'I've known him forever. He's my brother. More than my brother, because we chose each other. And I wasn't planning on a crowd of people. I just thought he could come down casually with me one day. I'd like you to meet him.'

'And I'd like you to meet Andrea and Mike,' Jessica said evenly. They know I'm involved with someone, and-'

'What have you told them about me?' His voice was sharp. He sat up and leaned forwards, elbows on his knees, staring into the fire. Oh, no! Here it came. 'What have you said?'

'Not a lot!' Jessica glared at him, 'What *can* I tell them? Only that I'm seeing someone called Nic and that you enjoy walking and music! I can't exactly tell them anymore, can I?'

And that summed it up. There was hardly any more to tell. She knew the things he liked doing. She knew she enjoyed being with him and talking to him. She knew he stirred her as no other man had ever done, making her weak with nameless longing when he took her into his arms, kissed her, touched her. But other than that, that he lived in London, worked in recording studios and his association with Andy, his life was a closed book.

She shook her head in distress. She didn't know where he lived. She didn't know who his friends were. And the only times she saw him was when he came here, to her house. She didn't even have a contact number for him! No wonder she felt uneasy. And to top all that, today there's been the invitation to his "secret" house, and the strange incident at the pub. She couldn't talk to David or Andrea about this, she'd feel such a naïve fool and they would agree. A naïve fool indeed to put up with a boyfriend who wouldn't tell her things? Who kept her incarcerated down here, a secret?

Without warning, a cold silence hung over the room.

Nic sank back onto the settee. 'I'm sorry,' he muttered, knowing his anxiety had precipitated exactly what he was trying to avoid.

Jessica took a deep breath. No matter what the outcome, she decided this was as good a moment as any to let him know she was going no further with their relationship until he was able to fully trust her, answer a few questions and open up his life to her. 'Okay, so when will you let me invite them down? And when will you invite me up to London to see where you *live*? And while we're on the subject, what was going on at the pub today? I didn't understand it at all. I don't understand, either, why you're so secretive about this house of yours in Cumbria! Don't you think it's about time you trusted me a bit more?' She poured out all the confusion and anxiety that had been building up over the last few weeks, her tone angry and hurt. 'You're asking me to…to keep you compartmentalised, almost. I only ever see you *here*, when you decide. You don't want to meet Mike and Andrea, or David and Stephanie. When are you going to become fully part of my life, my friends? And when am I going to become fully part of your life? It's gone on too long, this, and we're beginning to trip over it every which way we turn!'

They had to sort this out…or perhaps it might be better if he went away until he'd learned to trust her. She was horrified as these thoughts spiralled through her head. What had happened to the day? The beautiful day with the primroses and the sun, their carefree laughter of the morning? His confession he needed her as much, maybe more, than she needed him? How could it all turn to ashes as quickly as this?

'Jessica, I...can't you give me some more time?' Nic pleaded.

'Some more time for what? I don't see what the problem is. It's this total exclusion from your life I find so difficult to understand. I'm willing to introduce you to my admittedly small circle of friends but you always make excuses why you can't meet them. In the meanwhile, there's no suggestion I can join in with your London life-' She broke off and looked at him in growing horror, her face paling with shock. 'You're not married, are you?'

'No! No, I'm not. Jessica, I promise you, I'm not lying or trying to deceive you on that score. I'm not married!' His tone of voice rang with such anguished sincerity on that basis at least Jessica was reassured.

'Then why?' she asked helplessly.

He stared at her silently, unable and unwilling to give her what she wanted because he couldn't bear the change there would be once she knew. It *always* happened. As soon as people realised who he was, they changed, in one way or another. Why should she be any different? It was a rare person indeed who would be able to cope with it, he admitted. Maybe he'd found someone who could, but he wanted more time to be sure, more time for her to *see*, to accept him, as…as…ordinary. And this time he was so afraid. So very afraid that she might turn away from him.

Jessica stood up, tired and depressed. 'Okay. You can't tell me...you won't tell me. Maybe you'd better go now. Think about what I've said, will you? I really do feel you need to straighten all this out with me. One thing I thought we had was total honesty between us…there *has* to be total honesty between us….' Her voice broke and she turned away.

Nic's face was set in harsh lines of dismay as he rose silently to his feet. 'Jessica...'

'I just need some space to try to understand why you won't trust me. I don't know...maybe I'm asking for too much from you? After all, Josh said-'

'Forget what Josh said!' Nic exclaimed harshly. He pulled her into his arms and stared down intently into her face. 'I love you, Jessica. I want to marry you.' The words came unexpectedly, but he knew they were true.

Jessica drew back in shocked surprise. Love, yes. She knew she loved him. *Marriage*? If there were no clouds of doubt in her mind, maybe even that was a possibility, but as it was...

'It's been growing on me ever since I met you. You're so different from...I love you. Don't make me tell you...there are reasons. Not what you think...there are *good* reasons. What I do, who my friends are...none of it has any relevance to our relationship. I just think...I just feel it might be better if we had more time before I...Ah, I don't know what to do...' He shook his head, his eyes full of bleak doubt.

'I don't like to feel you can't trust me,' Jessica repeated. 'You say you want to marry me, you say you love me but so far you've shut me out of your life. I love you, as well, but I'm saying I want to know more about you and I think I've the right to ask that. *Especially* if you say you want to marry me. And as for more time...' Her hands fell open and she shrugged. 'It's what you've been saying ever since I began to ask questions. First, evasions, then more time. How much more? When will it be the *right* time?'

Nic groaned and covered her mouth with his own. It wasn't a gentle kiss, or an exploratory one. It was demanding and desperate. His tongue opened her lips and plunged deeply into her mouth as he slid his hands down her back to press her against him, making her aware of his passion and need. Jessica's body flared in response and she moaned deep in her throat, melting against the hardness of his body. Her fingers dug into his shoulders before one hand tangled itself in the thick profusion of his long hair, pulling his head closer, welcoming the kiss.

For a few ecstatic minutes she gave herself up to the sensuous pleasure, then, exerting all her willpower, she pulled away from him. 'No!' she exclaimed. 'No! You won't distract me that way. Not this time. *I want to know*!' Jessica trembled weakly, unable to tear her eyes from his face and the look of bleak hurt and anger in his eyes, but still determined to have an answer.

'You enjoyed that,' he said bitterly. 'I could go on, Jessica. It would be so, so easy to go on. You wouldn't say no. You wouldn't have a chance. It's good between us and if I did go on, you'd see just how good!'

'I know that,' she said harshly. 'I know! You've shown me enough to make me want you as I've never wanted anyone. And to not even care I probably don't have the experience to match yours! But I can't…I won't…make love to you until you can trust me! We can't build a life on evasion and half-truths!' What was she doing?

He stared at her, breathing hard, his hands clenched so tightly into fists by his side that Jessica could see the knuckles gleaming white. 'No!' he said harshly, stepping backwards. 'No, you're right. We can't! But equally I don't know if you would…if I…' His hand covered his eyes. If he went now, maybe there was still a chance. Think of a way to break it to her. Maybe contact her friends and enlist their help? How dramatic it all sounded. But dramatic or not, it was a situation he couldn't judge, didn't know what to do with. He'd never encountered anyone like Jessica.

He pulled her towards him, again kissing her with desperate intensity. 'Remember this...and remember all the...the good times we've shared in just this short space of time. You're demanding something from me that I can't give you yet. Ah, what's the use of talking?' His voice broke and he turned away.

'Nic...' Jessica said faintly. He paused in his journey to the door, not turning, his head to one side, waiting. After a few moments of silence, he continued on his way. Minutes later, Jessica heard the slam of the front door, followed by the roar of his bike as he gunned it into life.

'Nic...' she cried sadly, stumbling into the hall and pulling open the door.

It was too late. All she saw was the dwindling lights as he rode away into the darkness.

Chapter Ten

It was crazy. The flowers started to arrive next day. A single yellow rose with the message: *This reminds me of you. I'm sorry.* This was followed by two yellow roses. The card with it read: *I love you.* On the third day, he sent another three with the message: *I'm thinking of you.*

By the end of the week, Jessica had a bouquet of golden blooms, but she couldn't quite understand his reasoning because she couldn't ring him to thank him or to talk things over with him. She couldn't even write him a note. She didn't know his address or his phone number.

If she had but known it, the flowers were a prelude to his confession. Nic had decided he had to tell her. She was right. If he wanted her to share his life, then she had a right to know about *all* his life before she decided, and he began to feel confident that she would accept the truth in preference to feeling that he didn't trust her. If things stayed as they were, he'd lose her in any case. At the end of the week he'd go back and tell her everything.

Relieved, the decision made, he threw himself into his work, he and Andy striking sparks from each other as always. The new ballad was finished and the group made a tentative preliminary recording to decide what needed adding and what changes needed to be made to the backing. The long guitar solo, played by Andy, sent notes of love and longing echoing into the studio.

Late on Friday, Nic threw down his pen and grinned across at Andy. 'Okay? Call it a day? Time for a break, even?'

'Mmm?' Andy raised his head, eyes blank, obviously miles away. 'Oh. Yeah, I guess so.' He yawned and stretched, leaning back in his chair and linking his hands behind his head. 'It's going to be good, this release. It's incredible what you've come out with since you've met Jessica! I think I'm beginning to realise I've never been properly in love yet. Not even with Elise.' Andy smiled grimly as he mentioned his ex-wife's name. 'Aw, Nic! All these women, and each time here's me thinking this was it! I'm as foolish as you.'

Nic laughed. 'Yeah, know what you mean. So did I, often enough, until it dawned on me they loved my fame and money as much as they loved me. And now Jessica.' His face softened. 'Andy, it's unbelievable, it really is. Except...' he paused, a shadow crossing his face. His decision to tell Jessica may have been made, but it still troubled him what her reaction would be.

'Yeah?' Andy looked at his friend with affection. 'What's up? A problem?'

'You could say so...' Nic said slowly.

'So tell me.'

'You know you said I had to tell Jess who I was?' Nic stretched his long legs out in front of him, crossing his arms over his chest and looking speculatively at Andy.

'I did.' Andy replied firmly, one eyebrow lifted questioningly.

'I chickened out, as usual. Well, it was worse than that, actually. She asks questions...and I suppose I can't blame her. It must seem strange...she's right. Who are my friends, where do I live, all that stuff? But Andy, I like it that she doesn't know who I am, I really do. I mean,' Nic shrugged, 'we've just admitted we've never known what it's all been about, before, with the women we meet. Their motives, their...their general lack of genuineness! But with Jessica, I *know* it's just me she enjoys being with. It's the miracle you said could never happen, and it did! She's not there for the money, the fame, the bright lights or what I can do for her, and I like that. I really like knowing that.' He fell silent for a few moments before sighing and resuming. 'I'm still just terrified she might back off when she finds out and I'm going to lose it all anyway,' he confessed, anguish in his voice.

Andy nodded slowly. 'I take your point,' he conceded, 'but I think this has become an obsession with you. I think you've blown it up out of all proportion. I don't see why you should lose her. Okay, okay, okay, I know you keep telling me she's different, but that doesn't alter the fact she has to be told sooner or later and if she's that good, Nic, if she's *that good*, she'll work through it and stick with you. *Why* are you so convinced she'll back off?'

Nic shot him a look, worry clouding his eyes. 'I don't know,' he answered. 'Because...I guess...she's kind of conditioned and although she struggles against it, deep down her parents' prejudices are there. And her own insecurities. She'll see my world as being too fast, too sophisticated for her. She'll probably just panic and run. I don't *know*.'

Andy could see Nic was deeply troubled. 'And she might not. Well, okay, she might panic at first, maybe I can see that. But I guess if she thinks it all through, she'll realise this is *you*, not a way of life?'

Nic sighed, looking miserable. He wasn't so convinced as Andy that her initial reaction would be short-lived, but there was no going back now.

Andy stretched. 'What happened when you were going to tell her? I mean, why did you chicken out apart from these fears of yours, which I'm still sure you're blowing up out of all proportion.'

'I hope so,' Nic murmured. 'I hope you're right.' He rose to his feet, pacing impatiently across to the open window, standing with his hands thrust into the pockets of his jeans, his back turned to Andy as he continued. 'We went for a walk like we usually do, and she asked a few questions, and as usual, I avoided them and upset her. She's a very forgiving person and when we got to the pub, she was okay again. Then the waitress got the idea she knew me. Just as we were about to go the landlord saw something in the paper…it must have been some article about us, maybe about the new release, or the up-coming British tour, I don't know. I hustled out but the landlord and waitress followed us and were calling out. It was obvious something was up. Jessica kept giving me some very strange looks! Then I suggested you came down to meet her but said not to invite Mike and Andrea, which she wanted to do. Finally, add to that the fact I invited her to the house in the Lakes but asked her to keep it under wraps…!'

'You have to tell her.' Andy sounded subdued. 'It's gone on too long. You have to tell her, man. It's unfair not to and the longer you leave it, by my reckoning, the more hurt she'd going to feel that you implied this was something she couldn't cope with.'

'I know I have to tell her!' Nic's voice was impatient. 'She told me so...and told me to leave her alone until I felt I could trust her. It all came to a head last Sunday...I haven't seen her since. But I've sent her a few reminders,' he added with a grin.

Andy looked at him, one eyebrow raised.

'Flowers...every day.' Nic paused before continuing quietly, 'I know I've got to tell her. I'm going to do it this weekend, then I plan a quiet few days together up in Cumbria. You know that place is my real home. I always feel happier there than anywhere, even after all this time.'

Andy stood up and dropped a light punch on his friend's arm. 'That's the right idea. And I'll bet you find she won't take it too badly. After all, your lifestyle has generally been a bit on the quiet side, except for the odd escapade!' Andy grinned in delighted remembrance, before sobering quickly. 'Although this last couple of years you've let yourself down. Hey, but now you're a reformed character with regard to women and you're proving a real disappointment to the scandal sheets. The only human interest you ever provided them with was who the latest blonde was in your arms and now they don't know what's hit them...after all, how long is it now? Three, four months or so since you first started going around with her and suddenly became a recluse? I saw an article about you a couple of weeks back wondering if there was someone "serious" in your life...they'll dig it out sooner or later, so it's better you tell her first.'

'Yeah...well...' Nic looked faintly embarrassed. 'All those other women. You know I was bored, and looking for something...someone.' He shrugged. 'It was like taking out a succession of dolls...they all looked the same, all wanted to do the same things. I'm not that type.'

'Well, I know that,' Andy replied gravely, 'but you had me worried for a while, last year.' Andy had realised it'd all begun to depress Nic quite badly. Nic was a romantic at heart and had been searching for someone like Jessica for a long time.

'I know I went off the rails a bit. You helped me a lot, but...I think if it hadn't been for Jessica, I might not have come through.'

'Whatever. Glad to have you back, man!' Andy grinned and turned away, gathering together the sheets of paper they had been working on and stacking some into a pile while scrunching others into a ball and aiming them at the waste paper bin in the corner, usually missing.

'When I do take her up to Cumbria, Andy...I think I better warn you...' Nic's voice died away and he looked hesitantly at his friend's back.

'Yeah?' Alerted by something in his friend's voice, Andy's hands stilled in their task and he turned to face his friend. 'Yeah?' he said again.

'I'm going to marry Jessica,' Nic spoke quietly.

Andy stood in silence. For so long there had just been the two of them. Women. Oh, yes, women. Sometimes long-term, but they'd both known, always known, somehow, that none of them, not even Elise, Andy admitted now with a touch of shame, had been important.

Only Nic and Andy had gone on, unchanging, enduring, working together, an incredible friendship and partnership that had grown and lasted for over twenty years, since they'd first met as grubby little eleven-year olds in their first year at the local comprehensive.

But this time, he realised, it was important. Things would change. 'I'd like you to meet her. I'll arrange something definite, get her to ask you down sometime soon.'

Andy didn't move for a long time. Then he swallowed and grinned. 'Yeah,' he said lightly. 'I'd like to meet her, too. Invite me to the wedding and if you ask nicely, I'll even be your best man!'

Nic stepped forward and threw his arms round Andy, giving him a brief, hard hug of relief and affection. 'Thanks. Yeah,' his voice broke, 'I guess you'll be my best man. And, you know, Jessica and you, you'll get on all right.'

Andy glanced at his watch. 'Half an hour late! I was supposed to be at the fair Rosalind's at eight-thirty.' He pulled a face. 'She's going to some party and wants me along as her trophy. I don't think this is going to last much longer, even if she is good in bed!'

Nic choked on a snort of laughter as Andy continued. 'That Jess of yours, she got any mates going spare? If she's that wonderful, perhaps one of her friends will do for me? Seriously, Nic...I'm pleased for you. In our line of work, I guess you *have* managed the impossible because as you said, at least you do know it's you she cares for.' A sudden, bleak look crossed his face.

'We won't leave you out, I swear that. I don't know what I'd do without you to talk to anyway. And Jessica knows it too. Now get off to what's her name and I'll clear up in here. See ya!' He slapped Andy on the shoulder and stood watching as his friend lifted a hand in salute and walked out of the door.

Some ten minutes later Nic stood for a few moments looking at the work he and Andy had completed that day. With a grin of satisfaction, he dropped it on the table and settled down into his chair, reaching for the phone. It was time to ring Jessica.

He hesitated, head on one side, listening. He thought he caught the sound of his own name. It was surely Josh... calling him?

'Nic! *Nic*!'

What was wrong? Josh sounded weird, panicky. Nic leapt to his feet and stood still, listening, trying to locate the sound of the voice.

It was *outside*?

'*NIC*!' This time a frantic shout.

Nic ran down the stairs two at a time and let himself out into the street.

'Josh,' he said wonderingly. His employee was slumped against a lamp post, knees sagging, clutching the cold metal with clawed hands. Nic stepped forwards, his hand reaching out for Josh's shoulder. 'What's wrong, man?'

91

Josh raised an agonised face to Nic's. His mouth worked but no sound came out. Tears suddenly spurted from his eyes.

'Josh!' Nic spoke in real alarm now. 'What the *hell's* the matter with you?'

Josh shook his head several times as if to clear it and swallowed painfully. 'Nic...' he croaked. 'Nic! *Andy*...'

'Yeah, yeah. He left here, oh, I don't know...fifteen minutes ago. Why? Do you need him? Josh! *Tell me what's wrong!*'

'N-Nic!' Josh gulped and made a real effort to pull himself together. 'At the traffic lights. I-I hoped you'd t-tell me Andy was still here! There's been an accident at the lights. It's Andy's car...the Aston. Oh, Nic...it's a m-mess. It's a *mess!*' Josh slid to the ground, finally breaking down into sobs of anguish.

Nic raised his head and looked round wildly.

He started to run.

As Nic ran he felt as if he was running through sand. The faster he tried to go, the slower his body seemed to respond.

It was a nightmare come to life.

Sirens split the night, their harsh noise echoing from walls and pavement. The noise of the sirens rose louder and louder until they beat inside his head, together with his rasping breath and pounding feet, in a strangely insistent rhythm.

Nic reached the junction.

The world was full of lights. The traffic lights continued to change mockingly from red through to amber, to green and back. The lights of police cars revolved through the night, adding a strange carnival atmosphere to the darkness. Cars with headlights and indicators sat in patient queues, waiting for the policemen pulling on fluorescent jackets to restore order to the chaos by untangling the snarl of traffic building up on all four points of the junction, their drivers gawping surreptitiously at the sight of the red Aston slewed across the road with another car buried deeply, shockingly, into the driver's side.

Andy's Aston had been hit by a car coming down the dual carriageway. Hit at high speed.

A police car was angled behind the other two cars locked in their obscene embrace and a huddle of policemen stood in a nearby group, conferring in low voices.

Nic reeled and staggered forward. 'A-a-a-ndy-y-y!' he screamed out in agony. 'A-a-ndy-y-y!'

A policeman stepped forward as he approached the car and not unsympathetically took hold of Nic by his arm. 'Just a moment, sir. Please. Just a moment. We...we haven't fully assessed the situation yet. Do you know the driver in the car...the Aston?'

Nic struggled in the man's grip. 'Let me go! Let me go!' He lashed out wildly and broke away from the policeman, who stepped after him, looking indignant.

'Let him go, Dave,' one of the other men said wearily. 'We can speak to him in a minute.'

Nic ran to the Aston.

It had been hit full on the driver's side by the other car coming down the dual carriageway. This couldn't be Andy's fault, Nic knew it couldn't be. It was more than obvious that the other car had been travelling at a speed well over the limit to cause that amount of damage to such a strong, expensive car like the Aston Martin.

Nic wrenched open the passenger door and, abruptly controlling his agitation and movements, bent his long body to look in the car. His eyes met Andy's, dumb, pain-filled, agonised. Shock ran through Nic like a bolt of electricity.

'*Andy*!' Nic withdrew and shot round to where the group of police were still conferring. 'Why don't you *do* something? This man's alive! He's alive and he's *conscious*!'

The older policeman stepped forward. 'Yes, sir,' he said soothingly. 'We know. We're waiting for a doctor, or an ambulance, and the fire brigade. Unfortunately, we have to clear this...' he indicated the traffic, now being directed round them, 'to give them a chance to get through. We know they're fairly near. It won't be long, now. We can't get him out, you see. He'll need to be cut free. And he...he needs something for the pain. Is he...is he a friend of yours?'

Nic fell back abruptly against the boot of the car buried in the side of the Aston. 'He's my friend...my business partner...*my brother*...we work together. He was with me until a few minutes ago!' Nic spoke disbelievingly, shaking his head in pain. 'What happened? What the *hell* happened?'

The policeman sighed heavily. 'The car was stolen. We were following it. It went straight through the lights. It was...it was travelling at well over the limit. I'm...I'm sorry.' A silence fell on the group, broken by the rising crescendo of another siren.

'This'll be the ambulance or the doctor now,' the policeman spoke in terse relief. 'The doc had to abandon his car and one of our lads is bringing him through.' He glanced round. 'He'll help your friend. Stay around, sir, if you don't mind. We'll need to know a bit more about him.'

The doctor flung out of the police car and raced across to the Aston. Minutes later he emerged, looking depressed and weary. 'I've given him some morphine. He's still conscious. He's asking for Nic?' There was a question in his voice as he looked round the immediate group of people.

Nic stepped forwards. 'That's me,' he said quietly. 'Can I go and sit with him?'

The doctor looked at him in assessingly. 'He should be unconscious and I wish he was! He's going to suffer over the next hour. I haven't anything to put him out with! He'll have to be cut free and it's going to take some time. He's very, very badly injured. Can you cope with that?'

'For Andy's sake, anything,' Nic replied grimly.

'In which case, yes, you can stay with him. But if you start upsetting him...' The doctor glared at Nic, who stared stonily back, before moving once more to the passenger door of the Aston Martin and lowering his long length slowly and gently into the seat. He reached out and pulled Andy's hand into his own, gripping it firmly. Andy's head was turned towards Nic and his eyes were glazed. Nic swallowed and fixed his gaze on Andy's face. 'Andy.'

Andy's lips barely moved, a breath of sound escaped. 'Nic.'

'Hey, Andy! You didn't have to do this to get out of your date tonight! She can't be that bad.'

Andy's shoulders shook faintly and a gleam entered his eyes. He had to make several attempts before he managed to painfully swallow.

There was the sound of more sirens and within seconds the ambulance staff were there, cutting through Andy's buttersoft leather jacket, inserting a drip into his arm under the direction of the doctor, sliding on a blood-pressure cuff. Nic sat silent, watching the frantically controlled activity, carried out with terse, under the breath instruction and response, as Andy lay with his head back, white-faced and trembling.

The activity temporarily ceased. Andy slowly opened his eyes, dark with pain made just bearable by the drugs they had given him.

'You want something to drink?' Nic asked softly. Andy's eyebrow flicked up in a weak parody of its usual sardonic lift.

Perhaps no-one else would have seen these responses, but Nic, who knew him better than a brother, saw, and knew that he was comforting Andy by being here with him. He was the closest person to Andy, whose mother was dead and whose abusive father he hadn't seen since they'd left school behind them and embarked upon their long-held ambition to create a successful group.

Nic stuck his head out of the car. 'Hey!' he called with arrogant impatience. One of the policemen came round the car, followed by the doctor. 'Can he have something to drink?'

The doctor looked uncomfortable. 'No, better not...if he needs surgery...no.'

'Excuse me,' the policeman said. 'The press have turned up. One of them says this is Andy Lawlor's car. Is this Andy Lawlor?'

'Yeah.' Nic lost interest and turned back to Andy. 'Sorry, mate,' he said softly. 'Nothing to drink. They think you're going to need surgery and that means anaesthetics. They don't like you to have anything to eat or drink before you have surgery.'

A ghost of a smile flitted over Andy's mouth and his hand again gripped Nic's with a faint pressure.

The ambulance men closed in again for another session of monitoring. Fast, compassionate and caring, they were as gentle as they could be, as unobtrusive as possible.

Andy and Nic stared at each other, the agonising truth passing between them.

What was the point?

When would everyone else recognise the inevitable?

'In any case,' Nic continued, grinning at his friend through the grief and fear consuming him, 'they'd only offer you water, I guess. And you know you think that's only good for washing in.' Nic's voice cracked a little. 'Now if I had some whisky...' He looked at Andy who slowly turned his eyes in the direction of the glove compartment.

'Andy! Is there?' Again, a faint pressure on his hand. Nic reached forwards with his left hand and deftly flipped the catch on the small cupboard in front of him. Inside, amidst a tangle of odds and ends, lay a quarter bottle of Laphroaig whisky.

Grinning, Nic gently released Andy's hand and poured a small amount into the cap of the bottle. At that moment the doctor reappeared at the open door of the car. He looked at the whisky in Nic's hand and then at Nic. 'For you?'

Nic shook his head silently. The doctor stared into his eyes for a long, silent moment. 'Okay,' he said at last, giving in to the pressure of the truth. 'Give it to him.'

'It's his favourite drink, you see,' Nic explained in a low, broken voice. 'When we were young and we had no money, he always said...he said...'

'Give it to him,' the doctor repeated sadly.

Nic turned and cradled his friend's head as he tipped the capful of liquid into his mouth. The doctor stood by the car holding the bottle.

'Now then, Andy. How's that? More?' A faint negative movement of the head answered him.

Nic passed the cap to the doctor, who screwed it slowly back onto the bottle. 'Okay. If he asks for some more, or if he's in pain, let me know. He can...he can have some more morphine...a taste of whisky. It doesn't…matter.'

Nic turned back to Andy. 'Andy, do you remember that time we stole the boats from the café and went over to the island...' He began to recall for them both memories of adventures long since passed.

The fire brigade worked as quickly as they could. They stood around for a few minutes debating how to untangle the spears of sharp metal and hot engine trapping Andy.

They cut away the car that had crashed into the Aston first, using lifting gear to raise it up and swing it away. Slowly, carefully, they began to work out the jigsaw of crumpled metal that still encased and pinned Andy down.

Twice during that time the ambulance staff, standing close by, checked his condition and the doctor gave Andy another shot of morphine, and once more Nic gave him a capful of whisky.

Nic talked and talked, holding Andy's hand the whole time. His voice light and humorous, he dredged up escapades from their youth, recalled incidents in their early days, when they were just getting started, mentioned recent successes and triumphs. Throughout it all, Andy remained conscious, communicating with Nic by faint flickers of mouth or eyebrow and by faint pressure of his hand.

'Doctor!' Nic's voice was urgent. The doctor was there in seconds.

He'd largely ignored his other two patients, the teenagers who had stolen the car while high on drugs and who had caused all this carnage. They'd received first-aid from the ambulance staff and a cursory check from him to ensure their survival before the ambulance had taken one of them to hospital. The other was able to stand on his own two feet and was outside now, in the custody of an unsympathetic policeman.

The doctor had kept himself on call for the man who refused to give in, refused to descend into darkness, and by the sheer will-power of both himself and his friend, had stayed aware and so far survived the whole rescue operation. Now it was nearly over.

Somehow, they had to get him into hospital as fast as they could, but the doctor had little hope. Quite frankly, he couldn't understand how Andy had lasted this long.

'What is it?' He pushed his head in next to Nic's and looked across at Andy. His eyes were still fixed on Nic. There was still a faint awareness in them.

'He's...he's not...he hasn't answered me much in the last few moments. Does he need anything?'

'Nic...' the doctor hesitated. He was sure Nic had recognised the truth but from sheer desire not to let Andy see his despair, he was denying it up to the end. The doctor shrugged wearily. 'He's probably just tired, Nic. And you must realise the morphine has made him completely doped. Hang on there. We'll have him out soon.'

As if to prove his point, a fireman appeared at his shoulder and suggested the doctor should come round to the other side of the car, to supervise the removal of Andy, at last, from the wreckage. As he disappeared, Andy's eyes opened more widely and a thread of sound came from his lips.

Nic leaned towards him. 'Steady, Andy. What is it?'

'Don'...don' g-gi...give...up...pro-promise...promise...'

'You don't want me to give up?'

Andy continued to watch him. Not the right answer.

Nic hazarded another guess. 'The group?'

Andy nodded, faintly but perceptibly, a sheen of sweat on his brow.

'Never. You know that. But we'll wait 'til you're okay again.'

'Pro...*promise me*...'

'Yeah,' Nic said softly. 'Yeah, Andy, I promise.'

Andy spoke again, a tremendous effort of will driving him. 'Jess...Jess...'

'Yeah, I know. I've got Jess. She'll come and see you, Andy. She knows all about you...all about us.'

'Te-tell...her.'

'I will,' Nic said. 'Don't worry, Andy, I will.'

'Ha-hang o...o...on t' Je...'

'I will,' Nic repeated softly.

Andy's head fell back slightly. Once more Nic felt the faint pressure on his hand as Andy realised Nic had understood him.

His eyes fixed on a point behind Nic's shoulder. The faint grip of his hand loosened. Nic stared unbelievingly at his friend.

Why now? Why, when they were just about to get him out and to hospital?'

'Andy!' Nic screamed. 'You idiot! It's over now. The fireman said they'd finished! What are you playing at? Andy!'

The doctor was there again at Nic's shoulder. 'Has he gone?' he asked quietly, his voice filled with pain.

'What the do you mean' Nic stared at him in disbelief. 'What do you mean, *has he gone*?'

'Nic, I can't honestly believe he survived this long.'

'Do something!' Nic catapulted out of the car and grabbed the doctor by the shoulders, pushing him down into his place. '*Do something!*'

'Nic...' The doctor climbed out of the car and rubbed his hand over his face. 'Nic...Andy had massive injuries to the lower part of his body. Injuries to his hips and back...kidneys...liver...' The doctor shook his head.

Nic sank slowly back onto the passenger seat as he consciously began to accept what he and Andy had accepted together within moments of Nic's arrival at the scene of the accident.

'I think it was simply your love for each other that kept him going...trying, I suppose, to survive. But the shock to his system...the internal bleeding...Nic, I'm sorry.' The doctor's voice broke and he turned away.

Nic's shoulders started to shake with grief. 'We...we were...working tonight. Just before this...he...we were working tonight on the new...new...album...oh, hell! How can I bear this?' He dropped his head into his hands as sobs wrenched through his body.

The doctor waited patiently. Then slowly, he persuaded Nic to leave and let them take Andy away.

Nic stumbled from the car, unable to believe what had happened. Two policemen stood close to a youth of about sixteen or seventeen. The whole group stood in shocked silence as the ambulance men carefully removed Andy's body from the car.

'Who's that?' Nic asked harshly, indicating the boy with a jerk of his head.

The doctor looked round. 'The passenger.'

The youth turned from his horrified observation of the stretcher being loaded into the ambulance and stared at Nic.

'Nic Daniel.' He spoke in frightened recognition. 'We never meant...they keep saying it's Andy Lawlor in the car...?' He stepped forwards, one hand coming up towards Nic in a plea of disbelief.

'You…you…*damn* you!' Nic ground out, slowly and bitterly, a wave of red fury rising within him. 'It *was* Andy Lawlor! You've *killed* someone! He's dead, did you know that?' He suddenly lunged forwards and grabbed the boy by the throat. 'Dead! You've killed Andy! You've killed him! My friend! My *brother*! You...you... *bastard*!'

'Stop him! He'll kill the lad!'

'Who cares? It's all he deserves. Otherwise it'll be six months in jail and then back out again, won't it?' The policeman spoke in tones of exhausted disillusion.

'It's not the boy I'm bothered about!'

Two people stepped forward to pull Nic away.

'Come on, Mr. Daniel. Let him go! He's not worth it.'

Nic was beyond reason. Overcome with grief, fighting mad, it eventually took both policemen, the doctor and an ambulance man to pull Nic away from the youth, who sank to the ground, choking and gasping. They stood round him, uncaring, contemptuous, as the boy kept pouring out his remorse.

'The other lad, the driver, he's in a pretty bad way,' the doctor observed dispassionately. 'I think he's broken his back and there could be paralysis...he didn't seem to be able to feel anything in his legs.' Nic turned to look at him and broke into frantic laughter which slowly turned into sobs of anguish.

The doctor looked worried. 'I think you'd better let me give you something-' he began.

'No!' Nic spat out, suddenly resorting to icy calm. Only a muscle, tensing in his lean jaw, indicated the strain he was under. 'I'll need to ring Andy's father. I'll need to speak to Elise and Rosalind. All our friends...the rest of the group...' he shook his head and dragged the back of his hand across his eyes. 'I don't want to be doped up with anything. *I don't like drugs*. I thought most people knew that by now?' He turned to glare murderously at the boy, still in a defeated heap on the ground.

At that moment, there was a flash of a camera.

'Mr. Daniel...tell me, how do you feel?'

'Nic, how will you carry on without Andy Lawlor?'

'What's your opinion on joy-riders who kill, Mr. Daniel? Do you think we need to bring back the death penalty?'

'We all know your stance on drugs, Nic. What do you feel about Andy's death being drug-related?'

Nic wheeled round, his fists bunching, looking wild. Another frenzy of flash-lights dazzled him. He threw up his arm to shield his eyes. 'Get me out of here!' he shouted. '*Someone get me out of here!*'

A police car drew up silently alongside and the rear door opened. The two policemen helped Nic into the car, shielding him as best they could from the flashlights and thrusting reporters. Shattered, dazed, Nic fell into the car and it drew away before the door was properly closed.

Chapter Eleven

Nic went back to his flat that only a short while ago had been the scene of his last working session with Andy. And his last heart to heart talk with the friend, who'd shared his life for so long. He sank into Andy's chair at the table where they'd both been sitting and dropped his head onto his folded arms. He remained motionless for a long, long time, tears leaking from his eyes. Finally, he sat up and looked blankly at his watch. It was time to begin the phone calls. He had to begin the phone calls.

Andy's father. As always, he didn't care. He hadn't seen Andy for over sixteen years, resented his success and he wouldn't be coming to the funeral. The lack of affection between Andy and his father had been mutual. Nic wasn't surprised but knew he had a right to know of his son's death. He shook his head tiredly, existing and functioning in a state of dazed disbelief, and turned once more to the phone. The rest of their group had to be informed, Sam in the Lakes, and various friends.

The response here was everything Nic could have wanted. Complete shock and utter devastation from the group. Concern. Concern for Andy, concern for him, offers of help, promises of support that he knew would be honoured. Here at least Andy had made true and loyal friends who shared Nic's love for him. But nevertheless, he turned down every offer that was made for someone to come over and be with him. Not tonight. Tonight was for Andy.

Finally, everything had been done. Everything had been said. The possible date for the funeral was arranged and all the details were in the competent hands of Nic's team.

Nic remained alone in the room for most of the night, now dry-eyed and grieving, sometimes sitting staring into space contemplating a bleak future, sometimes rising to pace the room in order to cope with the agony of his feelings and the sense of panic he felt at having to continue without Andy.

He'd promised his friend he would continue but in this, his darkest hour, Nic felt it to be impossible. The promise loomed over him and he saw again Andy's intense look as he'd fought to get the words out, but Nic knew he'd never had to manage without Andy and wondered if he ever could. He was aware he was the strongest in the partnership, the most creative, but Andy had always been able to go straight to the heart of the matter when

Nic was having difficulties and point out what was needed to get things moving again.

Who could replace him, as friend, as mentor, as musician?

Nic flung himself down once more, wondering if he could actually live through this crushing pain he felt. Where could he turn? Who could help him?

Andy's face floated in front of him. Andy's words, jerked out in agony. Jessica.

Not caring about the time, he set off immediately, instinctively, to find her.

The hammering at the door caused Jessica to awake abruptly, her heart thumping. She peered at her alarm clock. Twenty past six! Who was knocking on her door at this time of the morning?

The hammering resumed, almost frantic in its sound.

Jessica leapt out of bed and hastily pulled on her dressing gown, fumbling to tie up the sash. She crossed to the window and opened the casement, peering down into the shadows by the front door.

'Who is it?' she called sharply.

A man stepped back from the door and raised his face. 'Jessica!' There was despair and appeal in his voice as he slumped forwards and rested his head on his arms, leaning against the door.

'Nic!' Jessica turned from the window and flew downstairs. What was wrong with him? Something, without doubt. Something bad! Tugging impatiently at the bolts on the door, she turned the key and flung the door open. Nic literally fell into her arms. Jessica staggered back, reaching out to support him. 'Nic! Whatever's wrong?'

He clung to her, burying his face in her hair, holding her so tightly he was hurting her. He was cold and his body shook convulsively.

'Come on,' she coaxed, feeling more than a little frightened in the face of his deep distress. 'Come on.' She turned to lead him into the house.

'Help me!' His face was ashen, his voice harsh and broken.

'Hush, oh, hush. Oh, darling, what's the matter? What's wrong?' She slipped her arm round his waist, aching to comfort him, to help him as he'd asked. Looking round wildly, she eased Nic to the bottom of the stairs and led him up to her room. It seemed the only, the best, place to take him, where she could be close to him. She pushed him down onto the bed and pulled him into her arms. He turned in one convulsive movement and buried his head in the warm curve of her breasts. Jessica pulled the duvet up to cover him because although Nic was fully dressed, he was still shaking, with deep tremors running through him from top to toe.

She settled herself so she could cradle him closely against her. Shocked, Jessica could feel the dampness of tears on her body. 'My love. Oh, my darling, hush.' Her voice broke with pain because of his grief. What could have happened to cause this?

Gradually, Nic stopped shaking, although he didn't loosen his grip and continued to cling tightly to her. Jessica repeatedly brushed his hair back from his forehead and bent to kiss him. 'Are you okay now? Can you tell me what it is?'

He raised his head. His incredible blue eyes were bright with tears and his mouth was tight with pain. 'I'm sorry. I just needed you. I had to come. Andy...Andy...' He drew breath harshly. 'Oh...*Andy*!' His friend's name was torn from him, agony in his voice.

Jessica grew still, cold premonition rushing through her body and leaving her faint with shock. 'Andy?' she whispered. Her teeth gritted together. What could he mean? Not...surely nothing that bad...?

'He's d-dead. Andy. *Andy*. He's dead!'

Despite her premonition, his words struck home like bullets. She knew what this would mean to him. '*Dead?* Andy? But...but...how? What on earth happened?' Jessica pulled him as close as she could, pain for his suffering flooding through her.

'I'll tell you...I'll tell you...'

Horrified, Jessica wondered what was coming. She knew Nic and Andy were more than working partners, more than friends. Nic had told her before, one of his few major communications with her about his personal life, how he and Andy had started with literally nothing and had struggled together until employment had come their way. She knew sometimes they'd shared their last loaf, had slept on park benches when the money had run out, had shared laughter and despair, and even when their worries were over, neither of them had wavered in their friendship. They still needed each other.

Slowly, dragging the words from numb lips, his head still cradled in Jessica's arms, agony in every word he spoke, Nic began to explain. 'We were...working together. We finished...we finished late...Andy...Andy...he had to go out so he left...he left and I was going to ring you and...and about ten minutes later,

103

Josh came. Josh came.' Nic's voice cracked. 'He said...he said...Andy's car...I ran. Jessica, I ran. It was like a nightmare. My legs wouldn't work.'

Nic closed his eyes and saw again the street, the stationary cars, felt the agonised slowness of his running steps. The words wrenched from him as he told Jessica.

Andy had still been alive.

Andy had been conscious.

A doctor had dosed him with morphine. Ambulance staff had strung him up with drips of all kinds and checked him over. They'd all stood around working out how to extricate him from the tangle of metal, the obscene embrace of the two cars.

It was silly, somehow.

Andy had known he was dying.

Nic had known it, too.

But they'd all tried. Tried to free him, tried to stop the bleeding, tried to lessen the pain. And Andy had tried. Tried to respond, tried to hang on, tried to be brave. But slowly, slowly, his eyes had dimmed, his weak grins faded, his hand fell slack in Nic's until at last the doctor had stepped back and shaken his head sadly.

Nic's voice died away and for several moments there was silence as Jessica rocked him and joined her tears with his, grieving for the man she'd never met, but in some ways felt she knew. There was nothing she could say, nothing she could do, except hold him and show him she was there.

Nic stirred. 'Jessica...' he hesitated. His eyes were red-rimmed and burning, his voice rough with pain.

'Nic, what is it?'

'I can't stay here. I have to get away. There's no need to stay down here. The funeral arrangements are under control. If I go back to London there'll be so much hassle...so much *hassle*...I can't face it yet...it would be better if I could get away. But I need you there. I...I don't think I can be alone...Jessica, please?'

She looked at him. White-faced, unshaven, hollow-eyed, he looked on the verge of a complete breakdown. She knew how close Andy had been to him and she knew the devastating grief he was feeling deep inside.

'Are you sure,' she asked carefully, 'that you should be away at this time? I don't know...there may be things you're needed for...' her voice trailed off uncertainly as she looked at him doubtfully.

'There's nothing,' he repeated emphatically. 'And in any case, if there is, they can ring me. They know where I'll be. It would be better if I did disappear, Jessica. I have to go. Andy would understand this.'

Jessica stared at him. He needed someone with him, for sure, the state he was in, if only to keep an eye on him and make him eat. She'd just started working on that new concert schedule but David would understand if she took some time off. It would only be until the funeral.

'Jessica?' Nic pleaded.

'Cumbria?'

He nodded.

'Okay, Nic. If you're absolutely sure you want me to know where this place is?'

'I was going to ask you anyway,' he spoke jerkily. 'You *know* that. Andy and I...we were only discussing it last night. Last night...?' His voice broke and he buried his face in his hands. 'Just don't let anyone know where you're going, please? You *mustn't* let anyone know...' Because if she did and someone made a connection, the pack would be baying after him within hours and wouldn't give up until they'd scented him out to wring every ounce of suffering from him they could.

Jessica eyed him doubtfully. He'd asked that before. Why? Why was it so important to preserve his secrets? Was there a good reason for all this, or...?

What of their quarrel? What of her demands to be let into his world? Why was the funeral "under control"? *Who* was controlling it? Why would he get nothing but hassle if he went back to London? How would they know where to ring him? Who were *they*?

Ah, now wasn't the time to hold out for answers! He needed her.

'Of course I'd promise you that,' she replied slowly. 'What do I need to bring?'

'Jeans. Sweaters. Boots. A coat.'

'Mmm. Okay.' She slid from the bed, stiff and gritty-eyed. 'Nic...don't you think you should rest today? We could go up tomorrow. You haven't had any sleep...it's a long drive.'

'No, Jessica. I have to get away. I'd rather get up there today. You can drive, can't you?' There was panic in his voice.

'Okay, okay,' she murmured soothingly. 'But what about your things?'

105

'I've got clothes up there. Sometimes I go at the last minute and it's useful to know I needn't pack. I need to go now, and I need you with me. I...I'll just ring Sam, let him know. Can I use your phone?'

They looked at each other for a long moment, a slight smile flickering over Nic's ravaged face as he remembered how they'd first met.

Jessica grinned back faintly. 'You know where the phone is,' she answered softly.

They were ready in less than an hour. They drove using Jessica's car. She'd been surprised to find Nic had come from London in a car. She hadn't known he'd got one because he'd always come before on his motorbike. But on her drive was a racing green TVR, which Nic asked if he could put in the garage. Jessica couldn't imagine why he wanted to use her Ford in preference but shrugged and acquiesced to his request.

Eventually, they left the motorway and drove west. The day was clear and fresh and the hills rose, fold upon fold, sharply green, the lower slopes thickly dotted with sheep and their lambs. A few trees were showing new, acid-green leaves and rooks rose in black flurries into the blue sky.

Their road lay through a grey-roofed market town, jammed with cars and early tourists, before climbing the flank of a large hill and dropping into a valley to run alongside a lake, placid in the late morning sun.

Nic directed Jessica to turn into a farmyard and draw up next to a barn housing a Landrover and various bits of farm machinery. Across the yard to their left was a whitewashed two-storey farmhouse and as their car came to a stop, the door opened and a burly, grey-haired man came walking across to greet them, a collie at his side barking in furious defence of the property.

'We're here,' Nic said unnecessarily.

He got out of the car and opened the boot, taking out Jessica's bag and bending to greet the collie, whose barks had changed to whines of delighted pleasure as she recognised Nic.

'Sam.' Nic raised his hand in weary greeting and moved to meet the advancing man. Jessica heard a terse response from the farmer before they turned away, Sam's arm briefly hugging Nic's shoulders, and their voices were lost to her as they continued a low-voiced conversation.

Jessica opened her door and climbed out. The dog came round and sniffed at her hand. Jessica stroked her smooth head

106

and the dog sank down onto the ground at her feet, leaning heavily against her legs.

Nic returned, Sam following behind.

'Come by, Meg,' the farmer spoke quietly and Meg slipped over to stand behind him, her tail waving, eyes bright.

'Jessica, this is Sam Longden. He and his wife Dorothy look after the house for me. Sam, Jessica Farndale.' Speaking in a flat, tired voice, Nic leaned against the car, his eyes closing, a spasm of pain twisting his features.

Jessica reached out and shook Sam's hand. He nodded at her, giving her a piercing stare from calm, grey eyes, steady in his weather-beaten and lined face, but when he spoke it was to ignore her. 'I've got them groceries you wanted, Nic. Are you coming in to collect them now?'

'Eh?' Nic turned his head. 'Yes, I'll do that. Just let me put Jessica and her bag in the Landrover, okay?'

Jessica felt some surprise. She had assumed her journey was over and that Nic's house must lie somewhere nearby but it seemed there was more travelling yet to be done. Nic swung away from the car and led into the gloomy barn. He slung Jessica's bag into the back of the Landrover parked inside, and opened the passenger door for her to climb in. He kissed her briefly on the mouth, his eyes sad. 'Won't be long,' he said.

He and Sam moved away.

'Bad, bad business, this, Nic,' Sam said again, as they walked across the yard, the dog following faithfully at Sam's heels. 'He were a grand lad, young Andy.'

'Sam, at the moment I don't quite know how to bear it. But I do know it was imperative to get away. What's actually been on the...?' Nic's voice faded away as they went into the house.

Jessica sat in the ensuing silence, staring across the road at the lake, which gave back the blue of the sky. The hills and trees opposite were reflected so clearly in the water that Jessica felt if she'd taken a photograph and then turned it upside down, it would have been difficult to tell which was real and which reflection. The peace of the scene stole into her heart. This was not an area she knew. She jumped as Nic silently reappeared, carrying a large cardboard box in his arms. He put it in the back and climbed into the driver's seat.

'Not far, now,' he reassured her with a brief, tired smile, the strain showing in harsh new lines round his eyes and mouth.

He started the Landrover and nosed slowly out of the barn. Instead of turning onto the road, as Jessica had expected, he

107

steered between the house and barn, along a rough stoned track. Sam stood leaning on an open gate at the side of the house and as Nic passed through it, he waved briefly. Jessica looked back to see Sam swinging the gate shut.

The road continued along the back of the farm before beginning to climb steadily, zigzagging up the side of the hill in a series of steep bends. They came to another gate. Beyond, Jessica could see a flagged yard, a sturdy grey stone, grey slated house set into the hillside, and a couple of outbuildings.

'Can you open the gate?' Nic sounded exhausted and depressed. Jessica got the impression that now they'd finally got here he was letting go.

She slipped out of the Landrover and lifted the catch on the gate, swinging it open so Nic could drive through. He parked at the side of the yard. A silence fell, broken only by the sweet, distant sound of larks and the occasional mournful cry of a curlew.

Nic crossed to the low wall that fronted the yard and Jessica followed. He slipped his arm round her waist and pulled her to him. Together they gazed down into the valley below, at the lake sweeping into the distance, the fields, flat by the lake shore and after that crawling up the hillsides until they gave way to rough grass, bracken and rock, grey and patched with lichen. The eye rose higher until the tops of the hills were discernible, tumbled with rock, looking dark and forbidding, but strangely beautiful. A few farms dotted the valley floor but up here it was isolated, the only way to reach the house being through the farm, and the silence was nearly absolute apart from the wind singing through the grass.

'How on earth did you find this place?' Jessica looked round wonderingly.

'I told you, I was born and brought up in Preston,' he said flatly. 'That's where Andy and Josh came from, too. We were all at school together. Josh sort of attached himself to Andy and me. He was younger.'

Jessica kept very still. Here was some of what she needed to know. More details of Nic's past which would in time lead to details of the present. His voice was soft and quiet. There was a bench nearby. Absently he pulled her across to it and they sat down, Nic holding her hand in his, staring across the valley, his eyes unseeing, his mind far in the past.

'Maybe also mentioned we were a bit delinquent? But fortunately, we came up here on the bus. As often as we could. We liked it, Andy and me, being able to wander anywhere. There was a sense of freedom and space we never had in town, a sense of adventure, I suppose.' He smiled at some memory, his bleak look temporarily lifting.

'We camped up the valley, by a stream. No-one cared then. We'd walk down to the village for our food. We could only afford beans and bread!' He laughed briefly, still staring across the valley as he remembered the careless, carefree days. Andy.

Andy laughing as he tried to build a camp-fire on which to heat the beans, balancing the tin in the damp sticks from which there was more in the way of smoke than flame, the tin tilting and the concerted rush to retrieve it before their precious rations tipped into the blackened twigs.

Andy, on his stomach, hands under water as he loosened the mooring ropes of one of the boats down by the café, the three of them laughing softly, looking over their shoulders in case someone heard them.

Andy, hanging on by his fingertips from a boulder and dropping to the ground, only to sprain his ankle and having to hop and stagger back to the bus stop, supported by himself and Josh. How many miles had that been...three? Four? And that time when Josh...

'We took some hellish risks, looking back now, but we survived. I can remember Josh... he was always weedy...getting stuck in a bog up to his waist! In the end we made a rope out of our jeans and threw it to him to pull him out. It was hard work, too! Nearly lost him that time. He never really liked it up here as much as Andy and I did, but he was determined to come along with us.'

Again, a thoughtful silence fell. A variety of expressions crossed Nic's face; amusement, sadness, deep tiredness. 'We first found this place then. It was a ruin. I think maybe it had been a small hill-farm. It took my fancy. I went down to the farm and asked whose it was. Sam owned it then. I asked him if I could buy it one day. He thought that was very funny, but I came back every year to look at it and dream. One day I asked him the price. I'd begun to earn by then and thought I had enough for a deposit at least. Sam said then it wasn't for sale. I couldn't believe it.' Nic gazed off into the distance, a slight smile lifting the corners of his mouth. 'Then he said it had been paid for over the years by my devotion and I could have it as it was no use to him. So I used the money I'd saved for the deposit to start doing it up instead. I don't think Sam thought I'd stay when I was faced with the reality of sorting it out and making it habitable, but I did. One room at first. One room to camp out in. Andy and I...Andy and I used to come...we worked on it every spare moment we had and then...well, then, the money came and we didn't have to...we didn't have to do it anymore, you see, but we still did. A lot of it. We did it ourselves.' Nic's voice cracked and he fell silent. At last he began speaking again, quietly, softly. 'And over the years I think I've repaid Sam for letting me have the house. He gave me the deeds, you know, the day I finally asked him the price.' Nic gave Jessica a faint smile but his eyes were still deep pools of sadness.

She stirred, her mind filled with images of three scruffy boys running wild up here through the summers of their growing years and how lucky they'd been to turn to this rather than delinquency in the town. 'He sounds a nice man.'

'He is. He's always believed in me.' There was a pause then Nic stirred. 'Come on, we've sat outside long enough. Let me show you inside.'

Jessica remembered that no-one else except Andy ever came here now. That now no-one else even knew where this place was, apart from themselves and Josh. She realised Nic was offering her the keystone of his life.

They went into a small hall with two doors and a flight of steep stairs leading upwards. The door on the left led into a room running from front to back of the house with a couple of wide windows taking full advantage of the magnificent views down into the valley. The window at the back gave onto a small flagged yard and a retaining wall from which the fellside rose steeply out of sight.

The room had been painted white, with some of the natural stonework left exposed in places. It had obviously been two rooms at one time, and both fireplaces had been retained. The furniture was soft, deep and luxurious, surprising somehow for such a plainly built house, and was upholstered in strong shades of teal, cerise and purple. The floor had been sanded, sealed and varnished. A few rugs, glowing like jewels, were scattered through the room, with two bigger ones in front of the fires. Both fires were lit, and burned softly, red embers and grey ash, with a faint smell of wood smoke lingering in the air. What startled Jessica was the sight of a small, upright piano tucked away at the bottom of the room.

'It's beautiful,' Jessica said softly, hiding her surprise and looking around. 'Beautiful.'

Nic stood watching her, arms folded, leaning against the wall by the door through which they'd just come. He straightened as

110

she spoke, coming away from the wall with smooth grace. He sighed and smiled faintly. 'Yeah. I think so too. I'm glad you like it,' he added softly over his shoulder as he led the way down to the far end of the room, past the piano. Jessica paused by it and touched several notes with light fingers. Perfect. But why was it here? For her? Or did Nic or Andy play? And if Nic *did* play, why had he never said? She looked at him enquiringly. His back was turned and he was opening a door, which gave onto a tiny, square lobby.

'Back door, store cupboard under the stairs and, through here, the kitchen.'

Jessica shrugged, left the piano and followed him into the kitchen. A large Aga dominated one wall. Again, the room was painted white and the original window had been enlarged to let in more light. The units were modern, but of a style which wasn't out of place in such an old house. As well as the Aga there was a large modern cooker.

'I had electricity brought up here about two years after I bought the place.' Nic gestured at the cooker. 'I used a generator before that but I didn't like the noise. As soon as I could afford it, I put electricity in. It's useful in the summer for water and heating if I don't want to light the Aga.'

Jessica shook her head wonderingly. This, then, was what he preferred to his life in London. This was the place he came to, to regenerate himself, to find peace. Admittedly it was luxurious enough, but its position was so remote and, apart from the times Andy had come, he must otherwise spend his time here alone.

Nic went into the dining room. A beautiful, old, dark wood table and chairs stood on a glowing red carpet. Another enlarged window gave a view out across the valley and to the mountains opposite. Jessica ran a finger lightly over the table.

Out of the blue, she realised he had to be well-off. She thought of his bike. This morning she'd seen his TVR, a low, sleek, sports car. Nothing she'd seen so far in this house had suggested a lack of money. And he owned a large enough property in London to be able to live there and run his recording business from it. At least, she had to assume it was his recording business, what with references to him and Andy working together, having dreamed together, started to make money together.

She dropped her eyes, uncomfortable with the thought of him being wealthy, wondering, as always, exactly how he earned his money. Was it just recording or something more? What on earth was it he did that led to such an air of sophistication and

111

authority and yet to his need, his preference, for such a place as this, which he was adamant no-one should know about?

It must be a very successful recording company and she was surprised she hadn't come across it, or Rodney, her agent hadn't.

With his bike and casual black jeans, she hadn't previously considered his job, his company, was very successful, and found it hard to come to terms with the possibility of Nic being wealthy.

'Okay, Jessica?' She realised Nic was standing by the door into the hallway looking at her quizzically.

'Mmm? Oh, yes. Sorry.' She moved to follow him again, as he led the way upstairs. 'Nic...' she began, hesitantly. But how did you ask someone if they were rich?

'Yes?'

'Oh, it doesn't matter,' Jessica murmured, following him up the narrow stairs.

'Two bedrooms and a bathroom,' Nic said briefly. 'This is the smaller bedroom.' He opened the door of the room to the right of the landing. Jessica looked in. A bed, some built-in furniture, an old desk, obviously antique and, Jessica realised, like many of the pieces she had already glanced at only casually, very valuable.

There was evidence of previous occupation. A jersey on the chair. A book on the bedside cabinet. A couple of pairs of shoes on the floor. Jessica looked in query at Nic.

'Andy's room.' His voice cracked as he abruptly closed the door.

Jessica opened the next door herself. 'This must be the bathroom and I need to use it.' She gave him a quick smile over her shoulder as she went in.

Uneasily she could see here was another room where no money had been spared. He and Andy may have started the house conversion off on a small budget and done much of the work themselves, but since then, it was obvious money had been spent on this house. A lot of money. Heated towel rails, thick carpet, deep bath, electric shower cubicle, built in linen cupboards round the hot water tank. Jessica dried her hands on one of the fluffy towels, wondering how all this stuff had been brought up here, before going out to re-join Nic. He was leaning on one shoulder, staring out of the window at the fell rising behind the house, his eyes bleak.

'Nic?' Jessica touched his arm. He stirred and sighed, straightening up, and without speaking led the way into the last room.

Like the sitting room downstairs, this room stretched from the front to the back of the house. Like the rest of the house, it was painted white. Like the rest of the house, the colours of teal, cerise and purple were predominant in curtains and coverings. And like the rest of the house, no money had been spared to make the room warm, comfortable and quite frankly luxurious.

Jessica sank down onto the large double bed.

'I'll sleep in Andy's room,' Nic said abruptly.

Jessica looked at him in surprise. 'No,' she said hastily. 'This is your room. If...if...' She hesitated, upset by the thought of him not wanting to let her share his bed. She'd assumed she would, had accepted coming here thinking at last they would sleep together. She swallowed her disappointment and rushed on, 'If you don't want me to stay in here with you then I'll sleep in the smaller room.' She couldn't bring herself to speak Andy's name, knowing how much it would grieve him, as he stood with his back turned, his eyes once more seeking the soaring hills across the valley.

His shoulders stiffened in surprise and he turned to look at her, uncertainty in his eyes. 'Jessica?' He spoke hesitantly.

'It's up to you,' she said hastily, 'but I don't see why you should give up your room.'

'But you'll...you'll sleep with me? I didn't want to rush you. I've never wanted to rush you. Don't feel sorry for me because of Andy...don't sleep with me for that reason...I couldn't bear that.'

'I'm happy to be with you. It's not just Andy, Nic.' She gazed at him steadily. 'I love you. I want to be with you if you want me. I've wanted it for some time.'

'Thanks,' he said softly, his incredible blue eyes fixed on her face with exhausted gratitude. 'I was...one day soon I was going to ask... thanks, Jessica.'

Pulling her up from the bed, he held her in a silent embrace, his arms crushing her to his hard body, his eyes closed and his throat working convulsively as he accepted her gift.

Chapter Twelve:

'Nic, you have to eat something,' Jessica pleaded. At Keeper's Cottage he'd refused her offer to make some sandwiches for the journey, refused to eat at their two brief service stops and was now pacing the floor, his hands restless, his eyes anguished.

'Jessica, I...' he paused in his restless pacing. 'I suppose you're hungry.'

'A bit. Come on, Nic. It would do you some good to eat a little. Please?'

'No. No need. I can't settle. I keep thinking...I keep thinking of him...of Andy...' he turned and abruptly left the room.

After he'd gone, Jessica drifted round the sitting room, looking at the books on the shelves, pleased to see plenty of her old favourites. No television. That was a surprise but it was possible reception was poor in this area. She shrugged. She was used to that.

She could hear Nic going out to the Landrover to bring in the groceries and moving round in the kitchen. Picking up a book, Jessica threw herself down onto the settee in front of one of the fires and tried to read. Restless, worried about Nic and his reaction to Andy's death, she put the book down and got to her feet to continue exploring the room.

There was a stereo system as good as her own and Jessica smiled to see two or three of her own early recordings stacked amongst the classical section. Nic had an amazing number of LPs and cassettes and the variety was interesting. She recognised several he'd brought over for her to listen to. She stopped, lifting her head, eyes widening in shock. If he'd brought cassettes over to her house it meant he had to have two sets, one in London and one here. Shaking her head slowly from side to side she looked again at the collection. In front of her were twelve recordings by Tunnel Vision, a name she recognised because they were Mike's ideal group. Pulling one out, she looked at the cover. It showed a tree, stark and leafless against a grey sky. Heavy lettering across the top read 'Root and Branch'.

Strange that she'd never listened to any of their music, considering Mike's interest in the group. Strange also that Nic hadn't brought one of their cassettes over with him, as he seemed to like them as much as Mike did.

She switched on the stereo, slipped the cassette from its box and put it in the player. After a few seconds silence, a cascade of

114

hauntingly beautiful guitar chords rang out, with a heavy drum rhythm behind. Jessica responded to the strong beat, head on one side, enjoying the tune. She picked up the box and turned it over. A list of songs. The first one was called, 'Baby, Let Me Know'.

Curious, about to open it and read further, Jessica was startled by Nic's voice. 'What are you doing?' He spoke roughly and strode across the room to snatch the empty case out of her hand, at the same time stopping the cassette playing.

'What...?' Jessica's throat tightened in sudden hurt at his roughness.

Nic stared down at the case in his hand, his features working. After a long silence he raised his eyes, agonised and despairing, to meet her green ones. 'Jessica...' he began, gazing at her with naked grief etched sharply on his face, stretching the skin tightly across the strong bones. His shoulders slumped and he dropped his eyes. 'I'm sorry. I...I came to ask you if you could...can you just keep an eye on things in the kitchen while I see to the fire in here? Here.' He thrust the cassette box back into her hands. 'I'm sorry.'

He stood there, waiting, watching her. Given no other choice, Jessica murmured incoherently and turned to put the case down on the table.

She went into the kitchen and looked round. There was a pan on the cooker. When she lifted the lid, she smelled mushroom soup. Salad, cheese and crackers lay ready on the table. Two bowls were warming on the rack. Rather helplessly, wondering exactly what she was supposed to keep her eye on, Jessica leaned against the table and stared out of the window, confused and puzzled by Nic's abruptness when he found her looking at, and playing, the cassettes.

She could hear him moving about in the other room. Eventually he came to join her and suggested they ate, although it was clear by now he was desperately tired and withdrawn. Conversation was minimal. Jessica swallowed her hurt and made an effort to be gentle, knowing his behaviour was all part of his grief and misery.

Soon after they'd finished, Nic hardly having eaten a thing, Jessica cleared everything away, and they went back into the sitting room. While Nic was taking her bag upstairs, Jessica moved casually over to the racks of recordings.

All twelve of the cassettes by Tunnel Vision had gone.

115

She stared in disbelief before turning her eyes to scan the rest of the cases, wondering if she'd been mistaken about their position. But no, they were definitely not there anymore. It seemed it wasn't playing music that had upset Nic, but playing Tunnel Vision in particular, else why would he have taken them away?

Maybe when Andy had come up here, the two of them had listened to that group in particular. Yes, that would be it, it had reminded him of Andy. Strange, though, knowing as he did of Mike's interest in the group, that Nic hadn't bought any of the cassettes over to Keeper's Cottage for her to listen to, although it was possible he only had the one set which was up here. Possible...but unlikely, she admitted uneasily. Slowly she followed Nic upstairs, her mind still puzzling over it. Was this another part of the enigma that was Nic, or was it something else entirely? She shook her head, bewildered.

That night Jessica held Nic in her arms until he slept. She lay awake for some time beside him, acutely aware that for the first time she had his warm, hard body next to hers, his smooth skin and the smell of him filling her senses, and she wished they were here for some other reason than to mourn Andy's death, because then...ah, then she knew Nic would have drawn her to him and covered her with kisses until she was weak with longing, before taking her beyond, to the unknown territory she knew was there and now longed to explore. But at least she was here with him, helping him, and she knew the rest would come. At last, worn out, she slept.

Startled awake, for a moment Jessica wondered where she was. The room was faint with early dawn light as she remembered. Her hand reached out.

Nic! Where was he?

Jessica sat up in bed in a panic, her eyes adjusting to the gloom in the room. A darker shadow stood motionless by one of the windows, the curtains pulled back. Nic stood, his bare chest gleaming in the faint light, his broad muscled shoulders hunched, hands bunched into fists as he leaned against the wall, staring bleakly out of the window.

Jessica slipped out of bed, shivering in the cool dawn air. She slid her arms round his unyielding body and gently pulled him against her. 'Nic! Nic, my love.' She laid her head on his cold, smooth back and continued to hold him in a loving embrace, rubbing her cheek softly on his shoulder. He stood rigidly for a few

116

moments longer before finally turning with a wrenching sob to hold her closely to him.

In an echo of the previous night, Jessica pulled him back to the bed and drew him down next to her, wrapping them both in the duvet. She pulled his head down to lie against her breasts and smoothed her hands over his back, murmuring mindless words of love and sympathy, aching for him, aching with her own needs that she couldn't, at this time, express.

'I don't know how I can...can go on without him...we've been together for...for...twenty years...we've worked together for sixteen of those years. I don't...I don't know if I can...if I can even work alone.'

Jessica was silent. This wasn't the assured, confident Nic she knew. This was a lost, frightened and lonely man, and somehow, she had to find the right words to help him. 'Andy...' she began hesitantly, 'Andy...he...what you did together, was it important to him as well?'

'It was our life,' Nic replied simply. 'We worked together and what we do...what we *did*...not only earned us money, but it was what we wanted to do...*always*. I've never worked...*never* worked without Andy. Jessica, help me!' An agonised plea came from Nic as he turned and buried his head deeper in her warm comfort.

'Nic...you can't give in. You can't throw it all away.' Whatever it is, Jessica thought despairingly. She didn't even know what she was pleading for, she just knew it was important to Nic. 'I know your world is in pieces but you're strong enough to go on and keep what you and Andy have built up as a memorial to him and all his hard work over the years.' She hugged him convulsively to her, her voice filling with pain. 'Oh, Nic, poor Nic. Poor Andy. Why did this have to happen? How will you fill the void? But you must...you must...you can't give in, Nic. I'm sure...Andy...he wouldn't have wanted you to give in!'

'Yes...I know...I know...He knew how I'd feel...He made me *promise*. He made me promise to continue. And I did. I did promise him...I said I'd keep going. I've made a promise to him but I don't know if I have the strength to keep it!' His anguish was great.

'I don't think Andy would've asked you to promise something he didn't think you were capable of.'

'Perhaps...I don't know...he...I had the main ideas...but he made them better...he changed them and polished them...and the things he suggested made me look at what I was doing in a different way.'

117

Slowly, listening to Nic's grief and self-doubts, answering them as best she could with words and loving gestures of comfort, Jessica gradually quietened him and at last he slept again, exhausted in her arms.

This time it was the sun shining brightly through the windows that brought Jessica awake. Muffled sounds from downstairs indicated Nic was up and about. Quickly pulling on sweater and jeans, and running a brush through her thick, blonde hair, Jessica went down to find Nic in the kitchen, drinking dark, aromatic coffee, eating nothing, eyes staring unseeingly into space.

She poured herself some of the coffee and sat down opposite him at the table. He focused his gaze on her face and gave her a brief, but tired smile. 'I'd like to go off by myself today. I need to walk...Do you mind if I leave you here? It's safe enough. There are books and music...' his eyes flickered with awareness and dropped, a faint stain of colour rising on his strong cheekbones.

'Can't I...can't I come?' Jessica swallowed, dismay filling her.

'Not today. No, not today.' His voice was gentle. 'I'm sorry. I've always used these hills to walk off my problems. I just need...it'll only be for today?' His voice was pleading.

Her shoulders dropped wearily. 'Go on, then, sweetheart. I'll see you later. When...when will you be back?'

'Late. About eight. I've written down where I'm going. If I'm not back by ten, go down to Sam's with my route and he'll sort things out.' Nic turned away and picked up a rucksack which lay ready on the kitchen worktop.

Jessica followed him as he moved into the back lobby to put on his boots and fleece. He straightened up and pulled her into his arms. 'Jessica,' he said huskily, 'I do love you. I do need you here, you're bringing me comfort, you really are. You're being so good to me. So patient.' His kiss was gentle but passionless. And then he was gone.

Jessica read and listened to some music. She went outside and walked a little way down the rough track leading to the farm. For some time she sat on the bench in the yard and gazed across the valley at the magnificent view, thinking about Nic and Andy and their work, although she still wasn't clear what it was they did. She thought about Nic's struggles to come to terms with the loss of his friend and her certainty that he *would,* eventually, keep going with the work that was so important to them both. She ate a solitary lunch, examining the note Nic had left which was a string of unknown place names beginning and ending with Bleathwaite Farm, which she assumed to be the name of the house.

The afternoon passed more slowly than the morning. Overcome with guilt at abandoning David, she practised her scales and ran through the new pieces she had been working on with him. He hadn't been pleased when she'd rung yesterday morning.

'You want to what?' His abrupt voice had almost deafened her. Smiling ruefully she had held the phone an inch away from her ear before continuing the conversation.

'Leave rehearsals for a while'

David had been clearly astounded. Jessica had *never* asked...was she even *asking*?...to do something like this before. He was more than astounded. A brilliant conductor, he had a temperament to match, and didn't hesitate to let her know his displeasure. 'No, I do not want to leave rehearsals for a while.' His voice mimicked hers but Jessica merely smiled. She knew, deep down, he was a lamb at heart.

'I'm sorry, David, but we have to,' she said softly.

'Oh, do we? Then would you mind explaining exactly why?'

'I have to go away for a few days.'

He knew her well enough to recognise she was being evasive. He pounced on it. 'Where? Would you mind telling me what it is that's more important than the work you are doing with me?'

'David...please...I haven't...look, I've never asked for time out from rehearsals before and it *is* only you and me at the moment.'

A silence fell. Then, 'Perhaps because this *is* the first time and rather out of character for you, I want to know why. And don't fob me off with milk-and-water reasons, because there's more to it than that.'

'My friend needs me.'

'Friend?'

'I...I told you about him...remember? In the new year?'

'That *biker*? It never even crossed my mind you might still be seeing him. I thought...Jessica, no. This can't be a good idea. He can't be suitable for you at all. You hardly know him and-'

'Oh, I do know him, David. I know him very well and I love him-' she broke off, shocked, but realised how true it was. 'And he needs me and I'm going.' Her tone was final.

'Je-e-e-ssica!' David's voice was filled with despair, but he recognised her mind was made up. '*Why* does he need you?'

'His friend's just died, a close friend. He's asked me to go away with him for a few days...just a few days, David, until the funeral.' Her voice trembled.

A silence fell.

'David?'

'Go. But do me a favour?

'What?'

'If there's any trouble from him, or he frightens you or...or tries anything on you're not happy with, Jessica, then ring me, okay?'

And with that, Jessica had agreed, replacing the phone softly with a sad shake of her head. She had nothing to fear from the grieving, broken man who had come to her last night for help. Nothing at all.

At about three thirty Jessica heard the sound of an engine and went outside to find Sam opening the gate into the yard, a tractor throbbing in the lane behind him. He drove into the yard and swung the tractor round. There was a trailer behind, filled with logs. Sam switched off the engine and jumped down. He came round the back of the tractor to where Jessica stood, a little wary after his cool scrutiny of yesterday. But she needn't have feared. Today, Sam Longden seemed disposed to accept her.

'Afternoon, Miss Farndale. Young Nic around, then?'

'No...no. He's gone walking for the day.' Jessica looked away, hurt to admit her abandonment to this keen-eyed farmer, but unable to disguise it completely.

'Aye, yes. He will have done, at that. He likes these hills, you know. Been coming here since he were a lad.' He smiled sadly. 'He needs them at the moment. They'll help him as none of us could. It'll do him a power of good.'

Jessica nodded her agreement.

'He tell you when he took a shine to this place? Came to me as a little scrubber...could he buy it? Could he buy it, eh?' Sam said quietly. 'But when he came back, year after year, I reckon he deserved it. I give it 'im, you know, in the end.'

'Yes...yes, he told me. It was good of you. You could have sold it, probably.'

'Nay, not as it was, nowt but a ruin. And at least I knew Nic. And then when he had electric put in, he had ours done as well. And he maintains this lane for us. And insists on paying rent to use the very road he's had made!' Sam Longden nodded emphatically and tipped his cap over his eyes as he scratched the back of his head, wellington-booted feet planted firmly apart. 'He's

120

a good lad,' he added quietly. 'A good lad, and it's a right shame about Andy. Unbelievable. Unbelievable. Those two lads...' He shook his head sadly. 'Tells me he's known you from last summer. He's never brought anyone here before, you know. Well, Andy...but never a lass.'

'I know, Mr. Longden. He told me.'

'Don't you take it too hard that he's gone out today,' Sam said again. 'That's Nic. The hills will help him. There's a lot of truth in that bible thing, you know. Lifting your eyes to the hills and all that. Whatever the reason you choose to look up there, it helps. They've been here longer 'n us. Puts things in perspective, somehow.' He nodded at her then turned and lifted a great armful of logs down from the trailer. Crossing to the smaller of the two outbuildings he pushed the door open with his foot before disappearing inside then re-emerging without his load.

'Can I help?' Jessica stepped forward and lifted several chunks of wood into her arms. 'I've got nothing else to do.'

'Aye, yes, all right.'

They worked in companionable silence together for about twenty minutes or so until the trailer was empty and the logs neatly stacked in the shed. Sam dusted his hands off on the seat of his overalls.

'A cup of tea?' Jessica suggested.

'Thanks, lass, but I've not really got the time. I want to get up the fell before dark and bring some sheep in for dipping tomorrow. But thanks.' He stood there, hesitating a moment before continuing. 'Now, Nic'll be back soon. He's known Andy a long time and it's going to be right hard for him over the next few months. He needs you, lass. If he's brought you here, then he trusts you and he needs you. Whatever he does, goes off on his own or what, don't forget that, will you?' His steady gaze bored into her as he spoke, then he swung himself up onto the tractor, started the engine. 'Can you shut the gate for me?' With a brisk wave he was gone from the yard.

Eight came and went. Jessica turned down the oven, concerned that the casserole she'd concocted from a variety of tins would dry up. The sun sank down behind the hills opposite and the clear sky turned milky blue then pale violet. Stars began to sparkle behind the house. Jessica moved restlessly outside and sat on the bench, breathing the cool evening air and staring unseeingly over the valley. Was she really any help to Nic, as Sam had implied? He seemed to be working his own way through his grief. Only twice had she felt she was being of any use. It was

121

so difficult when she still didn't know fully what it was that Andy and Nic had shared together, but this, she knew, was not, most definitely not, the time to ask.

Footsteps gradually approached, crunching over the loose stones of the lane. The gate creaked and thudded closed again. The steps crossed the yard, then hesitated. 'Jess?'

'Nic.' She rose to her feet. Briefly, he hugged her.

'All okay?' His voice was subdued.

'Yes, all okay. Sam came up. He brought some logs.'

They both turned and went into the house. The kitchen was warm and bright and the casserole and potatoes smelt inviting.

'Something to eat?' She faced him across the table.

'I'll just have a quick shower and get changed first, okay?' He looked tired.

Jessica warmed some plates, then served the meal as Nic appeared.

'Thanks for the meal. I-I hope you haven't been too bored?'

'It was quiet,' she admitted. 'Apart from seeing Sam, nothing happened. I read a bit, listened to some music, practised. Nic…' Jessica hesitated. She had been going to ask who the piano was for, but maybe not now. Not if it had been Andy's. Surely if it was Nic's he would have said something to her before this about being able to play? It had to be Andy's piano. Better not ask about it.

Nic sat down and lifted his fork, then lowered it to his plate. With an obvious effort he managed to eat a few mouthfuls before pushing the plate away. Abruptly he pushed back his chair and left the room. Seconds later Jessica heard again the plaintive guitar chords of the first song on the Tunnel Vision tape, so loudly played it seemed they must echo hauntingly through every room and even steal out into the night.

Why the cassettes had disappeared and why now Nic was playing them so loudly the music must be vibrating through him, totally enveloping him, was something else Jessica wasn't going to ask about. That it was probably to do with Andy seemed almost certain. She finished her meal and followed him through to the sitting-room.

The music assaulted her, almost drove the breath from her body, and yet she liked it. She had earlier lit the two fires which now burned with steady warmth, but Nic was by the window, arm propped against the wall, staring with those lost, bleak eyes out into the dark night.

By now, Jessica thought, as she moved slowly towards him, he must be exhausted and hungry, but it seemed he couldn't give in and rest, couldn't eat. She placed a hand on his back and rubbed gently, soothingly. Convulsively he turned to her. His arms went round her like a vice, pulling her close. Softly she murmured, smoothing her hands over and over again down his back. Poor Nic. Poor Nic. He was in a hell where she couldn't join him, which she couldn't share. All she could do was be there for him.

Chapter Thirteen:

They stayed at Bleathwaite for another three days before the phone shrilled an evening summons and he was told the funeral arrangements had all been put in place for the day after tomorrow, as planned.

In the morning, Jessica watched Nic as he locked the door and dropped the key into his pocket. She wasn't sure if she'd helped him or not. All she knew was that she ached for him, longed to take some of this burden of grief from him.

Nic had slept after a fashion, eaten bits here and there when she'd forced him, disappeared for more long walks without seeming to care that Jessica was left to her own devices, and he'd played album after album of what Jessica assumed to be Tunnel Vision, although the tapes and cases themselves were never apparent. She had no idea where Nic was keeping them hidden, or why. All Jessica thought with relief, as the voices, guitars and drums had pounded out, was thank goodness there was some depth to their songs and she liked their style, otherwise it would have driven her mad.

Now they were to return to her cottage and from there, Nic would go on to London. No, he didn't want her to come to the funeral. He'd been adamant that she was not to come despite knowing this had hurt her deeply, and he could see that she felt excluded yet again. But it just wasn't the best of times to introduce her to his life and regardless of her hurt, he was simply too tired and distressed to care.

Nic knew, despite the privacy they'd requested, despite the security set up around the whole event, that it would be a madhouse outside, with press, television and radio pushing ghoulishly for emotional reactions from anyone they could corner, and the crowds who would be coming to share their mourning waiting to catch a glimpse of the other members of the group and celebrities coming to pay their respects. Andy had been well-liked, a steady and gentle man who had quietly influenced many people without ever being aware of it.

That Jessica might see a report of it all in the papers was more than probable and at this point it was a risk he had to take, but Nic also knew she'd be going straight back to work with David, and he'd noticed before that she tended to ignore everything once she started practising new pieces. With no television, she wouldn't see anything there, and once back at home, after her day of rehearsing, she would no doubt leave the radio off and continue working on her interpretations. But much as he loved her, much as he'd valued her silent support these last few days, she simply wasn't his priority for now.

As they drove down to the farm Jessica glanced sideways at him. Nic had lost weight over the last few days and looked ill. He was in no fit state to drive anywhere and she'd been worried about his insistence that he would drive straight on to London once they got back to her cottage.

Hopefully that was now sorted. Unknown to Nic, the phone had rung a second time last night, while he'd been in the shower. Jessica had answered, speaking cautiously. 'Hello?'

'Nic? Who's that? Where's Nic?' She'd recognised instantly the belligerent northern voice of Josh.

'Nic's in the shower. Can I help?'

'No.' Josh had been no friendlier now than when she'd met him face to face. 'No. I'll ring him again later. Tell him Josh called, okay?'

'Wait! Wait, don't go yet.' An idea had occurred to her. 'Look, er, Josh…can you get to my house again? Keeper's Cottage, where you picked up Nic's bike last sum-'

'Oh!' His sudden exclamation had interrupted her. There was a brief silence, then Josh spoke cautiously. ''S you, then, is it? At Bleathwaite, are you then?' He didn't wait for an answer. 'Yeah, I remember, I remember. Why?'

'Because he's planning to drive from there back to London tomorrow, and quite frankly, I don't think he should. He's…' she paused, uncertain what to say to Josh, then decided the simple truth. 'He's a mess, quite frankly. Would he be angry if you came over to drive him back? Can you drive his car?'

'Angry?' Josh had snorted. 'If he's a mess, I doubt he's in a fit state to care, is he? Yeah, I can drive his car. What time?'

Jessica made some rapid calculations. 'About three?'

'Right.' The phone had gone dead and Jessica had slowly replaced it into the cradle. Strange man. But at least Nic had someone to drive him to London. In the state he was in, she doubted he would have made it, or even cared if he hadn't. Perhaps Josh wasn't so bad, she thought. He seemed to know Nic well, and care for him. He hadn't hesitated about agreeing to come over.

The drive back south was uneventful and very silent. True to his word, Josh was sitting on the wall of her garden when they

125

pulled onto the drive. Nic had made no protest when she'd told him about the call and what she'd arranged.

After a sharp glance at Nic, Josh silently transferred the few things he'd had brought back from Bleathwaite into the boot of the TVR. Nic stood on the drive with his arms wrapped round Jessica, his cheek resting on her hair, until Josh impatiently revved the engine.

'Jess, I'll be in touch,' he said dully, pulling reluctantly away from her. 'I'll be in touch. And…thanks.'

The car roared off down the narrow country lane, Jessica standing and watching until it was out of sight, before turning with a sigh to unpack the car. Nic, oh, Nic. How would he bear tomorrow? She felt he was verging on a total breakdown.

Inside, on the answering machine, there were three messages from David, all getting more and more impatient, wanting to know if she was back yet. Jessica listened to his voice, more irate with each call, and silently answered him. Yes, it was all right, she was safe, thank you David. Yes, she knew she was supposed to continue work on the new pieces and continue soon. Yes, she knew she only had six weeks before the concerts started. And yes, she would be in London tomorrow, to start rehearsals again and there would be no need for him to find another pianist, no need at all.

Three weeks of intense work followed, either in London or down at her cottage, as David and Jessica worked on the style and emotional interpretation of the music chosen for the six concerts in which she was to perform, when she would fill in for the international artist who had broken his arm.

Throughout it all, Jessica felt a constant nagging worry about Nic. Every time the phone rang she pounced on it, hoping, expecting, to hear his voice. There was nothing else she could do except wait. She still had no way of contacting him.

Almost a month to the day since Andy had died, the phone rang one quiet evening in early June. Jessica was sitting reading the paper, the windows thrown open to the warmth. She dropped the pages and scrabbled for the phone.

'Hello?'

'Is that you? Jessica?' The harsh tones of Josh.

'Yes.' She felt breathless, her heart beginning to pound. Surely nothing had happened to Nic as well? Surely he…'Yes, what is it?'

There was a long silence and Jessica's fears grew, before the rough voice continued in a slightly subdued manner. 'I got the number from out of Nic's book, see? I thought as how you might be the one to help him, like.'

She sank down onto a chair, her legs weak as she realised that at least Nic was still around. 'What do you mean?' she asked faintly, her hand gripping the receiver until her knuckles turned white.

'He seems to set some store by you, then, don't he? Ain't been messing round with no-one else, has he then? Not since he met you. He's different, like.'

'Josh,' Jessica said with ragged impatience, 'what do you want me to do?'

'Well, go and find him. He's gone back to his bolthole, see. Went straight off after Andy's do, like. There's people here what need him. Decisions to be made. Can you get him to come back? I could go, if you don't want to, but I reckon it'd be better if you went. I mean, you've been there, ain't you? He asked you. I know where it is but I don't bother to go there anymore, and Nic, he doesn't ask me anymore. If he took you there, it means he cares about you, see? And you might be able to get him back.'

The next day, Jessica once more found herself abandoning a furious David and their rehearsals, ignoring his protests, uncaring that there were only about two weeks to go until the performance, covering the long miles north, knowing that for the first time in her life something was more important than her music…Nic.

Nic was far, far more important than her music, no matter how much he hurt her at times.

Unsure of her reception, she left the car by the barn and knocked tentatively on the farmhouse door. Meg exploded into a flurry of barks to be silenced by a firm command from Sam. His kind grey eyes surveyed her with some relief. 'You've come, then,' he stated calmly, totally accepting her presence on his doorstep. 'He needs you. I'll drive you up.'

Jessica looked anxious. 'He hasn't asked me to come. Nic hasn't asked me to come. It was Josh who rang me and said he would be here. He asked me to see if I could get him to go back.'

Sam shook his lined and weather-beaten face and sighed. 'You'll maybe have bother, lass. He'll not do owt. Tramps the hills all day and seemingly sits up all night, staring out of the windows.'

'Do you think he'll want to see me then? I-I wasn't sure about coming but Josh seemed to think it was better if it was me, not him…' her voice tailed off doubtfully.

127

'I think he'll not give any sign he's glad to see you but I think he'll want you. The lad must need some human comfort and he was the one who brought you here in the first place. If he hadn't wanted to let you close to him, he'd not have done that.' Sam glanced up at the darkening sky which threatened a heavy downpour. 'I saw him come back an hour since. I'll take you up and drop you off in the yard but I'll not come in.'

True to his word, Sam took her and her bag as far as the gate into the stone-flagged yard. Jessica waited until Sam's Landrover had disappeared from view before turning with some trepidation to open the front door, finding there was a chill, damp feel to the old stone house.

Leaving her bag at the bottom of the stairs she quietly slipped into the sitting-room. Nic was sitting on one of the long settees, staring into the cold ashes of the fire.

'Nic?' Her voice was a breath.

His head whipped round and he half rose from the settee. 'Jess? *Jessica*?'

She was *here*?

'Oh, Nic...' Jessica's voice broke on a sob as she moved swiftly towards him, dropping down to sit next to him and take him in her arms.

It was clear he still wasn't eating well. It was clear he wasn't sleeping, either. No wonder Sam and Josh were concerned about him. By now, no matter how close he and Andy had been, by now he should be picking himself up and getting on with life. Andy himself would surely have been shocked at this thin, hollow-eyed travesty of the handsome man she'd found asleep in her garden last year.

'Josh rang me,' Jessica explained.

Dazed, Nic shook his head. Josh had rung her? Did that mean she knew? He'd told her? *And she'd still come*. She'd come to be with him.

'He was a bit worried about you. I don't think anyone's heard from you for a while.' She smoothed his wild hair back from his face and kissed his hollowed, stubble-covered cheeks. 'Come on, Nic. Let's make you a bit more comfortable. It's cold in here.'

Chattering lightly, Jessica cleared the ashes from the hearth and lit a fire, switched on the electric radiators and had the satisfaction of seeing Nic eat a few of the sandwiches she prepared and drinking a mug of hot, strong tea. She stifled thoughts of David's fury at this, her second disappearance, and was determined to stay, however long it took to rouse Nic from his grief. She could continue to practise on the piano here, not exactly top-notch but good enough to keep the pieces alive.

They slept that night closely entwined, Nic seeming to take comfort from the fact Jessica was there, but saying very little. But in the morning, when she awoke, he was gone.

It was late evening when finally she heard the sounds of his returning footsteps.

'Where have you been?' she greeted him tersely.

'Walking.' His voice was flat.

'But I thought maybe now I'd come…'

He looked at her blankly and she flushed, realising she was uninvited. Nevertheless, he needed someone to help him.

'Nic,' she pleaded, 'you have to try. There are…Josh says everyone needs you. He says you've got to make plans, decide what to do next. He said you have to come back.'

'I can't!' There was panic in his voice.

'But, Nic…?'

'I can't face it! I can't! Leave it, Jessica, okay?' His voice was muffled as he bent to pull off his boots.

As the next two or three days passed, the pattern of the first day and night repeated itself. During the day, Nic disappeared and walked, returning in the evening with shadowed eyes and lines of pain etched on his face, eating little, to lie at night in restless sleep in her arms.

They hardly spoke.

On the fourth day, Jessica stood by the low wall edging the yard and stared angrily down at the lake, ruffled and grey as the sweeping clouds and intermittent drizzle drifted across the hills. She clasped her arms tightly across her body. She was doing nothing! Nothing to help! Maybe at night, perhaps. At night sometimes, Nic awoke from a nightmare and turned to her, sweating and distressed, begging for comfort. But they hadn't even made love. She'd thought maybe now…this time…even if he only turned to her for comfort.

So why was she here? Why had she bothered to come when it was obvious she wasn't going to succeed in getting him back to London, as Josh wanted? All she'd managed to do was to enrage David, and she had to admit at this stage, barely ten days before the concert, he was justified in his anger. But she was frightened for Nic, really frightened. He seemed to be sinking deeper and deeper into an apathetic existence where nothing existed but his desire to physically exhaust himself by walking.

Jessica swung round as she heard the gate being opened. Nic fastened the catch then turned to see her standing by the wall.

'Why am I here, Nic?' Jessica asked, dangerously quiet.

He stared at her blankly, seeing the anger growing on her face, vaguely aware it was justified, unable to care.

Seeing this, her very fear for him made her continue. 'Really, I don't feel I'm doing any good. I don't know why Josh asked me to come up here.' Jessica folded her arms defensively and looked down at the ground, afraid to show the tears burning in her eyes. 'You spend every day alone on the hills. The only thing I do is cook for you and offer you some comfort at night. You couldn't care less about the former and a hot water bottle would do for the latter! And...and you're completely shutting me out! Me, and apparently everyone else. You need to pull yourself out of this! You *have* to pull yourself out of this! I want to help you! I want to help you get your life back on line!' She looked up, directly into his dulled eyes. 'I can't see Andy approving of this, can you? And you have all your other responsibilities, which you now seem to care nothing about! Ohhh!' Jessica whirled and ran to the gate. She fumbled with the catch. She wouldn't let him see her cry.

Nic watched her blankly before stepping forward, his hand on her arm to detain her. 'Jess, don't. Where are you going?'

Jessica finally lost her temper and her voice broke with fury and tears. 'I'm just going out. Might be back by ten tonight.' Deliberately she mimicked what he had been saying to her each day as he disappeared. 'Who cares? *You* don't! You don't need to know where I'm going or...or what I'm doing.' She shook his hand off her arm, flung the gate open and ran on, up the rough track which, once past the cottage, changed from packed hard-core to rough stone and sand.

'Jess! Jessica...oh, go, if you must! But don't go far,' Nic yelled at her fast-disappearing figure, startled for the first time in weeks from his depressed apathy. 'It'll be dark soon, remember, and you're not wearing the right clothes. Jess! Did you hear me?'

Jessica ignored him, shut out his voice as she slowed to a walk but continued to surge upwards, slipping on the smoother rocks, stumbling on the loose stones. Her anger carried her on and up for a long time. When she finally stopped, the cottage was out of sight and she was surrounded by quiet hills scattered with a few sheep, incurious and intent upon eating.

A ridge of rocks rose up in front of her, the path climbing to the top of them. They beckoned, tempting Jessica to go that little bit further, to the top. Then she would go back and tell Nic...tell Nic what?

That she was sorry. Very, very sorry, for having lost her temper with someone who was so obviously suffering. But otherwise she felt as Josh did, very worried. This was wrong. This was a total breakdown and maybe Nic needed some professional help to get him to start over again. She knew, of course, what frightened him so much...it was the thought of going back to his job without Andy at his side. But once he'd made the initial effort, she was sure he would manage. And he'd promised, anyway. It must have been very important to Andy if he'd made Nic promise to carry on.

She climbed on steadily. As she topped the first pinnacle of rock she drew back sharply, startled to see a steep drop to her right. More rocks rose in front of her. Where *was* the top? Determined now to see for herself the fascination this country had for Nic, Jessica climbed on, frequently having to draw warily back from precipitous edges, gradually ascending higher and higher until at last there was nothing further in front of her and she stood on a rough, wide plateau of smooth, worn rock, scuffed shiny by countless pairs of boots.

Panting, exhausted, Jessica stood and gazed down the way she'd come. It was an incredible view. Like being in a plane almost! But somehow more marvellous because her own achievement had brought her up here. Moving cautiously across the plateau, she looked carefully over the far edge. There was a dizzying drop plunging down to a small, dark lake secretively hugging the base of the rocks. Some more sheep wandered next to the edge of the lake, stopping, browsing, moving on. They looked like tiny pieces of fluff blowing lazily across the grass.

Jessica shivered and stepped back a few paces. This was different in every way to walking the gentle hills of the Cotswolds. She'd been up here long enough. It was time to go back. She turned round and gasped in dismay. There was nothing to see. A drift of grey swept over the rocks in front of her, the sudden dampness soaking into her jersey and reminding her that the heat of her climb had evaporated, leaving her chilled.

The mist disorientated her. She turned back to fix where she was by the cliffs behind her. But she must have walked forward a few steps as she had turned. They were no longer there. If she moved forward, she might reach the edge and fall over. Okay. Turn round again and walk forward. Then she would pick up the path. After all, it crossed this area of rock. If she just went forward, it would be easy to pick up.

Moving forwards slowly and cautiously, her eyes scanning the rock at her feet, she searched for a trace of the clear path she'd followed up here earlier, but then gasped in terror, heart beating hard in her chest as a sheer drop appeared in front of her. Impossible! She had been walking *away* from those cliffs! And where was the path? She turned wildly, panic rising in her, threatening to add to the chaos already around her.

Calm down! Calm down, she told herself firmly. There was only one sensible thing to do. Sit down and wait, either for the mist to clear or for Nic to find her. Except, she thought wildly, in his present state of apathy and depression, would he notice the weather? Would he remember how long it was since she'd been gone? Would he even bother to try and find her?

Jessica sank to the cold, hard ground, a knot of fear rising up in her throat. As time passed, she felt more and more chilled and frightened. The wind-swept ragged drifts of cloud across the rocks and a fine rain began to fall. The silence was absolute. No bird called. No sheep bleated. And slowly, imperceptibly, it began to get dark.

Occasionally she stood up and made a feeble attempt to warm herself but by now she was shivering too much to care. Gradually she sank into a miserable stupor, annoyed with herself for treating the hills so casually, frightened that the mist and drizzle showed no signs of lifting and soon it would be completely dark. She felt sleepy and rolled over onto her side, pillowing her head on her arms and pulling her legs up for warmth. Sleepy. Her mind drifted into peaceful darkness.

Nic glanced out of the window at the mist and the heavy drizzle which had drifted across the fells since Jessica left. He hadn't expected her to be long. An hour perhaps. Enough to get up to the start of High Ridge and come back.

Feelings began to stir in him. Part of him admitted that he'd shut her out even though she was so important to him. He took a deep breath. *So* important to him.

Andy had laughed at Nic when he'd suggested he might have to change if he wanted to keep her. What he hadn't told Andy was that it had been no penance to change. He'd very soon realised, by complete chance, he'd stumbled on what he'd always believed could be his, a beautiful and intelligent woman who loved *him*, him alone, and shared with him many of the same interests. He wanted to keep her.

In limbo for nearly a month, deep inside, Nic finally felt the desire to go on living.

He deserved Jessica to lose her temper and storm off. Lost as he'd been, in the shadows of his grief for Andy, he hadn't realised how lonely Jessica must be, with nothing to do but patiently wait for him as he walked off into his self-imposed solitude. And he no longer wanted that solitude. He wanted Jessica.

Nic looked anxiously at his watch. Over two hours now since she'd gone. She had to be somewhere up on High Ridge. He should be able to locate her. It was essential he located her before it was dark. Decisively now, Nic dressed in his outdoor gear and packed a rucksack with some spare waterproofs, food and a flask.

With the mist swirling eerily around, steep drops opened unnervingly both to the side and in front but Nic strode over the rocks with confidence. He knew this ridge well and was unworried by the cliffs. But his fear, steadily growing, was that Jessica might have lost her way, lost her footing, and plunged over the edge. He felt a sick, cold dread creep over him and fought to keep his thoughts firmly on deciding where she might be.

He reached the top. Visibility was limited and the rain was falling with persistence. Steadily Nic walked on, quartering the plateau, calling and calling Jessica's name.

An explosion of relief filled him when he at last saw her figure huddled on rough ground between the path and the drop down to Black Tarn. His heart lurched. Did she realise how close she was to that drop? Thank goodness she'd had the sense to stay still! Covering the ground between them swiftly, he bent down to take her in his arms, kissing her face and her lips, cradling her head in his hands and murmuring her name. Life definitely began to have meaning again.

'Jessica? Come on, Jessica, I'm here, now. Come on.' Nic rubbed her hands then pulled the extra clothes and waterproofs from the rucksack, swiftly dressing her to give her much needed extra warmth.

'Jessica! Come on, darlin'! Speak to me, will you?' He pulled her into an upright position and shook her slightly. Her head lolled and her eyes half opened. 'That's it! Come on, Jessica, wake up!' She couldn't have lost that much body heat, surely? 'Jess! Hey! Come on, will you?' He shook her again and this time her eyes opened.

'Nic?' She spoke vaguely, eyes glazed and unfocused. Nic sat back on his heels, relief again spreading through him. That

133

was enough. If she was awake, by the time she'd eaten something and had a warm drink, he'd be able to get her moving and off High Ridge before the last of the light went.

Just.

He pulled out the flask and poured out half a cup of warm, milky coffee. 'Come on, darlin'. Drink this.' He spoke firmly, new strength flooding through him.

Jessica bent her head to the cup, reaching out blindly with her hand to steady it. She drank then lifted her head. Their eyes met, Jessica's now fully aware. 'Nic!' She stared up at his stern face, relief at seeing him flooding through her.

'It's okay, darlin', I'm glad you're all right. I'm glad you had the sense to stay put,' he finished with feeling, glancing over his shoulder at the cliffs behind them.

Jessica looked down and dropped her hands, clasping them loosely on her knees, a flush staining her cheeks. 'I-I'm sorry. I lost my temper and now I've g-got us into this mess.' She raised tear-filled eyes to his. 'I'm supposed to be helping *you*. I'm sorry.'

'We're not in a mess.' He grinned faintly at her before pouring some more of the coffee and holding out the cup a second time. When she took it from him, he tore the wrapper off some chocolate and broke it into pieces, absently handing them to her and watching as she took them and ate them hungrily. 'I know this hill well enough to lead us down without worrying about mist.'

'I thought I was going to fall over one of the drops!' Jessica shuddered. 'I didn't know which way to go! I'm so *sorry*.'

He bent suddenly and kissed her, remorse sweeping through him as he looked at her white face and large, frightened eyes. 'I can't really blame you for storming off. I've been very wrapped up in myself...yeah, I know, understandably maybe, for a while, but...' He shook his head. 'You, though, I think you just did me a favour...made me realise how much I need you. I-I lost it for a bit, back there. You've shocked me into realising I don't want to lose you as well as Andy, so don't be sorry.' Nic reached out his hand and touched her gently on the cheek. 'It's going to take me a long, long time to come to terms with Andy's death, I know, but I think maybe now I can make it. It would be much harder without you. Even Andy saw that.'

Jessica looked at him questioningly. Nic's mouth twisted in a wry smile of sadness. This was the first time since she'd arrived he'd shown any emotion, or talked about Andy. 'Andy and I'd been talking just before he left that night, and I'd told him I was bringing you up here soon. I told him that I wanted to marry you. In the car, after the crash, we both knew he was dying. He...he told me at the end not to give up...on the...on work, and...and he told me I had you to help me. And I have...you *have* been helping...even though it seems I'm shutting you out.' Nic lowered his head to rest his cheek on her hair, still kneeling on the wet rock, folding her close, his voice breaking.

'Nic!' Jessica's voice was agonised. 'Don't! I don't deserve this! All I've done is lose my temper with you. Oh!' She threw her arms round his waist and clung tightly to his hard body. At last they broke apart and Nic dashed his hand across his eyes. 'Come on,' he said gruffly. 'It's time we got you home.'

For Jessica, the return was a nightmare. The clinging grey mists swirled and eddied around them, distorting the landscape, disorientating her. Nic guided her with steady confidence, totally at home both on the rocks and in the mist although, as he pointed out with a degree of wryness, he would never actually *choose* to come out so late, in such weather. At last the path turned into the rocky lane and before long, the lights of the house glowed through the darkness.

'A hot shower for you,' Nic observed, unlacing her trainers and looking at her white face and chattering teeth. He led her upstairs and undressed her with gentle hands. Switching on the shower, he pushed her into the warm spray. Her cold hands couldn't hold the sponge so Nic rolled up the sleeves of his shirt and shampooed her hair and soaped her body, disregarding the fine spray soaking his shoulders and moulding his shirt to his body.

Jessica leaned back against the wall of the cubicle and shivered at the touch of his hands. Despite the new warmth in her body, her nipples hardened in response to his touch. Nic's hands slowed in their movements and the soap fell from his fingers. He braced himself against the sides of the cubicle, his head bowed, shoulders tense. Jessica looked at him in startled dismay.

'Nic?' she said softly, putting out a hand and touching him on the shoulder. 'What is it?'

Slowly he raised his eyes to meet hers. 'Jessica,' he said softly, 'this is suddenly impossible...I can't do this, unless we...I want to make love to you. Please?'

For a long moment they stared at each other. Jessica swallowed as she saw desire glinting in his eyes, and her lips parted as her head dipped in assent. It was all she wanted as well. Ever since he'd taken her clothes off.

135

Nic stepped into the shower and slowly, slowly, uncaring of the water now soaking him, he gathered her into his arms.

'Yes?' he breathed questioningly. His mouth dropped onto hers and his hands slid down her wet skin to hold her close against him. His kiss went on and on, the water cascading down over them, running into their eyes, over their faces and mingling with their kisses. Alive again, his hands moved, touching her, caressing her, until Jessica clung to him, weak with need and longing.

She threw back her head in trembling ecstasy as his mouth traced down her throat and lingered on the smooth swell of her breasts before grazing her nipples and returning eventually to her lips, parted and welcoming. Murmuring soft endearments between his kisses, his hands explored every part of her body until she ached to have him closer, closer still. She ached for him to make her his, as her own hands pulled at his wet shirt, undoing the buttons so she could touch the warm skin of his chest.

Nic looked at her intensely, his eyes smouldering. 'Jess...Jessica...I love you. I want to make love to you, but you...?' His voice was hoarse with a passion barely held in check but he still wanted to be sure this was what she wanted. If she asked him to stop now, he could, just. In another moment he would be lost.

'Yes. Yes, yes, yes! Please...kiss me...touch me! I love you too. I love you so much!' She'd never expected to find such happiness, such joy, such a depth of feeling, with a man.

Within moments, he'd wrapped her in one of the luxuriously large and fluffy towels. He pulled off the rest of his own wet clothes with trembling fingers, leaving them puddled on the tiled floor, before snatching a towel for himself and scooping her up into his arms to carry her through to the large bed.

Once there, his restraint of the past few months crumbled. Hands touched, tongues explored and their bodies met in a fierceness that shook them both. As he drove into her body, she flinched. With startled eyes, Nic pulled back. 'Jessica...I forgot!' he buried his face in her neck, gritting his teeth as he held on to the force of his desire, remembering too late that Jessica was not only innocent in attitude, but also innocent sexually.

'I don't care,' she panted in his ear. 'Nic, I don't care! If you stop now, I'll...I'll kill...' She dug her nails into his back and pushed her hips into his groin, pulling him down with her legs. Lost then to all reason, Nic moved, gripping her hands and capturing her mouth with his, sweeping them towards a tumbling, explosive release which left them awed and shaken by its very power and force.

Chapter Fourteen

They made love again, gently this time, lovingly, exploring each other in rapt fascination, after waking to a dawn of pale blue skies and warm sun. The rain and mist of yesterday, the doubts and greyness, were all swept away.

Jessica lay in bed as Nic showered, her lips bruised, her body glowing and her mind full of contentment. Nic's eyes were still shadowed, there were new lines of pain on his face, but she knew now he'd let her in, he would at last begin to heal.

After breakfast Jessica wandered out to gaze down into the valley, waiting for Nic to complete some calls he said could no longer be postponed. And Josh would no doubt be glad of that, she thought dryly.

Eventually he came out to join her. He watched her as she stretched her arms and lifted her face to the sun. She fitted in here so absolutely. His throat closed as a welcome surge of love for her swept through him. Walking across to join her where she was gazing down at the lake, he slid his arms round her waist and pulled her back against him. 'Hey!' he exclaimed softly, 'I always said I'd teach you to kayak. Why not today? We have today just for us.'

Jessica looked apprehensive. 'Kayaking? I never have, before. They look so...so *narrow*. It'll just roll over as soon as I move.'

Nic smiled. 'No, it won't. There are different kinds of kayak, anyway. I've got a couple of general-purpose ones in the outhouse that I keep for messing about on the lake and they're broad, very stable. We can go up to Merefell and have lunch there, it'll make a good round trip, not too far. Come on, Jessica, have a go! I've got life-jackets, and anyway, I know you can swim. Let's just have a day out for us. It'd be good...oh, but do you need to get back? I forgot, I think you said you had a concert coming up, but I'm sorry, I really can't remember when.'

'Soon,' Jessica said briefly, 'and I have to admit David was a bit angry at me coming away. I do need to get back, but hey, one more day. He'll live. I've been practising here anyway, but I do need to ring him and he'll be pleased when I give him the news I'll be home tomorrow. But kayaking?' She sounded doubtful, but in the face of Nic's pleading, his obvious desire to do something for her, his welcome return to life, she capitulated. 'Well, okay then. But what happens if it does roll over? I can't bring it the right way up. I don't know how.'

'It won't roll, I promise. But if it does, you simply wriggle out and swim to the surface. You hold onto your kayak and I'll tow you to shore. We'll stay fairly close in, just in case.'

They piled into the Landrover, the two kayaks loaded onto the roof rack and Jessica wearing, as Nic had suggested, leggings and an old waterproof from Nic's collection of coats in the rear lobby. They drove down through the farmyard and along the road a little way until they could stop by a gravelly shore.

Nic unloaded the kayaks, showing Jessica how to step in before he secured her spray deck and pushed her out onto the lake. At first, she sat there, frozen, clutching the paddle across the deck of the kayak, hardly daring to even breathe. Moments later, Nic's boat skimmed past her, the paddles flashing at a dizzying speed. There was a sudden flurry of water as he slewed his kayak round and with a dextrous move of his paddles came to a total standstill next to Jessica.

She gazed at him admiringly. 'A man of many talents!'

'Huh!' He smiled briefly. 'Years of practice. We started by nicking the hire boats, you know, at dead of night! Me, Josh, Andy. We'd row across to the islands and light fires. How we got away with it I'll never know. Of course, they weren't locked up in those days. Now, push your rear end back into the seat and lean forwards, and wedge your knees up under the deck, one each side, okay? You have to dip your paddle in, edge first, then pull it back and lift it out of the water. Then you twist it...like this...' he demonstrated slowly with his own paddle. 'and repeat the movement on the other side. You need to keep the blade edge up going into the water and also when coming out, okay?'

Carefully, he showed her the movements of the paddle several times, then pulled a little distance away. 'Okay, you try now.'

'Nic...'

'Mmm?'

'I daren't even move!'

'Come on, darlin', try!' He grinned at her. 'You won't tip over. Look!'

He began to rock his kayak from side to side until his spray deck was dipping into the lake, first one side, then the other. Jessica gazed at him in horrified fascination.

'Okay?' He came upright, and stilled his rocking boat. 'Now try what I've told you to do. Slowly, until you feel happy.'

139

Nervously, knees pressed tightly in terror against the cockpit edges of the kayak, Jessica tentatively dipped her paddle into the water. The kayak rocked a little and moved forwards. She caught her breath and clamped her teeth over her bottom lip as she twisted the paddle and dipped the other blade into the water. Again, the boat dipped and slid forwards. Jessica breathed in fast through her nose. Dip, lift, twist, dip, lift, twist. This was awful. Why had she ever agreed to do it?

Half an hour later, she looked across at Nic, her face flushed and laughing.

'Hey!' he said in admiration. 'You're doing okay darlin'. I think you're a natural.'

'It's fun!' she said in amazement. 'I can do it! I can do it!'

He paddled alongside, fluid, at one with his craft, handling it with easy grace, his face still tired, and much too thin, but with eyes lit up for the first time that week. He leaned over, reaching towards her, his kayak dipping at what, to her, seemed an incredibly dangerous angle.

'Nic!' Jessica shrieked. 'Don't! I'll tip up! Don't!'

He took no notice and threw a casual arm over her shoulders. 'I'll let you go when you agree to marry me!'

She gazed at him, her fear forgotten. This wasn't the first time he'd mentioned marriage. A shadow touched her eyes as she remembered his apparent lack of trust in her, especially when he'd told her not to come to Andy's funeral, yet how could she deny him her love? But *why* couldn't he trust her?

'Please, darlin'?'

Jessica suddenly relaxed. She loved him too much to care anymore. 'Yes,' she said simply. 'I'll marry you.'

Nic brought her face towards him to kiss her soundly before releasing her and grinning at her panic. His face was cold and wet. He looked far more relaxed than he'd been ever since he'd come to her for help on the night of Andy's accident.

'Now earn your lunch. We still have to paddle to Merefell.'

They set off up the lake, Jessica concentrating profoundly on the action of her paddles and keeping in a straight line. After a while, as she relaxed, she found everything becoming easier until at last she could raise her head and look round at the scenery. Slowly, Merefell drew closer. Nic pulled towards a cluster of boats moored at some wooden jetties and ran his kayak on the gravel beach. He helped Jessica to get out and then pulled both of the kayaks up to rest by a wall.

'Won't they get stolen?' Jessica shook her hair free from the band she'd confined it in to keep it out of her eyes.

'No, it's unlikely. But in any case, I'm going to leave the paddles with the hire-boat man. He's Sam's nephew and he'll keep an eye on them for us.

They wandered hand in hand through the narrow streets until Nic decided on a small cafe in one of the side streets that he said he remembered from years ago, because of their simple but good food.

Opening the door, he hesitated. The cafe was full. The pleasant weather had persuaded quite a number of people to come out for the day. There were several middle-aged and elderly couples, a few parents with young children and, in one corner, a large group of cheerful students. A few casual looks were directed their way as they stood in the doorway.

'It's full,' Nic said in dismay. 'We'll have to-'

'Excuse me.' An elderly woman approached them. 'Me and my husband have just finished. We were just sitting talking but it's not fair to hold a table if you've not had your lunch yet. Over there, love.' She touched Jessica on the arm and pointed to where a man was struggling to his feet, pulling on his jacket.

'Thank you.' Jessica smiled at her. They crossed the busy room to the table just vacated by the elderly couple, Nic looking reluctant. When they sat down, Jessica turned to him. 'Not happy, Nic? It was you who suggested eating here, but we don't have to stay if you don't want?'

'I didn't expect it to be so busy. I don't often come into Merefell. We may as well stay,' he continued hesitantly. 'It'll probably be as busy wherever we go and at least we're in and sitting down.' Nevertheless, he looked round uneasily, caught the eye of a couple of the students and quickly turned back to face Jessica.

The waitress eventually made her way over to them and they ordered. As they waited for the food to arrive, Nic gave occasional quick looks over his shoulder. It was as he'd feared. The students were talking together in low voices, occasionally flicking glances at Nic and Jessica. Nic sat tensely, long fingers drumming impatiently on the table top, his face showing the strain he was under.

Jessica stretched out her hand and laid it gently over his. 'Hey!' she said softly. 'You're a bit on edge. Calm down. Are you okay, or would it be better if we went? I don't mind.' Her voice was full of concern.

141

He gave her a quick look. 'It's all right,' he reassured her. 'I just find crowded places worrying.' Unless he was well separated from the crowds...then he was okay, he finished silently to himself.

Two or three times, in the early days, as his popularity grew but before the money and prestige led to enough security, he'd been mobbed by groups of fans. It had been a frightening experience for someone naturally claustrophobic, and being in a crowded room still made him feel uneasy, that much was the truth, but in addition, he was waiting for the inevitable approach of the students. Oh, well. Jessica would just have to get used to it. She seemed okay about things so far, although he knew she was probably going gently with him because of everything that had happened recently.

Their food arrived and Jessica ate with some appetite after the exercise of the morning. Nic was right; the food was simple but good and she was glad to see even he managed most of his meal. He was far too thin and he still looked too pale. Soon they were sitting over cups of coffee, and Nic broke to her the results of his phone calls that morning. 'I'm sorry, darlin', but I've to be in London pretty early tomorrow, so we'll have to leave later today, maybe around five. I'll follow you down to your place then drive over to London in the morning, if that's okay? At least we'll have had this, and another night together.' He gave her a tired smile.

Jessica looked at him sharply. 'Time to get on with life?' she asked.

'I think so,' he admitted painfully. 'We have commitments booked, the tour, and I need to find a replacement for Andy.' His voice was low, his head drooping wearily as he reached out blindly for her hand. 'I have to face it, Jess. The sooner now, the better. I've lost a lot of time and been very selfish to a lot of people.'

A *tour*? What did he mean by that? Maybe of trade shows? Nevertheless, her fingers closed warmly round his and she brought his hand up to her cheek then pressed her lips on the back of it. 'Okay, Nic. That's okay. Whatever's best for you, whatever you want-'

'Not this! I never wanted this!' His voice broke. He couldn't go on. Jessica rubbed her thumb over the back of his hand, longing to take him in her arms, hesitating because of where they were, still at times diffident when she was with this glorious man.

'Come on, Nic,' she said softly. 'Let's go. Get me back in the device of torture and see if I can get back without turning turtle!'

At that moment a voice said politely, 'Excuse me?'

142

Jessica looked up. One of the party of students was standing by Nic's shoulder, hesitant, deferential.

Nic turned his head. 'Yes?' he asked, tired and, Jessica realised in surprise, resigned, almost as if he'd been expecting something like this. She watched curiously.

'We think...we'd like to ask you if...we wanted to tell you-'

Nic stood up abruptly. 'I'll come over there, shall I? Jess, can you wait here for me? I won't be long.' No need to expose her to it all yet, although this was minor in comparison to what she would eventually meet up with.

Nic followed the boy back to his table. What on earth, Jessica wondered, was going on? Nic seemed to know what the student had wanted. He hadn't really been surprised by the interruption.

And now what? Nic had sat down and was talking to the group, who leaned forward, their faces dark with sympathy. With *sympathy*? Did they know about Andy? Perhaps they were friends of Andy. A couple of heads at other tables turned to see what was going on and a small sea of silence grew round the island of students and Nic, broken by the occasional whisper and nudging of arms. Eventually a pen was thrust into Nic's hand and he wrote something on a piece of paper. Then he wrote again on another piece of paper. And again. And again. Jessica half rose in her chair. What *was* this all about? He was surely giving out his *autograph*, of all strange things! No. No, that couldn't be it. He had to be writing something else down for them.

Nic rose to his feet and turned. He beckoned Jessica and as she reached him, he pushed her gently in front of him, gave a brief wave of farewell to the group and moved through the tables to the door. On the way he stopped a waitress and thrust a twenty-pound note into her hand. She spoke in a startled voice, Nic shook his head and reached round Jessica to open the door. In moments they were walking quickly down the road in the direction of the lake.

Jessica stole a look at Nic. His face was flushed and his mouth tight. 'Sorry about that, darlin'. It doesn't happen all that often because I'm usually-'

'Am I allowed to ask what it was all about?' she interrupted quietly.

He looked startled. 'But you must know?'

'No. Why should I?'

'Because...because...' She *must* know...she *had* to know! How could she not have seen something in the papers, heard

143

something on the news? How could Josh have asked her to come up without telling her why he was needed? And everything she'd said to him, about having to meet his commitments, about everyone needing him…she *had* to know! He stopped and turned to look at her. This was a nightmare. He'd assumed…he'd thought…everything was all right now.

'I thought you knew,' he whispered. 'I thought you'd have seen the papers…I thought Josh…' his voice trailed off in disbelief

'Nic,' Jessica said patiently, 'I have no idea what that was all about. And if somehow it's all linked in with you…with you and Andy…then sorry, I still have no idea. As far as I know, you both work in a recording studio. That's what you told me. Josh said nothing. He just asked me to make you come back to London. And seen what in the papers? What should I have seen?'

Tell her, Nic. Andy's voice whispered to him from the shadows. You'll have to tell her now.

They stood and stared at each other. The tourists eddied lazily past them.

'No,' he said in anguish. 'No! *No*! I thought you *knew*! I thought you knew and everything was alright! That you'd accepted me despite knowing!'

Tell her.

'Enough's enough, Nic,' she said quietly. 'I *don't* know and I think this is as good a time as any for you to explain. You maybe owe me quite a few explanations. I was going to leave it until we got home, but after that...' she shrugged, waving one hand back in the direction of the cafe. 'Maybe this is as good a time as any to tell me why you've kept me out of your London life, told me not to come to the funeral, refused to meet my friends?'

'So leave it until we get home,' he said, panic turning his voice harsh. 'Forget it. We'll sort it out tomorrow.'

You have to tell her, Nic.

'Yes...but that's what we've always done, isn't it?' Jessica said slowly. 'Well, it's what *you've* always done...put me off. Told me some day, sometime, when you're ready, you'll tell me what it is in your life that's so mysterious. Well, I think I'm saying I want to know now.'

'What?' He gestured at the shops, the crowds. 'Now? This minute?'

She nodded.

'Okay,' he spoke brusquely. 'I just happen to be an internationally-famous rock star.'

144

'Ohh, Nic!' Jessica exploded, before she could stop herself. 'Be serious! I'm asking you to explain why you've kept me out of your life! I don't need facetious comments like that.'

He stared at her in disbelief. Then, not knowing what else to do, what else to say, he shook his head, turned and walked off.

They kayaked back to where the Landrover was parked in cold silence. Once on shore, Jessica threw down her paddle furiously. Surely he didn't expect her to believe that rubbish? He was simply fobbing her off again with that stupid remark. Rock star! Huh! Someone like Nic, quiet and sensitive, fit and healthy, a lover of classical music? And he tried to tell her he…words failed her.

She pulled off her spray deck and lifejacket, watching Nic shoulder the kayaks out of the water and onto the roof rack, his face set. Rock stars wore tight leather clothes. They had long hair. They took drugs and drank a lot. They drove large expensive cars and had an entourage of flashy women and heavies with wraparound sunglasses. They got into fights and were always being thrown out of night clubs, hotels and places like that.

She couldn't believe that she'd finally asked him for the truth and he was still determined to fob her off. Although she loved him and cared desperately about his grief for his friend, she was hurt that he should treat her with such contempt, especially in view of their passionate lovemaking. How could he respond to her in such a stupid, *stupid* way after that?

Rock stars had fans, a small voice inside her whispered. They gave out autographs. *Had* Nic been giving those students his autograph?

Back at the house, Nic threw his things into a bag. There was no point in staying for another two or three hours. He would be better off going back to London early. Jessica watched in silence, then followed his example.

They drove down to the farm, said goodbye to Sam and Dorothy and put their bags in the cars, the silence growing between them like a steel wall.

Jessica was reminded of his implacability and arrogance the first day she'd met him, and how coldly silent he'd been when she'd invited him back inside. Well, he'd had right on his side then. But *now*?

They stood staring at each other before Nic sighed and said quietly. 'I'm going straight to London.'

Jessica was startled into replying. 'When?' He'd said he was coming home with her.

145

'Now.'

'Why?'

'I see little point in prolonging this fiasco.'

'Look, all I asked was that you tell me why you keep me away from your London life! You want me to marry you. I think I have a right to know.'

'Yes, you do'

'So tell me, then.'

'I did.'

'Oh, come on, Nic!' Jessica turned her head away wearily.

'Having finally plucked up the courage to tell you, why is it so hard for you to believe?' Nic slammed the boot of his car. He stood there indecisively for a few seconds. 'Ah, what's the use!' he exploded. He slid into the driver's seat and within minutes he started the thrumming engine and without a backward look, he was gone.

Chapter Fifteen

Sitting in his flat, staring at the table that he and Andy had occupied the last time they'd worked in here together, his hands clasped loosely in front of him, Nic thought about Jessica and how their week had ended. He ached for her. He'd known they would be good together in bed. But it wasn't just that. He could have any woman, anytime, anywhere, and let's face it, it would probably be good.

But not, he quietly admitted, as good as it had been with Jessica. Because it wasn't just her body. Jessica. Quiet. Restful. Liked doing everything he did. Had even loved his house in Cumbria. Talked intelligently. Loved him passionately. Jessica was his friend as well as his lover.

He'd thought, when she came back to Bleathwaite in search of him, that she'd known everything, that everything was going to be all right, but it seemed not. So he'd finally told her and the unbelievable irony was, she hadn't believed him. Now what? Because he surely wasn't going to let her go.

He shrugged. The answer was simple. He had to replace Andy and the man he had in mind was the one person who would inevitably lead Jessica to Nic's world and force her into believing what he'd told her.

And then? Ah, then. Who could tell? But somehow, he had to make it work, make her see he was...just himself, the man she'd known for the last year. If he couldn't…ah, if he couldn't, it didn't bear thinking about.

Nic stretched out his hand and picked up the telephone. He knew he had to start again and had Jessica to thank for the simple fact he was sitting here, ready to go on. He owed it to Andy not to allow everything they'd worked for and built up together to collapse. He'd *promised* Andy! But...it seemed so final somehow, to replace him. It brought home the fact he'd really gone and wouldn't suddenly fling open the door saying breezily, 'Hiya, Nic. You know that bit where you were stuck? Well, I've got an idea...'

With stiff fingers he rang his manager. 'Greg? Sorry it's so early but you know we're starting back in today and-'

'Nic! What time do you call this?' But Greg was glad, nevertheless, to be disturbed. Nic had been worrying him badly for some time. 'I thought you weren't back in London until later this morning?'

'Yeah, yeah, I know. Change of plan...sorry.' His mind wandered again. Would Jessica accept what he did or would she, as he'd always feared, decide his world and hers were too far apart? He had to stop this...he really had to stop worrying about her, put her to the back of his mind. He had other things to do. He owed the band. Returning his attention to the call, Nic sighed and leant his forehead on his free hand. 'I thought seeing as I was back, we could get moving earlier.'

'How can we? We still haven't found anyone to replace Andy! We haven't even got anyone left to try out!'

'Well, yes, that's why I'm ringing...I do know someone-'

'Then why haven't you come up with him sooner? I've been looking all month, Nic. Whoever you're thinking of, he's probably just signed a five-year contract with another group! Six o' clock on the day you want to start back!' Greg sounded exasperated, although he knew, as they all did, about Nic's breakdown, his reluctance to acknowledge Andy was really gone.

Several names had already been put forward as successors to Andy and in the last week, in desperation, some had even been tried out, but so far, the group had been unhappy with them all, and without Nic no decision could be made anyway.

'Yeah, I know I should've told you about him before, but I couldn't bring myself to do it.'

'Yeah, I know, kiddo.' Greg sighed, his voice gentle. After a moment's silence, though, he continued in his usual brusque manner. 'But how do you know he'll do? This might just be another non-starter.'

'In which case we'll be no worse off, but...I've seen some stuff he wrote. He's good...well, at least on paper.'

'Okay, okay, I'll ring him for you,' Greg said hastily, hearing the pain in Nic's voice. 'Give me his name and number and I'll get back to you. What time do you want him for, if he's free?'

'Thanks, Greg. Eight-thirty? I let the others know last night it would be an earlier start. His name's Mike D'Arsace and this is his number...'

Greg rolled over in bed and swung his feet to the floor. Some coffee first, before he rang this Mike D'Arsace who Nic had dug up from somewhere. He pulled on his clothes. Great! They were moving again. Nic had sounded tired, but he was planning to go on. There would be a lot of very relieved people today. And happy. Most people liked Nic. They knew what he'd been going through since Andy died.

Coffee to hand, Greg dialled the number Nic had given him. 'Is this Mike D'Arsace?'

'Speaking.' Mike yawned and glanced at the clock. Six-thirty was a bit early for a phone call.

As if in recognition of the fact the caller apologised. 'I'm sorry to be ringing you so early but I've just been asked to contact you and see if it's possible that you're available today. I know it's short notice...have you anything else on at the moment?'

'Well, no, I haven't, as it happens.' Mike sat up, looking and feeling puzzled. Short notice was a bit of an understatement. 'What is this?'

'Oh, sorry! My name's Greg Spalding and-'

Mike drew in a sharp breath. '*What*? Tunnel Vision?'

Andrea shot upright in the bed, an eyebrow raised in a disbelieving question.

'Tunnel Vision, Mr. D'Arsace.'

'Call me Mike, it's easier,' Mike said slowly, his heart thumping, his mind racing. What was this? A joke? One of his friends winding him up?

'Nic Daniel asked me to contact you,' Greg explained. 'The group want to start back in...*have* to start back in, in fact. Everything's moving again. Just as well, really. I didn't want to cancel the next tour and they really should have started some more recording by now. As you know, they need a replacement for Andy Lawlor.'

Mike shot a glance at Andrea. This couldn't be a joke. It was too elaborate. And in any case, he didn't recognise the voice. And no-one he knew would be this cruel, knowing how much he'd admired Andy Lawlor. But...Tunnel Vision contacting him and suggesting he tried for Andy's replacement? *How*? Was he *awake*?

'In addition, if you fit in, in six weeks' time there's going to be a memorial concert for Andy at the Wembley Arena, with the proceeds being donated to Andy's favourite charities. The date was finalised yesterday.'

Mike swallowed and drew in his breath again. 'Six weeks' time! At the Wembley Arena! He doesn't ask much!' One of the biggest concert venues in Europe, possibly performing there with Tunnel Vision! Was he dreaming? *Was he*? 'Where did he get my name? My number, even?'

'I don't know. Quite frankly, I don't care. All I want to know is if you can make it for eight-thirty for a try-out?' Greg gave him the address of Nic's house.

'Eight-thirty?' Stop repeating things, Mike, he thought. This man will think you're a moron at this rate. Say something intelligent. Say something positive! 'I'm not sure...I'll try...*Yes*, I'll get there. I want to do this, yeah, but look, I might be a bit late...rush hour, you see...but I'm definitely coming, okay? What about my gear?'

'If you've got something you prefer to play above anything else, bring it. Otherwise...' Greg left the sentence unfinished, a shrug travelling along the line. Mike knew why...all Andy Lawlor's stuff would be available to him. All his fabulous guitars.

Mike put the phone down slowly. 'You get that?' he asked Andrea in disbelief.

'I'm not sure…' Andrea was hesitant.

'That was Greg Spalding, Tunnel Vision's manager, Andrea! *Tunnel Vision*!' Mike leapt from the bed and started pulling on his clothes at frantic speed. 'I've got just over an hour and a half to get across London. Andrea...' he stopped and stared at her, shaking his head in disbelief, his hands trembling. 'They want *me*! They want me to try out with them! Nic Daniel himself rang Greg Spalding and told him to ring me! But I don't understand. How's Nic Daniel heard enough about me to ask me to try out with them as a replacement for Andy? Furthermore, where did he get our number?'

'Who cares? But he has. Get moving, man. Oh, Mike…what a break!'

The journey was chaotic, but, somehow, he made it. A few minutes after eight-thirty Mike pushed open the door to the large terrace situated on a quiet side street. A uniformed member of security immediately stepped forwards. 'Mr. D'Arsace?'

Mike nodded, noticing the security cameras and the lack of any obvious exit from the spacious reception. One thing this outfit had always been strong on was privacy. They gave their all publicly, but after that they disappeared from view. Even the funeral of Andy Lawlor had been a private affair, the fans denied a chance to pay their last respects except for crowding hopefully in the street outside, laying tributes and leaving tealights and candles.

An announcement of the special memorial concert was in this morning's paper that Mike had picked up on his way here. As he'd been told on the phone, in six weeks' time at the Wembley Arena. A big, big event, to raise money for a cause that'd apparently been dear to Andy Lawlor's heart – support for projects and youth clubs for inner-city kids. Mike was very nervous indeed and still completely bewildered how they'd known about him.

'If you'd like to follow me, Mr.D'Arsace, Mr. Daniel would like a word before you start.' The security man led him across the floor, nodding to the receptionists seated at large and functional desks, and punched in a code onto the security lock on the far side of the room. Panels slid silently open and they stepped into a lift.

Within seconds the doors smoothly opened again and the guard led Mike across a thickly carpeted hallway, past some stairs, to a white painted door set to one side. He knocked and it was opened almost immediately by a man Mike didn't recognise.

'Mr. D'Arsace...Mike?' The man held out his hand. Mike put down his battered guitar case and shook hands. 'I'm Greg Spalding. We spoke on the telephone at rather an unearthly hour this morning. Glad you could make it. Nic'd like a word.'

He turned and went into the flat. Mike followed. They went into a large, light room, furnished with a big table, a piano, some comfortable chairs, a very complex stereo system and little else. Not really a sitting room. Not really an office. A cross between the two.

This time the man who turned from the table was instantly recognisable. He looked tired, he looked thin, his eyes were sad, but it was Nic Daniel. Lead singer and song-writer of Tunnel Vision, guitarist as well. Dressed all in black. As he always did.

'Mike D'Arsace? Hi.' Nic shook hands and gestured for him to sit down. 'Glad you could come. I'll explain what I want.'

Mike sat warily. He still hadn't spoken. Simply nodded. Three times now. Nic cleared his throat and paced over to the window. He stood with his back to Mike, gazing out over distant roofs, his long-fingers tapping restlessly on the sill.

'Greg,' he said abruptly. 'Can you go down and see if everything's ready? Mike and I'll be along in a minute.'

Greg silently withdrew and Nic turned to face Mike, leaning back on the sill, arms crossed. 'It's me who's asked you here to try out with us, as you've probably realised. We've had a few people in already who the others came up with, but one way or another, they apparently wouldn't do. To be honest, I've had you in mind for some time as a possible replacement for Andy, and even if he hadn't been...killed...' he brought his hand up to rub his forehead, eyes briefly closing, swallowing hard as a grimace of pain crossed his face, 'killed in that car crash, we'd have both been in touch with you.'

151

Mike sat forward, stomach churning partly in fear, partly in excitement. 'In touch with me anyway? But...why?'

'I've seen a song you wrote,' Nic began slowly. 'I was told it was one you'd probably abandoned as no good.'

He reached forward to the table and picked up two sheets of paper fastened together with a paper clip and tossed them across to Mike.

Mike caught them and stared at them, his brow creased. 'I wrote this...months ago. I was...I was at Jessica's! Where did you find it?'

'At her house.'

Mike raised his eyes to find Nic staring consideringly at him, arms once more folded across his chest. 'Look, Mr. Daniel-'

'Nic, please.'

'Okay, Nic, then,' Mike said impatiently. 'Quite frankly, I don't understand. When were you ever at Jessica's? How can you even know her?'

'Hasn't she mentioned recently she's going round with someone?' Nic's eyes were steady.

'Well, yes,' Mike said vaguely. 'Andrea mentioned she was seeing some guy called Nick but...' Mike's head came up in sudden comprehension. 'Nick? *Nic*! We never connected the name with *you*! We assumed Nick with a k type Nick! Jessica...and *you*?' A note of dismay entered his voice. 'What are you playing at? *You*...you'll eat her alive!' Nick...Nic...it just hadn't connected. But then, why on earth should it? Who would ever have connected Jessica...quiet, shy Jessica...*innocent* Jessica...with Nic Daniel?

The two men continued to stare steadily at each other, Mike's thoughts clearly visible to the other man. Mike half rose from his chair, suddenly angered by Nic's long silence. 'You'd better not be messing her around, you-'

'Cool it, Mike!' Nic's voice was sharply commanding even as he appreciated Mike's care of Jessica without even considering it might impact on his try-out. 'I'm not messing her around. I love her. Really love her...' Nic paused, his voice softening.

'How did you even *meet* her? This is beyond belief!'

'We met by chance. My bike broke down near her house. I called there to use the phone.' He smiled quietly at the memory. 'It just kind of grew from there...'

'Grew? What do you mean? With your...' Mike hesitated.

'Yeah,' Nic sighed. 'I know what you want to say. I don't...didn't...have a good reputation with women, I know that.

And I have to confess when I met Jessica it was all a bit of a joke, really. She didn't know who I was-'

'Doesn't surprise me,' Mike broke in. 'She was brought up by very old-fashioned, elderly parents. If your hair was more than half an inch long, you were degenerate!'

Nic laughed disbelievingly. 'Not that bad, surely?'

'That bad, believe me. Oh, they loved her enough, and when they discovered the talent she had musically they pulled out all the stops. Nothing was too good for her. But with all the practising, having a private tutor because she was already beginning to perform, enter competitions, that sort of thing, which involved travelling, well, hey,' a grin and a rueful shake of the head emphasised the words, 'she grew up so sheltered, almost naïve, you know?'

Nic smiled wryly. 'Yes, I know. She explained.'

'Yeah, well…' Mike hesitated before gruffly continuing. 'I still can't see what you're doing with Jessica. She's not your sort at all, I wouldn't have thought. Your experience and hers…' Mike shook his head.

'At the start, I wasn't sure what I was going to do or where it was heading.' Nic sighed. 'But I was attracted to her. I liked the peacefulness of her. Then we started going around together and she just grew on me. I fell in love. I liked it that it was just me she cared for. Not because of who I was. Not because of what I could do for her. Not because she knew how much money I have. You can never really trust people's motives until you get to know them well.' He straightened up and came across to the table and sat on the edge, idly playing with a pen lying there, swinging his long legs.

Mike thought of the price of possible fame and was glad he already had someone he knew he could trust implicitly. 'Yeah, I can see that's a problem,' he admitted. 'But, with Jessica…look, you really have to understand just how innocent she is. Okay, she came to college to study theory and stuff but as far as I can gather, she went nowhere, did nothing. It wasn't until Andrea met her in the local supermarket and took her under her wing that she at least updated her clothes.'

He shook his head at the memory and was silent a moment as he recalled the painfully shy girl. 'And although Jessica took to Andrea, even took to me, though I was everything her mummy had warned her about,' this spoken with a quick grin, 'and although we updated her image some, she's still totally innocent, trusting, and honest as well. Look, Nic…really…you have to

153

understand this, she's not experienced with men. I think you'd be better off leaving her alone, okay?' Mike looked away. He wasn't sure if it was his place to be saying these things to someone he'd only met half an hour ago, who was offering him the greatest chance of his life, but someone had to watch out for Jess.

'I know. I know all you're saying, believe me. I realised she was different. And somehow, it all attracted me. Her values, her outlook on life. It echoed how I always used to be and she kind of brought me back. I hadn't been too great and I was letting the band down, but she made me re-evaluate and I realised it was me who'd have to change if I wanted to keep her, and I *did* want to keep her. This honesty you talk about, her innocence, everything...' Nic's voice cracked and he swallowed. 'Well, as I said, I fell in love with her. Really in love with her.'

'Well, that's good,' Mike said doubtfully, not sure if he could trust what Nic was saying.

'I was in no hurry to push things. I was prepared to let her set the pace, but one thing I was definite about. I didn't want her to know who I was. She knew I worked with Andy, I told her we worked in recording. She knew about Andy being killed, but not even then who we were...' Nic paused. It was still hard for him to talk about his friend.

He shook his head, staring at the pen in his fingers. 'I still don't know how she never saw anything about his funeral,' he finally continued, when he could trust himself to talk again. 'I was expecting her to...and when Josh asked her to come and find me, to help me...I thought she must know everything and had accepted it.'

'Sorry, I'm not with you.'

Nic looked up, startled. 'Sorry...I was miles away then, trying to work out how she missed the reports in the papers...'

'Surely, she would have seen something about the accident, never mind the funeral?' Mike queried, raising one eyebrow.

'No. No. Not the accident. I needed her after Andy died. I asked her to go away with me. I have a place I go to...and she came with me and I only have a stereo system up there. No television, because the reception's poor. I'm so used to being out when I'm up there so I never miss it.' Nic shrugged. 'And we never bought any papers because we never went anywhere. But then we came back down here for the funeral and I left her at home, at Keeper's Cottage...' Nic moved restlessly back to the window, staring out at the garden behind the house.

'Was she in rehearsal?'

Nic nodded.

'Well, then. I gather from Andrea when she's in rehearsal she tends to bypass the world,' Mike offered.

'Yes, I suppose that'd be it. I suppose she went straight back into it, missed the relevant papers. I don't know. I was a little confused and...and after the funeral I kind of cracked up a bit. I went off again, went to pieces a bit. The group got a little worried and Josh, well, a few days ago he took it on himself to contact Jess.'

Went to pieces for a *bit*? About a month, by Mike's reckoning. No wonder the group had been worried! 'Josh?'

'Road manager.' Nic fell silent, his eyes troubled. Eventually he shrugged. 'Anyway, Jessica...thank goodness...dropped everything again and came to me, and this time I thought she must surely know who I was and it hadn't made any difference to her. But of course, she didn't.' Nic threw himself down in one of the chairs. 'You have to understand that without her, I don't think I would've made it, I don't think I would've survived. She came to me and helped me, made me want to go on again, for her sake, for Andy's sake. I pulled myself together at last, saw sense. Yesterday, I rang Greg and arranged to get going again. But even though it was essential to get everyone together and get in touch with you, I decided we'd have one day together, just the two of us. One day.' He fell silent, staring broodingly into space.

'Was it only *yesterday*? We were so happy...we went out, I taught her to kayak. We ate out in the local town. There were some students...they wanted to talk to me, tell me how sorry they were about...about Andy. And get my autograph. Obviously, she wanted to know what was going on and I...I was so taken aback...I mean, I was so sure she *knew*. I thought Josh would have said something even if she hadn't read about the funeral in the papers or heard about it on the radio. Anyway, I just came out with it, I told her that I was a rock singer, and she wouldn't believe me! She thinks I'm just being stupid with her!' His voice caught, his jerky explanation finally coming to an end as he raised his eyes to meet those of Mike's, his pain clearly obvious. 'We ended up pretty well not speaking, I was mad because having finally got it out, she thought I was messing with her. She was mad because she thought I was being flippant. So I came straight home last night, and Jessica went to hers.'

Mike sighed. 'Yeah, well. Is this the problem? So tell her again.'

155

'Obvious solution. Or you'll tell her. But then what? It seems a hopeless situation. She's been so sheltered and I know from things she's said, and what you've just told me only backs this up, that she doesn't have much idea about our kind of life. I can see things about us, the life she thinks we lead, might frighten her off and I'm afraid, Mike. I'm afraid I'll lose her. And I can't. I can't lose her!' A silence fell as Nic covered his eyes. Finally dragging his hand down his face, he looked straight at Mike 'But you know her…do you think she *would* accept it?'

Mike shook his head slowly from side to side, astonished at what he'd just been told. 'I don't know, I really don't know. Those parents of hers were well-meaning but incredibly narrow-minded. I'm afraid she'll think, deep down, all rock singers take drugs, drink, lead riotous lives, womanise...' he shrugged apologetically.

Nic groaned softly. 'There could be some truth in that last thing you said. But I confessed that part at least!' He paused and ran his hand through his hair in exasperation. 'Surely she's intelligent enough to realise that not everyone in the rock music world has to be like that?'

'She knows nothing about the rock music world. *Nothing*, you hear me?'

'We couldn't survive! People like Tunnel Vision, ones who've lasted a decade or more, they can't live like that...the stereotypical image! And she knows *you*.'

'Yeah, she knows me, but I'm not big time...I'm safe. I'm Andrea's husband, really. Even though she likes my stuff, to her I'm only playing at it.' He paused. Taking a deep breath, he spoke firmly. 'Nic...'

'Yeah?'

'You have to face the fact she really might find it too hard to accept. It'll make her wary…she'll find it hard to balance what she knows of you against what she thinks she knows about rock. She'll be frightened by what she perceives as the sophistication and glamour, the fame…the easy morals. She'll find it hard to trust you, maybe.'

'She should have no reason not to trust me,' Nic spoke slowly. 'I told Andy that I'd have to be the one to change and I did…I *did*. I vowed not to push her or hassle her until she was ready for me and I kept that vow. She has no reason not to trust me so far.'

Mike's eyebrows rose in startled disbelief.

Nic laughed dryly. 'Think what you like, it's true. I've been careful. I didn't want to destroy her, I wanted to awaken her. And

156

until yesterday, I would have said I'd done a pretty good job of giving her no cause for alarm, no reason to be frightened off. She *should* be able to accept this on what we've shared so far, she really should. And I was never that bad anyway! You're falling into the trap of believing all that rubbish they print in the papers! You know how the press exaggerate! Half the time they had me in bed with someone when I was sitting quietly at home drinking my cocoa!'

Mike let out a short laugh. 'Huh! That's stretching it a bit, especially in view of what's been in the papers this last year or two! Even if you take half of those reports with a pinch of salt, there's still plenty left! Look, the only advice I can offer is go see her. Explain. Apologise. Tell her exactly why you kept on not telling her.'

'Yeah. I hope...I think maybe it'll be all right. But I don't know!'

Mike wondered, really wondered, if it'd be okay. Jessica was easily hurt. Who knew how she would take this? He touched his guitar case. 'And now what? I hope I'm not here just because I'm a friend of Jessica's?'

Nic sighed and shook his head. Nothing Mike had said reassured him but he knew he had to put it all to one side for now. 'You're here because I found that song and I showed it to Andy. We both liked it and as I said, we were planning to get in touch with you anyway. It's our sort of stuff. I could work with that. I actually made a couple of alterations...hope you don't mind?'

Mike scrutinised the lines of words and music. 'Yeah,' he said suddenly. 'That's it! I knew I was wrong, but I simply couldn't sort it out.' He looked at Nic. 'Yeah, maybe we could work okay together, at that. I'd like to give it a try, in any case. And,' he added awkwardly, 'I hope you and Jessica sort things out. We'll help all we can. But tread carefully, okay?'

'I'll tread carefully. And I'll leave it for now anyway, because her concerts start next week. She's got five, I think, all just in the one week.' Nic stood and stretched. 'Now look, we ought to go down and meet the others. Just try to take it steady today, okay? Get a feel of how we operate. I always lead. You'll soon pick up the signs I use. We're going to have to rehearse pretty hard for the next three or four weeks, maybe include a bit of recording for the new album. Hopefully we can get in a break, then back at it in the final week before the memorial concert. Did you have anything else on, because if so, you're gonna have to cancel, okay?'

157

Mike went cold inside and stood up. 'Yeah, I guessed so. But maybe you won't like me…maybe you- '

Nic held up a hand and gave a tired smile. 'Hey! Slow down, okay? Let's see how things go, yeah?' He opened another door at the far side of the room to reveal a flight of stairs. Mike followed him down and through some sound-proofed double doors into a large room filled with recording equipment and musical instruments.

'Nic.' A tall brown-haired man straightened up from adjusting the skin on a drum.

'Jon. Hey, all of you. A word, okay?'

The three other men in the room drifted to gather round Nic and Mike. Mike ran a tongue over suddenly dry lips, aware of their curious scrutiny. He knew them all. Of course he knew them all. Jon Marshall, drummer. Adam Tyler, keyboards. Ian Green, bass guitar. The line-up had been completed by Andy Lawlor, lead guitar and co-songwriter, and Nic Daniel, main song-writer, occasional lead guitar, lead singer and, together with Andy, the founder of the group.

So what was *he* doing here? His hands were shaking so much he stuffed them rapidly into his jeans' pockets so no-one would notice. How he thought he could play with this lot, he didn't know. It was all a horrible mistake. He better stop wasting their time and tell them now. He better get out of here. He better-

'This is Mike D'Arsace and I have him in mind as a possible replacement for…for…' Nic's voice choked up. He swallowed hard before continuing steadily, 'for Andy, okay? Andy and I, we'd been intending to speak to Mike for a while. I came across a song he'd done and it seemed our kind of stuff. He knows what we do, so let's give it a try and see how he makes out. I know you'll all give him some help. We'll let him go easy today and after that, we're in for some hard graft if we're to be ready for this concert at Wembley, okay?'

There was a general murmur of agreement. Ian slung an arm round Nic's shoulder and gave him a casually affectionate hug, his look sharply discerning as he took in his friend's white face and the dark shadows under his eyes. Andy's death had hurt them all, but not as badly as it had hurt Nic. The three of them all knew he'd been a long, long way from them these last few weeks, and it would be hard for him to get through the next few days. After that, he'd probably do okay. He surely needed no more problems for now.

But then, apart from Mike, none of them knew about Jessica.

Everyone drifted into place. Mike looked at his battered guitar case and then at the gleaming electric steel-string guitar propped on a stand near the microphone. He hesitated before pushing his case aside with one foot and walking slowly forwards towards it.

Nic stood indecisively before scooping up a mike, only to let it hang listlessly from his hand as pain overwhelmed him. His throat closed. Andy. Andy. Why had it happened? How could he go on? What was he doing here? He couldn't...he couldn't...he *couldn't* do this.

Ian shot a look at Jon and Adam and nodded. Jon picked up his sticks and led into a strong beat, followed by Ian with an insistent bass. Adam placed his hands on the keyboard and joined in with familiar chords. Soon, soon, Andy would have joined in...

Mike panicked and looked wildly at the door then back at the gleaming guitar. Slowly, he stepped forwards and stretched out his hand, aware of the others watching and waiting. He glanced up at Nic and found him staring blindly at the guitar. Time was running out. He picked it up, slung the strap over his head, settled the guitar against his body. His fingers found their familiar places on the strings, his pick was miraculously between his fingers...the next chord...now...*now*!

His fingers moved of their own accord, the trembling fading as if it had never happened. Sweet notes echoed through the room.

Nic raised his head and stared at Mike. There was a collective holding of breath before he turned, lifting the mike, and added his voice to the surging music.

Chapter Sixteen

Jessica had spent all night tossing and turning, trying to work things out, the same thoughts churning round and round in her head.

Thoughts she could hardly credit. Nic? Telling the truth? The autographs? Were they autographs? Hardly, it was too impossible, surely? But then, what did she know about the world of rock music? Well, there was Mike. Admittedly he didn't take drugs...or even drink that much. But Mike...he'd studied music at *college*. He might have hair halfway down his back, but...he was...Mike...she'd known him years.

People in the rock world didn't produce serious music. No. That was unfair. She'd seen Mike's compositions. They were good enough. She'd listened to quite a lot of good music with Nic. Tunnel Vision especially. Layers of instruments. Good guitar playing. Sometimes quite lovely songs. But did the performers write their own stuff? She didn't know. Probably not. But then maybe they did. *Mike* did.

Her thoughts whirled round and round the possibility that Nic had told her the truth. He was rich. Yes, well, he would be if he was a rock star. They earned fabulous amounts of money. So why didn't he spend it on fast cars, parties, holidays, fancy clothes? Rock stars did, didn't they? They lived it up all over the world.

All of them?

The ones you heard about, yes. But perhaps there were others like Nic, who actually led quite private lives...like she did...except when they were performing?

But Nic did have a fast car...and a fast motorbike. Nic as a *singer*? A rock singer? Jessica shook her head. She couldn't reconcile the Nic she knew with such an alien idea. It was no good even trying. The two just didn't fit together. It just wasn't what she knew of Nic. And yet...and yet...it would explain why he'd had always been so careful about what he said his work was...recording. And how he kept her apart from his life in London. He must have known it might frighten her off. At the back of her mind, dismissed weeks ago, was Nic's admission that music dominated his life followed by his weak explanation that he listened to music a lot. It had puzzled her briefly at the time and now took on new significance.

Going round in circles was exhausting her and Jessica felt the need to confide in someone. Andrea was the only person she knew who would be able to answer her questions. As soon as it was decently possible, she dialled her friend's number. Mike was out, Andrea told her over the phone, suppressed excitement in her voice, and she would be delighted to see Jessica because she had some wonderful news to tell her. Jessica set of immediately to drive to London.

'Jessica!' Andrea threw open the door and embraced her friend. She looked happy and her eyes were glowing.

'You look over the moon! What's happened? You said you had some news...?' Jessica pushed her own concerns to one side as she followed her friend into the house to the large room at the back, a warm, inviting place to sit and eat, yellow and white and cream with the gleam of copper and carefully sited spotlights picking up and emphasising the warmth.

Andrea sobered. 'Yes, I do have brilliant news...for us. Unfortunately, it was caused by someone else's tragedy but...' She shrugged, a cloud passing over her face.

'Tell me.' Jessica sat down, intrigued, wanting to share her friend's happiness.

'Mike had a call this morning. Tunnel Vision contacted him and asked him to come and try out with them.' Andrea joined her friend at the table, unable to keep the note of excitement re-entering her voice.

'Tunnel Vision?' Jessica was immediately thrown back into her own problems as she recalled the strong and powerful music Nic had played over and over again at Bleathwaite after Andy had died. A group not only important to Mike, but to him and Andy as well, she thought, as she pictured Nic silhouetted against the window, staring, staring out into the darkness, his face set in lines of pain. Dragging herself back to the present, she asked, 'Aren't they Mike's idea of perfection? Oh, Andrea, I'm thrilled for you both! What happened?'

'Well now, that we don't know,' Andrea said slowly. 'Tunnel Vision are big, big time, Jess. International stuff and way out of Mike's league. Not that he's not good enough,' she added hastily. 'Simply that there's no way they could ever have heard of him at this stage of his career. But somehow they have.'

'What does this mean to you?'

'If they like him, if he's good enough, they'll have him as part of the group.'

'But that's fantastic!' Jessica leaned forward in delight, then saw again the shadow on her friend's face. 'But something's the matter, Andrea. What's wrong?'

Andrea looked up with a sad smile. 'Yeah, it's great for us, but the only reason this has happened is because they lost a member of the group a month or so back.'

'But they must think Mike is good enough to replace him?'

'He is. It's just that we like this group, always have done, and we were upset about this guy dying, is all. Mike thinks the chance of joining them is fantastic. It's just we wish it had been for a different reason.'

Dying? Jessica grew cold inside.

Tunnel Vision.

Andy. *Andy*. Andy had died.

Jessica clutched Andrea's arm. 'Who? Who was it died?'

Andrea looked at her, surprised by the urgency in her voice. 'Well, the lead guitarist, of course.'

Nic. Nic, losing his friend. Nic sitting in the dark room at Bleathwaite, rock music exploding through the house, rock music she knew was by Tunnel Vision, and she'd wondered why...why that group, why he'd hidden the cassettes. Nic, turning to her in the middle of a street crowded with tourists, blazing with sunshine, to tell her he was an internationally-famous rock star. Nic, with Josh at his beck and call, with...

'Yes, *but what was his name*?'

'Andy Lawlor.' Andrea watched as her friend turned away, ashen-faced, clenched fists pressed to her cheeks.

'Oh, no,' Jessica whispered. 'It was true, then. He was telling me the truth.' She sank into a chair and rested her head on her hands.

'Jessica, what is it? What's wrong?' Stepping forward, Andrea laid a concerned hand on her friend's shoulder. 'Come on, girl. It can't be that bad.'

'This is why I came,' Jessica said flatly, 'to find out the truth. I knew you'd know but I never thought it would be this easy.'

'Will you explain? No, wait. You look in need of a brandy to me. And a bit of food. Whatever you have to say can wait, although I've no brandy, but wine'll do.'

Andrea quickly put some cheese and rolls on the table before opening a bottle of wine.

'No,' she said, over Jessica's protests that she was driving. 'You look as if you need this. You'll be sober enough to drive home later and if not,' she shrugged, 'you can stay here. Won't be the first time. Now, quiet, and drink this, then eat at least a little. I can wait. I don't know how *you* of all people know something about Andy Lawlor, but I guess you must.'

162

Insisting Jessica had a little food and at least two glasses of wine, happier when she saw some colour return to her friend's face, Andrea at last made coffee and settled back in her chair, hands linked behind her head. 'Okay then. So what gives? You ask to come here to talk over some problem you have...which I assumed has something to do with this bloke you've been going around with, yeah? And now something about Andy Lawlor seems to have spooked you. I don't know where you want to begin. With your fella or with Andy?'

'Oh, Andrea,' Jessica sipped coffee from her mug and regarded her friend with sad eyes. 'I don't know where to begin myself.' She paused and sighed. 'At the beginning, I suppose. I met this man. I told you that.'

'Yes. And?'

'And I fell in love.'

Raising her eyebrows, Andrea leaned forwards and picked up her coffee. 'In love? Okay, it happens. Usually sooner than this with most people, and better if it's mutual. It helps. Is he a nice guy?'

'Yes, he's a nice guy. And yes...it's mutual...'

'But?'

Jessica looked at her in surprise. 'But?'

'There was a big but at the end there, and anyway, you've been crying, you look as if you haven't slept all night and you've asked to come here and talk to me. There has to *be* a problem, so tell me what the problem is. Does he beat you?'

Jessica smiled.

'Obviously not, then.' Andrea looked at her friend, head on one side.

Jessica sighed. 'It's got to the point where he's asked me to marry him.'

Andrea shot upright, staring at her friend in delight. 'Well, there you go! Jessica, this is great!'

'Yes, but you're forgetting the problem.'

'Ah, yes. And that is?'

'Ever since we met, he's been cagey about his life.'

'His life? How so?'

'Keeps me totally out of it. Totally. Shortly after we first met, he had to go abroad, said it was business, and since then, he seems to have been on the go all the time and quite often completely exhausted when he comes down to see me...' Jessica paused, beginning to realise why. 'But he's always been evasive and refused to discuss anything in detail. I got to the point of wondering if he was married and I was the other woman, you know? I even began to wonder if he was a drug dealer!' she laughed, slightly hysterically.

'Sounds mysterious and not you at all. No clues?'

'I'm not sure you could call them clues. Well, one was, to anyone not so ignorant as me.' Jessica shook her head. 'But anyway, he finally came out with it and told me what he did yesterday.' Was it only *yesterday*? 'And I didn't believe him.'

'What were the clues then? Tell me that before you tell me what it is he really does. Let's see if I can guess.'

Jessica looked at her friend sadly. 'Oh, *you'll* guess all right,' she said. 'Just me that's such a stupid, always so absorbed with my piano because that's the way I was brought up, head-in-the-sand *idiot*!'

'Don't be so harsh on yourself. Although...you could, maybe occasionally, be less intense and take a few days off here and there? Live a bit?'

'Hah! I could. In fact, over the last couple of months, I *have*, much to David's horror. But that still didn't help me to realise, work it out, whatever. But you most definitely will.'

'Try me. I might not.'

Jessica smiled wryly. 'Oh, you will. Then it began to dawn on me he's rich. Very rich. He has two houses, one in London, and the second one, the one I know, furnished with antiques and luxury everything else, and I'm not allowed to say where it is. Why, I wondered? But now I know why,' Jessica said sadly. 'I haven't seen the place in London so I don't know about that, but no doubt it's the same. He's got a motorbike, new, flashy-looking and large. He's got a sports car, a TVR. So, where does all this money *come* from?' Jessica watched her friend. As she spoke, she could see Andrea's eyebrows climbing up her forehead.

'I haven't a clue. But you said he worked in recording. He might own his own studio?'

'I suppose. He sort of implied he and his friend were in charge.'

'Okay, okay. Right...let's get back to clues. He's rich.'

Slowly, painfully, knowing this was the deal breaker, Jessica continued. 'He worked very closely with a friend called Andy, who died recently.'

'Who?' Andrea shot upright in her chair, eyes flying wide open. Andy? Andy Lawlor? Nick? *Nic*? *Nic Daniel*? It couldn't be!

'Yes. Andy....Andy Lawlor, he was called.'

It *was*! And for how long was it, about a year, Jessica had obviously not known who she was going around with until *now*. But how had she *survived*? How had she not found out? Andy's death and funeral had been massively covered by the news. She said he'd asked her to *marry* him! How had the press not got wind of it? Andrea stared at her friend, thoughts racing as she slowly shook her head in total disbelief at what she was hearing.

Jessica continued to explain. 'They'd known each other years and then he...Andy...was killed in a car crash, which you obviously know all about. Yesterday it all came to a head.' Jessica paused, remembering again the crowded cafe and the group of students.

She glanced at Andrea who was sitting bolt upright in her chair, her hands clasped together so hard the knuckles gleamed white, staring in fascinated horror at Jessica, who continued rather uneasily. 'He told me yesterday he was a rock star. I blew up at him.' She shook her head sadly at the memory. 'I thought he was just being facetious, stupid, putting me off again. But he was really angry and we didn't speak much again. He went straight to London. And today, I came to talk to you about it. I knew you'd know. And then you told me about Mike...and mentioned Andy and Tunnel Vision. Nic kept playing Tunnel Vision after Andy died. And I can tell by the way you're looking at me...Nic told me the truth, didn't he? And he *is* something to do with Tunnel Vision, isn't he? Does it add up?'

'Look,' Andrea said wildly, 'what did you say Nic's second name was? I'm not sure you've ever told me.'

'He's called Nic Daniel. He's fussy about his name...Nic without the k and Daniel without an s.'

Nic Daniel...Andy Lawlor! Andrea stared at Jessica, her mind racing.

Oh, *she* understood why he'd been so evasive. And Nic Daniel had heard of Mike through Jessica. Goodness knows he left enough of his stuff at her house. If she'd been going round with him for nearly a year then Nic would have had plenty of time to come across Mike's songs there.

'Jessica...I don't understand...you say you're going round with Nic Daniel? Nic without a k and Daniel without an s? You sure? Tall guy, long black hair, very good-looking, always wears black?'

'Yes.' Jessica sounded subdued. 'Do you and Mike know him?'

'Not personally. Not yet.' Andrea jumped to her feet and restlessly paced the floor, her hands gesticulating. 'If Mike gets in the band then yes. Oh, yes, Jessica, it adds up...he *is* Tunnel Vision! He and Andy Lawlor...they started the group, oh, about sixteen years ago, when they left school. There were four of them originally. Two of the guys overdosed and were told to leave after about four years because of the drugs. Nic was serious about his group...he wanted success with a capital S, hence the name, I guess...Tunnel Vision! They expanded then, took on a keyboard player and found two other guys to fill in for the ones Nic had kicked out, and the five of them have been together ever since. They're international. They're...' Andrea's voice died away.

Jessica? Jessica and *Nic Daniel*?

'But, Andrea...a rock star.' Jessica was dismayed. 'I-I just can't take it in. He's so quiet...he's...I don't understand... rock stars are so wild...'

Jessica had such fixed ideas, culled mostly from her elderly and conservative parents, and from the press, about rock stars, and Nic quite simply didn't fit into her preconceptions.

Andrea wasn't sure she understood either. Did Jessica realise what she was saying? That apparently Nic Daniel had asked her to marry him? *Nic Daniel*! Certainly, he was a very private man in most respects...the whole group were...but one thing he'd never been able to hide was the fact he went through women like a hot knife through butter. He'd never managed a steady relationship.

Jessica? So innocent! So honest and trusting! The bastard! Andrea lifted her head sharply. He'd better not be messing her around! Jessica couldn't cope with his brand of fun and games! Love them today, leave them tomorrow. But what was that she said? He's so *quiet*? And they'd been together a whole *year*? And he'd asked her to *marry* him?

'And,' Jessica continued, after the long, dismayed and somewhat horrified silence on Andrea's part continued, 'by the way you're behaving, he...he can't really be a very...pleasant person.'

'Oh, no! No, don't think that. It's just that he's always had a bit of a reputation as a...there've been...well...ohhh!' Andrea turned to face her friend and continued harshly, 'Women, Jessica. You may as well know. Stories about him and...but the papers exaggerate and Nic...he's a natural target, simply because he's so well-known.'

166

'Yes, okay. I'll agree he's a natural target. And he's admitted it to some extent. But some of what was in the papers would be the truth.' And it hurt to hear that it was common knowledge. That it would be inevitable the newspapers would be watching them both to see if Nic's attention strayed yet again.

And how soon would his attention stray? Leopards and spots and all that. She stared sadly at Andrea. 'I can't really see we have a future, can you? Is he likely to change after all these years? If even *you* are telling me he has a bad reputation for running through different women? I'm only one in a long line and he'll get bored soon enough with me. Right from the start I couldn't see what he saw in me...he's so experienced and sophisticated compared to me, I realised that. Oh, Andrea!' A sudden thought struck her and her eyes brimmed with tears. 'What a novelty for him to amuse himself with! He must have been laughing his head off the whole time at my ignorance of who he is!'

'Jess! Not necessarily so. And think about this. Nic Daniel has *never* had a relationship before, which has lasted for a full year!'

Mike returned late that evening, after Jessica had wearily decided she would prefer to go home, her doubts still there and her problems still unresolved. Andrea could barely let him through the door before she clutched the lapels of his leather jacket and backed him into their tiny sitting-room. She was desperate to hear how things had gone, down to the last detail, and also wanted to communicate the stunning news about Jessica.

'Mike, how did it go? Did they like you?'

Mike slumped wearily into a chair, exhausted by the day's rehearsing and the knowledge he was on trial for something that meant the world to him. 'It was great. They were really helpful, kind. And apparently he and Andy Lawlor were going to contact me anyway.' Mike had been dazed by that piece of information and it had given him a terrific surge of confidence for the ordeal to come.

'Jess came to see me today.' Andrea said slowly.

Mike raised his head and they stared at each other.

'You know, then?' she asked softly.

'I know,' Mike admitted heavily. 'He found some of my work at her house.'

'I can't believe this. Much as I admire Nic Daniel as a singer, a writer, a performer, he hasn't led a blameless life. Okay, nothing he's done has been particularly bad, but I think he's way out of

167

line, chasing after Jessica. She thinks...*thought*, perhaps I should say...he's in love with her but now she knows who he is, she thinks maybe he's just messing her around...and let's face it, she's going to end up hurt...' her voice tailed off as she ran a hand through her shock of hair, looking exasperated. 'It seems he's led a pretty quiet life with her, but now she's convinced he'll revert to type, get bored with her, throw her over as he's thrown all his other women over. Nic will walk out of it unscathed but Jessica will be *hurt*. She has that excessive pride of hers...I don't know what's going on but she's not happy with what I had to tell her and feels he could have been more honest right from the very beginning.'

'I told Nic she wouldn't like it,' Mike groaned, dropping his head into his hands, 'but one of the reasons he didn't tell her was just this...her reaction to it all. He became convinced she'd run away from it, so he held off. He held off from telling her because he was frightened of losing her.'

'You told Nic...? He *talked* to you about it? Mike, is he playing her straight? I can't quite come to terms with someone like Nic Daniel taking up with Jessica. He's so experienced and she's a babe in arms when it comes to men! If he's messing her around, I'll-'

Mike looked up. 'Hang on there, he's okay. From what I know of Jessica and heard from Nic, this is one hell of a serious relationship. Or *was*...until he told her what it was he did. He changed with Jessica and I believe he means everything he's saying about her. He says if it hadn't been for Jessica, he's not sure he would have survived Andy Lawlor's death. Yeah, we had quite a talk.'

Andrea threw up her hands. 'Okay, so if it's really genuine...if he really does care for her and wants a quiet life, we may have difficulty persuading *her* to believe *him*. I don't know,' she sighed. 'She's very upset and confused. Are you absolutely *sure* he's genuine about her?'

'I really do believe he is,' Mike answered slowly. 'He pointed out to me most of the rubbish in the papers is just that, rubbish. I know she's not his usual type but yes, I think he really loves her, strange though it may seem. I think maybe he *needs* someone like Jessica. Someone grounded.' He sighed and stretched his arms above his head, flexing stiff fingers. 'He knew she didn't believe him yesterday, when he told her what he does, but he realised she'd learn the truth from us soon enough, and maybe see something about him and Andy in the papers. They'll be running a lot of stuff about the group again, because of this memorial fund-raising concert. I warned him of her rather narrow upbringing.' Mike stood up and moved restlessly round the room, keyed up by the whole day. 'The stuff in the papers might not do his cause much good, though,' he muttered, stretching his arms above his head again before swinging them round in wide circles.

'And you...oh, Mike, how did you feel about playing with them? Was it as good as you'd hoped? You want in with them? I hope this doesn't spoil things for you. Do you think...have they said anything about joining them?'

'I think...I got the impression that if everyone was happy today...especially Nic Daniel...then I maybe *was* in, for now.' He turned a face blazing with hope to Andrea, eyes bright despite his extreme weariness. 'Nic was already predisposed in my favour because he and Andy had intended to contact me anyway. And I think we got on okay.' Mike leaned back against the windowsill, looking thoughtful. 'I just hope he can sort things out with Jess, though.'

'Ah, she thinks it's all been a big joke to him, that he's been having a good laugh at her ignorance.'

'Oh, no.' Mike shook his head with conviction. 'He hasn't been laughing at Jessica because she didn't know who he was. Quite the opposite. As I said, he *liked* the idea, and he didn't want to tell her at all. He said when you're as well-known as he is, you can never be sure of anyone's motives in a relationship, but with Jessica, he knew she loved him for himself. I reckon maybe that's why he's never settled down before. Oh, no, no, no,' Mike shook his head again. 'He never laughed at her.'

'Yeah, but she thinks otherwise. She thinks he's just been using her to amuse himself.'

'I realise. Quite frankly, I think he may find it hard to persuade her to accept all this. She'll back herself into a corner. Hurt pride because she convinces herself it was all a big joke, and she'll refuse to see what's under her nose. Whatever.' Mike shrugged. 'I can do no more. Now, my dearest one, I'm starving. They want me back tomorrow so I need to get to bed pretty soon. We're rehearsing for that concert every day, from now on.'

'Mmm,' Andrea nodded at him and led the way into the kitchen. 'I know. It was all on the news. A memorial for Andy and fund raiser for inner city kids.'

'After all this time together, the rest of the group know exactly how they react to each other. Nic directs a lot but they need to know if I can pick up on that, what I'm going to do, so we'll have some pretty intensive rehearsing to do. Oh, Andrea...' Mike wheeled round, appeal in his face. 'I hope they have me!'

The newspapers couldn't, from Nic's point of view, have planned his destruction better as far as Jessica was concerned. Apart from Andy's death, Nic Daniel had been out of the news for some time and now the group was moving again, they raked up as many of his past amours as they could, amiably shredding his reputation as they did so. The trouble was, none of it was totally uncomplimentary and all of it had sufficient truth to render it a waste of time and money to sue. All Nic could do was keep his head down and hope Jessica hadn't seen reports of the worst excesses he was supposed to have done.

If Nic hoped Jessica would be immersed in rehearsing and wouldn't be interested in reading about him, this time he couldn't have been more wrong. The concerts were over and done with at the end of two weeks. She and David had only just started to think about material for a recording, so she had time on her hands.

Knowing about him at last, seeing his name in almost every paper in the newsagents, she bought them all, and discovered, according to them, his supposed reputation as a womaniser. She read about his fame, his lifestyle, his money and, more specifically, details about all the women he was supposed to have slept with, proposed to, nearly married, lived with, abandoned. It was impressive reading and she couldn't help wonder why, again and again, he'd taken up with someone like her, the very opposite to the type of woman who seemed to appeal to him.

Staring out of the window, her heart was breaking inside as she reached her bitter conclusions. It was what she'd suggested to Andrea. It *had* to be what she'd suggested to Andrea! Nic had found someone who knew nothing about him, and the novelty must have been irresistible. He'd had a great few months laughing up his sleeve at her unworldliness and ignorance. Yes, okay, David was right. She had some talent and she supposed she was fairly attractive, but Jessica knew she wasn't sophisticated or glamorous. She knew she didn't enjoy parties very much. She knew she hadn't been sexually experienced...but then that, she admitted bitterly, was something he'd obviously intended to remedy as soon as possible.

No! That was unfair! He'd never made *any* attempt to seduce her until she'd indicated her total willingness. Had, in fact, she now realised, probably exerted some considerable self-restraint there.

Jessica shook her head sadly. She wasn't going to stay around and try to enter his world, to be shown up as quiet, plain, unworldly. To have everyone laugh at her and wonder what on earth Nic saw in her, and then watch as he gradually reverted to what he'd been previously. She couldn't face the pain and humiliation she knew would be hers when he wanted to disentangle himself because he was bored with her, as he'd become bored with all the others. Better to end it all now. No point in becoming further enmeshed. Further enmeshed? She smiled bitterly. Wasn't she enmeshed enough? How could she bear life without him?

A tear ran slowly down her cheek and pain crushed her as she made her decision. She knew he would soon come to see her. She'd convinced herself it wouldn't work and she knew she'd be sending him away.

Although worried about Jessica, and still trying to come to terms with his raw grief over Andy's death, Nic pushed everyone to give their best through the intensive rehearsing that followed Mike's inclusion in the band. Now, after nearly four weeks of continual, exhausting practice, Nic felt confident enough to take a few days out. He intended to go and see Jessica that evening. She'd had time to cool down, think about things. He'd sort everything out, hopefully bring Jessica back to London with him. They could spend one more day of rehearsing tomorrow, then he'd give everyone the weekend off and maybe take Jessica up to Bleathwaite for two or three days before returning for the final rehearsals.

He'd wanted to see her before this but he'd felt, after his previous weeks of total withdrawal and neglect, that his first priority had to be the band. Over and over, they went through certain songs, including the ballad Nic and Andy had written shortly before he had died, the initial tentative recording with Andy already released as a single and now at the top of the charts, when there was an interruption. There was a phone call for Mike.

They were all glad to call a break.

Mike stopped in the middle of a complicated run on his guitar, sweat pouring from his face. He'd never worked as hard as he'd done in these last weeks. He'd never had so much help and companionship. And he'd never enjoyed himself so much, although he still hated the reason for being here.

'Go on. Take it. We could do with five minutes.' Nic, short of breath, dropped to the floor and stretched himself out full-length. Jon abandoned his drumkit and went over to the coffee machine.

172

Adam played a run on the keyboard and then tried it again and again until Nic called out impatiently, 'Break, Adam, *break*! I'm exhausted.'

Ian had followed Nic's example and taken to the floor. Now he lazily raised his voice. 'Never complain about enthusiasm, Nic!'

Nic aimed a paper cup at Ian's head. 'Shut up,' he said amiably. A silence fell and minutes passed. Then Ian stirred. 'He's okay, is Mike. Yeah?'

'Yeah,' Nic murmured, an arm thrown over his eyes, knowing this was final decision time. 'What about you, Adam?'

'Eh? Oh, Mike. Yes, he's fine. He fits in well. I like the guy.'

'Jon?'

'Not Andy. Never Andy. But perhaps the nearest we could ever hope for. We've been lucky to find him. Where *did* you find him, Nic? I don't think we've ever asked. We were just so glad to see him!'

'Oh, hey, I told you. I came across a song he'd done, and someone who knew where he could be contacted. Andy and I had intended to see him in any case. We thought we could bring him in sometimes, perhaps use some of his stuff.'

Mike re-entered the rehearsal room. 'Nic. Can I have a quick word?'

Nic twisted his head round and pulled his arm from his eyes, giving Mike a long look. 'Okay.' He jumped lithely to his feet, the exhaustion disappearing as if it had never been.

Outside the studio door, he paused. He knew Mike had something to say, but it seemed important to tell him what they had all just decided. 'Mike…' he stopped, his throat closing as he remembered Andy. But Andy would have applauded this. 'We've all just agreed. You're in. Permanently.'

Mike's clasped Nic's hand in his. 'I won't let you down,' he promised. 'Thanks. Thanks, Nic!' His face sobered. 'I don't really know how to tell you what this means to me but I want to say I wish it'd been for any other reason.'

'Yeah, well. Thanks. Thanks, I know that. I'm glad we found you. Huh! If nothing else, I owe Jessica for that! Anyway,' Nic's voice became brusque. 'You wanted me?'

'That was Andrea,' Mike said quietly. 'She has this idea of getting you and Jessica together the day after tomorrow, having you both down to our house, and trying to sort this out.'

Nic swallowed. He knew Andrea and Mike were motivated by love of Jessica and, he believed, growing affection for him. After that first day, there had been no awe in Mike for Nic or the

173

group. He'd found confidence enough in his own ambition and abilities to take his place alongside them, and Nic knew enough of Andrea by hearsay from Mike and Jessica to know her fierce loyalty would soon be directed his way as well.

'Mike...' Nic paused, shaking his head with tiredness. They both stepped aside to allow one of the sound technicians access to the door before Nic continued. 'That's really kind of Andrea. What's today? Thursday? I've lost track of time!'

Mike nodded. They'd *all* lost track of time with the intensive rehearsing.

'Look, I'm going to see Jessica tonight so I'm hoping everything'll be cleared up anyway. I'll see you tomorrow at rehearsal and let you know what's happened. Then, yeah, maybe we can get together Saturday night?' Bleathwaite could wait. Why add to his tiredness with the long drive up there? They could spend the time here, or at Jessica's place instead. 'I'd like to meet Andrea and tell her myself how much I appreciate what she's trying to do.'

'Okay. I'm glad about that, I'll look forward to hearing about it.' Mike hesitated. 'Tread carefully, won't you? Jessica has a stubborn streak that can sometimes be infuriating.'

Nic grinned ruefully. 'Thanks for the warning. But I think it'll all be okay, I really do.'

Mike shot him a doubtful look as they moved back into the studio to start the rehearsal again. 'I hope so,' he said under his breath. 'I really hope so.'

Because Mike could see, under all the surface hard work and energy, that Nic was driving himself and was still under considerable strain, and he knew from long acquaintance that Jessica could be unbearably stubborn if she had made her mind up about something.

To him, it was an explosive situation.

Nic set off as soon as he could after the rehearsals had ended. Although expecting arguments, it never crossed Nic's mind to think that Jessica would reject him out of hand. No-one ever had, before.

When she did, it came as a complete shock.

'What do you mean, you don't want to see me again?' Nic rose abruptly to his feet, his chair spinning backwards with the force of his movement, his face whitening in shock.

But Jessica didn't see that. She was staring at the polished wood of the table in the kitchen, tracing her finger round and round in a circle as her heart broke inside her. She was determined not to raise her head. Her distress would be too apparent and she didn't want to let him know how deeply in love with him she'd become. She wasn't going to be needy or clinging.

Her world and Nic's were as far apart as ice and fire.

She'd convinced herself that now she knew who Nic was, the novelty she'd been for him would wear off and he'd get bored, revert to what he'd been like before, going round again with the kind of woman she'd seen in the papers, glamorous blondes moulded closely to his side, who, let's face it, probably suited him better than she ever would and certainly fitted better into his world.

Jessica was a realist. She knew she wanted a quiet and unsophisticated life and she was sure this would eventually irritate Nic.

'I want you to leave, Nic,' she repeated now, keeping her voice even with tremendous effort. She dropped her hands onto her lap, her fingers clenching until the knuckles turned white. 'I want you to collect together all the bits and pieces of yours that have ended up here, and go. Now.'

'But...why?' Nic shook his head, bewildered, unbelieving, shaken to his very core, in a total panic. He'd expected tears, anger, recriminations, but not this quiet dismissal.

'Because I think we're wasting our time.' Jessica's head was still bowed.

'*Why*?' Nic was implacable.

'Because we're so different. Your life...parties, night clubs, I don't know, maybe even drugs...' she looked up at him swiftly, doubtingly, 'Nic, it's just not my scene.'

'It's not mine, either,' Nic said grimly. 'Have you noticed me going in for any of that in the past months?'

She stayed silent. No, she hadn't. But nothing would convince her now that he hadn't been...experimenting in a different way. Experimenting with her innocence and her naivety.

'Well?' Nic's voice was harsh. 'Have you?'

'At first, it must have been such a novelty to you, to try out my way of life. And then...and then...Andy died. I appreciate you maybe needed me then. For a while.'

'Needed you *then*? For a *while*? Jess! I need you *forever*, get that into your head, will you?' Nic turned away, pain burning in his eyes, arms folded tightly across his body. He continued in a low voice. 'I admit the fact you didn't know who I was interested me...at first. Yes, okay, I'll even admit it had...*novelty value*, as you so neatly put it. But now...now I *love* you. I didn't plan it, I didn't intend it to happen, but I fell in love with you. And,' his voice rising, Nic suddenly swung back to face her and slammed his hand down on the table, 'if you think my lifestyle's so wild and decadent then tell me where does the house in Cumbria fit in?'

'Oh, Nic.' Jessica was close to breaking down. 'It won't work.'

'Jessica! You're being stupid! Can't you understand that some rock musicians can take their music seriously and live a reasonable life, just like you do? I work, Jessica. I write songs, I record, I perform. *Just like you.* I can't afford to mess around!' He smacked his hand down on the table again, too tired to exercise caution, and leaned down to look into her face. She turned her head away, still refusing to meet his eyes. 'Do I have to be wild? Do I have to take drugs? Once, maybe, when I was young and stupid, but not now. Years ago, I said no more drugs and anyone in the group who wanted to stay had to agree. I wanted to succeed!' He straightened up and began to pace the floor. 'It might surprise you to learn I invest my money carefully, that so much goes to charity, that my anti-drug stance is well known, that I lead a clean life! That sort of news doesn't make the papers, now does it, because it's not what everyone wants to hear! Okay, maybe there are a few rock players around who mess up their lives, but *I'm not one of them*, hear me? And neither is anyone else in my band!'

Jessica rose to her feet, her arms tight round her body, and resorted to anger herself. It was that or give way. And her pride wouldn't let her give way. She had worked herself into a corner. Nic had deceived her...never mind that deep down she could understand why...Nic had deceived her, had used her, had tricked her.

So now, her eyes blazed and she turned to stare at him accusingly. Here at least she had ammunition enough to shoot him down in flames. 'Huh! A clean life? You're famous...or perhaps I should say *infamous*...for your treatment of women. You use them and discard them. I've been reading and hearing nothing else, these past few days. Even Andrea admitted you were a womaniser! *You* told me you were a womaniser!' She crossed to the sink, back turned to the pleading Nic.

'Oh, yes. I knew it would come down to this,' he muttered. 'I won't deny that. But not now...I don't any more. I haven't since I met you.'

'*Ten months*! Have you reformed in such a short time?' Her voice was scathingly bitter.

176

'Okay, then. Let's have the truth of this, okay? Yes, I did go around with a lot of women! So what? There was no reason why I shouldn't, was there? I wasn't married. I wasn't seriously involved with anyone. And as for treating them so *badly*...don't you realise to be dropped by me meant an end to a pretty lucrative and publicised relationship, and some women can be incredibly bitchy when they're politely told this is the end of a beautiful friendship and they realise they're gonna lose all that? I was *bored*, Jessica. I was looking for someone...*always* looking for something special...' his voice broke, 'and then I met you! All the time...*you're* what I've been looking for. Can't you see...you cared for *me*! Not what I was, what I had, what I could do for you! Don't you realise how much that means to me? Jessica, please, please, *don't let this go!*'

'How can I trust you though?' Jessica said wearily, staring out of the window at the clouded evening, hearing the wind and the sudden lash of rain against the glass. 'How soon will you become bored with me as you did with those other women? How can you be so sure I'm what you're looking for? Get out Nic.' Jessica said, unable to bear this any longer. 'Just get out.'

'Are you *listening* to me at all? I won't get bored with you! That's what I'm trying to get through to you!' he shouted. 'All those other women, they were empty-headed and greedy. You...you...you're different. That's how I know it's you I want. You never wanted *anything* from me. You like everything I like. You like books and reading and music and walking. You like Bleathwaite. Doesn't that mean something to you, that we both like Bleathwaite? If I'm going to spend my life with any woman, she has to like it there, surely you can see that? Where would all these sophisticated women you think I want so much fit in up there, tell me that?' His voice changed, he sounded depressed and quiet. 'Jess, listen, please? I'm saying again, I love you. I'm begging you to give us a chance.'

'Have you seen the papers, Nic? Even the more sober ones?' Jessica dropped the subject of women and changed onto a new tack, another aspect of Nic which disturbed her. She still wouldn't turn. Still wouldn't look at him.

He stood in the middle of the kitchen, hands by his sides, his eyes fixed pleadingly on her back, convinced he could turn this round, and sighed. Yes, he'd seen them all. Now what?

'I don't want to put up with that kind of thing.' Jessica spoke wearily, still staring blindly out of the window. 'Speculation, intrusive photographers, impertinent questions. If you remember, when we first met, I said I loathed all the back-biting and jockeying for position that goes on even in my world. The sort of person *you* are, it would be an integral part of our lives!'

'Jessica,' he said desperately, his hand coming up in mute appeal, a gesture she didn't see. 'It won't last. Most of those photos you've seen this week are old ones! If we give a press conference and answer all their questions, it'll all be over in a day or two. And believe me, no-one gets in to see me who hasn't been screened. The people around me are my friends, good friends.'

She shrugged. On that score she could probably believe him. It still didn't alter things. 'There's nothing to give a press conference about, Nic. I haven't changed my mind.'

'*Why*?'

'Oh, is there any point in repeating myself? I don't want to be just another notch on your bedpost! I'll see the real you-'

'You *have* seen the real me! Ask Greg! Ask...hell, I wish you could ask Andy! Ask some of the band! Ask Josh!'

'Isn't the real you the one I've been reading about in the papers?'

'Come off it, Jess! You know the rubbish that gets into the papers! The inaccuracies! You *know* the real me!'

Briefly, he managed to silence her. But then, 'As for asking Josh,' Jessica laughed dryly, 'that little man who's always been so unpleasant.' She pushed to the back of her mind his care of Nic, his grudging acceptance that she held an important place in his life when he'd rung her and asked her to go to Bleathwaite. 'Huh! He implied, if I remember rightly, that women were always flinging themselves at you and you were always in need of rescuing! I don't think he's a good person to ask about your lifestyle!'

'You have no justifiable reasons for doing this, Jessica.' His voice was dangerously quiet. 'You're throwing away something very precious.'

Jessica sighed wearily, her breath catching in her throat. 'This is just repeating things, Nic! Going round in circles! *I'm not your type.*' Her head drooped and her chin rested on her collar bone, eyes burning with tears that threatened to spill down her cheeks. She would not, she *would not* cry.

'That's *your* opinion! Surely it's what *I* think of you that's important?'

She ignored him and continued. 'I don't like the thought of all the publicity and the image you have to keep up.'

'How many times do I have to tell you, I do a job, that's all? Most of the time, I just work in the studio, as I always told you. Otherwise...at least give it a try? Give us a chance?' He stepped towards her, his voice softening, pleading, and placed a gentle hand on her shoulder.

She shrugged it off violently. 'Don't touch me!'

Shocked by her reaction, he stepped back. He tried again, helplessly, beginning to feel a rising tide of fear and disbelief flood through him. 'Jess, I love you. *You*, do you hear me? I can't bear it if you leave me! Please!' Nic stood there in crushed, pain-filled defeat.

A cold silence fell on the room. Nic stood immobile in the centre of the kitchen, his face buried in his hands, fingers gripping his hair, shoulders hunched. He couldn't take any more, he really couldn't. He'd lost Andy and turned to Jessica...what would he do if she, too, abandoned him? *What would he do*?

A black void yawned in front of him.

Jessica failed to hear the note of real terror in his voice. 'Please, Nic, just go, will you?' she begged, her voice distraught. This was awful! '*It won't work*!'

'Only because you won't let it,' he shouted. 'You won't even give it a chance. I love you, Jessica.' He ran his fingers through his hair in agony. 'Look, if we part now, you'll never know what might have been.'

'If we part now I won't...oh, how can I get this across? I won't be hurt. Nic, we've just started to sleep together-'

'Yes! And it was fantastic, you know that!'

'You can't base a relationship on that!'

'I would agree, and say we've done a pretty good job of building our relationship *without* that, wouldn't you?' he flashed back. 'Look at me!'

She turned slowly at last, and raised pain-filled eyes to meet his wild ones. 'I couldn't bear it if we...if we continued, became even more committed and then you...then you...'

'*I won't change*! I won't revert to past behaviours because I won't need to! I asked you to marry me because of the love, *the love and trust and sharing* I thought we both had. I don't understand why you're telling me to go, Jessica, I really don't. I haven't changed, I'm no different. I still love you. I still want to marry you. Is it any wonder why I kept postponing telling you what I did? I *knew* this would happen!' He stood there in total despair, not knowing what else to say to her which might change her mind.

179

Finally, she stirred and turned away from him again. 'How you must have been laughing at that,' she said bitterly. 'Me, not knowing who you were. I must have been the only woman of my age in the whole of Britain to be so ignorant! What a joke!' All the remembered pain and humiliation of realising how different she was to other girls when she had finally gone to college rose up in her again.

He stared at her aghast. What if he'd told her sooner? But…he shook his head in bewilderment…he doubted it would have worked even then. She would've still shied away, convinced they were wrong for each other. It was illogical, it was unreasonable, and he couldn't understand it! But it looked as if he wasn't going to be able to shift her. This was a no-win situation!

What was he to do? *What was he to do*? Without her, what was left? Even the band didn't seem important any more.

'Jessica…' his voice cracked, 'I didn't laugh. I *never* laughed at you.'

Jessica already regretted saying that. She didn't really believe it. Her hands gripping the rim of the sink, she watched a drip form on the lip of the tap and slowly gather and grow big, before it dropped into the bottom of the bowl. A tear rolled down her cheek to land in the bowl and mix with the water.

Suppose she considered what he was saying, and stayed with him? What then? Ah, what was the use? He'd lied and evaded, knowing that to tell her what he *was* would expose what he was really like! He'd used her, right from the beginning! She wouldn't risk the possibility of losing him later. It would hurt even more...although, would it? This was dire enough. Like nothing she'd ever previously experienced.

'I don't care, Nic.' Her voice cracked. She paused and swallowed. 'I don't care if you laughed or not. I don't care what you say, I know it won't work. There's nothing left to say. We're going over and over the same things and it's painful and it's a waste of time. Will you go? Just get out of my life…' And I wish you'd never come into it, she finished in silent agony.

A long silence fell then Nic turned on his heel. 'I can't believe this!'

The kitchen door closed with a resounding bang. Jessica whirled round to see the room was empty. Seconds later, the slam of the front door echoed the closing of the kitchen door, causing the whole house to shake. Her hands went up to her mouth and the tears she had fought dripped from her eyes and ran down over her fingers as great sobs wrenched out of her body. She doubled up and collapsed against the sink. How could she bear this loss?

The car door slammed, the engine revved in screaming protest and he shot off from the drive in a spurt of gravel. Jessica looked up just in time to see the back of the car disappearing at high speed down the lane.

She laid her head down on her arms and continued crying, her tears dripping into the bowl to mix with the drips from the tap. She'd convinced herself Nic was in love with an idea rather than herself and now she'd destroyed what little they'd shared, and sent him away.

Ah, be honest, she told herself, the pain twisting through her even more deeply. They'd shared a lot more than a *little*. He was right. They *had* built a relationship first, a wonderful, marvellous friendship, and then…and then…finally making love with him had been so natural and so right. Had been ecstasy.

Her support for him after Andy's death had been laced with an aching, empathetic feeling for his pain, a deep and selfless desire to lift the burden from his shoulders. Oh, yes. They did love each other.

But it was no good. It wouldn't work. His lifestyle was so different, so exotic; she felt it would be impossible to share and there was no way she could compete with the likes of his previous girlfriends. She would simply have to learn to live with this feeling that part of her had been torn out and she was slowly bleeding to death.

But perhaps what he'd been saying was true and he did care and he wouldn't change and he *had* been searching for someone to trust.

Someone to trust.

How hard it must be to live your life always wary of people's motives, and how sure he must have been of hers…her eyes flew open as too late she realised the other side of the coin when it came to her not knowing who Nic was, and her tears fell faster.

Nic fled. Dismayed, shocked, bewildered, for years being able to have anything he wanted and now denied what he knew was his whole life, his whole future, he drove blindly into the evening, his eyes gritty, his reactions automatic, and eventually, late, *late* that night, came to Bleathwaite, a wind howling round the eaves, cold rain lashing at the windows. There were no fires. Sam and Dorothy hadn't been expecting him, hadn't prepared the house.

Nic made no preparations either. He sat in the dark, staring out at the gradually dawning day, grey and ragged, clouds tearing over the tops of the opposite hills, and was swamped with depression and despair. He'd thought it was bad before when he had lost Andy, but now he had lost Andy *and* Jessica.

This couldn't be him, surely? He leaned forwards, elbows resting on his knees, hands clasped together, knuckles showing white. He could have any woman he wanted! All he had to do was walk out of here, go back to London, ring any one of dozens of numbers in his phone book. He didn't even have to do that. He only had to go to a nightclub anywhere, *anywhere*, and he'd be guaranteed a nubile, glamorous woman willing to go to bed with him before an hour had passed. That was what all the papers said! He laughed hysterically, a shocking sound in the empty room. That was what Jessica thought, wasn't it? That he could have any woman he wanted?

He stood up and paced restlessly over to the window, gazing out across the gloomy, rain-torn valley. Somewhere in the distance an owl shrieked. Nic shoved his hands in his pockets. Trouble was, he didn't want to take up with an old flame, nor did he want to pick up *any woman*. He'd finished with all that. He'd got Jessica now.

He shuddered as he recalled the tenderness and passion of making love to Jessica, so moving he had lain in silent awe, wrapping her in his arms when at last it was finished.

A muscle flickered in his jaw. Well, he'd *had* Jessica.

But not now. It couldn't be true! She couldn't mean it! It seemed there was one woman he couldn't have...and she was the only one he wanted. Black depression settled on him and his fist smashed into the stone wall next to the window. Nic didn't notice the pain, or the blood trickling down his hand.

Jessica pulled herself painfully upright and dragged herself over to the table. She had cried for hours and dawn was breaking. The wind was coming up and rain spattered against the glass doors. She stared blindly out into the dull greyness. She'd thought, once she'd told Nic to go, she'd be able to pick herself up and get on with life again, but this pain was crushing her. Quite how she was going to face her life, to play again, she didn't at this moment know or care. All she could think of, over and over again, was Nic. Nic, lonely. Nic, needing someone, needing *her*, and she'd turned him away. She trembled with cold and shock.

Slumped on the settee, Nic buried his face in his hands. He couldn't sleep, didn't want to eat. All he could see was Jessica.

Jessica laughing with him, Jessica looking at him tenderly as he cradled her in his arms, Jessica's clear eyes regarding him steadily, demanding from him loyalty and commitment.

And now that he was prepared to give it, Jessica's unyielding back turned implacably, rejecting him, telling him to go.

Shivering in the chill of the stone house, he dragged himself upstairs and flung himself on the bed, his arm over his eyes, uncaring of the tears which leaked slowly from the corners of his eyes.

Grey light seeped more fully into the kitchen. Jessica lifted her head from the table and pulled herself wearily to her feet. She drank some water and moved restlessly through into the sitting room. Touching the piano, all she could remember was Nic sitting there the first day she had met him, casually asking questions about the song Mike had left behind.

Did it matter so much who he was or what he did? She had to consider what he'd told her, that he'd been bored and looking for someone to share his life. Sitting down on the stool, she crashed her hands down on the keys, over and over again, a cacophony of discordancy that echoed from the beams and washed back in waves from the stone walls. Impossible to go to London today, to rehearse for the recordings. Later, the phone rang, and rang again. It would be David. She ignored it.

Still and silent, Nic lay on the bed getting colder and colder. As the weak evening sun drifted behind banked clouds he rolled over and pulled the duvet over his legs, his raw knuckles stinging as his hand closed over the cover. He no longer cared what happened to his life. He could fight no longer. He was tired.

The phone rang, and rang again. He wouldn't answer. He didn't care.

Where had Nic gone in such a tearing hurry? Jessica hoped he was all right. She remembered his laughing face as he taught her how to kayak, before this mess broke round them. He'd never shown anything but enjoyment of how they had spent their time, and look at Bleathwaite. He was right. No-one who liked to live the high life all the time would have a place like that...or the respect of a man like Sam. He'd never been able to take anyone there, before he'd taken her, because, as he'd said, which of his sophisticated girlfriends would have tolerated the place? She flung herself down on the settee. Papers would print anything. They could create an affair from one photograph. She bit her knuckles as the tears began again.

As the darkness of the second night deepened, the owl silently glided across the yard of Bleathwaite and alighted on the gatepost. It shrieked into the wind, listening for the answering cry of its mate from across the valley. Nic stirred briefly, his head turning on the pillow, cheeks unshaven, lines of pain etched on his face, before slipping back into the darkness he sought. There was nothing now to come back for. *Nothing*. Andy was gone. Jessica was gone. He had nothing left.

Chapter Eighteen:

The doorbell shrilled an urgent summons. Jessica sat up, startled, and pushed her hair away from her face, looking blearily at her watch. She'd spent the last two nights dozing or pacing the floor and was still wearing the jeans and sweater she'd put on two days ago. She'd fallen asleep at about three this morning, the first sleep she'd had since Nic had gone.

She felt awful and knew she looked awful, with unbrushed hair, swollen eyes and bleak expression.

The bell rang again.

'All right, all right. I'm coming,' she muttered as she stood up. In the hall, she quickly pulled a brush through her hair and straightened her jumper before opening the door. When she saw the group of people waiting on the path, her eyebrows rose in surprise and shock. Josh was the only one she recognised. The others were all strangers but she thought she might hazard a guess as to who they were if asked.

'Uh...umm...' Jessica didn't know what to do. She wasn't sure why they were there.

A tall blond man stepped forwards. He was incredibly good looking with a narrow face, strong nose and chin, and a lean, rangy body that moved easily.

'Hi.' His voice was deep, gravelly, pleasant to listen to. 'I'm Ian Green. Part of Tunnel Vision. Is Nic here with you?'

'N-no,' Jessica stammered.

The group on the doorstep exchanged concerned looks. One of them stepped forwards and murmured something to the man who'd introduced himself, who now spoke tersely. 'Then I hope you don't mind...we'd like to come in and talk to you.' His eyes were coldly steady, his attitude determined.

Jessica felt it would be little use trying to deny them entry. She stood back silently as they filed into the hall, and gestured to the door on the left. They moved into the sitting room.

'Sit down.' Jessica said abruptly as she drew back the curtains to let the sun stream in the windows. She noticed it in vague surprise. Somehow all she had was a memory of rain. 'Coffee? I'm having some, anyway. I won't be able to make much sense of anything 'til I've had some coffee.'

There was a general murmur of acceptance. Jessica shot into the kitchen and plugged in the kettle, gathering mugs, milk and sugar onto a tray. She spooned coffee into the cafetière and leaned with her back to the sink, her mind now awake and racing. Why were they here? Obviously, something to do with Nic. Had he sent them to plead his cause? Surely not?

The water boiled. Jessica poured it onto the coffee and carried the tray to the sitting room. She paused outside the door. She could hear a Beethoven piano concerto. A bit rude, she felt, to be using her stereo system. Pushing the door open, she glanced across to the stereo. It was off.

Much to her surprise, Josh leapt to his feet and took the tray from her, putting it down onto a table. Jessica looked round. Sitting at her piano, his hands just coming to rest on the keys, was the man with dark hair touching his shoulders.

'Sorry.' He stood up, looking genuinely apologetic. 'I couldn't resist trying it out. It's a beautiful piano. I've heard you play,' he added abruptly. 'You're very good.'

Jessica stood with her mouth open in complete surprise. Was she continually going to be surprised by this new world she'd found herself in?

'You're quite good yourself,' she said, astounded. 'I'm sorry, I don't know your name...or yours.' She turned to the fourth person, sitting quietly in a chair, thick brown hair tousled over his forehead, steady green eyes observing her closely.

'Jon Marshall. And the guy playing your piano is Adam...Adam Tyler. Yes, he's good. He can play anything. And Nic, now. Have you ever asked Nic to play you any classical guitar? And did you know Nic can also play the piano? Not as well as Adam here, but pretty well. But no, of course you don't know. I forgot. You only discovered just recently he fronted a group, so Mike tells us.'

Jessica sat down slowly, staring at the man who had introduced himself as Jon Marshall in a dazed fashion.

'Steady on, Jon,' Ian stood up and poured the mugs of coffee, handing one to Jessica before helping himself and sitting down again. 'We agreed. Gently.' He swallowed a mouthful of coffee and sighed, looking tired and worried.

Jon made a noise deep in his throat and subsided. A few moments of silence passed before Ian carefully put his mug down and leaned forward, hands clasped loosely between his knees. 'We came because we know...*now*...that you and Nic have been seeing each other for quite some time. He kept it pretty quiet, although I gather Andy knew all about it and certainly we'd all noticed how much better he's been since last summer. Whatever.' Ian shrugged. 'We thought he might be here. We learned quite a few things yesterday, you know,' he added conversationally, although there was a distinct edge to his voice. 'We found out Nic's asked you to marry him. We know you have preconceived ideas about...*us*...our type. We discovered you didn't actually know what Nic did until a couple of weeks back...that he told you he was a rock star but you didn't quite believe him until Andrea made the connection for you. Nic *is* Tunnel Vision. Its founder member and lead singer, and one of the lead guitarists. We also understand you'll have read and heard quite a few stupid remarks about Nic and his attitude to women these last few days in the papers.'

There was a long, silent pause. Jessica looked from one man to the next. They all had their eyes fixed steadily on her.

Ian eventually added, very softly, 'We want to try to make you understand his side of it and, more importantly now we know he isn't here, try to track down where he is.'

'He shouldn't have told you these things!' Jessica spoke sharply, not hearing the last part of his speech.

Ian stood up and drifted over to the window. He leaned one shoulder against the wall, hands in his pockets, staring out across the garden. 'Nice garden,' he said idly, then continued, still speaking softly. 'Oh, no, no, no. Don't go blaming Nic again. *Mike* was the one who told us all this. And he told us,' Ian straightened accusingly, abruptly, one finger now pointing stabbingly at Jessica, 'he told us because Nic never turned up for rehearsals yesterday. The last day of rehearsals before we planned a short break, and we had a lot to get through. There's no way, *no way* at all, do you understand, that Nic would have let us all down, either professionally or as friends, so you can understand if we all feel a little concerned about him. He's just lost his closest friend of many, many years. That should tell you something about his loyalties! He's still looking ill, tired and much too thin. We have a gig in just over two weeks. A massive gig that he's been working on extremely hard as a tribute to Andy, okay?' Ian frowned and rubbed a weary hand across his eyes. 'And now it seems Nic's disappeared. We thought he might be here with you and that would have been okay, but it seems he's not, so no-one knows where he is or how to contact him. We tried ringing Bleathwaite all day yesterday, off and on. No answer, Miss Farndale, no answer at all. And we did try ringing you...Mike gave us your number...but again, there was no reply.'

187

Jessica half rose from her seat, aware of the accusing eyes. If this was what Ian called gentle, she was glad she'd been spared...what was his name...Jon's interrogations.

'And?' She asked defensively. 'What has that to do with me? If he chooses to disappear?'

'What do you mean, *what has that to do with you*?' He looked at her sourly, his voice incredulous. '*You*, of all people? Quite a lot, I'd say! And *we* happen to be quite fond of the guy. When he just drops out of sight like this, we feel a little concerned. Obviously, we went up to his flat.' Ian crossed the room and sat down again opposite Jessica. 'He wasn't there. His bed hadn't been slept in. We didn't know if any of his stuff had gone or not. But we got worried. Nic doesn't, *has never*, just *not turned up.* If he said he was going to be at rehearsal yesterday, then he would have been at rehearsal yesterday. Even when he cracked up after Andy's funeral, we knew where he was. He's reliable and considerate, Miss Farndale. Do you get those two words? Reliable and considerate. Has he been here at all?' He shot the last words at her abruptly, his narrowed gaze fixed on her face.

'Yes. H-he was here on Thursday night. He wanted us to go on...to stay together.'

'And?'

'I-I couldn't. He...a rock star...I couldn't. I told him he'd better go.'

'Why?'

Jessica shrugged.

The group exchanged glances.

Ian sighed. 'Perhaps,' he suggested with bitter quietness, 'that's why he's disappeared. That thought cross your mind, Miss Farndale, now you know no-one can locate him?'

Jon was the next to launch his attack into the ensuing silence. 'As to why you told him to go, we understand from Mike you're maybe frightened about continuing your relationship with Nic because you feel he might suddenly become, I don't know, wild? Inconsistent? You feel his lifestyle and yours are incompatible...Yeah, I know a few long words. I read English at Cambridge and performed with the band at weekends to supplement my grant. Then we hit the big-time.' He shrugged and spread his hands. 'But back to Nic. He's known Josh here for twenty or more years and didn't abandon him because he wasn't musical. He found him a job moving our gear, as soon as we could afford someone to do it instead of doing it ourselves. He and Andy stuck together for longer than that, and I think you're aware, Miss

188

Farndale, he was genuinely upset when Andy was killed. We joined him fourteen years ago when he and Andy wanted to expand the band, and never once in that time has he let us down, or been inconsistent, apart from a short period of time last year when he was depressed. But it didn't last long...I think because he met you? Now are you beginning to get our drift, Miss Farndale?'

Yes. Jessica dropped her face into her hands. She was beginning to get their drift. When it came to people he really cared about, Nic was loyal, Nic treated people well and stuck by them. Nic wasn't inconsistent. And they were also telling her that rock singers weren't uncouth yobs. Adam...playing Beethoven nearly as well as she herself could. He'd had classical training, no doubt of that, and still practised seriously to produce that quality of playing. And Jon Marshall, the cold-eyed man to her left...a Cambridge graduate, of all things. Her prejudices were indeed being thrown overboard.

Josh silently rose to his feet and collected the mugs. As he put them on the tray in front of her, she was surprised to see a look of sympathy on his face before he picked the tray up and left the room.

Out of character, Nic had disappeared...tired and miserable. He'd lost Andy and now...her? A thrill of horror ran through Jessica. Her face paled and she clenched her hands into fists, a variety of emotions chasing themselves across her face.

'No, Miss Farndale. I...*we*...don't think Nic would harm himself.' Ian leaned forward, a note of sympathy entering his voice for the first time. 'He's a very strong man indeed. But he's taken a lot these past few weeks, what with Andy's death and now you ditching him. I'm afraid we're not happy about that.' Ian jumped to his feet and again paced restlessly to the window. He turned and swept his hand through the air to emphasise what he was saying. 'We'd really like you to think again, please. He *has* gone around with a lot of women previously, we can't deny that, but he was never deeply involved with any of them. He complained often enough of being bored. He always had an air of loneliness. This job isolates you, *makes* you lonely. Some of us cope with that. Some of us are so egotistical that we're happy with lots of superficial relationships that give us occasional comfort. Some of us, like Nic, are constantly looking for one genuine person who will give us, perhaps forever, the love and support we need. I understand from what Mike said, Nic thought he'd found that person in you. And it had made him a very, very happy man, insofar as he was able to be happy after losing Andy. Mike said Nic'd told him if it hadn't been for *you*, after Andy was killed, he didn't think he would have made it through.'

Jessica raised her eyes and looked directly into his brown ones, still unswervingly fixed on her face. She could almost guess what was coming.

'I read Life Sciences,' he said wryly, 'which includes psychology. Also at Cambridge. That's where Jon and I first met Nic and Andy. They came to play at a May Ball and we were the supporting group. They weren't quite so rich and famous then. Adam had just joined them. A year later they needed two other people. Their previous two group members...' he shrugged. 'They both seemed determined to ruin themselves with drugs, so Nic kicked them out of the band....but maybe you know about that?'

Jessica nodded. 'Andrea...Andrea told me.'

'Nic came back to the university when these guys left. As I said, he'd seen us play...and he remembered us. He said he needed some extra players. Nic asked the two of us,' he nodded at Jon, 'to join him. We were happy to earn some extra money but it made the final year difficult because Nic was beginning to get recognition then. He and Andy wrote some brilliant stuff, it was bound to happen. In the end, we got our degrees, but there was little point in looking for an alternative career, now was there?'

Jessica swallowed, her gaze moving once more round the group of men sitting so calmly, so implacably, in her sitting room. She rapidly reassessed her ideas about the type of person who went into rock music.

Again, as if reading her thoughts, Jon interjected harshly, 'The keyboard player, Adam here. He was a few years ahead of you at the Capital Music College. He won the Latimer Trophy in his final year.'

Adam made a quick gesture of dismissal. Jessica turned to him, another shock of surprise buffeting her mind. 'The Latimer Trophy?' Then why, her voice implied, are you doing this kind of thing?

Ian sighed. 'Still not accepting our work is valid, are you?'

Jessica blushed, ashamed her reaction had been so obvious. She, too, had won the Latimer Trophy. It was awarded to the best pianist of the full three years in college and although it didn't bring any financial rewards, the prestige of winning it could take you very far indeed.

Adam shrugged. 'I'm an extrovert and life in a rock group appealed. I wasn't sure I was suited to the grind and dedication a

190

concert pianist needs. I thought there was maybe more to life. I've never regretted my decision.'

Ian stirred. 'So okay, what else is bothering you? Oh, yes. Mike mentioned publicity. There's an occasional flare of interest in one of us...Nic especially...usually connected with a woman, but otherwise, unless we choose to generate some publicity before an album release, a tour or a gig, we're left pretty well alone. There's not much news value in us, you see. We're all too clean living and too well-behaved. So, Miss Farndale, we'd really like you to reconsider, and if you know where Nic is, then go to him and tell him. We know he has the bolt hole in the Lakes. If he isn't here, which we'd hoped, he might have gone there, even if he isn't answering the phone. Which is in itself worrying. Josh knows Nic's taken you there. That at least must tell you something, lady! So go and find him.'

'I-I...he...I'll think-'

'You do that.' Jon Marshall stood up menacingly and towered over her. 'You think hard, and think rapidly! I hope we've convinced you about Nic's character and shown you we're not uncouth monsters. I know you tour as well. I'm sure you can arrange for your tours to coincide. I really can't see what the problem is. *You're* the one behaving like a spoilt star, not Nic. I, I, I, all the time. I can't cope with this, I can't put up with that, I don't want the other!' He turned away in disgust, thrusting hands into the pockets of his jeans.

'Jon,' Ian interrupted, 'cool it. Miss Farndale, we're really worried now, about Nic. I know I said I didn't think he'd harm himself...well, I'll stick by that...but only just. He's a very unhappy man. It's a long time since I studied psychology but I still tend to indulge in it as a hobby, and the last few days, before he disappeared, were painful to watch. Of course, we didn't know about these extra pressures he was under. Andy's death and getting the band back on track was enough, without you complicating things. So if you do know where he might be, and let's all hope it *is* this place in the Lakes, could I strongly advise you to find him? Soon? Preferably telling him you'll at least give him a chance? I assume you do really love him?' he asked, suddenly severe. 'Mike said you'd mean it, if you'd said it.'

'Y-yes. I-I love him more than anything.'

'Hell of a way of showing it,' Jon muttered.

Jessica turned on him. 'I thought it was for the best!' she shouted. 'I thought he'd get bored with me, being so quiet, leading the sort of lifestyle I do! I only knew what I'd read in the papers

191

about people like you! I knew I couldn't cope, didn't want to cope, with fast living, parties, glamour!' She dropped her face into her hands, crying bitterly. Their combined onslaught of the past hour had shaken her completely. Ian jerked his head and Josh, Jon and Adam went quietly out of the door.

Ian slipped his arm round Jessica's shoulders. 'I'm sorry,' he murmured. 'Perhaps we've been a bit hard. But you see, we didn't know, in turn, what you were like. Mike said you were okay, but the way you've just told Nic to get lost...well,' Ian sounded uncomfortable. 'It riled Jon, you see. And we're worried, Jessica. Very worried now. If you love him, do something, please?''

Jessica continued to cry without restraint. 'I-I love him. I do love him. When I found out who he was...I thought...he'd not want me anymore. I thought my attraction for him was just my i-ignorance of who he was. I thought I-I'd let him down. I can't make bright, witty conversation. I don't like the bright lights.'

'But neither does Nic, except when he's performing. Surely you realised that?'

'I-I thought it must just have been the n-novelty value. I decided h-he'd been trying the quiet life out for a b-bit of fun.'

'No, Jessica. Tunnel Vision...all of us... we value our privacy. It's a joint agreement. We're all private people, as much as we're able to be. Some groups enjoy publicity and, yes, they actively seek it. If they enjoy it, that's okay.' He shrugged. 'We don't. Nic was telling the truth. He is, quite simply, what you've seen so far. Go find him, okay? And let us know he's all right, won't you?' He gave her one more brief hug and followed his friends out of the house.

Briefly, Josh poked his head round the sitting room door. 'I'm sorry,' he said awkwardly, 'about that day last year. So many women throw themselves at Nic just because he is who he is. But you...I was wrong, wasn't I? You really love him and he knows it. That's why he's so upset, see? Please,' his ugly face twisted in distress, 'find him for us.'

192

Chapter Nineteen:

Jessica had to walk from the farm. She'd set off for Cumbria as soon as the group had gone, worry churning her stomach, and arrived in the late evening.

In the summer dusk, the Longdens' house was in darkness, but she was relieved to see Nic's TVR in the barn. At least he *was* here. Thank goodness for that. He'd meant it when he'd said this was the place he came to whenever he was in need.

Now, as she walked steadily up the rough lane, her stomach contracted nervously. He might be here, but was he all right? What would she do? What would Nic say to her? Perhaps he'd be so angry he would tell her to go away. After everything she'd said to him, he would be justified. He might be especially angry that she'd followed him here, to the place that was a secret from everybody, his refuge.

Jessica paused to catch her breath, the peace of the evening stealing into her heart and easing the pain and trepidation she felt. The moon rose full and bright over the shoulder of the hill behind her as the daylight gradually faded.

At last she stood before the gate. The house was in darkness, the Landrover standing in the yard. Jessica advanced to the door, hovering there in uncertain misery. She couldn't understand why there were no lights. Hesitantly, she knocked softly on the door.

No reply.

Jessica tried turning the handle. It gave under her hand and she found herself in the dark hallway. The house felt cold and damp. A shiver passed through her body and she closed the door quietly behind her, before slipping into the sitting room, where she'd found him the last time she had come up here. The hearths were cold and swept bare. The room was neat and tidy. No books, no papers, lay scattered in comfortable disarray. If it wasn't for the vehicle outside, and the unlocked door, Jessica would seriously doubt Nic was here at all.

She felt deeply troubled. If he was here, he'd made no attempt to make himself comfortable or warm. Her fears, pushed aside once she'd seen his car in the barn, rushed back in full force.

Jessica passed through the lobby at the back into the kitchen.

Again, all was cold and silent. The Aga sat unused in the corner. The sink and drainer were bare of any signs of cutlery or plates. All the jars stood in neat lines that spoke of a cleaner's conscientious hand rather than the owner's careless one.

The dining room was just as deserted.

Upstairs, she peeped into the small bedroom that had been Andy's, when he'd come to visit. It was just as she'd seen it last, still with a few possessions scattered around the room. Jessica closed the door softly, her hand shaking.

Unless Nic had gone out walking in the dark, or had walked down to the farm and gone somewhere with Sam and Dorothy, he had to be in his bedroom.

Jessica eased the door open. Relief flooded through her making her legs weak. In the light of the moon flooding through the uncurtained windows, she could see Nic lying hunched on the bed asleep. It was all right then. He was all right.

She tiptoed across the thick carpet and gazed down at him, gently brushing the wild tangle of black hair back off his beloved face. Swallowing convulsively in relief that he was here and alive, she sank down onto the edge of the bed. The simple fact that Ian had voiced concern meant he thought it was possible Nic might have had enough, and Jessica hadn't realised until this moment just how afraid she'd been.

Doubt began to creep through her. There were shadows under his eyes and his jaw was dark with stubble. His hair was unbrushed and he was still fully clothed in what looked, to Jessica, like the same clothes he'd worn when he'd come to see her. Lines of suffering had etched themselves onto his face and he lay in complete stillness, his breathing hardly perceptible. He was hunched over, his hands forming fists close by his cheek and on one hand she could see severe bruising and dried blood. It looked painful. This was not an easy or relaxed sleep.

She shook his shoulder. There was no response. No stirring. No fluttering of the eyelids. No sighs. No rolling over. She shook him again, panic stirring deep within her. Had he taken something? She looked round wildly, but there was no trace of glass or mug, no empty bottle of pills, nor had there been downstairs, and she knew Nic had a pathological hatred of any substances, based on his experiences with those two group members who had freaked out on drugs all those years ago. No, he hadn't taken anything, but she began to realise he might have just given up.

194

Realising it was her selfish actions which had brought him to this withdrawal, Jessica slid to her knees by the bed, filled with self-loathing and deep dismay. How to bring him back? How to let him know she was willing to stay with him? She bowed her head and cried silent, bitter tears of remorse, knowing she had to tell him...she had to tell him she was sorry, so, so sorry, and she loved him as she would never love again. Her decision was made. Whatever the risks, she was now prepared to try.

As remorse swept over her, words broke of their own accord in a ragged murmur from her lips and hot tears fell on his hand as she laid her cheek against the back of it, desperate to feel some part of him against her skin.

In the black depths surrounding Nic, a voice echoed meaninglessly and he knew someone was trying to reach him. He closed his mind to it. He'd had enough. No more. No more. *Nothing* mattered anymore.

'I love you, Nic,' Jessica sobbed in an agonised whisper. 'What have I done? Oh, what have I done? I'm sorry. So, so sorry. I love you.'

The owl called mournfully somewhere out in the darkness of the night, a sad sound which echoed Jessica's grief.

Nic stirred, his mind grey and disorientated. He'd retreated from his unbelievable pain and wasn't sure there was any reason for returning, but something seemed to be calling to him...someone...the persistence was reaching him even as he tried to resist.

He didn't want to come back. There was no point anymore.

He struggled through the layers of mist, dizzy and unable to properly understand what it was he'd heard, but surely... '*Jessica*?' he said roughly.

Her head shot up. Nic's voice. Dazed, doubtful, questioning, but definitely Nic's voice. Her eyes met his, Jessica's wild with pain at what she'd done, Nic's wide with dazed disbelief.

'Jessica?' he said again, struggling to lean up on one elbow and rubbing his hand across his eyes in bewilderment. She continued to stare at him, transfixed, tears silently running down her face, unable to say a word now she knew he was awake.

'Did...did I hear you say you loved me?' His voice was still low and hesitant, but a faint light entered his eyes and he pushed himself further upright on the bed. '*Jessica*!' he said urgently. '*Did you just say you loved me*?'

She nodded mutely, still kneeling on the floor. Nic swung himself unsteadily round, sitting on the edge of the bed, his hands coming forward to cup her face, hurting her. 'Say it again!' he commanded. 'Say it again! What you were saying when I was...asleep. Tell me!'

'I'm sorry,' Jessica said in a low voice. 'Yes, I-I love you. I should never have told you...told you to go away.'

Nic stared down at her, his eyes slowly blazing with light. His hands gripped tighter and Jessica winced. 'Do you mean it?' he asked sternly. 'Jessica, the time for games is long past. Don't...don't torture me anymore. Don't torture me! *Do you really mean it*?'

If she'd held any doubts, they were all swept away now in the face of his intensity. 'I...yes. I really mean it. I knew I couldn't live without you. I thought I c-could...I thought it wouldn't work, but...oh, hold me, please...just hold me...?'

'*Jessica*.' He held out his arms. After a moment's hesitation, Jessica flung herself forwards.

'I'm sorry. I'm sorry.'

'Hush, hush, darlin'. We've both had a bad few days. It wasn't all your fault by any means,' he said roughly, rocking her in his embrace. 'If I'd been honest with you from the beginning it wouldn't have come as such a shock to you...'

'No. If you'd told me right at the start, my lack of self-confidence would have killed off anything we might have had. But when you did tell me...I was a fool. I was so convinced I was nothing but a novelty to you, and so sure I couldn't fit into what I thought was your lifestyle.'

'Never. You were never a novelty apart from the first hour or so when I met you. Can't you understand the trust I could put in you simply *because* of your ignorance? That for the first time I knew I was loved because of myself, not my position, or money, or the favours I could give. Until I met you, I was never sure, I could *never* be sure.'

Jessica pulled back and looked at him with searching eyes. 'That must have been hard,' she observed sadly.

'As for lifestyle, I understand from Mike that you had preconceived ideas about what rock stars were like, but you *know* what my lifestyle is like.' He laughed wildly in almost drunken relief and buried his face in her hair. 'I can't believe this! I can't believe you're really here. What made you change your mind, darlin'?'

Oh, the joy of hearing that lovely, easy endearment again. 'I changed my mind because I found the thought of living without you was unbearable and, in addition, your whole group turned up to convince me that you really were the good guy and that rock

196

stars could be quite civilised. They succeeded on both counts.' Jessica laughed nervously, remembering the ring of stern faces, Jon's sudden attacks, Ian's attempts to keep everything on a polite footing and the surprising sympathy from Josh.

'The *whole* group?' Nic was incredulous.

'Well, except Mike. Josh came instead. I think Mike felt he ought to keep out of it, being aligned to both sides, as it were. They pitched in a bit, but it clarified my thinking!' Jessica confessed wryly. Then she self-consciously touched her hair. 'I must look a real mess. I haven't been sleeping very well and then I drove up here without stopping.'

With an incoherent murmur, he pulled her into his arms again and crushed her against him, burying his face once more into her hair. 'I don't care what you look like! All that matters is you're here!'

Jessica wound her arms fiercely round him, relief flooding through her as she felt herself safe in his embrace. The roughness of his chin grazed her cheek as he rubbed his face against hers. All at once he set her away from him. His eyes blazed and a grin split his face. 'You've no idea how glad I am you're here. But Jessica, I'm sorry. I really should have told you straight away.'

'No, no. It wouldn't have done you any good. Back then, I'd have definitely been frightened off, you were right about that. And I can understand,' Jessica said softly, touching his lips gently with her fingers, unable to stop looking at his beloved face. 'You...it must be hard wondering all the time why some girl is there with you. I can understand now why you didn't tell me. I-I over-reacted. If I'd just thought about it all a bit more and not been so convinced you were laughing at me…and not let all the media hype get to me...'

'Oh, Jess!' He bent forwards and kissed her swiftly on the forehead. 'I can't blame you! They make me sound like a cross between De Sade and Lothario. It was enough to frighten anyone off!'

'Sweetheart...' Jessica said softly, 'hush. Enough now. Make love to me? I want to be close to you.'

His face filled with a joy, shadowed by pain as he realised how close he had come to losing her forever. He laid his cheek on her hair. 'My darlin', my love, *yes*. But not now. Not until I've showered and,' his voice was rueful as he touched a finger to his chin, 'shaved. Do you mind?'

'Not at all,' Jessica replied demurely. 'As long as you don't object to sharing the shower?'

They had very nearly shared a shower before. This time the sharing was complete. They soaped each other and washed each other's hair, the water cascading down in silver drops, warm and caressing on the skin, running into their eyes, over their faces and catching on their lips as they stopped to gently kiss.

As Nic shaved, Jessica leaned dreamily against his back, watching over his shoulder as he scraped two days' growth of beard from his face, her hands idly stroking his body until he complained he couldn't concentrate and then complained again because she stopped.

Jessica giggled. 'I quite liked you with all those whiskers!' she exclaimed. 'It made you look wicked and sexy!'

He lunged round and caught her close. 'Don't worry,' he breathed into her ear. 'I still feel wicked and sexy!'

He caught her up in his arms and carried her through to the bedroom, throwing her down onto the bed. Her breath caught in her throat and she looked up at him, her eyes filling with tears.

'What? Tears, darlin'?' His finger touched her lips.

She lifted her hand and let it drift over his thigh. He shivered at her touch. 'Oh, Nic,' she whispered, all laughter gone, her eyes darkening with passion and love. 'Oh, Nic...if I'd lost you! As I walked up here, I thought...I thought...what if you sent me away? How would I live? And I realised what I'd done to you! How I'd made you feel! And I was so ashamed! And so frightened you'd...you'd-'

'Hush, darlin',' Nic lay down by her side, his hands slowly stroking her body, brushing over her breasts, his touch feather light on her thighs. 'Hush, darlin'. Nothing matters now. Nothing matters...' And his mouth came down on hers in a kiss deep with passion and promise.

It was dawn when they awoke, and the sun pouring in through the window heralded the new day. Jessica lay, sated and glowing, in the curve of Nic's arm. There were still shadows under his eyes, still sadness in their depths, but his face was clear and a smile of pure contentment lit his handsome features.

'You do realise we have to go back today?' Nic asked her, kissing the top of her head and sliding his hand further round to cup her soft, warm breast.

She ran her fingers over his rough chest and inhaled the unique smell of his skin, full of sensual pleasure. 'I know,' she admitted. 'You're rehearsing. And anyway, I need to contact

198

David. I suspect he's been trying to get hold of me this last couple of days!'

'We only have fourteen more days until the concert,' Nic said, 'and Mike needs as much time with us as he can get. I'd hoped,' he added carefully, 'to spend this break with you. When I came on Thursday...I thought you might be a bit angry still, but, oh, Jessica,' his voice darkened with remembered pain. 'I never thought you'd send me away!'

'Ssh, don't!' Jessica buried her face against his chest. 'Oh, please, don't! I'm so sorry-'

'Ah, c'mon! I didn't mean to upset you! And I'm sorry we have to go back, darlin', but I can't let the group down. They need me to integrate Mike...I sort of lead them, you see. You do understand?'

Oh, yes, she understood now. She saw again the three men, Josh simply an observer, sitting round her in an accusing circle assuring her of Nic's steadfast loyalty. She could hear the steady beat of his heart under her cheek and felt cherished and protected in his arms. 'I understand,' she said softly. 'Let's just drift round the house, okay?'

'Okay.' He kissed her again. 'Until we need to go back, later on. Now I hate to sound prosaic, but I have to admit I haven't eaten for a day or two, so do you mind if we get up and have some breakfast?'

'Nic, we have to ring someone! I said I'd let them know if you were here.'

'I'll do that now.' He rolled out of bed and crossed to the wardrobe, pulling fresh clothes out.

'Lucky you to have something clean to put on,' Jessica grumbled.

He laughed at her as he dressed. 'Can't help there, darlin', except to offer you a teeshirt and jumper, but they'll swamp you.'

'Maybe better than the ones I had on!'

Downstairs, Nic decided against lighting the Aga but switched on the electric heating and lit the two fires in the large sitting room as Jessica prepared something to eat.

His next job after breakfast was to ring round the group members and tell them he was fine.

In the now welcoming sitting room, Jessica smiled as she flipped through the cassettes. All the ones by Tunnel Vision were back in place. Out of curiosity she pulled out Root and Branch, slipping the cassette into the player and taking out the sleeve. It was in the form of a booklet. The band were listed inside the cover. Photos of them were scattered through the pages. Nic put the phone down and turned as she was reading the words to one of the songs. He leaned over her shoulder, grinning as he saw what she was doing.

'Hey, Mr Daniel! This is a flattering photo!' Jessica flicked the posed shot of Nic with one of her long fingers, swinging her hair out of her eyes as she turned to smile at him. 'I wouldn't have recognised you anyway!'

'Why, you...you...' Nic grabbed her round the waist. 'That deserves some penance! Six kisses. Each...' he bent to kiss her, his lips tender and demanding at the same time.

A shiver ran through her.

'More...' he kissed her again, his eyes darkening. 'Passionate...' his voice roughened and his hands ran down her back, pulling her closer. 'Than the one...' Jessica stared into his blue, blue eyes, mesmerised by the love she saw in them. All the laughter had gone from his face. 'Before.'

Then he spoke no more. Only the music played on, masking the soft sounds of the lovers on the rug in front of the flickering fire.

They were later than they'd intended when they finally set off. Nic laid his hand over hers as they cruised down the motorway in the TVR. They'd left her car in Sam's barn and Nic had promised Josh would come and collect it as soon as possible. 'Darlin'...'

'Mmm?'

'I have to be in the studio pretty well all the time, at the moment. It would be difficult driving over to Keepers Cottage. But...this time, I don't want to be parted from you. Will you come back to London with me? And...if I can get a special licence for the register office, how about we get married quietly, the morning of the concert? I think, under the circumstances, it can be done. Because of who I am, you see, otherwise it'll get out and there'll be a complete riot. And I don't want that. Don't suppose you do, either.'

Her heart turned over and she turned luminous eyes to Nic. 'Oh, sweetheart, yes. Yes to London, yes to getting married quietly. Yes, yes, yes!' She paused before looking down at her crumpled jeans and continuing on a more prosaic note. 'But have we time to go round by my house? I really could do with some clothes. Especially as I'll need to meet with David to get some of my own work done. And,' she glanced shyly at Nic, 'tell him we're going to be married, if you don't mind?'

Nic glanced at her, smiling. 'Go ahead and tell him. Invite him to the Wembley concert, why not, and I think also, a party afterwards? To let everyone know we've married? But as to calling at yours, we don't really have the time...we're so late as it is...' he hesitated. She looked at him, detecting a strange note in his voice. 'You'd better get used to the fact you're marrying a rich man,' he said ruefully. 'Now, while I don't want you frittering money away,' he flashed a quick grin at her, 'I do think we could run to a few replacement clothes. I have accounts at several of the larger stores and all you'll have to do tomorrow is order what you want and someone'll bring it round for you, okay?'

Jessica was stunned into silence.

'Jess...' A note of desperation entered his voice. 'Please...it's a part of me. I can't help it and sometimes it's useful to have a bit of money. Please?'

She gave him a sideways glance. That bleak look was entering his eyes again. She couldn't bear to see it. 'It's all right, Nic,' she hastily reassured him. 'It just comes as a bit of a shock, that's all.'

And so did his flat, although by now, Jessica scolded herself, she should have been prepared for it. She followed Nic as he showed her round. It covered the whole of the top two floors of the tall London house and, as at Bleathwaite, everything was to the highest standard of luxury. The flat was reached by a private lift but there was also an internal staircase going down through the house to the recording studio and the basement where Nic kept his motorbike, the TVR and, she discovered, a BMW saloon. Nic explained the rest of the house was given over to offices for the fan club, merchandise and administration, the recording studio, a rehearsal room and reception, which was the only way in and out of the building apart from the basement garage.

He explained. 'I have one strict rule. No-one can get in without giving a personal code or having an appointment. Otherwise...' He spread his hands and shrugged.

Jessica had already noticed knots of people outside the house, staring up at the windows. Sometimes they tried to gain access but were always moved courteously on, with the gift of a signed poster, by the security men.

'Now perhaps you can understand why I love your place so much?' Nic asked softly. 'Jess...we have to sort out what we're going to do.'

'How often do you tour?'

'It depends. We did a fairly big European tour last autumn and we have a short British tour booked in for later this summer. We...we were going to work on recording the new album before that. After this concert I'll try out some ideas with Mike. We'll probably still record, get the album out before the Brit tour, then come spring, we'll be away for a while again. We'll be going to America. The dates are all booked now.'

'You plan that far ahead?'

'These tours take a lot of organising. We have quite a few people working for us you know. Roadies. Technicians. Publicity and secretaries. Security staff. We have to arrange to transport all our gear and all the personnel. We've a couple of lorries and a couple of coaches. Then all the accommodation has to be sorted out, publicity, advertising, marketing...it goes on and on!' He grinned and shrugged.

'It's vast, isn't it? Can I come with you? All the time?'

Nic stared at her, his face lighting up. 'But...your piano? Practising?'

'I think I'd probably be able to manage that. My agent can probably make some bookings for me. I've had a few requests from America but so far, I've been too nervous to go by myself. And anyway...' it was her turn to shrug, 'I think maybe you're more important to me. I think I might give up. It's time to live and enjoy it.'

'I don't think it's wise for you to give up.' Nic looked serious. 'You'd miss it. You're only just starting out, darlin'.'

'Maybe.' She didn't look too convinced. 'Maybe. I'll see what my agent says. I won't stop playing for a while, but...' Thoughts of children floated into her head. She knew Nic would like that. Too early to talk about it yet, though.

'We fly everything out there and hire transport for everyone when we get there. We...the group...usually have a base somewhere and fly in by jet or helicopter to the gigs. Would you really come with us?'

'Yes,' Jessica said softly. 'Yes, I'd really come. And okay,' she came to a decision, 'get someone to give me your planned itinerary for the American tour and I'll see about arranging some dates that link in with yours.'

Nic folded his arms round her. 'Ah, I love you, darlin'.' He kissed her hungrily, aching to possess her body. She pressed herself close to him, her mouth opening under his passionate demands, her bones melting as he caressed her. They slid to the floor onto the thick grey carpet in front of the open fire. The

202

flickering flames danced over them as they twined together, clothes soon abandoned in the heat of their love-making.

'Jess?' Nic raised his head, eyes intense, burning into hers, lips swollen with their bruising kisses.

'Nic?'

'Promise me...promise me...never again. *Never* leave me again, darlin'?'

The day after their return to London, Jessica ordered some replacement clothes, which, as promised by Nic, arrived within the hour.

Andrea had come over to be with Jessica on her first day in this new world, but in fact, she saw no-one else. The flat was an oasis of calm peacefulness and she and Andrea started to decide what Jessica might wear at her wedding.

'Nic said low-key,' Jessica said. 'He'll be wearing black, no surprise there, and I suspect just jeans and a shirt, maybe a jacket slung over the shirt. I don't want a wedding dress, just something classy, I guess.'

'Mmm,' Andrea turned over the pages of a couple of fashion magazines which one of the secretaries had gone out to buy and have sent up. 'Look at this...I think it'd look good on you.'

Jessica leaned over to look where Andrea was pointing. A slim sheath of a dress, in coppery tones, with three-quarter length sleeves.

'*What*? Have you seen the *price*?' Rearing back, eyes wide, and mouth open, Jessica looked far from elegant.

Andrea laughed at her. 'Get used to it, kiddo,' she said. 'You...Nic...can afford a dress that cost ten times this amount. This is cheapskate!'

Falling silent, Jessica looked thoughtful before looking once more at the dress. 'Well, I don't want anything that costs ten times as much,' she said reluctantly, 'and I do like this, so...'

'So let's go shopping, today, and sort the dress, some shoes, maybe a necklace. Have you got an engagement ring yet?'

'Nope. Not that bothered. I suppose Nic might buy one. But we decided on the wedding rings. Just plain gold, quite simple ones. Okay, let's shop. But I really have to ring David and let him know what's going on, and invite him and Stephanie to the concert and party. You okay here while I ring? Nic has a sort of sitting-room office place. I'll ring from there.'

'Okay here?' Andrea raised an eyebrow. 'Oh, I think I'll manage!' Jessica swiped her over the head as she left. Minutes later, she heard the phone ringing at David's end.

'Brunskill.'

'David? Jessica here.'

'Jessica,' he exploded. 'Where have you *been*? You just disappeared again. I've been ringing your place for a few days and no answer! What's going on?'

With a big sigh, Jessica settled herself at the large worktable. 'A lot, if you want the truth. It's a long story so I hope you've got some time?'

Intrigued now, his voice came soothingly down the line. 'For you, all the time you want. Is this going to explain all these absences and rebellions I've had to put up with recently?'

'Yes, but you're being overly dramatic. Do you remember when I was so upset, at the start of the year, when my friend who'd been in the audience never came round to see me afterwards?'

'I do. A biker who worked abroad. Not someone I ever thought you should be seeing.'

'Well, maybe I better break this bit of news fast then, because one point of this call is to invite you to my wedding party next Saturday night, after a concert. Although not the type of concert you would usually go to!' She grinned, even though he couldn't see her. 'And I know you're not conducting that night, I checked. Stephanie too, of course.'

His voice was soft with shock. '*Your* wedding party? To...to the biker? Jessica, are you sure you know what you're doing here?'

'Ah, it's not what you're thinking. Nic fronts a rock group.'

'What? A *what*? Who? Which group?'

'You're familiar with such things?' she teased.

'More than you, yes, probably. Anyway, the kids can let rip on occasions and I sometimes ask who it is they're playing. Their favourite at the moment is Tunnel Vision. Apparently they lost a group member recently in some tragic accident and there's a single out that's taken the country by storm. Guitar solo by the guy who died. It's quite a nice song, actually,' he admitted, a note of surprise entering his voice. 'And I understand the lead singer goes to quite a mix of music events, gives him ideas apparently. He's called Nic...Jessica, did you say your *biker* was called Nic?' His voice rose in shock.

'No more explanations needed, David. You've nailed it. Now, can you and Steph come? Pretty please, otherwise I'll only have Mike and Andrea at the party. Oh, you won't know that bit...Tunnel Vision has asked Mike to take Andy's place.'

There was a long silence at the other end of the line. So long that Jessica said, 'David? Are you still there?'

205

'You've floored me,' David said faintly. 'Some biker.' Another silence followed, then, 'Yes, we'll come. Oh, and by the way, can the kids have a signed poster please?'

Laughing, Jessica went back to Andrea and they set off for the shops.

The morning of the memorial concert dawned bright and sunny. It was also the day of Nic and Jessica's wedding. Only Mike and Andrea would be there, and, in place of Andy as best man, Nic had asked Jessica if she minded him asking Josh to take on the role.

'I wouldn't know which of the group to ask, and Josh works so hard and asks for so little. I think he'd be honoured and after all, I've known him as long as I knew Andy. I'll ask him to keep it quiet.'

There was sadness that Andy was not with them, brought home even more by the fact it was the day of the concert. Nic and Jessica, however, had decided enough was enough and they wanted to commit to this relationship which both knew had had Andy's blessing, so were going ahead.

Before the wedding, there was a press conference about the concert and the planned British tour. Jessica wasn't going to be there. This conference was about Andy, the group, Mike, and their future plans.

As soon as that was finished, Nic, Jessica, Josh, Mike and Andrea changed upstairs.

'Whoa,' Nic breathed, when he saw Jessica in her dress, 'that takes some beating. You look lovely, darlin'. But then, to me you always look lovely.' He pulled her into his arms and kissed her softly, before whispering into her ear, 'All good?'

Gazing up into his thickly-lashed, glorious blue eyes, she nodded. 'All good.'

'Then let's go do this thing,' he grinned, taking her by the hand and leading her to the lift.

Josh was amazingly spruced up, probably the smartest of them all, in a suit and tie. Nic, as predicted, wore black jeans and a black, open-necked shirt, with a black linen jacket to complete his outfit. Tall, slim, his thick, curling hair waving down round his face, he was, quite simply, stunning. Mike also wore more casual clothes, although new and very smart. Andrea was Andrea, in a flurry of long skirts, layered tops and scarves.

Leaving from the underground garage, one of his staff driving the very luxurious minibus with tinted windows, they soon reached the registry office. The ceremony was quick and simple,

206

Josh's pride in producing both rings successfully was almost comic, and Andrea predictably sniffed and dabbed her eyes.

'Hey,' said Nic in wonder, as the ceremony ended and he turned towards her. 'Hey...*Mrs Daniel.*' He bent his head and drew her close, kissing her deeply until her knees sagged and he laughed, having to almost support her weight. 'Later,' he promised, in a deep husky whisper, meant for her ears alone. 'But hey, maybe not until after the concert, okay?'

Laughing back at him, Jessica murmured, 'I'll keep you to that.'

They ate at a restaurant, in a private room, where Josh proudly toasted the bride and groom, before returning to the flat so Nic and Mike could rest before the massive performance they'd planned in Andy's memory. As far as Jessica was concerned, as a wedding day, it'd been pretty good.

Chapter Twenty-one

Jessica got out of the taxi and turned to Andrea, standing waiting on the pavement. They were both tense and nervous, Andrea because this was Mike's debut with the group and Jessica because she was meeting Nic after the concert and would, for the first time in public, be acknowledged by him, and she knew the press would be there, watching his every move. Nic himself, with Mike and the rest of the group, had set off a couple of hours previously, to check the equipment, the sound system, and try to relax.

Their passes were scrutinised intently and eventually they were led to a cordoned-off area of reserved seating with an excellent view of the stage. Andrea explained who the other occupants would be.

'Some of them are girlfriends of the crew, but some are press, critics, backstage or office people.' Andrea explained.

Press. Jessica cringed, then put them out of her mind. 'Andrea! The noise they're making!'

'This is a bit different to what you do, you know!'

'You're telling me.' But Jessica was determined to enjoy this as much as possible for Nic's sake. 'Oh, look. David and Stephanie are here already!' She reached them quickly and hugged them.

'Cacophony,' David said tersely, after greeting them. 'You do pick them, don't you? Not a plastering Hell's Angel, just the biggest name in rock imaginable! Congratulations, by the way'

Stephanie grinned. 'Take no notice of him,' she said, eyes sparkling. She kissed Jessica on both cheeks. 'Indeed, congratulations! I think it's amazing....and I also confess to having a sneaking liking for Tunnel Vision. Can't believe we're joining you tonight at the party!'

The two of them settled into their seats next to David and Stephanie, Jessica continuing to look round in fascinated interest. It was all so alien to her. The Wembley arena was enormous, holding thousands and thousands and thousands of people, and every seat was taken. Coaches had brought people from all over Britain. This was a new way of performing, one she knew nothing about.

Multi-coloured lights split the air, synchronised to flash on and off, and swing round, in time with the music that was playing over the sound system. The crowds were singing, chanting, swaying. Some were on their feet and dancing. The rest of the arena was dimly lit, only the exits brightly illuminated, which made their own stylised pattern in the vast building. Jessica shook her head in bewilderment. 'I couldn't...I just *could not*...perform in this!'

'Glad to hear it,' David said promptly, 'because that makes two of us!' Despite his comment, however, he was smiling and, like Jessica and Stephanie, was taking a keen interest in everything.

'Just wait,' Andrea said, 'until Tunnel Vision come on. You'll be amazed by the atmosphere. Everyone knows every word of their songs. Well,' she added, laughing dryly, 'perhaps not you lot, but everyone else who's here tonight!'

Jessica protested. 'I've been educating myself! I've been listening to all their stuff while Nic's been rehearsing!' Still rather shy about Nic's world, she'd declined to sit in on the rehearsals themselves, despite his suggestion that she should. 'But...what on earth must it be like, to be faced with this? So many people!'

'When Nic's on, he can do anything with them. Mike and I were at one of their concerts once, when he brought the whole audience into total silence. That was for a particular song, but they'll probably do it again, tonight, for Andy. But they're going to be pretty tired by the end of tonight, you know. This is a long performance time for them, but Mike said Nic only wanted Tunnel Vision playing.'

Time passed. Gradually the crowd settled down, moving up from the shops and stalls in the corridors behind the seating, drifting to their seats. A song was played over the sound system. There was a roar from the crowd, several screams, and then a muted chorus joining in with the words of the slow love ballad. Jessica put her head on one side. 'Is this Tunnel Vision? I'm not sure I recognise it.'

Andrea nodded, a lump in her throat. She couldn't believe Mike had a chance with this group. 'Their new single...'

The atmosphere was unbelievable. Jessica could see many people crying as the soft singing about needing someone to love and trust went on, and when a haunting guitar entered the song and eventually took over in a solo, the crowd rose to their feet, all sound dying away.

'What's going on?' Jessica whispered, pulling at her friend's sleeve as they, too, stood up. Andrea dashed a hand over her eyes and shook her head.

'Andrea,' Jessica demanded again, 'what *is* all this about?'

209

Andrea turned and looked at her. 'It's for Andy,' Andrea explained simply. 'It's one of the songs he and Nic wrote and recorded together just before he died. It hadn't been properly recorded, it was just a try-out, but it came out as a single, as a tribute to him. It went straight to the top of the charts.'

Jessica stared at her. 'Oh, Andrea,' she exclaimed softly. 'I'm glad Mike's got his chance, but I'm so sorry about everyone losing Andy.'

A sudden roar from the crowd cut Jessica off. Andrea clutched her arm. 'They're coming on,' she gasped. 'Oh, Jessica, I'm so nervous for him. You heard how Andy played. Can Mike match that?'

Jessica peered up at the stage, her excitement matching Andrea's. She recognised Jon Marshall. So he was the drummer. Cold, good-looking, frightening. And the man with the bass guitar was Ian Green, incredibly sexy, also frightening. Adam Tyler took his place at the keyboards.

'There's Mike!' Andrea clutched Jessica's arm even harder, her fingers digging in.

Still on their feet, the crowd roared and chanted as the group quietly settled into their places, checking their equipment, talking to each other, occasionally laughing. Mike ran his fingers over his guitar and the notes echoed out above the noise. There was a sudden run on the drums, a chord on the keyboard, a deep, strong note from the bass, then a silence before a crashing chord as the band broke into a strong rock tune with an insistent beat. The crowd exploded, clapping and cheering.

Andrea literally wrung her hands together, her face white. 'This is where Nic comes on. This is one of the first songs they ever wrote...it's an instrumental to begin with. Mike's playing lead guitar. Oh, Jess!' Her hand went to her mouth before she clutched her friend's arm yet again.

By tomorrow it would be black and blue, Jessica thought ruefully.

'He's good! I always knew it, but hearing him with this lot just shows how good he really is! And tonight they're going to sing two of his songs! They've done some work on them, obviously, he and-'

Jessica couldn't believe it. The noise of the crowd rose yet again in intensity, almost competing with the loud rock instrumental the band were throwing out. A dazzling spotlight swung into the back of the stage and a figure dressed all in black,

210

shirt undone to the waist, a guitar slung over his shoulder, ran to the central microphone.

Nic.

This is what he did. It was so unreal.

Suddenly a voice, deep, powerful, was pouring out lyrics at the screaming, cheering crowd, rising above the instruments, blending in with them, now rough, now smooth.

Slowly the crowd calmed and settled into a mass of swaying, singing humanity, totally supportive of the group on stage. Nic had his back slightly turned towards Andrea and Jessica. Then he turned. The song slowed a little. He seemed to look directly at Jessica. He walked down the stage. Hands reached up to him. He put his own hand out, stretched towards where he knew Jessica must be. The words were of love. Finally, the song came to an end. Cheers, screams, calls of 'Nic!' 'Nic!' filled the air as the band swung straight into another song, this time slow and full of passion. Massed hands swayed in time to the music, muted voices sang along with the band.

Jessica turned her head to Andrea and found her friend's eyes waiting for her. 'Well,' she said at last, 'he's good, I'll grant him that. It's amazing! The way he sings! I'd no idea! I know I've been listening to his records but to see him live...!' Jessica was stunned by the power of it. Tears filled her eyes and pride filled her heart.

'That keyboard player has some talent,' commented David.

'Talk to him tonight,' Jessica murmured. 'I think you might get a shock!'

She turned back again to watch as Nic strode now down to the other end of the stage. His energy and dedication were intense. Everything went into his performance. He was never still. Singing or playing, he moved constantly, restlessly, prowling the stage, controlling the crowd, directing the band.

Song succeeded song. Nic sometimes offered a brief introduction. Sometimes he paused and talked to the crowd between songs. Sometimes he stopped singing altogether and let the crowd and the band carry the song. Sometimes he simply called a title and the band plunged straight into the new number. Sweat poured off them all. She could see the dampness of their shirts, the gleam of sweat on their skin as they continued to perform for around ninety minutes, to create a non-stop torrent of music, a tribute to a much-loved performer, friend and fellow band member.

The music was fascinating. Sometimes slow, sometimes fast, sometimes loud, sometimes soft, sometimes a mixture. Layer upon layer of guitars, drums and keyboards, every one of the players pushing himself to the limit, with vocals running over the top in Nic's strong voice which sometimes caressed, sometimes threatened, sometimes cajoled, sometimes directed, backed with harmonies coming in from the others.

Oh, he was *good*. Andrea had told her he and Andy had written the lot, words, music, everything. She knew now why he'd collapsed after his friend's death. He must have wondered how he could keep this up. He must miss Andy unbelievably. Quite how he'd the courage to get through this night, the first without his friend by his side, Jessica didn't know. Her heart went out to him.

After each song the crowd clapped, cheered, whistled, chanted. Jessica's eyes turned from the stage, to the people, to the stage again, concentrating, listening, intent, interested. She'd never experienced anything like this, never imagined she would...never, ever thought such a man as Nic would be her fate in life.

Finally, the group put their instruments down and ran off stage. Recorded music, sounding surprisingly flat, replaced the band. The volume of noise decreased to a manageable level. People moved again, out of their seats searching for drinks, food and souvenirs.

Andrea was right about Nic's ability to control the crowd. At the start of the second half he brought everyone to total silence.

'Hey! We all know why we're here. This night is for Andy, okay?'

'Okay!' The crowd roared in response.

'This...he would've liked this...' For the first time that night, Nic's iron control slipped. His throat closed and his eyes shut, every move caught and magnified by the giant video screens to each side and above the stage set. The crowd sighed. There were soft calls of 'Andy' from various places, the sound of a sob.

'You're a great crowd...he loved you, you know that?' His voice cracked and his hands clenched. A silence hung over the arena, broken by the occasional sound of Andy's name.

'A great crowd...We're all gonna miss Andy...you, the band...me...hey, Andy, Andy.' Nic might have finished on a broken whisper but his voice was still caught by his mike and amplified throughout the arena, and his head dropped.

This time, the silence continued for too long. Jessica could see Jon and Ian exchange worried looks. The crowd murmured

212

and shuffled, willing to remember Andy but unsure now what should happen next and getting uncomfortable with Nic's long silence. Nic was in control. Nic shouldn't let them down. Nic should tell them what to do now. Nic shouldn't stop...

Jon and Ian looked across at each other again and Jon half-rose from his drums. The silence in the vast arena was uncanny and frightening.

He needed her.

Jessica knew without a doubt he needed her help. Without thought for herself, she called to him, as strongly as she could. *'Nic! I'm here!'*

Just the sound of her voice was all he needed. His head lifted. He blinked in the spotlights, the merciless video cameras catching every expression in his pain-filled blue eyes, including the glimmer of tears, and looked over to where he knew she was sitting. Anyone near the sound of her voice craned to see who had called out and her face flamed, hidden in the welcome darkness.

But she'd broken his bitter reverie as perhaps no-one else could have done, and the band gave a collective sigh of relief as Nic threw out an arm and half-turned to Mike, swallowing hard. 'Yeah, we'll remember Andy, but I want you to meet Mike! Andy and me, we were gonna ask Mike to maybe join us anyway. We liked his stuff. And now, well, here he is, and I know you'll give him your support!'

There was a roar of approval from the crowd and the band swung into the new ballad, the one that had been put out earlier on the sound system, when Andy had been playing. Mike was brought to the front to play the slow solo and the audience went wild cheering him when he'd finished. Andrea's fingers, still digging painfully into Jessica's arm throughout the whole solo, finally relaxed and she sobbed quietly on Jessica's shoulder.

The rest of the concert was as fast moving and as good as the first part. At the end, though, Jessica could see the effort it took all of the band to keep going for the last two or three numbers that they played as encores. It didn't surprise her. The energy that had gone into the performance astounded her. She had been honestly impressed by Nic and was beginning to understand his firm avowal that groups like his couldn't go on performing with such dedicated energy if they were constantly abusing themselves. She was also beginning to understand why he had so often looked tired when he'd come out to see her, and had wanted the peace and relaxation which the country and walking had given him.

The final encore was sung, the band had gone from the stage and the lights had come up. The crowd were reluctantly beginning to move, to shuffle slowly towards the exits, still singing snatches of the songs which had been played that night, clutching tee-shirts and programmes as they good-naturedly waited to leave.

David and Stephanie said a temporary goodbye. They weren't coming backstage but would see them later, at the party for close friends to be held in Nic's flat. Both seemed to have enjoyed the concert.

Jessica and Andrea moved instead to the front of the stage. Their way was soon blocked by a couple of burly security guards. Again, Andrea produced the passes she'd been given and they were both waved through the barrier and went into the regions behind the stage.

'Why all this?' Jessica asked in a subdued voice.

'Would you like it if Nic was totally mobbed? Unfortunately, the fans aren't quite as civilised as yours...or perhaps I could say they're more demonstrative? Either way, if there wasn't security there would be hordes of screaming females down here by now. The band is kept well-shielded, Jessica. You were worried about intrusions into your life, but it'll rarely be a problem.' Andrea paused indecisively. Several doors opened off the area they now found themselves in. 'We're supposed to wait for Mike and Nic in one of these rooms. There's drinks and some food available for friends, critics, whatever. I don't know, which door, I wonder?'

At that moment a tall, conventional-looking man strode past them before pausing and coming back. 'Can I help?' he asked, politely veiling his suspicion.

'Mmm. I'm Andrea D'Arsace and-'

'Hi, there!' The man held out his hand, smiling in welcome. 'Greg Spalding, Tunnel Vision's manager. We're pleased that Mike's joined us. He's done really well to fit in this quickly. Come on, I'll show you where to go. Hi,' he said, turning to Jessica. 'Are you a friend of Mike's, too?'

'This is Jessica Farndale,' Andrea supplied.

Greg shot Jessica a startled, curious look. Nic's girlfriend. They all knew her name by now. And after the little episode out there in the arena, they all knew what effect she had on him. Later tonight there was that party at Nic's for his close friends, to introduce her. Beautiful, yes, but in a quiet, calm way. Little make-

214

up, casual clothes. No hard edges and, he guessed, no sharp repartee. A lamb amongst some pretty ferocious she-wolves. He could see why Nic was taken with her. He guessed her key words were honesty, integrity and loyalty, and he imagined going home to her was like a haven in a continual storm.

Slightly more warily, Greg led them to the room they wanted. It was crowded with people all talking at once. He pushed through the crowd, brushing off the many attempts made to stop him, hoping this gentle and reserved girl wasn't noticing the sharp looks of curiosity directed at her. Not because anyone here knew she was connected to Nic, but simply because her face wasn't known and somehow...somehow, she obviously wasn't the type usually found in this world, whereas Andrea...now she could probably hold her own. He found them a relatively quiet corner, away from the acid mainstream of guests, realising he was already trying to protect this quiet, self-contained beauty.

Suddenly he smiled. She *would* survive...simply because that's what all of them would do, the group, the roadies, the technicians. They would be as captivated by her quiet charm as Nic had been and they would all protect her fiercely. He relaxed a little and acquired three glasses of wine.

'Sorry!' he shouted above the din. 'It's a madhouse in here tonight! The concert was such a success, everyone's here to say congratulations. Even,' he grinned wolfishly, 'the critics!'

Andrea laughed. 'How long will Mike be?'

'Don't know. Not long. They're having a shower and changing. But...he'll be as high as a kite. That's what these performances do to you, and this one was extra long, you see. No supporting band. Nic didn't want that. He wanted just Tunnel Vision and he hoped that by promising a long performance, he'd pull in the fans to raise money for Andy's pet project. And he was right! But as a result, the band's exhausted, and they take ages to come down. Look,' he turned to Jessica, his voice gruff. 'Thanks for what you did tonight out there. Nic...well, he's had a rough time coming to terms with Andy's death. You've done a lot for him.'

Jessica's face flamed and she dropped her eyes. 'I nearly didn't,' she muttered quietly, shame filling her as she recalled her initial spoiled rejection of Nic.

'Yeah, well. 'Greg smiled. 'You made up for that tonight, okay? You're a performer yourself, aren't you?'

215

'Mmm?' Jessica had been scanning the crowd with slightly wary eyes. Now she turned her attention back to Greg. 'Oh, sorry. Yes, I play the piano.'

'Nic mentioned it this morning, after the press conference. He...he was a bit worried you'd find this...how to put it?...find the music a bit basic?' He could tell she was nervous. The hand holding the glass trembled and her speech was disconnected and vague. He wanted to help her, make her feel more at ease.

'Oh no, not at all. I actually enjoyed the band. They're very good. And Nic and Andy have written some lovely songs. I like quite a lot of different music but I haven't been able to listen to it much. I have to practise a lot and...and...' Jessica's voice trailed away and a glow filled her face. Greg looked at her sharply and swallowed at the naked love he saw blazing there, then followed the direction of her eyes. The door had opened and the band were coming into the room. They looked exhausted but, as Greg had warned, they also looked tense and elated.

Jessica saw Nic. No-one else. Nic, all in black.

The shirt was damp and clung to his broad shoulders, and the jeans outlined his narrow hips and lean legs. His thick, black hair clung to his forehead and curled over his collar onto his shoulders. And this man loved *her*. She still found it hard to take in.

Accosted from all sides, he held up his hands, long fingers open in supplication. Jessica was too far away to hear what he said, but she saw the flash of white teeth as a grin split his face and caused his blue, blue eyes to crinkle in amusement at something someone said to him.

A woman suddenly catapulted from the crush of people. She was a redhead, dressed, like Nic, in black that clung to every curve of her voluptuous figure. She flung herself at him, pressing herself blatantly close.

'Uh-oh,' Greg muttered under his breath in dismay, flashing a sideways look at Jessica. 'Trouble.' He moved towards Nic and the glamorous lady wrapped round him, but before he could reach them Nic himself firmly took hold of the arms round his neck and removed them, at the same time stepping backwards and sideways to avoid her forward movement again intent on embracing him. Then pointedly, rudely, he turned his back on her and moved into the crowd, his eyes searching the faces, looking...

'And who was that?' Jessica asked Andrea in a low voice, a touch of amusement in her eyes. She could afford the

216

amusement. She had been through all the storms possible and was now secure in the knowledge that Nic loved only her.

'She's an actress. Louisa somebody. She and Nic were an item, oh, ages ago now. But he's looking for you, Jessica.'

Yes. She knew he was.

The noise in the room subsided as everyone watched Nic to see who he was so intent on finding, while at the same time pretending they had no interest at all. Heads turned, voices stilled. The redhead laughed in a brittle way and returned to the side of the rather disgruntled man she had come with, but even she could not resist following Nic's progress through the room, as he stopped here and there to talk to people, but all the time disengaging himself as quickly as he could before moving on and searching with his eyes...

Jessica's steady green eyes remained fixed on his face...his *beloved* face.

His eyes met hers, passed briefly on, swung back, and a smile of relief and love crossed his features. Greg looked from Nic to Jessica and back again, shaking his head. It had happened then, at last. What they'd all decided never would. Nic had been snared. Completely. It was obvious to everyone here he was in love. And it was equally obvious to everyone here that he'd never been in love before.

In two quick strides he was at her side, his hands gripping hers, eyes for no-one else in the room. 'Jess...' he breathed. 'Darlin'. I'm glad to see you...and, hey, sorry about Louisa.' He looked at her pleadingly.

'It's okay,' Jessica said softly. 'It's okay. I know you love me.'

'And thanks...oh, *thanks* for being there for me tonight.'

They stared steadily at each other before Nic, oblivious to the curious crowd, bent his head, his lips tenderly brushing hers as he pulled her closely to him.

A flashbulb flared, then another and another. Jessica looked startled and drew back, but Nic kept his arms firmly round her.

'Nic...this lady...can you tell us...?'

'Nic, that was a superb concert. You've done some brilliant stuff recently. It's been suggested you're in love. Is this...?

'Mr. Daniel, you were seen at one of Miss Farndale's concerts. Is that when you met...?'

A barrage of questions followed which Nic fielded neatly, laughing down at Jessica, holding her firmly by his side. 'It will only be for a while,' he whispered. 'Be patient, darlin'. They'll get tired of us in a day or two, okay?'

Soon after that, they returned to the flat for the party Nic had planned.

Jessica was wary of meeting the group again. She'd sensed that at best, Josh had been truly sympathetic and Ian had been prepared to give her the benefit of the doubt, but Adam and Jon had both felt contempt for her. Perhaps this was only her imagination, based on the heightened feelings of that dreadful day. She hoped so, but it still made for uncomfortable feelings as she and Nic went ahead of the others for the gathering after the concert, because the main purpose was to announce the fact she and Nic had been married that morning.

Nic had sent a press release of the wedding to the papers. The story would break the next day, but he wanted, he said, the rest of his own friends to know first.

Mike and Andrea arrived before anyone else, with David and Stephanie in tow, having picked them up from their house on the way from the Wembley Arena. Jessica had asked them to follow as soon as possible, to give her moral support. Josh arrived next, quickly followed by Greg and his wife.

Jessica found Josh shadowing her footsteps, always there to fetch and carry, always prepared for a word if Jessica found herself with nothing to do.

Nic drifted across. 'He approves,' he whispered in her ear. 'He does that all the time with me.'

'It's very sweet, but doesn't it drive you mad?' Jessica murmured under her breath.

'Not after twenty or so years. You kind of get used to it! And he's very careful not to trip you up.'

Jessica snorted inelegantly with laughter.

'Seriously, Jess, he's devoted to me...and was to Andy. He tried to play an instrument, you know, to be like Andy and me, but he was never musical. I never had the heart to throw him out. Bear with him...for me? I know you've never liked him since last summer. But you understand now he was protecting me?'

'Ah, I've forgiven him that,' Jessica exclaimed. 'He said he was sorry, you know. And he did a great job this morning and was very proud, too, to have been asked. That was kind, sweetheart.'

'I love you, Mrs. Daniel.' He took her hands in his and pulled her forward to kiss her on the nose.

'That sounds strange!' Jessica laughed. 'You know I shall retain Farndale for performing?'

'Call yourself what you like,' he said roughly, under his breath, 'as long as you stay with me. When I thought you'd

218

gone...when I thought it was hopeless...it was a black time. I...I'd lost Andy...and...and I thought I'd lost you as well and I...' He shut his eyes and shook his head, lips held tight in remembered pain.

Jessica clung to him. 'I'm sorry,' she whispered. 'I'm sorry. I promise, never again.'

Over his shoulder she saw the door open again. Jon, Adam and a woman.

'Jon's here. He frightens me a little,' Jessica confessed.

'He's okay,' Nic said briefly, turning to greet his friends.

Ian was the last to arrive. Jessica was careful to keep in the background at first. She really wasn't sure if they approved of her and if they would like the idea of their marriage this morning, but slowly she was drawn into the mainstream of conversation. Adam had a long discussion with her about various interpretations of classical pieces she'd played. Jessica was right in suspecting he kept up his classical work. It seemed he took tuition from a very highly regarded but now retired pianist. Jessica was still intrigued that he found Tunnel Vision to be enough.

'Oh, yeah! It suits me. Long periods of intense energy then equally long periods of laziness! Yeah, I know I still practise classical but it's because I want to, rather than because I must, like you.' He grinned down at her, amused by her concern, before a look of seriousness crossed his face. 'But hey, I just wanted to say, I'm glad you and Nic have sorted things out. I was worried when Ian said he was ill, but he looks loads better now, and I gather we start recording tomorrow.'

As they finished talking, David pounced on him, a long and deep discussion following which went on for some time.

Stephanie seemed at ease with everyone, drifting from person to person, laughing delightedly at everything. Jess was pleased her friends were mixing so well, but not surprised. It was, after all, Mike's and Andrea's world anyway, and David and Stephanie were good company whichever group of people they were with.

Ian drifted over. 'Thanks for reconsidering. Sorry about the hard arm tactics, but he really had us worried. Andy's death knocked him out, but this was something else again. And, hey, we surely needed you tonight back there, when he kinda cracked a bit. Thanks for that. You're going to stick by him?'

'I'm going to stick by him,' Jessica replied steadily.

A grin creased his strong, good-looking face. 'That's great! Nice to meet you properly...Jessica.'

Later, as Jessica was talking to Andrea and a girl called Samantha, Jon joined their group. He listened for a few moments then neatly edged Jessica away.

'You okay?' he asked abruptly, his green eyes narrowed in concentration on her face.

'Yes. Why?'

He shrugged. 'You look happy, but a bit edgy, too.'

Jessica looked at him thoughtfully. Incredibly good-looking and nobody's fool, this man. Only the truth would do. He would either accept it or be offended by it, but it was the only way.

'You're right,' she admitted slowly. 'I am happy...very happy...but I've been feeling very nervous about meeting you all again, especially you.'

His eyebrows flew up, green eyes snapping wide in surprise. Much as she loved Nic, she could sense this man's animal attraction. Dynamite if you liked living dangerously, Jessica thought in amusement, waiting to see what he would say.

'Me? Because of what I said to you?'

Jessica nodded.

'I'm not apologising. What I said was true,' he said uncompromisingly. 'But at least you thought things over and did something about it. Nic was in hell, woman.'

Well, at least that was an improvement on Miss Farndale, spoken in sneering contempt, thought Jessica.

'If someone treated your friend like that,' he turned to indicate Andrea with a nod of his head, 'don't you think you might feel a bit riled with the person who'd done it?'

'I take your point.'

'Nic's okay now. Make sure he stays okay.' He grinned suddenly, his whole face lighting up. 'Welcome, Jessica. And I have to say, after what happened in the arena tonight, I'm quite glad you're around!'

Nic waited until everyone had arrived. Gathering Jessica to his side, he called for silence. 'Jessica told me how you all tried to help when she and I had a slight difference of opinion.'

There was a general laugh at this understatement.

'She wasn't totally to blame for what happened, you know. If I'd been a bit more honest with her then perhaps everything wouldn't have come as such a shock to her. Mike was the only one who pitched into me about that and he was quite right, too. Still, it's all okay now and I just wanted to tell you Jess and I...we were married this morning by special licence.'

A sudden cheer drowned out the last part of his announcement. Someone found the champagne in the kitchen and soon corks were flying and golden, bubbling wine was spilling into glasses while overlaying everything was a babble of excited chatter. Everyone came in turn to slap Nic on the back, or clasp his hand, and to hug her and kiss her cheek.

Jessica looked at everyone's face in turn. Adam, Ian and Jon looked delighted. They'd been the first to rush up to Nic and to shake his hand, punch him on the shoulder and unashamedly embrace him.

There was no doubt. They were pleased.

When everyone had finally gone, and they were alone again, Nic was still strung up. He paced the floor as Jessica watched him from a chair.

'Ah, you're exhausting me,' she said. 'Come here. I bet I know how to calm you down!'

'Yeah?' Nic leered at her.

'Yeah,' she laughed.

'Hey, you're learning!' he exclaimed softly, coming to stand beside her. 'You looking forward to the tour?'

'Mmm. I'll come to your concerts if you'll come to mine.' Jessica now had several dates booked around Britain and in America which tied in with the dates of Nic's tours.

'I don't care if you don't come to any concerts,' he said huskily, into her hair, 'as long as you're there afterwards.'

'I'll be there,' she promised as she pulled him down onto the floor at her feet. 'No, stay there. Sit still.'

She ran her hands slowly over his tense neck and shoulders, smoothing the tight muscles and caressing his neck and hair. Her hands passed over him again and again until he sighed and she felt his tight frame at last begin to loosen.

'I have to warn you,' he turned his head to grin at her. 'This could lead to things.'

'Good,' she breathed, leaning forwards and running her tongue round his ear. 'I rather hoped it might.' Her hand ran down his chest and felt the muscles of his stomach tighten in response.

'Tonight,' he murmured, turning and scooping her into his arms. 'Tonight, we go to bed first.'

Later, curled up together in the big double bed, Nic said drowsily, 'Why are you frightened of Jon?'

'Mmm? Oh, that.' Jessica kissed the corner of his mouth. 'He was a bit harsh when he came to see me...I didn't think he approved of me at all. But...we sorted it out tonight. He explained.

221

It's okay now.' She sighed and snuggled deep into his arms, sensuously aware of his warm skin under her fingers. 'Ah, Nic, I love you.'

'You were right, you know.' He laughed at her. 'That was a really good way to calm me down. Care to take on that role after every concert, darlin'?'

She looked intently at him. His face lost all trace of humour as he gazed back deeply into her eyes. They leaned towards each other and kissed, very gently.

'Every concert. For always,' she vowed, a catch in her throat. A promise.

Printed in Poland
by Amazon Fulfillment
Poland Sp. z o.o., Wrocław